The
Archangels
of
Dreamland

The
Archangels
of
Dreamland

STEVEN L. FAWCETTE

THE TROPHY GROUP, INC.

For further information contact:

The Trophy Group, Inc.
1368 Turnbull Bay Road
New Smyrna Beach, FL 32168

Book design by Arbor Books: www.arborbooks.com

Printed in the United States

Steven L. Fawcette
The Archangels of Dreamland

1. Author   2. Title   3. Fiction
Library of Congress Control Number: 2005908722
ISBN: 0-9773709-0-9

FOREWORD

$\mathscr{I}$n every story, there are protagonists and antagonists who battle each other over some sort of goal. This is certainly the case with 'The Greatest Story Ever Told', the Holy Bible, which chronicles the eternal conflict between good and evil, with the disposition of humanity hanging in the balance. It is an epic saga, from The Book of Genesis, which recounts the beginning of the world and mankind's expulsion from paradise, to The Book of The Revelation, which cryptically discusses the end of the world and how the Devil and His minions are overcome by God and His trusted Archangels.

Unfortunately, the story does not end there. The book you are about to read follows events which take place before and after the Biblical Revelation. If that sounds impossible — read on. As the author, I can only tell you this story was revealed to me in a series of dreams which I did not wish for nor felt worthy to receive. Something has disrupted God's Divine Plan. It is up to you, the reader, to decide whether this is fiction — or present and future fact.

Acknowledgment

I would like to take this opportunity to thank the Trophy Group, and in particular my business partner Michael, for his unswerving support on this project. For many years, we have recognized the inherent talents in each other and I appreciate his vision and counsel.

Dedication

I would like to dedicate this book to four precious individuals.

First, to my three sons, Kevin, Christopher and Casey, whose names I've honored in this story. Although we have been separated by circumstances, I am with you in spirit and love each of you now and forever.

The other person is my reason for living. I promised God I would write this story if He'd direct me to the woman of my dreams.

Three days after finishing this book, my sweetie walked into my life. She is my gift from God... and my love for her is eternal.

Thank you, Eva... for everything.

"And there was war in Heaven:
Michael and his angels
fought against the Dragon;
and the Dragon fought and His angels."

Revelation 12:7

CHAPTER ONE

❧

ROSWELL, NEW MEXICO — JULY 4th, 1947

*L*ightning surged through the night sky, bridging the void between Heaven and Earth. The approaching tempest pushed a welcome breeze across the floor of the desert, producing a sound no known instrument could duplicate. The residents of Roswell scurried inside their homes making sure their windows were secure. Thunderstorms were the norm this time of year and everyone in town knew what to expect.

They were wrong. The future of the world was about to change.

A few miles outside of town, Bobby Kirke drove his pickup along a rural dirt road and parked next to a large rock formation. Seated next to him was his date for the evening, Mary Ellen Hart, a virginal, raven-haired 18 year old. At least he thought she was a virgin. The word around Roswell High School said she was a good Catholic girl who took sadistic pleasure in upsetting a boy's well-laid plans. This was the reason he'd chosen to go to the senior prom with another girl whom he knew would provide a more satisfactory completion to the night. But, Bobby remained intrigued with Mary Ellen enough to give her a try. Hope springs eternal in all 19 year old boys.

"What are we doing here?" she asked, certain of the answer.

Before he could respond, a loud clap of thunder shook the vehicle. "The engine was overheating. I thought I'd let it cool down before we head back."

"I see. Does this happen often?"

"It depends. My engine's very sensitive."

A grin crept upon her face. "Most guys' engines are."

Bobby began sliding his fingers up and down her bare arm. Mary Ellen sighed, aware she'd have to stop this in short order. She didn't really want to because she did like Bobby and this was starting to feel better than she thought it would. However, she was determined not to give herself to a man before her wedding night. Bobby arrived at the base of her neck well ahead of schedule. Now she'd really have to stop this. Soon. A little longer. Almost time. A few more seconds. *God, does this feel good. Chastity is so overrated.*

Just as her will was nearing catastrophic meltdown, a percussive shockwave vibrated through them. "What was that?" she squealed.

"Just thunder. I'll keep you safe."

"No. That was more than..." She was cut short by another noise, like that of rending metal coming ever closer. Bobby jerked his head up in awareness.

"What the hell?"

Mary Ellen froze with fear as another flash of lightning lit the area. She saw a silver mass tumbling across the ground, with shards of metal shearing off in a blizzard of debris. The mysterious object then disappeared into the darkness beyond. The two sat motionless, unable to comprehend what they'd just witnessed. Bobby swallowed hard in an effort to act brave. Lust had been driven from his body, if only temporarily.

"Turn on the headlights," she implored.

He nodded and reached for the knob. The beams flared into the night revealing a few small pieces of whatever crashed before them. Lightning continued to illuminate the area beyond the beams, but a clear view was obscured by a cloud of dirt saturating the air. At that moment, a steady rain began to fall further impeding their gaze through the windshield. Bobby grabbed a flashlight under his seat and checked to see if it worked.

"There's another in the glove box."

She reached over and removed it from the compartment. "Bobby, I think we should get the Sheriff."

"We will," he agreed. "I just want to check this out."

He opened his door and stepped into the storm. Before he realized, Mary Ellen grabbed a jacket, draping it over her head to join him.

"Stay in the truck."

She shook her head in defiance. "I want to see this, too."

They started walking, remaining within the outline of the beams. Intense thunder rocked the area with lingering echoes and tremors. Bobby spied one of the metallic pieces before his feet and bent down for a closer inspection. The object looked like aluminum foil. He crunched it in his hand and the metal magically returned to its original shape.

"Shit!" Minding his language was now a distant concern. "Nothing does that."

"Maybe, because it's wet?" she speculated. He shook his head, tossing it to the ground in confusion. They proceeded with caution until arriving at the outer range of the headlights. Another flash of lightning revealed a large object jammed into the rock formation about 20 yards further on. The rain was falling heavier, making them trudge through newly-formed puddles. Despite the jacket, water was streaming down Mary Ellen's face, smearing her make-up and making it difficult to see. After another fearful step, she felt something roll onto her foot. The girl stopped, shining the flashlight before her. A pair of huge, black eyes stared back.

Mary Ellen shrieked in terror. She dropped her flashlight and tumbled backward into the mud. Bobby was beside her in an instant, leveling his light at the object.

"What the fuck?"

The pair ignored the raging storm, their eyes riveted upon the lifeless being. It was a grotesque sight. The head had been sliced open by a sharp rock allowing a viscous liquid to ooze onto the wet ground. The bug-like face was frozen in shock and the creature's belly swelled with an alien rigor mortis.

Mary Ellen cupped her hand over her mouth. Suffering a series of convulsions, she glued shut her eyes in an effort to stem a tide of hysteria.

"What is it?" she whimpered.

Bobby looked upon the corpse in disbelief. The open head wound was producing a nauseating smell which eventually forced him to back away. He then pulled Mary Ellen from the mud.

"Let's get out of here."

After beginning their retreat she abruptly stopped. "Did you hear that?"

"Hear what? Just thunder."

"No. It sounded like 'Help'."

"You're imagining..."

Then, he heard it too. A breathless plea for aid. Bobby spun around, scanning an area closer to what he could only guess was some sort of craft or ship. He waded through a minefield of curious debris, trying not to disrupt the crash site. Over the noise of rain and wind, he heard the voice again. Five to six yards from the ship was another body. This one was face down in the mud — and was moving. Mary Ellen ran up alongside, gasping in awe. It was a living being, but not of this world. The creature twisted its head toward them and peered into the light.

Help, came the anguished voice. Mary Ellen noticed the small slit which should have been it's mouth didn't move. The being seemed to be in direct contact with their minds. She was suddenly overcome with empathy.

"Bobby, we have to do something."

"What?" crying in dismay. "I don't even know what it is."

She dismissed his callous remark, bending down to communicate. "Don't move. We'll get a doctor. Someone who can care for you."

The creature continued to writhe in pain. It attempted to crawl toward the damaged ship, its labored efforts causing Mary Ellen to squirm in discomfort. Bobby walked over to the craft and looked inside the cockpit. Another body was strapped inside, impaled with a metallic bar through its chest. The entire cabin resembled an elaborate prop from a science fiction movie. The instrument panel was dimly-lit with writing that reminded him of Egyptian hieroglyphics. In the center of the console was a device like that of a small TV set, but glowing in color. It also had a strangely shaped keyboard underneath, but unlike any typewriter he'd ever seen. On the screen were various unknown words and groups of numbers scrolling past. Bobby shook his head in bewilderment and withdrew from the cabin. The tortured figure remained on the ground, still groping its way toward the ship. Mary Ellen stood nearby, scanning Bobby with wet eyes.

"Should we put him back in there?"

"Hell, no!" he exclaimed. "He could grab a ray gun or something."

She gasped in exasperation. "Oh, please."

"Mac Brazel's ranch is nearby. You could drive there and call for help."

Mary Ellen stood as stone. "No, you better go. I'll stay here until you get back."

"Are you crazy? You can't stay here with this — thing."

"He's hurt. Nothing's going to happen."

She didn't say it, but Mary Ellen knew she had less to fear from the creature than she did from her Earthly date. Bobby sighed, aware she'd made up her mind.

"All right. I'll be back in 15 minutes. But, let me give you something first."

He ran to the truck, then hustled back with a shotgun. He loaded the weapon and made her take it in hand. "Just in case."

She nodded at the logical suggestion. Bobby stole a last look at the injured being, kissed her on the cheek and dashed back through the headlights. In a moment, he was speeding toward the Brazel ranch.

With the rain swirling about, Mary Ellen had become a fright-ful mess. But, vanity was no longer her concern. She continued to hear the anguished cry in her mind. "He's gone to get help. They'll be here soon. Just try and rest."

Her words agitated the creature. He appeared desperate to return to his ship, venting a torturous groan upon realizing it wasn't to be.

"Is there something you want in there? Something I can get for you? I want to help."

He pointed toward the craft, extending all six fingers at the open cabin door. At last, he exhaled in despair. *I know,* came the response. *You would not understand.*

A chill seized her body. She wanted to cry, but bit her lip at the thought. "I'm sorry. I'm so sorry. I know you hurt."

The being looked up at her, pausing in apparent meditation. *You are chosen,* he said, reaching forth with a quivering arm. His sudden motion caused Mary Ellen to back away. In response, the voice she heard was soothing and calm. *Let me touch you. No harm.*

The creature advanced. She remembered the shotgun in her hand, but just as quickly dismissed the idea. Before she realized, one of his fingers was probing her navel. It was warm to the touch. Soon, a pleasing sensation was flowing through her. She was acute-ly aware of a vibration in her ovaries and uterus, followed by a feel-ing of contraction and cramping as experienced during her periods. An overwhelming burst of warmth then caused Mary Ellen to gasp in ecstasy. She felt more alive than ever. A freedom she never imag-ined. The rain abated as her spirit drifted in rapturous flight. All she could feel was elation. Harmony. A communion with the universe. She wanted it to last forever. However, when Mary Ellen heard another vehicle approaching, she was thrust back inside her flesh and bone cocoon.

An air traffic control operator at Kirtland Air Force Base in Albuquerque had detected the mysterious object on radar, alerting the Army Base at Roswell once it disappeared from his scope. The Duty Officer at the Base dispatched a team of armed MPs for a search of the downed craft — made much easier with the assistance of Bobby Kirke whom they'd intercepted down the road. Prior to the military jeep cresting the hill, Mary Ellen became filled with dread. She felt something was terribly wrong, but unable at first to grasp the seriousness of the situation. It suddenly occurred to her. The discovery of alien life. A ship from another world. If these were the authorities, they wouldn't let them live to tell the tale.

Don't let them have it, the voice gasped in terror.

She looked puzzled. "Don't let them have what? What do you mean?"

The creature dropped his head in the mud. *Go.* There was a silent pause, then a more forceful warning. *Go!*

Mary Ellen jumped behind the rocks, retreating to a higher vantage point about 30 yards distant. The jeep pulled up to the crash site, stopping with a sudden jerk. Three soldiers bounded from the vehicle and were led to the wreck by Bobby. She could see the four standing around the tortured figure, guns drawn. It was hard for her to hear their muffled conversation, but could tell the soldiers were clearly agitated. Bobby started yelling for her. She ignored the invitation, crouching lower in the rocks above. As he called for her a third time, Mary Ellen slumped over in horror. One of the soldiers, visibly gripped with fear, placed his rifle at the creature's head and fired multiple rounds. The helpless being jerked rhythmically with each shot — channeling an extended, final breath. At that moment, the senior officer grabbed Bobby by the arm and marched him to the jeep. The others remained as sentry at the site while he drove the boy away. Two gunshots soon echoed through the night. Mary Ellen refused to move lest she be discovered. The jeep then returned and the lone soldier jumped out.

"What happened?" another wondered.

"The kid tried to escape," he explained. "What else could I do?"

On a night of incredible events, what followed exceeded belief. The three exchanged nervous laughter.

"Call the Base and report our status," the senior officer barked. "Have them seal off this area. No one gets in or out without the Base Commander's approval."

Another soldier saluted, walking back to the jeep to call in on the portable radio. Mary Ellen caught her breath so she wouldn't hyperventilate.

"What about his girlfriend?"

A cigarette was lit. "We know who she is. Where she lives. How hard can it be?"

There was no reason to stay. Mary Ellen knew she had to get back to town and tell her parents. The Sheriff. Somebody. She placed Bobby's shotgun on the ground and darted into the wilderness using her flashlight.

Panic grew stronger with every stride. She was now a hunted animal and the desert was as unforgiving as her pursuers. During her trek across the bleak landscape, the girl was swamped by every conceivable human fear. However, as time wore on Mary Ellen brought forth an inner strength she didn't know she possessed. A feeling that God would protect her from harm. Soon, her rapid breath became the wind. Her pounding heart became fire. A seemingly endless supply of spiritual fuel propelled the youngster onward. It allowed her to reach the main highway before dawn, hitching a ride with a passing trucker.

Several military vehicles flashed by in convoys speeding to the crash site. The frightened teen said nothing to the driver for fear of getting him involved. They stopped at the first gas station where she asked to borrow a nickel for the phone. The man obliged and the girl ran to call her parents. It rang four times before her mother answered.

"Mary Ellen! Where are you? I've been worried sick."

"Mom, I'm fine. No, I'm not fine," she said, confused. "Just listen, Mom. You've got to listen!"

Mary Ellen caught her breath so she wouldn't babble. Before she could finish recounting the story, a click was heard. The line went dead.

"Mom? Mom?" her voice broke in panic.

She hung up, unsure what to think. The girl walked back to the trucker who was finishing his morning coffee and doughnut. He agreed to drive her home.

As the truck droned into Roswell, a kaleidoscope of disjointed images tumbled through her mind. *Did this really happen? Is Bobby dead? Are my parents in danger? What did that creature do to me?* She wondered if she were going crazy. All these thoughts! Could she survive this whirlwind of insanity? Getting home would bring some comfort. *Only a few minutes more.*

As they turned into a modest, tree-lined neighborhood, Mary Ellen squinted into the dawn's early light. She spotted two military jeeps parked in her parents' driveway a few hundred feet ahead.

"Which place is yours?" the trucker asked.

Recognizing the threat, she shrank into her seat, blurting forth the first thing that came to mind. "It's further. Please keep going."

The truck continued on, passing the house she could no longer call home. Her mother and baby brother were being led outside by an armed MP. Her father stood in the doorway, arguing with two other soldiers.

Tears fell as her anguished heart refused to beat. *Are they going to harm my parents, too?* Mary Ellen knew now she could trust no one in authority. Certainly not the military. Without her family, the only place left for her was the Catholic Church.

"I'm sorry," she stammered. "I'm supposed to be at morning mass. Could you drop me off at the Church of the Immaculate Conception? It's over on West Sixth Street."

The trucker shrugged approval. Mary Ellen peered into the rear-view mirror, watching in disbelief as the life she knew receded in the distance.

Upon arrival at her family's church, she found Father McCarthy eating his breakfast in the rectory. It took the better part of an hour for the girl to tell her story. The priest had known the Hart family for many years and had watched them raise Mary Ellen to be a truthful servant of the Lord. He couldn't bring himself to doubt her.

After promising to help her family, Father McCarthy escorted Mary Ellen to the Roswell bus station, placing her on the morning bus to El Paso, Texas. The terrified girl sat alone, one of only five passengers aboard, wondering if she'd live to see the rest of the day. Unknown to Mary Ellen, the nightmare had just begun.

CHAPTER TWO

✆

Many Years Later… In Our Immediate Future
WASHINGTON, D.C. — FEBRUARY 9th

𝒜lmost three months had passed since President Petersen died from cardiac arrest. During the state funeral in the Capitol rotunda and burial at Arlington National Cemetery, Susan Webber allowed the impact of the event to touch her on many levels. She was shocked because President Petersen was a good friend and only 54 years old. He'd kept himself in excellent physical condition and it seemed inconceivable he could die at so young an age.

Due to his untimely death, Susan had been forced to take the oath of office as President of the United States. Obviously, she was aware of the historical significance by being the first woman to hold the office, but she had wanted to win it on her own in the upcoming general election after Petersen had completed his second term. Still, the savvy former Governor was honored to have been placed in this position and knew she possessed the requisite experience and wisdom to be a great leader. She was very photogenic, with long, auburn hair and deep pools of chocolate-brown eyes that sparkled in the light. Even after pregnancy, she'd kept her svelte figure and was sure her looks gave her an advantage in the predominantly male world of politics. Perhaps more than she knew.

President Webber leaned back in her Oval Office chair and forced a sigh. She looked at a picture of her two adolescent children and reveled in the joy of being their mother. Susan had recently celebrated her 45th birthday, a milestone she wasn't particularly happy to admit. At least her children kept her young at heart.

Webber's next appointment was at ten this morning, called by her National Security Advisor, Richard Stern. The meeting was to be held downstairs in the White House Situation Room. This struck her as odd. Usually this room was used only during a crisis, such as war or covert military actions, when information had to be kept absolutely secret. The room was heavily reinforced and protected with sophisticated electronic jamming equipment. She shrugged, aware the NSA was the most paranoid of all Federal agencies. Holding the meeting at this location was probably their way of making themselves feel important. President Webber rose from her chair and informed her secretary she'd be down in the Situation Room. She was escorted to the basement of the White House by Steven Yeager, a member of her Secret Service detail. The agent would wait just outside the door.

As she strode in, surprise registered on her face as 12 individuals rose from their seats. Most of them she knew.

"I didn't realize standard NSA meetings were so well attended," she stated, attempting to size up the situation. The door closed behind her with a sound that seemed strangely permanent.

"This isn't a standard NSA meeting, Madam President," Stern replied. "If you'll please take your seat, we'll begin the briefing." He pointed at the President's chair as her hesitation became obvious. "We've much to discuss," he added. His black hair and mustache perfectly framed his dark, brooding eyes. He'd never been known to sport a friendly face and Webber disliked men who never smiled or laughed. She always sensed danger around him, as if he were more than appeared. However, Stern was competent and had served President Petersen well for more than three years. She saw no logical reason to replace him.

The President took the cue, positioning herself at one end of a large conference table. The room had a sterile feel in spite of the dark wood paneling, with fluorescent lights recessed inside a drop ceiling. Adorning the walls were global and regional maps, topographic charts of every country and sea, and a 72 inch plasma television to display slides, transparencies or to view satellite transmissions from foreign fields of battle.

In front of her was a printed list of attendees and an agenda for the meeting, as well as several folders with the designation 'BLACK MAJIK — EYES ONLY'. The President first scanned the room, then the list to place a name with every face. It read as follows:

NSA MEETING — MAJIK-12— FEBRUARY 9

ATTENDEES

National Security Advisor — Richard M. Stem

CIA Director — Dr. Walter J. Langlois

FBI Director — Judge Harold S. Monroe

Attorney General — Judge Sharon Ortiz-Bennett

Secretary of Defense — Phillip C. Roth

Chairman, Joint Chiefs — Fleet Admiral Curtis L. Holliman, USN

Member, Joint Chiefs — General Frederick R. Stevenson, USAF

Member, Joint Chiefs — General Kenneth G. Connolly, USA

Commanding Officer 'Dreamland'
— Brigadier General Michael T. McKay, USAF

NASA Director — Dr. Matthew P. Leonetti

Defense Advanced Research Projects Agency (DARPA) Chairman
— Professor J. Robert Blau

GG&E Chairman — Dr. Pierre K. LeClerke

President of the United States — The Honorable Susan N. Webber

The military men, all resplendent in their dress uniforms, occupied seats on the opposite side of the table psychologically distancing themselves from their female Commander-in-Chief. As she studied the list, her eyes locked on the title of General McKay. *What the hell is Dreamland? Some sort of military fun park?* She briefly stole a peek at McKay. His steel gray eyes matched the color of his short-cropped hair. His age was something of a mystery, but he was the epitome of the spit and polish soldier. It was clear this man was nobody's version of Walt Disney.

She quickly scanned the agenda sheet. The primary focus of the meeting was '...to fully inform the President of the existence of MAJIK-12, Dreamland and of all pertinent R&D activities relating thereto...'. Webber began to realize the importance of the discussion and was anxious to find out what this was all about.

"All right, people. You have my attention."

Stern rose from his chair. As he cleared his throat, a look of cold professionalism gripped his face. "Madam President, in accordance with Executive Order 47-142 signed by former President Harry S. Truman, the disclosure of the MAJIK-12 must be made to each succeeding President within the first 90 days of assuming office."

She found herself taking a quick headcount. "This is the MAJIK-12?"

"Yes, Madam President," he continued. "The codename MAJIK — Major Investigations and Knowledge — was used by the original members who first convened in September, 1947."

"Is there significance to that date?"

Stern paused. "First, I must make sure you appreciate the sensitivity of this information. As you know, within the U.S. Government, there are several levels of security clearance. The highest level, which doesn't officially exist, is MAJIK-12 data or BLACK MAJIK. The only people cleared to see this data are before you. What you are about to hear is the most extraordinary information possessed by our Government."

"I understand."

"You must further understand that once you've been informed of this data, you are under oath, and under penalty of death, not to discuss what you hear in this room with anyone. Ever. You take what you know to the grave."

The President forced a voluntary gulp. "Richard, you don't have to patronize me. I'm well aware of my obligations as President."

Stern nodded. "Do you know anything about the alleged UFO incident in Roswell, New Mexico back in 1947?"

She pursed her lips. "Just what every conspiracy buff knows. A UFO crashed there — and the U.S. Government covered it up?"

"It was more involved than that, Madam President," Leonetti joined in. The NASA Director was a short, balding man of 52 and looked every bit the part of the typical adult nerd. "In fact, a craft of staggering technical and aerodynamic design was recovered in the desert roughly 23 miles outside of Roswell. The military cordoned off the area and removed the craft to Wright-Patterson Air Force Base in Ohio for scientific analysis."

"Am I to presume this craft was unmanned?"

A difficult pause. At last, General Stevenson spoke. "No, ma'am. Three bodies were recovered and flown to Fort Worth, Texas for autopsy. There were no survivors." His fully shaved head dropped, reflecting the lights from above.

"Well, that's not quite true," the Attorney General interjected. "One occupant survived the crash, but when our soldiers arrived — the creature was killed."

The President immediately expressed her horror. "We killed it? What kind of monsters do we have in the military?"

General Connolly squirmed in his chair. Sharon Ortiz-Bennett flicked a moistened tongue over her lips, unsure how to respond. She was a few years older than the President and certainly less attractive. Her decision to sit next to Webber had been deliberate. An 'us girls' against 'these guys' mentality.

"I assure you Madam President, the responsible party was court-martialed and spent ten years in prison for that...," her voice faded, "...and other abuses."

The President shook her head in disgust. "Do we know anything about them? Where they're from?"

"We know a great deal, ma'am," chimed in Blau from DARPA. "It's not so much a question as where they're from, as it is when they're from. You see, after completing the autopsies, it was evident these beings were remarkably human in skeletal structure, as well as possessing similar digestive, respiratory and circulatory systems." He removed his eyeglasses to wipe them with a cloth. Blau was a burly man of 58 years and looked distinguished with his snow-white head of hair. "The major difference was an enlarged brain with superior frontal lobe and cerebrum development — 52 chromosomes in the DNA instead of the normal 46 — six fingers per hand — as well as a curious lack of genitalia. To this day, we still don't know exactly how they could reproduce."

"What were their conclusions?" Webber wondered.

Blau replaced his eyeglasses and folded his hands in a scholarly manner. "That these beings are our descendants. That they underwent some sort of genetic mutation, utilizing a matrix of computer-mapped genomes from different species."

Another uncomfortable lull in the discussion. "Of course, that's conjecture on our part," Leonetti blurted forth. "But, we have good evidence to back it up. NASA has conducted thousands of experiments with the craft and the equipment found inside. According to the craft's own internal log, it didn't originate from another planet or system. It definitely came from Earth. Earth of the future."

CIA Director Langlois, the most colorful of the group with his reddish hair and beard, continued with the thought. "This craft yielded a treasure trove of scientific data which the U.S. Government of 1947 wasn't able to readily assimilate. After we realized this wasn't some Soviet plot to confuse our scientists, we began to inspect each system and subsystem. Of particular interest was a small device which proved to be the most important discovery of all. The world's first computer."

"The first computer?" Webber echoed in surprise.

Blau nodded. "We knew we'd been handed a quantum leap in technology, but it took us many years to adapt it. A lengthy process called reverse engineering. But, it's safe to say that every major technical discovery in the past 60 years has come as a direct result of what we found in Roswell."

The President remained tomb silent, reflecting on the startling information.

Langlois continued to elaborate. "As far as the CIA was concerned, the discovery in Roswell turned the tide against the Soviet Union. With the computer in our possession, we were able to design more sophisticated weapons and electronics. We beat the Russians to the Moon because of the computer. The United States developed technology with such precision, the Soviets simply couldn't keep up. Their economy collapsed under the weight of trying to duplicate our technical feats. The fact is, there was no way they could win. After Roswell, we had the proverbial stacked deck."

Webber stared at the man, absent of any outward emotion. He forced a smile, exhibiting smugness befitting a spy. "An amusing bit of history, wouldn't you say?"

The President acknowledged with a limp nod, refusing to respond. The NASA Director, who seemed uncomfortable with the prolonged silence, could contain himself no longer. "We're still reaping huge benefits from the Roswell crash, such as improved aerodynamic designs for our space program. New metallic armament that'll make the H-Bomb obsolete. Exciting things, Madam President."

She looked over at McKay. "General, according to this you're the Commanding Officer of an installation known as Dreamland. Is this where all these 'exciting' discoveries are happening?"

"Yes, ma'am," said the General, ramrod stiff in his chair. "For the past 12 years I've overseen all military activity at the Groom Lake Test Site in Nevada, otherwise known as Area 51. Our codename for the facility is Dreamland."

"Why Dreamland?"

"It was one of our engineers, ma'am," said LeClerke, amused.

"He made a comment that having so much advanced technology to play with was like being in dreamland. I guess it stuck."

The President scanned her list. "You're Mr. LeClerke of GG&E?"

The rotund 62 year old seemed delighted to join the conversation. He appeared most jovial and not the least concerned with formalities. "Yes, ma'am. GG&E has been the chief contractor for Dreamland since it was built back in 1958. We have over 1,700 engineers who work at the site on a revolving basis, ferried in from Nellis Air Force Base and McCarran Airport in Las Vegas."

"How can this be a secret with that many workers?"

He broke into a smile. "All our people have some military background. They're used to receiving compartmented data, specialized to their area of expertise. No one knows more than they need to know."

"And the Air Force is there to keep them in line," McKay responded. "We have over 3,400 military personnel assigned to the site. There are shipping bays with railroad spur lines, laboratories, wind tunnels, assembly hangers, miles of underground passageways and the most sophisticated armories in the military. All ultra-secret weapons in various stages of test. In addition, the entire 50,000 acre site is ringed with over 200 Titan and MX missiles all carrying nuclear payloads."

Webber was perturbed by his militaristic enthusiasm and chose to respond with sarcasm. "Are you certain that's enough firepower, General?"

McKay stared her down. "Enough to hurl the Earth into the Sun, Madam President."

She could tell he wasn't joking. This man was starting to scare her.

"I suppose everything I need to familiarize myself with Dreamland are in these BLACK MAJIK folders?"

"That's correct, ma'am."

Webber forced a purposeful sigh, certain the full story was yet to be told. "Well, this was quite a briefing. Is there more I should know?"

Stern walked over to fill a glass of water, then offered it to the President.

"Thank you." She downed two lengthy gulps. Webber appreciated the gesture, thinking nothing further of his courtesy.

He sighed, reluctant to continue. "Yes, I'm afraid there is. The MAJIK-12 doesn't meet unless we have a new member to bring up to speed or an external development which impacts security or research. Such a meeting was called three months ago. It involved a major breakthrough with the computer which our engineers have been working on."

"The computer from the Roswell crash?"

Stern nodded and returned to his seat. "Professor Blau?"

On cue, the man leaned forward. "We've been trying for years to decipher various symbolic messages within the computer database. Recently, we unlocked these cryptologic algorithms and discovered two fascinating stores of data. One of the encoded files details how to design a computer which will think on its own. Artificial Intelligence or AI. It's been an unrealized dream of computer scientists. We now have the information necessary to construct a computer capable of independent thought. A new life form. This computer, codenamed Socrates, is being assembled at Dreamland. It should be ready for beta test within the next six to eight weeks."

The President understood the implications of such a device. "Are you serious? What if this computer becomes self aware? What if it doesn't like what we are or what we do?"

"We have that under control, ma'am. I assure you."

"Without specifics, your assurance is hollow, Mr. Blau. Before I approve activation of this computer, I want those specifics."

The room again fell still. Stern turned to the President, seemingly prepared for confrontation. "It's not your call. We've already approved the activation."

An unwelcome chill came over her. She'd known Richard Stern for many years and he'd never spoken to her in such a condescending manner. *What's happening here?*

"All of you work for me. I'm the President. You serve at my discretion."

"That's true, Madam President," replied Stern. "But, not in this room. There's no rank among the MAJIK-12. No one answers to any other. In fact, we're completely autonomous. As far as the Government's concerned, we don't exist."

The discussion had become most uncomfortable. It was about to get worse. Stern leaned back in his chair, showing a flair for the dramatic.

"The other encoded file was historical in nature. As Mr. Blau stated, these beings were time travelers from our distant future. The irrefutable evidence of this lies within this historical file. We know this file is genuine, because it accurately chronicles various natural disasters which have occurred since 1947. The 1980 Mt. St. Helens eruption. The 1989 San Francisco Bay earthquake. The 2004 tsunami in Thailand and Indonesia. It also records all data up to the end of the world — October 19th, 2007."

"October 2007?" she gasped. "That was years ago."

Stern nodded. "The reason their history is wrong — is because we've changed what should have been. These beings were from a different Earth. One that had gone through the final conflict."

Silence. Thick, impenetrable silence. Stern continued without being prompted. "Because of the Roswell crash, the U.S. Government received technical data from the future which allowed us to defeat the Soviet Union. That wasn't supposed to happen. After review of this file, it's our belief that we've not only changed history — but biblical prophecy as well."

President Webber lost her breath. She wanted to respond, but found it impossible to summon her voice. Stern used the opportunity to place a positive spin on the revelation.

"This is really a blessing in disguise. No apocalyptic end of the world scenario. No world-wide famine, disease or war. And, our Government continues to survive. I think we've engineered a much better situation than God ever intended."

The President eyed her National Security Advisor in abject horror. "What in Heaven's name have we done?"

"Complete secrecy is essential," he resumed. "If the American people knew the truth, it would be disastrous."

"Why do you say that?" inquired FBI Director Monroe.

"This nation is mostly populated by people who believe in the Judeo-Christian ethic and the Bible. Suppose they found out we destroyed God's plan for the future? Can you imagine the kind of panic and hysteria that would cause?"

President Webber struggled with the inconceivable conundrum. Her tortured thoughts labored to congeal. "I — I have to tell them. The people. They have to know it was an accident. Maybe we can change it."

"You'll do nothing of the kind, Madam President," Stern shot back. "The MAJIK-12 must not be compromised."

"Are you insane?" cried Webber, snapping in moral outrage. "To hell with the MAJIK-12. We're talking about the fate of humanity."

"Madam President, you're sworn to secrecy and that must be honored," Langlois implored.

"Honored? You don't know the first thing about honor. I took an oath to preserve, protect and defend the Constitution of the United States," came her indignant reply. "Not to baby-sit a bunch of self-righteous cowards with a God complex." She stood, scooping the BLACK MAJIK folders into her arms. "This material needs to see the light of day."

"Please, Susan. Don't do this," pleaded Roth, her Secretary of Defense. He'd known her the longest and could always address her on a first name basis. "You don't know what you're up against."

"This is the right thing to do, Phillip. Something you're obviously not capable of." Webber finished collecting the folders and turned toward the door. "I hereby declare the MAJIK-12 officially out of business." No one doubted her resolve. No one, but Stern.

"Sit down, Madam President," he demanded. "Sit down or you won't leave this room alive."

She froze in mid-step, disbelieving it had come to this. Her Secret Service bodyguard was just beyond the door. For a second, she thought about screaming for help, but the room was designed to be soundproof. She'd have to face this threat alone. The President turned and sucked in some air to compose herself. "I don't think I quite heard you, Mr. Stern. Would you mind repeating what you said?"

He gazed at her with laser intensity. "As you can see, there's no knob on the door. It's opened by a combination lock. Before the Secret Service could break in, you'd be dead. The poison I gave you is very effective."

Webber's eyes bloomed wide. "Poison?"

"Yes, Madam President. In the water you drank. Stops the heart. Leaves no trace for the autopsy. Guaranteed results. It worked exceptionally well on President Petersen."

She nearly fainted from the announcement. "My, God. You are insane. All of you. Do you have any idea what you're doing?"

"It's happened before, Madam President," stated the CIA Director. "You don't really believe President Kennedy was killed by Lee Harvey Oswald, do you?"

Webber felt disoriented, grabbing hold of the back of her chair to steady herself. Stern eyed his watch with mock concern.

"Madam President, you must make a choice. I estimate you have about three more minutes." He placed a small vial containing a clear liquid on the table. "This is the only antidote to the poison. It's yours in exchange for your silence."

The President was having difficulty breathing, her heart galloping faster. Webber thought of her children. Her responsibility to them as a single parent. She couldn't afford to leave them alone. Not now. *Oh God, what else can I do?* There was no other option. Weakened and humiliated, she forced her hand toward Stern. "Give it to me. I won't say a thing."

After initial hesitation, he slid the vial across the polished table. Webber bobbed her head back, quickly consuming the contents. Stern was amused by the President's sudden change of heart, confident she'd cause no further trouble.

"Very sensible, Madam President. I commend you. Did you know President Petersen was on his hands and knees sobbing at this point?"

Her fear was replaced with righteous anger. The President looked upon Stern as nothing more than a parasite, one she personally swore to eliminate. He rose from his chair and came to her side.

"I don't believe in accidents. What happened in Roswell was meant to happen. It allowed our Government to survive. To defeat its enemies. That ship from the future was a holy instrument. A tool of God."

"More like the Devil," she gasped.

A satanic smile leapt across his face. "As you wish." He then shook her hand in specious greeting. "Madam President — welcome to the Unholy 13."

CHAPTER THREE

❧

JUAREZ, MEXICO — MARCH 12ᵗʰ

*H*er body twitched, rocking back and forth with agitation. She attempted to scream, but all that came was a muffled groan. Once again, then twice more, as the frightening scene played on in her mind. Deep inside she knew it was just another bad dream, but each night they seemed more focused. More intense. Real. She tried to force open her eyes and deliver herself from this hell. Against her will, the vision continued until the final horrific moment. Only then was she released back to reality.

Maria Elena de la Cruz caught her breath and sat up in bed. The clock on the nightstand read 3:12 in the morning. She reached a trembling hand for the glass of water kept by her bedside, splashing a small amount on her face and neck. Leaning back on the bed, she noticed her shadow projected on the wall from the nightlight in the room. Maria Elena always left it on. She hadn't slept in the dark since the summer of her 18th year.

Not wishing to rejoin her dream, she came to her feet and put on her slippers. Stopping once to check herself in the mirror, she brushed her thin, gray hair back over her head and held it tight with a clip. The elderly woman ran her fingers over an ocean of wrinkles, stretching them taut in the hope they would magically disappear. A sly smile crept across her face. The wrinkles were there to stay. Taking her robe from the closet, she slipped it on and quietly left the room.

The great hallway linking the private sleeping quarters was empty. She walked as gingerly as she could, trying not to wake the others. The old Mission's thick adobe walls echoed any noise easily. Above, the ancient wooden ceiling beams kept most of the chilled night air out, but sometimes a stiff breeze would whistle through without welcome. The Nuestra Señora de Guadalupe Mission dated back to the 17th Century. It had weathered many storms over the years, while providing shelter to thousands of God's children in their time of need. Maria Elena noticed the initials MEH carved in one of the crossbeams above. *So long ago...* One of God's children had never found the courage to leave.

As she pushed open the oak door leading to the kitchen, she could hear some dishes rattling within. Sister Juanita Chavez stood before her like a deer caught in the headlights.

"Madre Superiora! I did not know you were awake!"

Maria Elena closed the door, begging the Sister to modulate her tone. "I may be old, but I'm not deaf."

"Sorry," she whispered. Juanita pulled down another cup. "Coffee?"

"No. But, I'd like some tea and honey."

As Juanita hurried to heat some water, Maria Elena sat down at a large table. The Sister soon joined her. Of all the nuns at the Mission, Juanita was Maria Elena's main friend and confidante. They'd known each other for more than 40 years. Maria Elena cared for her when she was brought to the Mission's orphanage at the tender age of two. The fact she grew up and wanted to help other children through their troubles spoke highly of her kind spirit. She soon became the Orphanage Director. Juanita was an attractive woman with long brown hair and a dark, flawless complexion. She would have had many men in her life, if she hadn't chosen to commit her life to God. She was also a very cheerful person, always ready to flash her winning smile to brighten someone's day. Maria Elena needed that now and Juanita happily obliged.

"Could not sleep?" she probed.

The Madre hung her head. "Nightmares. They've been getting worse. Ever since I've known about the baby." She reached down to rub her belly in a circular motion. Juanita noticed that she was starting to show.

"Do you wish to talk about it?"

"I suppose..." She paused, as the fetus kicked inside her. Maria Elena's secret past and the actual story behind her miraculous former pregnancies were known to a chosen few within the Catholic Church hierarchy. At the Mission, only the Padre Superior, Sister Juanita and Sister Josephina, who handled Administration and Personnel, were aware of what really happened in Roswell all those years ago.

Mary Ellen recalled how she was sent to the Mission by an El Paso area Jesuit who was a close friend of Father McCarthy's. She adopted her new name from the former Madre Superiora, Liliana de Ia Cruz, who'd jealously guarded the girl from any outside harm, convinced Mary Ellen was the present-day embodiment of the Virgin Mary. *Oh, how I miss Liliana...*

Maria Elena was jarred from her thoughts by the teapot whistling on the stove. Juanita poured the tea, then coffee for herself and returned to the table.

"Thank you, Sister," she sighed.

Juanita dropped some sugar in her coffee and stirred it through. "These dreams you have are not good?"

"Not good," she affirmed, as she mixed honey in her tea. "Tonight, I saw a great city with many lights. I floated above as though a spirit. There were many people below. They seemed happy, but there was terrible emptiness. The kind of emptiness caused from drifting too far from God. They had money and jewels, but it brought them no comfort because they wanted more. They filled themselves with sex, drugs and drink and the emptiness remained. It was the Devil's home and God had utterly forsaken it."

Maria Elena paused for a sip of tea. Juanita remained spellbound, forgetting the cup of coffee in her hand.

"Then, the city shook with such fury — such force — it crashed down into the Earth. Huge buildings fell over onto the people. They screamed for God to save them and He would not. The ground opened wide — and they were plunged into Hell's heart."

A leaden silence. Sister Juanita felt a chill roll up her back and accidentally spilled some coffee onto the table. She mopped it at once with a napkin. "Forgive me, Madre. I am clumsy."

She ignored the comment, downing another sip of tea. "God is commanding me to this city to deliver His final child. Then, He will reveal Himself to the people there and punish them with His wrath."

Juanita's eyes swelled the size of saucers. "Do you know where this city is?"

She nodded. "Las Vegas. In the State of Nevada. I must go there soon. The time of the birth is near."

"But, you must remember Papa is coming for the blessed event."

Maria Elena had forgotten that the Pope had scheduled a pilgrimage to Mexico to coincide with the birth of her tenth child. Of course, there was no official recognition of this on the Pope's itinerary. The word had come directly from Cardinal Morales of Mexico City that the Holy Father desired a private audience with Maria Elena. This was nothing new. Over the past 60 years, she'd received visits from Pope John XXIII, Pope Paul VI and Pope John Paul II, all under a tight veil of secrecy. Each of them had wanted to meet the modern-day Madonna and the current Pope was no exception. Due to concerns for her safety, Maria Elena's unique status remained one of the most closely guarded secrets in the Vatican.

"I'll have the Padre send a message to Cardinal Morales with my apologies. I'm sure Papa will understand."

Juanita was shocked anyone would decline an invitation from the Holy Father, but she'd always known the Madre Superiora to be faithful to God. Her trip to Las Vegas must be part of a Divine Plan.

"I will come with you, Madre."

Maria Elena smiled, then sipped more tea. "No, Sister Juanita. The children of the orphanage need you here."

"You will not go alone?"

"I was thinking Roberta and Benjamin would join me."

She was proud of her two youngest children, both of whom still lived at the Mission. Maria Elena wanted them to be present for the birth of their sister. The Madre knew it would be a girl. From the first, every birth had alternated gender and, much to her astonishment, race as well. She drifted into thought, wondering what had become of her first six children given up for adoption years ago. It made her sad to think of them and even sadder to realize she probably would never know. Juanita swallowed the rest of her coffee and broke the uncomfortable silence.

"Madre, are you feeling well?"

"Just recalling my life. What a strange journey I've had." A final sip of tea. "Do you know I haven't been in the United States since..." She stopped suddenly, lost in a quagmire of emotion.

"The incident?" Juanita completed her sentence.

Maria Elena nodded, exhaling wearily. "I don't trust the authorities. Because of them, I was forced to flee the country of my birth. Amidst the good, there is evil. Monstrous evil." She flopped her head back in frustration. "And, the worst part is no one knows it's there."

Juanita was wise not to mention Moses, Maria Elena's 21 year old son who was a Sergeant in the elite Army Rangers. His choice of career was a sore point with the Madre. So much so that Moses and his mother hadn't talked in over three years, even though he was stationed just ten miles away at Fort Bliss, Texas. Sister Juanita raised Moses from a baby and regretted the separation between the two.

At that moment, the kitchen door creaked open and in walked Sister Alicia Sanchez, startled to see the women before her.

"Oh, pardon me Madre Superiora. Sister Juanita. I didn't know..."

"That is all right, Sister Alicia," said Juanita as she took her cup and the Madre's to the sink.

"It's almost five and my turn to make breakfast for the children," Sanchez continued to explain.

Sister Alicia was only 24 and new to the Mission, having transferred from another convent in Mexicali. Her pixie-like 5 foot 2, 96 pound frame was accented with golden hair — a result of enough bleach to do a year's laundry.

Maria Elena rose from the table. "I didn't realize it was so late. I'll try to get another hour or so of sleep."

Sister Alicia's eyes followed the pregnant Madre as she walked toward the door. Sanchez was an expert at keeping her feelings to herself and didn't reveal the disgust that welled within. "Good morning, Madre Superiora," came her passionless reply.

Juanita wasn't fooled. She considered herself an excellent judge of character and this young nun smelled like trouble. She made a mental note to watch her closely.

Later that day, Sister Alicia met her brother Juan at a nearby restaurant. She'd transferred from Mexicali so she could see her brother more often since he was the only family she had left. Juan Sanchez was three years older than his kid sister and was a newly hired reporter for the _Diario de Juarez_, the local newspaper. Juan looked nothing like Alicia, with his shoulder-length brown hair, stocky build and Latin good looks. Most people in the restaurant presumed he was a matador or actor, and Juan was certainly vain enough to enjoy the attention. The two sat down, realizing they made a most unlikely pair.

"I guess you won't have a drink with me?" he teased.

"Not a chance. But, I could use one."

The waitress came to take their order. Juan never missed an opportunity to flirt and was a smooth, shameless player. As the waitress left, Alicia expressed her displeasure.

"So, was it good for you?"

"Most definitely," he smiled, watching the woman from behind.

"How do we have the same blood in our veins?"

"I just know how to live," Juan maintained. "You're the one who chose to be holier than thou."

She snorted defiantly. "At least I have morals. I'm not trying to score with every member of the opposite sex."

"Sounds like a plan to me."

"I guess you should hang out at the Mission."

Juan eyed her in amusement. "Do you think the Sisters would appreciate my kind of religion?"

"Ask the Madre Superiora."

He paused in confusion. "Am I missing something here?"

Alicia leaned forward to discuss the juicy gossip. "The Madre Superiora is pregnant."

"What?" chortled her brother in nervous laughter.

"It's not funny, Juan."

He motioned for her to tell the story. "Okay. Let's have it."

Alicia frowned. "The Madre is pregnant and has been several times before. None of the Sisters will even talk of it. And besides, the woman's older than dirt. I can't believe she just walks around with that belly hanging out."

Juan stifled another laugh. "Oh, this is good. Tell me more."

"I don't know more. I told you nobody wants to talk." She bit into a tortilla chip. "It's a disgrace. She's turned a house of God into a brothel. And, what do I tell the children when they ask questions? I can't understand why the Padre permits this."

"Maybe the Padre's the one responsible?"

Alicia's eyes flew wide. "You don't suppose…That would explain why the Sisters won't speak."

Her brother had an inspiration. "Aren't you the secretary for the Orphanage Director?"

"Yes. Her name's Sister Juanita. She's very close with the Madre Superiora."

"Then, you can access the files. Find out what's going on and I'll write the story for the newspaper."

She immediately balked. "I can't do that. I won't expose one sin with another."

"I'll keep your name out of it. You'll be an anonymous source and I'll write the story under another name."

Alicia continued to question the plan. "What if I get caught? This is really serious."

"You're right," Juan agreed. "And, it'll make a great story. Get the files and I'll take it from there."

Although Alicia had severe reservations, she agreed to check the files and assess the information. She was a good Catholic and saw it as her holy duty to protect the sanctity of the Church. After promising to call her brother at home that evening, she settled in to her recently delivered plate of arroz con pollo.

Roberta de la Cruz slapped chalk on her palms, then began her routine on the balance beam. Her flawless performance was no surprise to Sister Lupe Guerro who volunteered three years ago to act as her gymnastics coach. Not that Lupe had any experience as a coach, but she was the only one of the Sisters who recognized the God-given athletic talent in Roberta and thought it a waste not to cultivate it. Although the Madre Superiora didn't understand her daughter's fascination for contorting her body through such unladylike gyrations, she approved the conversion of a storage room to a makeshift gym and the purchase of some secondhand exercise equipment.

The Sister looked on with pride at her one and only student. Lupe was a few days shy of her 30th birthday and wanted to stay 29 at least a few more years. With her brown hair in a pigtail and her thick glasses, she looked more like a librarian than a gymnastics coach. When Lupe was Roberta's age, her parents discouraged her athletic development because she was female. Subconsciously, she was reliving her life through Roberta's training and issued guidance at every opportunity, especially now during her difficult double flip dismount.

"Concentrate, Roberta. Concentrate."

The young gymnast held her handstand for several seconds, then launched herself into the air. She executed the double flip and nailed her landing without a hop. Lupe clapped her hands in appreciation.

"Oh, that was wonderful."

"Sister Lupe, let me try the triple."

The coach smiled. "There's no need for that, Roberta. You have nothing to prove."

"But, is it showing off if I can do it?" she asked. Lupe was caught off-guard by her candid remark.

"Maybe you can try tomorrow. Time to get changed."

Roberta grabbed a towel to wipe the sweat from her neck, but avoided drying her face lest she rub off the small amount of make-up she was forbidden to put on. The young gymnast was already displaying feminine development in her breasts and hips, proudly wearing her exercise leotard long after the workouts were complete. Her jet black hair was cut short, framing a bright smile and sparkling brown eyes. This was one girl who couldn't wait to become a woman.

As Lupe turned, she saw Sister Juanita entering the room from the furthest door. She walked over to greet her.

"Sister Lupe. How is our star athlete?"

"She has the beam perfected. A bit more training on the floor exercises. Still, I think she's a lock for the Pan Am Games."

"You mean the Olympics," corrected Roberta.

The Sisters giggled. They knew she had the talent for such a lofty goal, but a real coach in a real facility, on an official Government team, would be required to secure a trip to the next Olympic games. Unfortunately, the chance of that happening were nil and none. Juanita pulled Lupe closer to keep their conversation private.

"Is Roberta caught up on her studies?"

"Yes," Lupe whispered. "She just took her midterms in Algebra and Literature. She's holding high marks all around."

Juanita nodded. "The Madre will be taking a trip soon. She may want Roberta to accompany her."

"Oh?" Lupe hoped she'd reveal the destination without being asked. Juanita took the bait.

"They are going to Las Vegas."

"Las Vegas!" screamed Roberta from across the room. "Vegas is the bomb. I've got to buy some new clothes."

"There's nothing wrong with her ears," grinned Lupe as they watched the youngster bolt from the room.

Juanita sighed. "God help her mother."

The Madre Superiora was in her study when she heard the church organ blaring an unfamiliar tune. Maria Elena put her reading glasses back in their case, placing her Bible on the desk. She walked toward the door, then down the empty corridor to the adjacent chapel.

Benjamin de la Cruz Nighthawk was at the organ. His small four foot, 90 pound frame was almost invisible, as he had to stretch to reach the bass foot pedals. The precocious child was a true musical prodigy. There wasn't an instrument the youngster couldn't learn to play within record time. He'd composed his own symphony at the age of five and won the national piano concerto competition in Mexico City just two months earlier. When Maria Elena entered the room, all she could see of her overly-talented son was his black mop-top hair over the edge of the ancient Wurlitzer.

"Benjamin!"

The music ceased and her impish son appeared sporting a Cheshire Cat grin. "Yes, Madre?"

"What are you doing? I thought Sister Diana told you to practice the classics?"

"I am, Madre. *'Layla'* by Eric Clapton. One of the true classics."

Maria Elena sighed, plopping herself into a nearby pew. "Can't you play something more uplifting? Spiritual?"

Benjamin produced a mischievous, jack-o-lantern smile. "All right, Madre. How's this?"

He began playing a new tune, one with a strong bass rhythm. The Madre Superiora didn't know the music, but felt it was an improvement. "Fine, Benjamin."

The music continued with Maria Elena keeping time with her right foot. Suddenly, Roberta ran passed the door. She braked, appearing in the chapel breathless.

"Madre, is it true? Las Vegas?"

"How did you hear that?"

"Sister Juanita."

She nodded. "I'm thinking about it."

Roberta knew that was as good as a 'yes'. She kissed her mother on the cheek. "I'm so excited," she exclaimed, pausing to listen to the music. "Madre, I didn't think you wanted him playing songs like that in church?"

"What is it?" she asked with mounting concern.

" *Like a Virgin* — by Madonna."

Maria Elena's eyes opened full. "That's enough, Benjamin! Stop it right now!"

Sister Alicia waited until midnight before entering the storage room where the Orphanage Director's files were kept. She maintained a wary eye on the door, hoping Sister Juanita was sound asleep. The filing cabinets were an old wooden type with a layer of dust caked on top. Using the keys she borrowed from Juanita's desk, Alicia opened all the drawers to locate the required folders. In the fourth cabinet, she removed a file labeled 'Maria Elena de Ia Cruz'. She took the folder to a nearby desk to examine its contents. What Sister Alicia read sent her reeling in astonishment.

"This can't be true," she whispered to herself.

Each page delivered another stunning blow of information, propelling the nun into a state of disgust. *How could the Church allow this to happen? This is an abomination to God. No righteous person could read this and not do something.* Clearly, God wanted her to get involved. To expose this woman as an infidel and sinner. She then called her brother as promised.

"Juan? I can't talk long, but I have the file on the Madre Superiora."

"And?"

"It's worse than I dreamed. This woman has borne nine separate children over a period of 60 years — and there were multiple fathers."

"Does it mention their names?"

"No. Not a single father is identified."

"Then, how do you know?"

She snorted in exasperation. "Because, the first two babies were Black."

"Are you shitting me?"

Alicia turned a sour face. "Why would I do that?"

"Tell me more." His interest was now superheated.

"On March 7, 1948 she gave birth to a Black male child. The baby was adopted by a couple in Philadelphia, Pennsylvania. On June 11, 1955 she gave birth to a Black female who was adopted by a family in Nassau, Bahamas. Then, on November 1, 1962 a Caucasian male was born and adopted by a couple in Dallas, Texas. A Caucasian female was born on March 27, 1969 and taken in by a family in Simi Valley, California. Then, a..."

Alicia stopped short after hearing a noise in the hall.

"What is it?" Juan gasped in concern.

"Wait a minute," she whispered. Alicia heard footsteps approaching, then the sound receded in the distance. "That was close." She forced a cleansing breath, keeping a watchful eye on the door. "Then, two Asian babies, male and female, were born on April 18, 1976 and August 5, 1983. The adoptive families were in Downer's Grove, Illinois and San Mateo, California. The next two children were born February 16, 1990 and January 26, 1997, and were Hispanic. Both of them were raised here at the Mission. The final child was born on March 4, 2004 and is of Native American descent." She shook her head at the thought of Benjamin. "He's a real little know-it-all."

Juan reflected on the news. "That's interesting. She has a baby about every seven years. Anything else?"

"Isn't that enough?" she whined. "This woman's had nine chil-dren out of wedlock — had interracial sex with several men — and instead of kicking her out of here, they made her the Madre Superiora. It's an absolute outrage."

"Okay. When can you get me this?"

Alicia stalled, biting her lip. "Are you sure you can keep my name out of it?"

"Absolutely," Juan assured her. "No one will know."

"I'll make a copy and leave it in the box outside the Mission gate. Can you pick it up tonight?"

"Sure thing. This is going to make a dynamite story."

"I'm only doing this because I'm sure God wants me to," she boasted. "I'll have the file outside within the hour."

Sister Alicia made the duplicate on the office copy machine, then placed the original back in the filing cabinet. 30 minutes later, she tiptoed outside and left the copy for her brother. The 'holy' deed was done.

The next day passed uneventfully. Sister Alicia talked to Juan that afternoon and was told the story would break in the morning paper. The editor of the *Diario de Juarez* decided to print it as a front page headline, with full detail of all the Madre's mysterious offspring. Upon hearing this she expressed regret, but Juan told her the story had already gone to print. It was too late to back out now.

That evening, Sister Alicia resigned herself to the consequences and found it nearly impossible to get sleep. Her conscience played havoc with her. She stayed in her room all night, so none of the Sisters would see how nervous she was. Alicia checked the clock. *3:52 AM. Just another couple of hours. Then, it'll be over.* She kept telling herself God would reward her for exposing such sin within His house. Strangely, this provided no comfort and she continued to suffer silently until dawn.

Curiosity got the better of Sister Juanita. She noticed a small gathering of women outside the Mission gate and couldn't begin to guess why they'd assembled. It was a chilly morning, so she donned a woolen shawl and walked down to the unruly crowd. They yelled various epithets at the Mission, most of which were shocking to the nun.

"House of sin!" one woman screamed.

"Den of shame!" shouted another.

"What is happening here?" Juanita cried, hoping to make sense of the chaotic scene.

Another woman nearest the gate shook a righteous finger. "As if you don't know." She shoved a copy of the morning paper through the rusty metal bars. "Tell us it isn't true."

Juanita scanned the front page story and felt her heart stop. "Oh, my…"

A different woman approached the gate, unable to contain her ire. "We want to see the Madre Superiora! Bring her to us now!"

"Sluts! Harlots!" an anonymous voice rang out.

Juanita ran back inside the Mission, still clutching the newspaper. "Madre! Madre!" she yelled, stumbling down the hallway. Two nuns appeared before her in a doorway. "Where is the Madre?"

"I saw her earlier in the study," Sister Josephina admitted. "What is the matter, Sister?"

Juanita bolted from them without response, trying not to trample several youngsters being escorted by Sister Alicia. She saw the paper in Juanita's hand and knew what this meant. "To your rooms, children. Quickly!"

Maria Elena was immersed in the Bible when Juanita dashed in, breathless. She placed the newspaper before her.

"Madre, I do not know how this happened. I swear. I can not understand." Sensitive adoption information had leaked out and Sister Juanita's responsibility was to keep such matters strictly confidential.

The Madre appeared stunned by the disclosure and the depth of detail to which the story lay claim. Juanita saw Maria Elena's face turn ashen. She tried to stand up, but her aged body went limp, striking her head against the table on the way to the floor. Juanita screamed out and held her stricken friend.

"Someone, come quick! The Madre needs help!"

Sister Alicia was first to the room, acting surprised by the turn of events. She grabbed a pillow off a nearby couch and placed it under Maria Elena's head. "Did she faint?" wondered Alicia.

"Yes," Juanita cried. "She hit her head as she fell. Someone, get Sister Victoria."

Sister Victoria was the resident nurse at the Mission. The Padre Superior next ran into the room and demanded to know what happened. By this point, Juanita was in hysterics and in no position to explain the situation. Alicia then made a fatal error.

"The Madre fainted after reading the story."

"What story?" the Padre asked.

Even in her despair, Sister Juanita knew Alicia was the one who'd betrayed them. Both women stared at each other without a word exchanged. Juanita had promised herself to keep a close eye on Alicia. She had failed.

When the Madre Superiora awoke, she saw Sister Victoria examining her head. "Where am I?" she mumbled in a woozy voice.

"The infirmary," Victoria stated. "You took a nasty spill."

It all came back to her. "Oh," she sighed. "I thought I dreamed it."

Sister Victoria, a kindly 62 year old with gray hair and striking green eyes, continued to hover over Maria Elena placing an ice pack on her scalp. "Leave this in place. You'll be fine."

"The baby?" she asked with concern.

"No problem."

The words gave her comfort. She saw Roberta and Benjamin standing in the doorway, looking puzzled.

"Madre, are you okay?" inquired her son.

Maria Elena struck a weary smile. "Yes, Benjamin. Thank you for asking."

"Is it true, Madre?" probed Roberta. "What they said in the newspaper?"

She paused, thinking through her response. "I didn't read it all. What I saw was true, but not the whole story."

"Why didn't you tell us?" her daughter queried further.

The Madre struggled for an answer. "Sometimes, it's best not to know everything."

She held out her arms and her children filled them willingly. It hadn't yet occurred to Maria Elena that all her offspring were now in mortal danger.

Sister Alicia knew the Padre Superior took confession at 4:00 PM each day in the chapel. She waited for the right moment, then slipped into the booth without being noticed.

"Forgive me Father for I have sinned."

"Yes, my child," the Padre responded. "Tell me your transgression."

Alicia paused to draw a breath. "I read the adoption files on Maria Elena de la Cruz. My brother is a reporter at the *Diario de Juarez*. I let him see a copy of the file."

The arctic silence continued far too long. Sister Alicia began to wonder if the Padre was still there.

"Why?" came his belated reply.

"I felt God wanted me to. I cannot be silent in the presence of sin."

"Sin?"

"A Madre Superiora who has sex with multiple men? That is a sin, Father."

The Padre channeled a leaden sigh. "Child, you've made a horrible mistake. An innocent woman has been crucified by your hand."

She was stunned by his strong rebuke. "Father, I don't understand."

"I want you to go back to the files and look at the folder marked 'Mary Ellen Hart'. You'll then learn what you've done."

"I will Father."

"Say ten Hail Mary's for three weeks and ask the Lord to help us all," the Padre implored. "Go and sin no more."

Sister Alicia wasted little time returning to the scene. The Padre's words haunted her as she rifled through the files. *At last!* The one he mentioned. She loosed the seal on the folder and began to read what happened to the Madre Superiora when she was a girl of 18. After a few minutes, the overly righteous nun dropped her head, spilling an ocean of tears onto the pages of the secret Roswell file.

"Dear God, what have I done?" she sobbed in anguish. "Forgive me, Lord Jesus. I didn't know. I didn't know."

At that moment, she felt a gentle hand on her shoulder. She looked up through swollen eyes to see the Padre Superior also weeping.

"Now you know what you've done. The seed of God entered Maria Elena many years ago. She's been the chosen vessel of His creations. Even our Holy Father in Rome knows of these miracles. The American authorities wish harm to come to her. Not only have you put her in grave danger, but you've placed all her children in jeopardy."

Her angst intensified. "I didn't know, Father. How can I be forgiven?"

The Padre tried to console her through his own torment. "God's mercy is limitless, my child. He will never turn His back on you."

She dunked her head in her hands, crying openly. Alicia felt she'd thrown her soul away. The Padre left the room, respecting her need to be alone.

An hour later, Sister Juanita returned to her office after resting from a headache which had plagued her since morning. As the nun opened the door, she froze in position. There before her was an electric cord slung over a wooden ceiling beam. And hanging from the end of it — was the body of Sister Alicia Sanchez.

CHAPTER FOUR

~~

WASHINGTON, D.C. — MARCH 18ᵗʰ

*E*xhaustion was the diagnosis of the White House physician. He prescribed extra rest. But, President Webber's sleep deprivation was the least of her problems. She was experiencing an inability to concentrate on her work and had lost ten pounds in the past five weeks. Of course, the cause of this remained a mystery to most. But, it was clear she hadn't fully recovered from her introduction to the MAJIK-12.

Therefore, it was less than welcome news when Richard Stern called, requesting her attendance at an NSA meeting to be held in the White House Situation Room at 2:00 PM. She instructed her secretary to juggle her busy schedule, then asked for the Secret Service agent on duty to meet her in the Oval Office.

A moment later, Agent Steven Yeager was before her. With his 6 foot 2, 210 pound frame, the dark-haired, blue-eyed 33 year old could've been the poster boy for *GQ*. The President tried hard not to notice.

"Yes, Madam President?"

"Please close the door."

Yeager complied, remaining at attention. The President seated herself, showing more than casual concern. "There'll be an NSA meeting at 2:00 PM down in the Situation Room. 12 people should be attending. I'd like you to search each of them."

The agent raised an eyebrow in surprise. Webber displayed a harsher tone. "Especially Richard Stern. I want you to give him the Full Monty."

A smile burst across Yeager's face. "I'll do a thorough job, Madam President."

She nodded in response. "I'm sure you will."

President Webber needed to use extreme caution in opposing the MAJIK-12. Out of 107 former members, 94 of them were no longer alive, meeting their demise through an assortment of heart attacks, strokes, car accidents, plane crashes and other 'Acts of God'. Aware that her life and the lives of her children were at risk, she concentrated on subtle intelligence efforts that remained clandestine in nature. She sought private counsel with two former Presidents via telephone. The first, a member of her own political party, remained cordial until the forbidden subject was raised. Without apology, he immediately terminated the call. The other was less fearful, sharing a modest amount of information. He told the President about the Blue Star Trading Company with a banking relationship in the Cook Islands. Blue Star was a front for the CIA, NSA and military to funnel proceeds from illegal arms sales into a slush fund for black programs. This was how the MAJIK-12 received money for its operations. President Webber thanked her predecessor, then called the Secretary of Homeland Security. She requested him to begin an investigation of Blue Star for possible ties to the Al-Qaeda terrorist network and attempt to have its assets frozen. Impressed with her own guile, this act of subversion was just what the doctor ordered.

At 2:00 PM, the President stepped off the elevator and was joined by Steven Yeager a few feet from the Situation Room.

"Everyone was thoroughly searched, Madam President," reported the agent. "They were madder than hornets, but I guess they've cooled down. I took the liberty of another sweep of the room as well."

"Thank you."

"Madam President, I don't pretend to know what goes on in there, nor is it my business to know. However, it is my job to protect you." He handed her a digital beeper. "If you need me, push the button. I'll be in there before you draw your next breath."

She smiled at his consideration. "Thank you, again."

The President entered the room and found her seat as the door latched behind. She noticed two chairs were empty. General McKay and Pierre LeClerke were seen on the wall-sized television in front of the conference table. Before her was the same list of attendees as before with a special notation of the secure satellite videolink from Dreamland. The stated agenda was '...to discuss the recent discovery of the sole surviving Roswell witness and finalize plans to deal with the security breach...'. The President found this intriguing. There had been no previous mention of a witness.

Stern began the briefing, trying to conceal his humiliation regarding the all-too-intimate search. "I trust, Madam President, you enjoyed your little power trip with the Secret Service?"

"Being President does have its benefits," she stated, repressing a reflex to laugh.

His voice resonated with contempt. "Not in his room." Stern paused to collect an agenda sheet from the table. "Because of the emergency nature of this meeting, we couldn't wait to recall General McKay and Mr. LeClerke to Washington. Therefore, they're joining us via satellite link from Dreamland. Gentlemen, can you hear us?"

"Yes, sir," McKay responded.

"Quite well, thank you," added LeClerke.

Stern turned to CIA Director Langlois. "Walter, I think you should begin."

The wiry redhead rose from his chair and straightened his tie in fluid motion. "As most of you know, the CIA hires a staff of people whose only task is to read and synopsize printed articles in foreign magazines and newspapers. If there's anything identified as having national security interest, it's flagged and sent to the Director of Information's Office and, if appropriate, on to my attention. If you'll look in the BLACK MAJIK folders before you, there's an English language translation of an article which appeared in the *Juarez Daily* four days ago."

As pages turned throughout the room, he continued in a halting manner. "For those who haven't had a chance to read this, let me summarize. It seems the missing witness to the Roswell crash has finally been located. Her name is Mary Ellen Hart. Since 1947, she's resided at Our Lady of Guadalupe Mission in Juarez, Mexico. Over that period she's given birth to nine children of different races and gender and is expecting another child in a few weeks."

"How can that be?" gasped the Attorney General. "This woman's over 80 years old. She's 30 years past menopause."

"Something extraordinary must have happened to her that night in Roswell," the NASA Director added. "Perhaps the creature..."

"Bullshit! That thing was killed the moment the MPs got to the scene," retorted Admiral Holliman, his pointed finger twitching with uncontrolled palsy. The 64 year old Chairman of the Joint Chiefs was in poor health from Parkinson's Disease, and the deep hollows and lines in his face made him appear closer to death than he was. He also never minced words. "I ain't gonna listen to nobody's crap about how this damn alien must've fucked her."

Blau issued a smile. "Admiral, since the creature had no genitalia, I think that might have been difficult at best."

The President saw her chance to deliver a well-placed dig. "Mr. Stern, how was this allowed to happen? You knew this girl was a loose end. Didn't you think this would come back to bite you on the ass?"

Stern clenched his hands, refusing to retaliate verbally. "General Connolly? Please inform the President of the procedures taken to capture Miss Hart."

The Army General stood to address her. Connolly was 61, with dark, ebony skin and short, gray hair on the back and sides of his head. His pleasant face and smooth as silk voice seemed out of place for such a top military official. "Madam President, the MPs intercepted her date that evening, a boy named Bobby Kirke. He was on his way to phone for help and had left her back at the crash site. When they arrived, she was gone. Mr. Kirke was placed in custody and killed trying to escape. Other MPs went to the Hart household and arrested the family. However, Miss Hart never returned home." General Connolly returned to his seat.

After an icy pause, Stern acknowledged Professor Blau who was busy clearing his throat. "Is there something you'd like to add, Professor?"

"Yes, there is," he stated, still examining the Juarez article. "Mary Ellen Hart's first child was born nine months after the Roswell incident. According to her parents' testimony, she was a virgin at the time. Therefore, since the first baby was Black, Bobby Kirke couldn't have been the father."

"So, the alien did do something to her," theorized Leonetti.

Blau winced. "Alien's not the right word. If we believe these beings to be our descendants, then they too are human. Just more genetically advanced. As for what happened, I can only speculate."

"Then speculate," commanded Stern.

A forced sigh punctuated the moment. "It seems the surviving being did impregnate her through a more evolved method than sexual intercourse. The fact she bears a child once every seven years is fascinating. Somewhat analogous to a perennial flower that grows year after year without having to be re-seeded."

"We're not talking about a plant, Mr. Blau," Roth contended.

"Indeed, we aren't. In fact, this is something completely new to humanity. And if I'm right, it could be a very disturbing turn of events."

"What are you trying to say?" Langlois demanded.

"Her children are the next step in human evolution. They're probably stronger, smarter — even more gifted than any of us. And, if they were to breed within their own group..." His voice suddenly abandoned him.

"A super race of humans," Leonetti murmured, deep in thought. "And, we'd be left behind. They'd look at us, like we look at — chimps."

Stern recoiled in his chair. The military men appeared especially agitated. President Webber grasped the impact of the revelation, nervously massaging her ballpoint pen. She began to wonder if any positive news was heard at a MAJIK-12 meeting.

"We have a volatile situation here," Stern conceded. "Fortunately, we have time to contain it. I call for a vote. All those in favor of issuing termination warrants for this woman and her children."

"What?" the President gasped. "You can't kill people because they're different. Their purpose could be totally benign. They have a right to live, dammit!"

"And the MAJIK-12 has a right to defend itself," Stern fired back. "In any war, there's always casualties."

"This isn't a war, Mr. Stern."

"Please don't be naive, Madam President," Langlois interjected. "There isn't a country on Earth that wouldn't kill us all to gain the secrets of Roswell."

Webber squirmed with agitation. "This woman didn't ask for this. What about her rights? Her civil liberties? This is a nation of…"

"There's no time for debate," Stern interrupted. "I call for a vote."

"I second the vote," exclaimed Langlois.

Stern grabbed a pad of paper to record the results. It was over in seconds. With just the President and Ortiz-Bennett voting no, and Roth and LeClerke abstaining, the fate of Mary Ellen Hart and her children were sealed. The votes were tallied and Stern proclaimed the verdict.

"With nine yes votes, the motion is carried. How do we proceed?"

"We'll need the FBI to locate the six adopted children," admitted Langlois. "Once acquired, we'll hire mercenaries to finish the job. Less attention that way."

"Agreed," FBI Director Monroe responded. "I'll have the Bureau track down the adoptive families and isolate the children as soon as possible."

"What about the four known targets?" inquired Stern. "I understand one is yours, General Connolly."

He nodded, scanning a fax in hand. "Yes, sir. Moses de la Cruz Castaneda. Sergeant in the U.S. Army Rangers. Currently stationed at Fort Bliss. Damn fine soldier by the looks of this. Hate to lose him."

"What's your plan, General?" Stern continued to probe.

"I'll have Colonel Wright, his Commanding Officer, neutralize Castaneda. Then, we'll send a squad of Rangers into Juarez. They'll attack the Mission, eliminating Hart and her two children."

Stern came to his feet, stopping adjacent to the video screen. "General McKay, any chance this could compromise Dreamland?"

"No, sir," he stated. "As long as the job gets done."

He acknowledged the assessment, turning back to the others. "I want those termination warrants issued tonight. Call it 'Operation Black Widow'."

Langlois and Connolly nodded in unison, their responses overlapping. "We'll do it." "Yes, sir."

"Don't forget the baby," Blau whispered. His lack of conscience was compounded by Stern's.

"When they get Hart — the baby will go with her."

The President was horrified. Although she'd never met Mary Ellen Hart, she shared a bond with her that all mothers possess. She feared for the children's safety as if they were her own. Webber knew she had to do something, but her game plan had yet to be implemented.

"Listen to me," Stern implored, thrusting his finger at the BLACK MAJIK folder before him. "These people don't exist a month from now. Am I understood? No excuse is acceptable. If anyone gets in the way, eliminate them, too. Smoke this whole family — before they discover how special they are."

CHAPTER FIVE

EL PASO, TEXAS and JUAREZ, MEXICO — MARCH 19th

The bed in room 618 at El Paso's Embassy Suites Hotel had seldom seen such acrobatic activity. As their bodies thrust in tandem, time and space began to dissolve. They entered their own world, at last merging into combined flesh.

After three blissful hours, they returned to reality. Both were spent, each secretly admiring their own stamina. They toweled the sweat from each other and shared a welcome shower. The two kissed with a passion few have known. An insatiable hunger nothing but the other could satisfy. They separated long enough to stare eye to eye, immersing themselves in the deep brown oceans which held their souls. Their frantic union gained speed as he again filled the limits within her. They then helped each other from the shower and donned robes provided by the hotel.

Moses de la Cruz Castaneda plopped himself onto a sofa in front of the TV. His black hair was spiked in different directions, since he didn't have the strength necessary to lift a brush. At 5 foot 10, 190 pounds, he wasn't the biggest member of the Army Rangers, but it wouldn't do to underestimate his lethality. He'd graduated top of his class and mastered firearms training, desert and jungle operations and hand-to-hand combat, as well as attaining expert status in tae-kwon-do, ju-jitsu and karate. In fact, his buddies nicknamed him 'Taz' because of his wild, superhuman speed and moves. His reputation was well earned and, at times, he even surprised himself. Equally impressed was Atali Castaneda who, after blow drying her long brown hair, sat beside him.

They'd known each other for more than five years. Moses and Atali met at a high school dance in El Paso while he resided at the Mission in Juarez. Their less than discreet romance upset Maria Elena who fought a losing battle to teach Moses the virtues of sexual self-control. His mother's constant harping on the issue forced him to leave the Mission and he was taken in by the Castanedas who owned a large hacienda on the outskirts of El Paso. Atali's father welcomed Moses, treating him like the son he'd never had. Moses eagerly took the family name as his own. If he and Atali were to have a future together, Moses realized he'd have to select a profession. His choice of the United States Army caused Maria Elena great distress, something he never completely understood. Because of this, the Madre and her son hadn't spoken in more than three years.

Moses was granted assignment to Fort Bliss, the massive Army complex in El Paso. Although he lived on-base, he was always able to secure a 48 hour pass to see Atali. They usually spent 47 of those hours in a hotel.

Atali was as beautiful as her name, chosen by her grandmother from an ancient Mayan text about a goddess of love who could capture any man's heart. Her curvaceous figure left no doubt she was a woman. Moses couldn't keep his hands off her and she couldn't live without his touch. The two were hopelessly in love and both wanted the world to know it.

Having surfed the TV channels, a pay-per-view movie was selected. Moses was ravenous. He checked his watch. *10:45 PM. Still time to order room service.* He snatched the in-room menu from a nearby table.

"What do ya want, babe?"

"I'll have a Chicken Caesar."

As he went to call in their order, Moses noted the message light was on. Earlier, he'd requested the hotel operator to place a 'Do Not Disturb' on their phone so they wouldn't be bothered during the heat of passion — the very reason he and Atali never brought their cell phones along. Moses dialed the operator for the message.

"Yes, Mr. Castaneda. You received a call at 9:26 PM from Abraham Rodriguez. He said it was most urgent and to contact him on his cell phone. He told me you had the number."

"I do. Thanks." He hung up, then dialed Abraham's number. *What could be this urgent?* One ring, then two. Finally, an answer.

"What's up, Pops?" Moses asked. 'Pops' had been Abraham's nickname since the two had met at the Mission orphanage. "Worried I'm getting too much?"

"Man, the shit's flying over here. Don't come back to the Base."

"Say, what?"

"The Colonel's sending us into Juarez on a turkey shoot. They're after your mom, man. The fucking Rangers are going after your mom."

Moses was incredulous. "What do they want with her?"

"I dunno, Taz. But, she ain't the only one. They want your brother and sister, too."

"When's this going down?"

"0400 this morning. The MPs are out scoping for you now. Better warn your mom, then disappear. And, Taz..."

"Yeah?"

"This call didn't happen, man. I ain't catching a bullet over this."

Moses understood. Tipping off a secret military operation could mean a court-martial — if you were lucky. He tried to sort through the thoughts stampeding in his mind. One thing was clear. Dinner would have to wait.

"Thanks, Pops. I owe you a big one."

"Already got me a big one, Taz," letting slide an ill-timed joke. "Just keep your head down, okay?"

As he hung up, Atali could sense his mounting concern. "Moses? What's happened?"

"Nothing yet. Get dressed."

Clothes flew across the room. He explained the situation as best he could while nearly ripping the buttons from his shirt. The first thing was to escort Atali safely home. A few moments later, he knew that wouldn't be easy.

As they left the room, Moses peered into the cavernous atrium of the hotel. Beyond the fountains and a bank of imported palms stood a Military Police officer, dressed in jungle fatigues, his assault rifle at the ready. Another MP was at the front desk, questioning the clerk. *How did they track us down? Did they tap Abraham's phone?* If so, they'd be after him, too.

"Shit," exclaimed Moses through his teeth. "Go down the rear stairwell."

They completed a few steps when the MPs noticed them from below. "Castaneda! Halt!"

Moses and Atali bolted toward the stairwell door. The armed MP fired a burst of gunfire, blowing out two glass windows and shredding the facade near several sixth floor rooms. Shrieks of terror echoed through the atrium as stunned hotel guests dropped to the deck. The other MP grabbed the rifle, pointing it to the ground.

"Not in the hotel, fuckhead. Get some backup here fast."

They split up, with one running to their jeep as the other dashed through the atrium in pursuit. People clustered outside their rooms to investigate the commotion, while others screamed for lack of knowing what else do to.

As Atali reached the third floor landing, Moses pulled her through the door leading to the corridor.

"What are we doing?"

"Head for the front stairwell. He thinks we're coming down the back."

They sprinted through a crowd of stunned guests and descended the other stairwell until exiting a fire door to the outside. The alarm blared, piercing the night air. In a state of confusion, Atali turned to Moses for guidance.

"Now what?"

"Get your car. Don't worry. They're after me, not you."

Moses kissed her, then jumped over a waist-high hedge disappearing from view. Atali ran toward the parking lot to find her fire-red Chevrolet Corvette. A few seconds later, the MP appeared at the exit and saw her running through the wet grass beyond. He drew his .44 automag with laser sight. With lightning speed, Moses jumped back over the hedge, grabbed the gun and bent the MP into it. Three rounds erupted through the soldier's arched back. Moses ignored the splattered blood on his face, keeping the weapon as his own. He leapt back over the hedge and circled to the front entrance.

The other MP was in the military jeep, talking on the field radio with two other units. Both confirmed they were minutes from the scene. Moses approached with stealth, using a stretch limousine parked along the blind side for cover. The next thing the MP heard were the cervical vertebrae snapping in his neck from a powerful headlock. Moses showed no emotion. He was in kill mode and a nagging conscience could prove fatal.

The radio was on, with one of the approaching units requesting a response. "Say again, Unit Alpha. Say again. We didn't copy your last message. Say again."

Moses grabbed the mike, pressing the button to transmit. "This is Unit Alpha. Castaneda here. Both MPs down for the count. Hope you brought some music, boys. I'm ready to dance."

"Shit," clamored the other unit. "Break communication."

The radio went dead, followed by light static. Moses shoved the MP's body into the passenger seat and took control of the vehicle. He noticed another jeep speeding toward the hotel, coming off a nearby Interstate 10 exit ramp. Moses strapped himself into his seat, then gunned the vehicle through the parking lot. The jeeps collided head-on, leaving the arriving soldiers dazed and sending the cadaver headfirst through the windshield.

"Better buckle up, soldier," stated Moses in mock concern. "That'll hurt like hell in the morning."

He climbed out of the jeep, steam escaping from a burst radiator. Atali sped over in her top-down Corvette.

"Come on," she cried.

Moses didn't argue, jumping in beside her. She floored the car down the adjacent service road and onto the eastbound lanes of Interstate 10. It was late night and traffic was light on the roadway.

"Are you all right?"

"I'm fine," Moses assured her. He then cursed Atali's sense of timing. "I shoulda taken care of business back there. They'll be after us. Another unit's on its way, too."

"Shouldn't you call your mom and warn her?"

"Good idea. Let's find a phone."

They exited the Interstate at the next opportunity, crossing back under the roadway to stop at a gas station on the corner. Moses ran to a payphone to make the call. As he waited for the connection, he looked back at Atali's car bathed in the overhead lights. It didn't occur to him they were far too easy to spot. He was greeted by a most unwelcome busy signal. *What nun would be on the phone at this hour?* Moses forced a sigh and walked back toward the car. From the corner of his eye, he noticed a military jeep emerging from the highway underpass. They were out of time.

"Go!" he yelled, jumping inside.

Her vehicle spun in a tight arc with the jeep a few yards behind. Atali swerved, cutting off another car and accelerated up the ramp of westbound Interstate 10. Moses heard a collision. He looked back to see the jeep broadside the other car, forcing it from the road. The MPs narrowly avoided the ramp abutment, maintaining pursuit. Next came the clatter of automatic weapons fire. Atali could have outrun the jeep if not for several trucks blocking a clear path of escape. Another burst of gunfire struck the rear of the car, shattering the taillights and forcing Atali to scream. Moses waited until the jeep was directly behind, then forced his leg between hers to depress the brake pedal. The MPs rammed them from behind. Before Atali could summon a breath, Moses jumped from the Corvette and onto the jeep. The car surged forth, leaving the military vehicle in a cloud of spent rubber. Moses windmilled his legs, slamming his right foot through their windshield.

"Jesus!" the driver yelped, as shards of glass covered him. Castaneda flung his boot into the MP's face, transforming his nose into a reddish paste. As the other MP drew his gun, Moses pendulumed over, hanging just outside the driver's door. The MP fired the weapon, accidentally lodging half a clip into the driver. Moses tossed the corpse out, then hurled both feet into the cab pummeling the MP with a series of rapid fire kicks. The final blow cracked the MP's jaw, propelling the bone into his brain. Castaneda jettisoned the body with little effort. The Rangers hadn't named him 'Taz' for nothing.

A few hundred yards ahead, the jeep which Moses had crashed into cut across the grassy median in pursuit of Atali's Corvette. Gunfire flashed across the westbound lanes as nearby trucks entered into a chorus of locked tires and burning brake pads. Moses stood on the accelerator, trying to draw the jeep's fire. As he pulled even with the MPs, another tongue of gunfire lapped at the Corvette, shredding the driver's side of the car. Atali dropped back as Moses rammed his jeep into the other. He grabbed the .44 automag from his belt and shot their right rear tire. The MPs' jeep rolled counterclockwise forcing the driver to lose control. The doomed vehicle burst into flames, then cartwheeled over a bridge. There was no need to check. The MPs were incinerated.

Anxious moments later, Moses returned to the bullet ravaged Corvette. His heart sank as he noticed blood drenching Atali's sweater and jeans. She'd been shot in the left arm and breast.

"Hold on, babe," Moses implored. "I'll get you help."

Tears welled in his eyes as he gingerly placed her in the jeep. He wrapped a blanket around Atali's shoulders, then sped to El Paso Regional Hospital five minutes distant. It was the longest drive of his life. Along the way, he continued to reassure her, knowing no one was there to comfort him.

Upon arriving at the Emergency Room, Moses scooped the precious cargo in his arms, wasting little time getting her inside. After explaining the nature of her injuries to an attending nurse, Atali was placed on an awaiting gurney. They rushed her into the Operating Room which was off limits to Castaneda.

"Doctor Ziegler. Doctor Hernandez. Report to the Emergency Room — Stat," the PA blared above. The urgent message was repeated.

Moses stood alone in the waiting area. The Army taught him how to act on impulse, but now there was nothing more he could do. His only thought was of Atali and how he failed to kiss her as she went to surgery. His mind was a mass of raging impulses. He blamed himself for allowing harm to come to her and vowed the Army would pay.

Another nurse entered the Waiting Room with a clipboard. She directed Moses to sit in a nearby chair, assuring him Atali was in the best of care. "I need some information," the nurse stated. "Her name, address, next of kin, any allergies she has or medications she's on. That sort of thing."

Moses answered her questions. Afterward, the nurse shook her head. "Strange. Two shootings in one night."

"Two?"

"Yes. Automatic weapon fire. We don't see much of that, thank God."

"Who was the other?" he probed.

She flipped a few pages on her clipboard. "His name was Abraham Rodriguez."

"Was?" his voice rising an octave.

"I'm afraid so. Pronounced dead when he arrived. Was he a..."

She stopped mid-sentence as Moses fled to the jeep. The police would soon be there asking all sorts of questions. There was no time for that. He gunned the vehicle and headed for the International Border.

Moses remembered the imminent attack on the Mission. *One hour left*. The heads-up Abraham provided had cost 'Pops' his life. His best friend was dead. The love of his life in critical condition. *What had mother done to make the Army do this?* Moses would stop at nothing to find out.

Another group of candles were lit in the chapel. The Madre Superiora was joined by the Padre Superior, Sister Juanita and Sister

Josephina who lowered their heads in silent reverence. Maria Elena knelt at the altar and prayed for guidance. A minute later, she made the sign of the cross, opening her eyes to be greeted by the others' concern.

"Maria Elena, we must make plans for your safety," the Padre urged.

"Yes, Madre," Sister Juanita agreed. "You cannot ignore this warning. That call was ordained by God."

Maria Elena rose to her feet. "Sister Josephina, you're certain you didn't know the caller?"

"I did not, Madre Superiora. He did not tell me his name, but did say the Army would attack the Mission in four hours — and that you and your children were in danger."

The Padre addressed Josephina. "When did you take the call?"

"About midnight, Padre. Almost three hours ago."

He shuddered with the news. "Madre, that leaves little time. We must get you, Roberta and Benjamin out of the Mission as soon as possible."

Maria Elena paused as the baby moved within, settling down after finding a more comfortable position. She mulled through her limited options. "Padre, I feel like I've been running for years. I'm tired of the chase. Besides, we don't know if the caller was telling the truth."

"It was the truth, Madre," came a deep male voice. Maria Elena knew instantly who it was. Juanita turned to see Sister Lupe in the doorway standing next to the young man who'd left more than three years before.

"Moses!" she exclaimed. "How long have you been there?"

"Just a minute. Sister Lupe let me in."

Sister Juanita ran to hug him, leading Moses to the others. In an uncomfortable moment, he greeted the Padre Superior and Sister Josephina before finally addressing Maria Elena.

"Madre?"

She stared at him with hopelessly wet eyes. "Yes, my son?"

He bit down on his lip, fighting back emotion. "You were right. They are evil."

Maria Elena smiled and absorbed him in her arms. Tears fell the length of Moses' face. "You were right all along," he admitted.

Maria Elena held her son, basking in the glow of the Mother and Child reunion. He composed himself in short order. "The Army's sending a strike squad to the Mission. They'll be here at anytime."

"How do you know?"

"Abraham's dead because he alerted me. They attacked us, Madre. Atali was badly injured. It's the truth. We must get Roberta and Benjamin and leave while we can."

Maria Elena finally nodded in agreement. "Sister Lupe, please wake my children and bring them here."

"At once, Madre Superiora."

"What's this about, Madre? Why's the U.S. Army trying to kill you — a Mexican nun?"

"Sister Juanita, would you please bring the newspaper article to my son?"

"Yes, Madre." She left immediately to fetch the item.

"I'll use this time to pack for you and the children," Sister Josephina stated. The Padre Superior agreed to go with her to help speed things along. At last, Moses and Maria Elena were alone.

"Moses, since you are now a man, I will tell you what I know. I owe you that."

The Madre Superiora disclosed her true identity and what happened that night in Roswell years ago. She recounted the events as if they'd occurred yesterday. Moses listened without interruption, finally scanning the newspaper article Sister Juanita handed him. Incredibly, it all made sense.

"Do Roberta and Benjamin know this?" he asked.

Maria Elena nodded. "I had to tell them the other day."

Moses expressed concern about her obviously pregnant state. "How much longer, Madre?"

"A few weeks. Certainly not tonight."

He smiled. "Where do you wish to go?"

The Madre Superiora gave Sister Juanita a knowing glance. "Las Vegas. The Padre has prepared a safe place for me there."

At that moment, Sister Lupe returned with Roberta and Benjamin in tow.

"Moses!" his sister cried in joy.

They hugged each other. Benjamin was still half asleep, trying to understand the fuss.

"Hi, Ben." Moses bent down to hug the youngster. "I guess you don't remember me."

"Sure, I do," he yawned. "You're the one who ran away."

Sister Juanita stifled a laugh. *Leave it to Benjamin to break the ice with an icicle.*

"What's going on?" wondered Roberta, pulling a sweater over her shoulders in response to a chill in the air. Moses' eyes flew open. A small laser targeting dot was lit over Roberta's chest. Time was up. The enemy was here.

"On the floor! Now!" Moses screamed.

He pulled Roberta and Benjamin down in swift reflex. The three of them landed behind one of the long, wooden pews. Looking up, Moses saw Sister Lupe falling backward after taking a round from a sharpshooter.

Sister Juanita saw another laser dot on the bulging belly of Maria Elena, three feet away. Instinctively, she moved in front of the Madre to protect her. Juanita was shot in the back, collapsing into Maria Elena and sending both to the floor.

Moses pulled a gun and shot the fluorescent lights above them, shattering the glass tubes and plunging the chapel into darkness. Muffled screams flooded the room, much to Moses' chagrin. "Quiet. Don't move."

"Sister Lupe," cried Roberta, slithering a few feet toward her. The nun was clutching her left shoulder, moaning in agony.

Moses grabbed his sister by the foot, sliding her back across the floor. "It's a shoulder wound. She'll live."

"But, she needs me."

"She doesn't need you dead. Stay here with Ben."

"He's not the one shot," Roberta sobbed.

"They're not after her. They're after us."

She finally nodded in compliance, flinging tears from her face. "Oh, Madre..." Juanita gasped in pain. "I did not mean to fall on you."

Maria Elena comforted the nun by stroking her hair. "You've always been there for me and I'll always be here for you."

Juanita smiled bravely through her injury. The Madre pulled her closer, noting the blood now gushing from her back. She kept her hand over the Sister's wound in an attempt to keep the precious fluid from escaping further.

Moses raised up to peer over the pews. The shots were fired through a stained glass wall depicting Christ's Last Supper. Four laser beams projected into the room in a frantic criss-cross search for another target.

"Stay down," Moses implored, falling back to the floor. He knew the worst was yet to come.

Outside the Mission, a dozen commandos from the elite Army Rangers assessed the situation. There were six sharpshooters brandishing HK-416 assault rifles with laser sights and infrared night scopes, two light artillery men with Rocket Propelled Grenades, two logistics men in the support truck parked a block away, as well as a field spotter and Unit Commander who were communicating on a walkie-talkie.

"We have two down in the church, but I don't think they're the ones, Commander," the spotter relayed. "No visible targets remain."

"Pull the shooters back," came the order. "RPG units, prepare to engage."

Two soldiers knelt just outside the Mission perimeter, inserting the bulbous, front-loaded weapons through the wrought iron gate.

"Fire!"

The grenades sped toward the Mission, spewing a trail of exhaust and smoke. They crashed through the stained glass, exploding in two simultaneous fireballs within the chapel. Six soldiers then began to scale the fence and storm the Mission.

Thick smoke and fire now saturated the room. Moses jumped to his feet, barking out commands. "We've gotta get outta here. The smoke'll give us cover. Move!"

He grabbed Sister Lupe and draped her over his shoulder, running for the door. Appearing in the hallway, Sister Josephina and the Padre Superior were aghast at the scene. He handed them the injured nun and returned for Maria Elena.

The fire was burning the pews as well as ornate curtains and tapestries. A massive hole was blown through the confessional and the life-sized crucifix of Jesus on the cross was torn from its mountings, hanging loosely on the wall. Smoke blanketed every corner of the room, making it difficult for Moses to locate his mother. At last, he found her underneath one of the pews. Maria Elena looked up at her son, still cradling her best friend.

"Sister Juanita is now with God."

He hesitated only briefly. "Come on, Madre. We must get out of here."

Moses helped Maria Elena to her feet, slinging Juanita's body over his shoulder. He safely led his mother out of the fire-drenched chapel. Once in the hallway, he noticed someone was missing.

"Where's Ben?"

"I thought he was with you," Josephina cried.

Moses ran back into the room, choking on the smoke. Through the murky haze, he saw the youngster pushing his prized Wurlitzer in front of the stained glass wall. Incredulous, he dashed over. "What are you doing?"

"I don't want it to burn up."

"Fuck that," forgetting he was in a house of worship. "I'll get you a new one. Come on."

At that moment, two soldiers crashed through a portion of the wall, falling into the back of the awkwardly placed organ. They destroyed the instrument, snapping several bones in their legs and feet. As they screamed in agony, Moses leveled his gun.

"Stop that whining."

Two bullets later, they complied. Moses turned to his little brother and shook a righteous finger. "You didn't see what you just saw."

"Sure," he stated. "As long as I get a new organ. You promised."

Moses didn't have time to argue with the little extortionist. "Get outta here."

Benjamin ran out of the chapel and into the hall with the others. Castaneda knew the soldiers would advance in staggered two-by-two cover formations. He perched himself upon a low wooden crossbeam and awaited the next wave of the attack. Hearing a creak, he saw Roberta climbing up to join him.

"Now what?" exclaimed Moses.

"You'll need help."

"Not from you. This is way too..." He was cut short by the sound of two more soldiers crashing through the wall, sending a shower of multicolored shards across the room. They were wearing night vision goggles and carrying HK-416s. Moses paused to judge the distance, then swooped down. In whirlwind fashion, he struck the right knee of one, buckling him to the floor. After ripping the goggles from the other, he twisted the soldier's head half-around, snapping his neck. As he removed a hunting knife from its sheath, two more soldiers crashed through, shattering the remainder of the stained glass. He plunged the knife into the neck of the hobbled soldier, twisting it a quarter-turn for good measure. Before Moses realized, Roberta swung down over the wood beam as though working a routine on the uneven bars. She caught one soldier square in the face felling him to the ground while dropkicking the other toward her brother. Castaneda grabbed the off-balance soldier and flung him against the far wall, then hurled his knife into the back of the other. The soldier collapsed, gagging on his blood. Moses spun to face the remaining commando, noting the man's laser sight lit upon him. Without warning, the ten-foot crucifix jarred loose. It plunged to the floor, cleaving the soldier open in a stomach churning mass.

Moses looked upon the scene in reverence. "Thank you, Jesus," he whispered.

He ran to Roberta, pointing to the fire now engulfing the confessional booth, choir dais and half the wooden pews. "Thanks, sis. Now get some people to fight this fire."

"What are you going to do?" she wondered, awed by his lethal handiwork.

Her brother grabbed an RPG from one of the dead soldiers. "I'm taking this fight to them. Now go."

Roberta bolted from the room, remembering some fire extinguishers stored in her makeshift gymnasium. Castaneda pointed the weapon through the breached wall, taking aim on the unit's logistics vehicle parked about 100 yards away. Suddenly, the grenade streaked through the night. The soldiers inside were consumed within an orange fireball which lifted the vehicle 30 feet in the air while other munitions aboard detonated with fury. Moses grabbed one of the rifles and using the backglow from the explosion, picked off two more commandos silhouetted in the darkness. Lights across Juarez popped on as frightened residents witnessed the mayhem. Castaneda drew upon his experience. A military strike team consisted of a dozen men and two were still unaccounted for. There was only one answer. They were circling around to the rear of the Mission.

Moses dashed out of the chapel, past his family and down the length of the great hallway. He stopped to comfort some of the terrified orphan children who were being herded together by Sister Diana.

"Be quiet guys," he said with a forced smile. "It's almost over. Stay there."

He trotted further down the hallway to the kitchen, hearing the soldiers enter through the service door beyond. He knew they'd be wearing their night vision goggles. Moses reached into the room, flipping on the overhead light. The soldiers cried out, blinded by the brightness. Storming into the room, he windmilled his legs into one, chopping him to his knees and coldcocking him with his pistol butt. The other fired a shot, grazing Moses' right arm, before being the unlucky recipient of a series of bruising kicks and blows. The soldier lunged for a butcher's knife on the kitchen counter. Moses caught his arm on the way back, desperately grappling with the much larger opponent. He noticed a grenade attached to the soldier's belt and pulled the pin from the weapon. Summoning all his strength, Moses dropkicked the soldier toward the sink. He dove clear, pulling the heavy oak table to the floor as protection from the imminent blast. An instant later, the soldier was consumed in an explosion of shrapnel.

Moses located a kitchen towel to use as a tourniquet for his bleeding arm. He grabbed the butcher's knife and placed it to the throat of the now semiconscious soldier. He knew the man. Master Sergeant Randy Hicks, the Ranger Team leader.

"On your feet, Sergeant," yanking him from the floor. He kept the knife square to the man's neck.

Hicks focused on Moses. "Castaneda. I shoulda known."

"You've got five seconds to explain."

"Explain, shit. You know as much as I do," Hicks shouted, rubbing the back of his head. "Colonel Wright's orders. A Ranger does what he's told. You know that."

Moses understood. "Anymore out there?"

"No. Standard unit. 12 men."

"Did you kill Abraham?"

An uncomfortable pause. "That was the MPs."

Castaneda felt woozy from the loss of blood and rigors of the fight. There was just one thing left to do. "Let's go."

He led him to the main reception area where a number of the Sisters were now congregated.

"Strip," ordered Moses.

"What?"

"You heard me. All the way."

After initial hesitation, the man complied. He eventually stood there fully naked, resembling a Greek statue come to life. The Sisters all feigned shock, keeping hands over eyes, peeking only when necessary.

Castaneda opened the door and motioned him out. "Go tell 'em you failed."

Hicks snorted in disgust. "Like this?"

"Could be worse," Moses teased. "Won't take you long to clear Customs."

The soldier walked off having lost the battle as well as his clothes. Moses knew this wasn't over. The Army would never allow themselves to be humiliated in this manner. However, he let a shallow smile bloom forth. The good guys had won this round.

He returned to the chapel to find the fire extinguished. The room was filled with smoke, as well as several unpleasant cadavers.

The Padre approached Moses, placing his hand on the young man's shoulder. "The chapel can be replaced, but not Sister Juanita. God now has one of His brightest angels."

Moses had been as close to her as anyone and felt the loss keenly. "It won't be the same without her," he stated. "How's Sister Lupe?"

"Sister Victoria called for an ambulance to take her to the hospital, but she's sure she'll recover." The Padre eyed the young man's arm with concern. "Come, my son. Sister Victoria needs to look at you, too."

The view through the shattered stained glass caused Moses to freeze. Three police cars were already outside the Mission gate. A number of officers were examining the bodies and securing the area. Distant sirens were getting louder. It was clear the authorities would soon have them in custody.

"My arm can wait, Padre," Moses affirmed. "But, our departure can't. Is there any other way out of here?"

His mind raced for an answer. "There might be," he mused. "Find the Madre. We must leave at once."

The Padre Superior was intimately familiar with the design of the ancient Mission and its unique history. The Nuestra Señora de Guadalupe Mission was built in 1659 by a group of Franciscan Friars and the local Piro Tribe. In 1681, the Nuestra Señora del Carmen Mission was constructed over a mile distant by the neighboring Tiguas. An early 19th Century flood changed the course of the Rio Grande, effectively separating the two missions. The Mexican-American War of 1845 allowed Texas to join the United States and the Rio Grande became the International Border. What was never disclosed to either country was that an elaborate network of underground catacombs linked the two missions…and this tunnel system could function as an escape route.

Prior to leaving, the Padre called the El Paso mission to inform them of their plans. He also arranged for Sister Josephina and Sister Victoria to drive the Church minivan over the Border with the Madre's luggage later that day.

Before the police could detain them, the Padre Superior led Maria Elena and her children through a fake fireplace facade and down into the underground labyrinth. The musty air assaulted their senses as he directed them by flashlight. They boarded a small rail handcar used for transporting coffins to their burial crypt. Moses and Roberta worked in tandem to propel the platform down a narrow track while the Padre searched the darkness ahead. Benjamin was awestruck, in disbelief such a fascinating world had eluded his discovery. The Madre remained silent, remembering her journey through this tunnel years before when she was smuggled into Juarez. She closed her eyes as long dormant emotions washed over her like ripples in time. It occurred to her that the fullness of life can only be measured when one is near the end.

Drops of subterranean water now fell from the catacomb roof, signaling their presence underneath the Rio Grande. Roberta was becoming fatigued from operating the hand mechanism, but refused to voice a complaint. The seeping water eventually saturated their clothes, making a difficult journey all the more unbearable. Soon, the drops abated and they were overwhelmed with another sickening draft of air. Minutes passed like hours. The ghastly surroundings continued to sap their spiritual strength. A welcome sense of relief came when the Padre announced their imminent arrival. With a minimum of delay, they ascended a flight of steps and were delivered out of the hellish tomb.

The Sisters at the El Paso mission took immediate care of the refugees, providing them with robes and hot refreshments. Within two hours, Sisters Josephina and Victoria arrived with the Church minivan and their luggage. They dressed while their wet clothing was being laundered and dried.

Moses used a phone in the mission's study to call El Paso Regional Hospital. His strongest prayers were answered. Atali was out of surgery and resting comfortably. She'd be able to receive visitors later in the day. He thanked the nurse, then made a call to Atali's parents to inform them of her condition. They agreed to meet at the hospital later that afternoon.

Moses hung up as the Madre entered. "Good news. Atali will be okay."

Her voice seemed distant. "I'm happy for that, my son."

"Madre, are you all right?"

She sat in a chair and channeled a nervous breath. "I'm worried about the others. My elder children before you. They're in danger as well."

"Then, contact them. Warn them."

"That won't be easy. They were adopted many years ago and even I don't have access to all the records," she stated in despair. "However, one of them..." A fleeting memory stalled her words. "Sister Josephina was somehow involved."

"Do you wish me to find her, Madre?"

She nodded, submerged in thought.

Moses left, returning a few minutes later with Sister Josephina who'd been informing the Padre of what the authorities had done after their dramatic escape.

"Sister, I need your help."

"Yes, Madre?"

"I must ask you to betray a confidence. Something you agreed to keep secret many years ago. My third child. Wasn't he adopted by a family who were close friends of yours?"

"No, Madre. He was adopted by a family who were close friends of my close friends."

She nodded with understanding. "If I can, I must get word to him. I need you to contact your friends and see if they know what happened to his family."

The Sister sat down, feeling an unanticipated weight on her shoulders. "Madre, I did make a promise. The adoption was supposed to remain strictly confidential, with no communication between the parties."

"I'm aware of the adoption guidelines," Maria Elena conceded. "But, I'm asking you as a friend — as a good friend — will you please do this for me?"

She sighed, ignoring her burdened conscience. "All right, Madre. I'll make some calls."

Sister Josephina contacted her friends. They provided the phone number for a Mrs. Connie Reese living in San Antonio, Texas. She was the adoptive mother of Mary Ellen's third child. Another call was placed. The Sister explained the situation and heard no objection. It was time for two strangers to discuss their common bond. Maria Elena's heart raced as she accepted the phone.

"Hello?" her voice quavered.

"Madre Superiora? This is Connie Reese. I'm Kevin's mother." She caught herself. "I mean, his other mother."

Maria Elena was breathing harder, trying to calm herself. "Kevin? His name is Kevin?"

"Yes. I told the Sister I'd do what I could to help. I'm widowed now and live in San Antonio. However, Kevin lives in Scottsdale, Arizona."

"Arizona?" came the ecstatic response. "I'll be driving through Arizona tomorrow."

"But, this week he's on vacation in Cabo San Lucas. He'll be calling me soon and I'll get a number where he can be reached. Will that be all right?"

She took a moment to catch her breath. "Will it? Of course, Connie. Of course. When shall I call you back?"

"Tomorrow night. I should know then."

"Thank you, Connie. God bless you."

Maria Elena handed the phone back to Sister Josephina, wrapping her arms about her in a tight hug. "And, thank you, Sister," tears of joy spilling forth. "God bless you, as well."

Moses returned from the hospital, having informed Atali of his plan to escort his mother to Las Vegas. The Padre Superior granted them permission to use the Church minivan for their journey. He handed the Madre Superiora a letter which would explain her unique circumstances to the Bishop of Las Vegas who'd see to the Madre's safety while there. After tearful goodbyes were exchanged, Moses drove them from the mission and onto the westbound lanes of Interstate 10. Maria Elena felt a sense of relief with three of her children by her side. Soon, there might be a fourth. The Madre could only pray for such a miracle.

Mary Ellen Hart had returned to the country of her birth — now on the road to destiny.

CHAPTER SIX

❧

CABO SAN LUCAS, MEXICO — MARCH 21ˢᵗ

*K*evin Reese wondered where she'd been all his life. This hot oil backrub was as good as sex. *Well, almost. Nothing's as good as sex.* But, this girl really knew how to stroke a guy. He was thinking she'd be just as talented at more intimate activity, but he didn't know how to ask. His Spanish was no better than her English. Still, body language was universal. He'd get her to understand what he wanted without words.

The Hyatt Regency's Cabo San Lucas Golf and Ocean Resort was the crown jewel of the Southern Baja Coast. Sitting atop a rocky bluff, the 500 acre site included 780 rooms and suites, an 18 hole championship golf course and a mile of gorgeous white sand beach for the private use of resort guests.

Kevin had previously stayed at the resort, this time remembering to slip the male concierge a C-note for his help in providing a selection of willing females, all available for dinners, dancing and — oil rubs on the beach. He realized he was pushing his luck. The young lady who'd accompanied him from Arizona might show up unexpectedly. Right now, that would be most unfortunate. She'd never forgive his roaming desires. There isn't a female alive who understands the only woman that matters to a single man is the one who's touching him at the moment.

Kevin Reese was a blond haired, blue eyed, former pro football player who craved publicity and adulation. Most people had seen his face and name lent to various products and charitable causes. This was one man who loved being in the spotlight and felt naked without a camera in his face or an adoring fan begging for an autograph. He'd even allowed his vanity to lead him to a brief, but unsatisfying career in the motion picture industry. His heart wasn't in acting. He was happy being himself and had no desire to behave any other way.

Kevin thought he'd like to settle down, but knew he could never be faithful to a woman. His addiction to sex was too strong for any one female to satisfy. He was in excellent physical condition, with his 6 foot 2, 235 pound chiseled body exuding the aura of a mythical Greek god. Unlike his buff brethren, he possessed quite a few brain cells and often used them to his financial advantage. In fact, Kevin was a very wealthy and influential person.

He'd been a first round draft pick of the Los Angeles Raiders in 1983 from the University of Texas. As an outside linebacker for the Longhorns, he'd set many NCAA records and became an invaluable starter for the Raiders backfield. In his rookie year, he was voted to play in the Pro Bowl, the same season the Raiders won the Super Bowl. He became an instant celebrity and garnered many endorsements. In 1988, he was traded to the San Francisco 49ers where he won another three Super Bowls, then to the Denver Broncos as a free agent where he won another two championships. He retired as the only player in NFL history to have six Super Bowl rings. Kevin parlayed his financial success in football into lucrative real estate and stock transactions which made him a millionaire many times over.

He flipped over to face the Mexican girl, motioning for her to remove her bikini top and rub the oil into his chest with hers. Without hesitation, she complied. Copying his move was Kevin's business partner and long time friend Reggie Peace. The girl massaging him also obliged. *Ahhhh! This is much better.*

Reggie had been drafted by the Raiders the same year as Kevin. They had teamed to become a fearsome duo in the backfield. When a tight end or wide receiver foolishly came over the middle of the field, Kevin and Reggie, the outside and inside linebackers, would sandwich him with a vicious hit, making the victim known as 'Reese's Peace's'. The two had even filmed TV commercials promoting the candy. Reggie was traded to the Dallas Cowboys in 1990 and won three Super Bowls there before finishing his career with the Arizona Cardinals.

Reggie convinced Kevin to move to Scottsdale and establish the Reese's Peace's Agency, or RPA, which in 12 years became the most influential sports agency in the country. Since the two ran an integrated, colorblind company, they were able to represent most of the top collegiate prospects as well as a good number of professional athletes. Their business was very profitable, but also demanding of their time. They decided to have the corporate jet fly them to Cabo San Lucas for a much needed break from their schedule, but would have to return to Phoenix in less than a week to prepare for the upcoming NFL Draft.

As they began to slide out of their swimwear, two long shadows loomed over the foursome. Shielding his eyes from the sun, Kevin looked into the dour faces of Lynda Knight and Saundra Davis, the two women he now regretted bringing with them from Arizona.

"What the hell is this?" Saundra cried in hurt tones. "I'm not good enough for you?"

"Baby, that's not true," said Reggie trying to conceal his excited state. "We're just being friendly with the natives."

She flashed a look of disgust, walking back toward the hotel. Reggie leapt to his feet to join his lady.

"Come on, sugar. You know I only want you."

Kevin shook his head at the nauseating, kiss-ass scene. He'd never let a woman lead him around like that. Still, Reese supposed he could forgive his partner. Reggie had told him how special Saundra was and had even mentioned the 'M' word. He knew they'd patch things up. Saundra just wanted to teach Reggie a lesson. Soon enough, they'd be kissing like two lovebirds, expressing their undying love for each other. *Oh, God.* He had to stop these thoughts before he lost his lunch.

Lynda Knight remained Sphinx-like, arms crossed in frustration. She was a very attractive 33 year old with bleached blonde hair draped halfway down her tanned back, hazel eyes that captured attention without excess make-up and a tall, thin frame. Her breasts could have been a cup size larger and her booty a little rounder, but Kevin's biggest complaint with Lynda was her mouth. It simply moved much too often.

"I suppose you have a good excuse for this?" she whined.

"Yeah," he retorted. "I wanna get laid."

Lynda couldn't believe he was using honesty as a weapon. "Is that all you can say, 'I wanna get laid'," mocking him. "What about me?"

Kevin stifled a laugh. "Jump on in."

She snorted in righteous indignation. "I didn't come all this way to have sex with the three of you."

The Mexican girls eyed her as though she were some sort of religious nut. Even with the language barrier, they could tell she was the walking antidote to Viagra.

Lynda continued her attack. "You don't know where those girls have been."

"I know exactly where they'd have been, if you'd kept on shopping."

"I can't believe this. You're the one who invited me on this trip. The least you could do is show me some courtesy, starting with keeping that — that — thing..." pointing at his evident maleness, "...tucked out of sight. Not everything has to be public, you know?"

He seemed puzzled. "What planet did you say you were from?"

"It's not a joke. Just act like a gentleman and treat me like a lady."

She turned, heading back toward the hotel. Lynda was sure he would come running up alongside, apologizing like a puppy who had just wet the carpet. But with each plodding step she realized it wasn't to be. She had too much pride to stop and look back. Lynda wasn't a prude. Far from it. This woman had made a lot of mistakes with men over the years and discovered the biggest was to be too easy. She liked Kevin very much, but didn't want to lose him as she had so many others. Kevin was a hunk and would make a great catch. In fact, Lynda had made plans to move into his palatial Scottsdale home. She smiled with confidence, certain she'd see a different man at dinner. Unfortunately, this woman was clueless.

The four agreed to meet at 6:00 PM at the hotel pool bar, then for dinner at the Costa del Sol restaurant, one of three four-star eateries on resort property.

Reggie and Saundra were already poolside, sharing a frozen margarita, when Lynda arrived. He motioned her to their table, pulling out a chair.

"You look nice, Lynda. Jumbo margarita?"

"Yes, that sounds good," she admitted, seating herself.

"It is good," Saundra chimed in, closing her mouth back on the straw.

"Make mine strawberry."

Reggie summoned a waitress and placed her order. Lynda scanned the area. "Have you seen Kevin?"

He separated himself from his drink. "Not since the beach."

Lynda eyed her watch, casting a sigh of annoyance. She could only imagine where he was. On second thought, she didn't want to imagine it. Maybe she was being unreasonable. After all, they weren't married or even romantic. But, she had to make sure Kevin respected her. That was important. Her margarita arrived and she stared at the two straws before her. A wave of depression struck without warning. Reggie and Saundra were so happy together. Why did she feel this way? Lynda tried to free Kevin from her thoughts, but nothing worked. *Damn this man! Why can't he be what I want him to be?*

It was almost 6:20 PM when Reese arrived. His mischievous swagger spoke volumes. "Sorry. Something came up."

"I'm sure it wasn't that big a deal," Lynda fired back.

An uneasy pause, broken only by Saundra's straw sweeping the bottom of her empty margarita. She smiled without apology.

"I was on the phone with my mother."

"Yeah? How is Connie?" his partner wondered.

"She's okay. Told me something weird. Said I might be hearing from my real mom."

Reggie looked up through a drink-induced haze. "Your real mom? I didn't know you were adopted."

Kevin nodded with a vacant stare. "They told me years ago. I just never talk about it."

The poolside waitress came to their table. "Anything else?"

"These margaritas are off the hook," proclaimed Saundra. "I'll have three more."

"No," Reggie insisted. "We'll have dinner soon. You can get something then."

"Party pooper," she yammered in disappointment.

"How about you, sir?" the waitress addressed Kevin.

"I'll have a cerveza. Dos Equis."

"Wait a minute," Lynda moaned, pointing at the massive margarita for two. "You don't think I'm drinking this myself?"

Kevin scrunched his face. "I'm not much on ladies' drinks. Saundra will help you with it."

"Fuckin' A, I'll help," said their well-oiled companion.

The waitress took Kevin's order to the bartender at the pool bar. He was a burly man with tattoos running the length of both arms and wild, curly hair which hadn't seen a comb in years. The bartender was a new hire and, unknown to the waitress, had been keeping his wide, pig-like eyes on Kevin.

"Dos Equis for Table 6. It'll be a room charge."

The bartender nodded. He turned away, grabbing a chilled mug to pour beer from the tap. Deftly, and without notice, the man removed a vile of clear liquid from his shirt pocket and dumped it into Kevin's drink. It was the same deadly mixture used by Richard Stern on the President. The same liquid poison now used by all CIA assassins.

Reggie and Saundra were grinning like two horny teenagers. Kevin poked his head under the table, watching as their bare feet probed each other's crotch. "Whoa! You guys need to get a room."

Lynda dropped her head down by instinct. "What the hell's going on?"

Reggie rose from the table, sliding his shoe on and taking Saundra in hand. "We'll see you in a few."

His lady giggled as they made their way back to their hotel suite. Kevin's smug look was too much for Lynda to ignore.

"And what are you smiling about?"

He refused to cloak his amusement. The waitress returned to their table and set the beer before him. He acknowledged the delivery with a quick nod. "Everyone's happy but you. I wonder why?"

Lynda knew full well where he was going with this. "I suppose you know how to make me happy, huh?"

Kevin lifted his brew and held it in midair. "Damn straight. You'll thank me when I get those cobwebs out of there."

She recoiled from the insulting remark, dumping the lethal beer in his lap. "You're a pig."

Lynda stormed off, leaving him soaked and embarrassed. He came to his feet, drying himself with a napkin. The waitress hurried to his side.

"I'm sorry, sir. Would you like another?"

Kevin paused red-faced. "No, I think I've had enough. Thanks, anyway."

The bartender cursed under his breath while his prey re-entered the hotel. The would-be assassin knew an easy opportunity had been wasted. He'd have to come up with another plan to eliminate Kevin Reese.

The next morning, Kevin and Reggie planned to take in a round of golf at the resort, but Reggie phoned at 8:00 AM to inform Kevin he'd promised to take Saundra into town.

Kevin and Lynda remained cordial at breakfast and even apologized to each other. Neither meant it. Although not much of a golfer, Lynda agreed to take Reggie's place for their 11:00 AM tee time. *Maybe this vacation won't be a total loss after all.*

Since he didn't have his golf clubs, Kevin left word at the Pro Shop they'd need to rent some equipment. Upon arriving, he failed to realize the man running the Pro Shop was last night's bartender. The assassin had juggled his schedule with another temporary employee so he could be here at this crucial moment. He replaced the Number 3 wood in Kevin's bag with a duplicate club head containing an explosive charge of C-4, triggered when the club struck the ball. The assassin was amused by his cleverness.

After equipping them with their clubs, balls, tees and shoes, the man provided an electric cart and sent them off to the first tee. His parting advice was to use the 3 wood on the short Par 3 holes of 4, 9 and 13. Kevin thanked him for his assistance.

It was a beautiful, sunny day with no wind. A perfect day for golf. The course was built high on the rocky bluff with breathtaking ocean vistas from every hole. Lynda seemed more interested in the scenery than the game, but Kevin had other distractions. She was wearing a white tennis outfit which revealed her bare, well-tanned legs. With every bump of the cart, he kept willing the dress to creep higher on her thighs — inch by inch — all the way to the promised land. What Kevin had failed to learn was that having a woman was often not nearly as sweet as wanting one.

They approached the Par 3, Number 4 hole and Reese remembered the man's advice. He withdrew the 3 wood from his bag, waiting for Lynda to go first. A straight drive, 30 yards off the tee box. Kevin stepped up for his turn. Just as he placed the ball down, a strong gust of wind blew it from the tee. He reset the errant golf ball, but the wind continued to howl. Realizing he'd never make the green in this wind, Kevin went back to his bag and substituted the club for his driver. After the swing, he was surprised when the wind became a gentle breeze, then went completely still. He thought it strange, but played on without comment. The gusts never returned.

The two continued the match without further incident until coming upon the Number 9 hole, another short Par 3. As before, Kevin watched as Lynda teed off first. It was now his turn. He prepared for the shot with the 3 wood firmly in hand. Suddenly, the sprinkler system activated around the tee box, sending forth multiple arcs of water. The two of them were getting drenched. He dropped the deadly club and both dashed to the cart for shelter. Once there, they brushed off as much of the water as they could.

"Those things aren't supposed to be on during the day," Kevin whined.

Lynda shrugged. "It'll stop in a minute. Until then, there's not much we can do."

Kevin's mind snapped to his favorite subject. "Oh, I don't know. I'm sure we could think of something."

She gazed at him, incredulous. "You've got to be kidding."

"No," maintaining a straight face. "I should be able to get these seats to fold down. If not, we could lay out here in the grass. That'd be romantic."

"That'd be stupid and I'm not doing it."

Kevin's frustration with Lynda was exceeding tolerable limits. "Why did you come on this trip? Just to screw up my vacation?"

"You invited me, remember?"

"Yeah. But, I thought I was inviting a woman. Not a little girl."

"Oh, and I'm only a woman if I spread my legs?"

"What do you think you're here for? To carry my bags?"

"You know something, mister. Go fuck yourself."

"That's gotta be better than getting frostbite inside of you."

Lynda pushed him from the cart, tears pooling in her eyes. "Get out!" She turned the vehicle in a tight arc. "I'm going back to the hotel."

Kevin stood dumbfounded as he watched the cart disappear over a small hill. Leaving the deadly club behind, he began his return trek on foot. The sprinklers soon stopped.

Upon returning to the hotel, Kevin changed clothes then met Reggie in the lobby. He handed him a pair of certificates for the exclusive Cabo Exotic Life Spa, the resort's ultimate attraction for couples. The facility boasted saunas, steam rooms, mud baths, massage, Jacuzzi and whirlpool therapy, all with erotic pleasure in mind. Reggie was stunned by the offering.

"What gives, man? This must've cost you over a grand."

Kevin shrugged. "I'd rather you and Saundra have some fun than let 'em go to waste."

"Nothing doing with Lynda, huh?"

"Only thing she's giving me is a pain in my 'nads. I've had enough of her shit."

His partner eyed the coveted certificates. "They're in your name."

"So? You can be Kevin Reese for a few hours."

"This is the tits," slapping his pal on the shoulder. "Wait 'til I tell Saundra." Reggie turned sympathetic. "What are you gonna do tonight?"

"There's a 'Gilligan's Island' marathon on TV," he joked. "That'll help pass the time."

The phone was ringing when Kevin returned to his suite. He dove across the room, knocking over a chair on his way to the receiver. "Hello?"

An unusual pause, then an elderly woman's voice. "Is this Kevin Reese?"

"Last time I checked. Who's this?"

"Oh, my… This…This is Mary Ellen Hart. I'm your mother."

Reese forced himself to swallow. A sudden chill caused the hair on his arms to stand at attention. "I think I need to sit down." He pulled the chair from the floor and fell into it. "My mom — Connie — told me you might call."

"Yes, Kevin," Mary Ellen said in a giddy tone. "I told her I needed to talk to you."

Reese rubbed his hand over his face, making sure this wasn't a dream. "But, why? After all these years?"

She sighed. "There's so much I want to tell you. All I can say now is your life is in danger. It hurts me to say that. I'd love to talk to you under happier circumstances. But, it's the truth. Please, be careful."

"Someone wants to kill me?" he asked. "Why? What did I do?"

"I know it's difficult to believe, my son. But, you must believe. Your life depends on it."

"You didn't answer the question."

"It's a long story," she conceded. "One which will be hard for you to accept."

Kevin remained skeptical, but could sense genuine concern in her voice. He decided to give her the benefit of the doubt. "Where are you now?" he asked.

"We're in Tucson, Arizona on our way to Las Vegas."

"We?"

"I'm with your brothers and sister."

He was intrigued by the revelation, but chose not to display interest. "I'll be returning in a couple of days. Go to the Phoenician Resort in Scottsdale. I'll call the manager and have a suite reserved for you. Stay there until I get back."

"Thank you, my son."

Kevin hesitated. "If you're my real mom, can you tell me who my father is?"

An excruciating delay. "Let me tell you when we meet. I'll answer all your questions then." Her voice broke with emotion. "I love you."

He wanted to return the sentiment, but felt it premature. He'd meet her first and decide how to deal with this.

"I'll see you soon," came the belated reply.

"Please be careful," she said. "God bless you."

He hung up, realizing his life would never be the same.

At the Cabo Exotic Life Spa, Reggie and Saundra were immersed in the Jacuzzi after a relaxing massage. Staff interaction was kept to a minimum to encourage intimacy of the couples. In fact, a sign on the door read: OCCUPIED BY REESE PARTY — DO NOT DISTURB.

Reggie positioned Saundra on his lap. They caressed each other as though playing a symphony with their flesh. Their sexual union became complete and the crescendo of love was magic. As the pleasure lingered, Reggie realized he was falling in love with Saundra. She was the missing piece of his life puzzle. He knew it wouldn't be long before he'd ask her to marry him.

They rose from the Jacuzzi with unabashed pride in their wet, naked state. The two entered the steam room and sprawled onto a wooden bench. Consumed in the wonder of love, they failed to notice that someone else had entered the spa.

The assassin moved into position, aware Kevin Reese had booked the spa at this time. He heard them in the steam room. *At last!* It would be an easy kill.

As he flung wide the door, clouds of steam shrouded the couple within. He pulled a pin on a sarin gas grenade and lobbed it inside. "Hey, Reese. Compliments of Uncle Sam."

Reggie and Saundra couldn't see what happened, but the grenade was already emitting the lethal gas. He rose to his feet, but the deadly vapors overwhelmed him. Saundra had time to yell once, but no one could hear. Their love chamber had became a gas chamber.

Kevin made two calls. The first to the manager at the Phoenician Resort in Scottsdale, reserving the suite he'd promised Mary Ellen Hart. The second was to the hotel concierge to arrange another visit by the lovely Mexican girl he'd experienced on the beach. She was summoned and arrived at his suite within the hour.

Reese was in a silly mood. Although neither could understand anything said by the other, they had fun playing naked parlor games. The two of them were on his bed as another rerun of 'Gilligan's Island' blared from the TV.

"Now, you'll be Mary Ann and I'll be the Professor," said Kevin, amused. He then altered his voice for the impression. "Mary Ann, I have an experiment I'd like to try."

The girl began to giggle. Kevin continued, pointing at his anatomy. "This instrument package, cleverly disguised as a male appendage, will help both of us get off on this island." He started to inspect her body which was now convulsing with laughter. "Now, where can we hide this so Gilligan won't find it?"

At that moment, they heard the door unlock. In stepped a hotel security guard and two officers of the Cabo San Lucas Police. The Professor and Mary Ann grabbed nearby robes.

"What the fuck is this?"

"Who are you?" the security guard responded.

"I'm Kevin Reese and this is my room."

An uneasy pause. "You're Kevin Reese? That's not possible."

He marched to his dresser, showing them his wallet containing several picture IDs. One of the officers handed the wallet back with a nod.

"I'm sorry, Señor Reese," said the guard. "There's been a terrible mistake."

"I'll say! What gives you the right to barge in here like this?"

The security guard, who was the only one to speak English, continued to apologize. "We're so very sorry to disturb you, but we didn't know. We were looking for evidence."

"Evidence of what?"

"Any clue as to who would want to kill you, Señor. You see, we thought you were the party murdered in the spa tonight."

"What?"

"The reservation for the spa was yours. You signed your name at the register."

Suddenly, Kevin shook with fear. "Oh, my God," his voice failing him. "Reggie..."

"Did you know the victims, Señor?"

Reese forced himself to nod. "Reggie Peace and Saundra Davis. In suite 510." He paused to sit in a chair, his body quivering from the news. "They took my place at the spa."

The security guard explained the mix-up to the police officers in their native language.

"How were they killed? Who did it?"

"The police investigation is still underway. But, it seems a poisonous gas was used in the steam room. A security camera shows a person leaving the spa, but he's still at large."

Kevin recalled Mary Ellen's warning. There was no way this could be a coincidence. The young girl walked over to him, placing her hand on his shoulder. Kevin looked into her warm, caring eyes.

"Get your clothes. Playtime's over."

He spent the next few hours completing the necessary, but unenviable tasks of identifying the bodies, answering more police questions and contacting Reggie and Saundra's immediate families. Kevin was also in touch with his company, RPA, to inform them of the tragedy, recalling the corporate jet so he and Lynda could return to Phoenix as soon as possible. The bodies of Reggie Peace and Saundra Davis would follow by cargo jet the following day.

The luxurious RPA corporate jet, a twin engine Gulfstream VIII, landed at the Cabo Airport a few minutes earlier than planned. The jet taxied up to the terminal and a single pilot emerged. Usually, two pilots would accompany the craft, but due to the emergency only one was available. After paying the ground crew for the fuel, the pilot walked to the Customs Control office to file his flight plan back to Phoenix. The jet was left unattended for several minutes, allowing the burly man with tattoos on both arms and wild, curly hair to stowaway in the cockpit. The assassin knew this was the best way for him to elude the Cabo Police — and to kill Kevin Reese once and for all.

Upon arriving at the airport, Kevin and Lynda emerged from the hotel limousine and their luggage was transferred onto the jet. The pilot met them on the tarmac, expressing his sincere condolences. They entered the craft and a few minutes later were airborne over the spectacular Baja Coast.

They sat in leather captain's chairs, trying to accept the bizarre fact their friends were no longer with them. Since the shocking news, they'd bonded together in grief and at least buried their petty differences.

Kevin went to the well stocked bar and poured himself a large Scotch on the rocks. "Want anything?" he asked over the drone of the engines.

Lynda nodded. "I'll have a Bloody Mary."

He prepared the drink, spilling some tomato juice due to a pocket of unexpected turbulence. Kevin mopped up the mess, handed her the glass and returned to his seat. He proceeded to down his Scotch without comment, stopping only to stare out the window.

Lynda felt it necessary to break the silence. "What's going to happen with your company?"

He slammed the rest of his drink. "It'll stay RPA. I owe Reggie that. Maybe I can convince his brother Calvin to be the new general partner. Try and keep it in the family."

"When will the funeral be?"

Kevin shrugged. "A couple of days. His relatives have to fly in from the East Coast."

He continued to wallow in depression. Lynda sipped her drink, thinking of something else to say. "So, you believe someone was trying to kill you instead?"

Before he could respond, a deep voice answered. "I certainly was, Miss Knight."

The assassin entered the cabin, gun drawn. Lynda gasped in terror, spilling the remainder of her drink into the plush carpet.

"You're the golf pro," Kevin cried.

The man smiled, revealing two missing teeth in his tobacco stained front grill. "Call me, Scorpion. That's my code name at the Agency."

"The Agency?" Somehow, Kevin knew he wasn't referring to William Morris. There was little chance this encounter would be pleasant.

"You keep thwarting my plans to cause an amusing death for you. In fact, you're really making me look bad."

Kevin snarled in disgust. "Not me, pal. It's your mirror."

The man ignored the insult, catching his balance as another buffet of air jostled the jet. "Shooting you would've been ridiculously easy," the assassin continued. "I tried to poison you, but Miss Knight spilled the beer. The 3 wood you didn't use was filled with C-4. Then, you gave the spa time to your partner." Scorpion shook his head in disbelief. "Imagine my surprise when I saw the paper this morning."

Kevin started laughing at the absurdity of the news while Lynda eyed him in shock. "What could possibly be funny about this?"

He continued to chortle with amusement. "You're telling me I'm alive because I couldn't get in her pants?" Another hysterical burst of laughter. She looked upon him with a combination of distain and horror.

"Kevin, stop it. This isn't funny at all."

"No?" he responded, tears blurring his sight. "How many other guys have you frustrated from certain death?"

"He's drunk," she moaned. "He had two in the limo and another just now."

Scorpion smiled. "Maybe he'll find it funny when he falls out of the plane?"

Kevin's laugh warbled to a stop. "I knew it was too good to last."

The man walked to the cabin door and turned the latch. With a great gust of air, the metal hatch fell back against the bulkhead. "We're at 10,000 feet, Reese," yelled Scorpion over the engine noise. "You can laugh all the way down."

Kevin paused in subdued thought. "Why are you doing this?"

"The Agency wants you dead. I don't ask why."

"What about the pilot?" Lynda wondered in due concern.

"He's earned his wings, Miss Knight," said Scorpion, lifting his gun with silencer attached. "We're on autopilot now."

"What are you going to do with her?"

The assassin exhibited a lecherous smile, drooling from the corner of his mouth. "I intend to have fun with Miss Knight. Lots of fun."

Kevin started to giggle. "Forget it, pal. This is one girl who really doesn't know dick. You might as well throw her out with me."

"Kevin! Shut up!"

"How's this, Horndog? When we get to Phoenix, I'll take you on a trim hunt and get you laid. Deal?"

Scorpion flashed an empty grin. "No deal. On your feet, Reese."

He motioned with his gun. Kevin rose from his seat with justified trepidation. "First, get the pilot. He's going to lead the way."

Kevin went to the cockpit, sliding the body of the pilot back to the open hatch. Exhibiting pure contempt, Scorpion kicked the corpse into the whistling air. The body spun like a pinwheel to the waiting Earth below.

"Your turn," laughed the assassin. "Can't say this isn't a pleasure."

Kevin forced a sigh. He'd been waiting for the right moment, but it hadn't yet occurred. Then, Divine Intervention. Another pocket of clear air turbulence rocked the jet, hurling the man against the bulkhead. Kevin was on him in an instant, wrestling the gun from his hand. They tumbled onto the cabin floor locked in a death struggle. Lynda jumped from her chair, freezing with fear when she noticed how close she was to the open hatch.

"What do I do, Kevin?"

"Kick him! Bite him! Do some damn thing!"

She slammed her foot into the flailing mass of flesh.

"You bitch! That was me!"

"Sorry." She looked on in terror as the two tumbled within inches of the great beyond. "Kevin! Look out!"

He grabbed hold of Scorpion's unkempt hair and rammed his face into the metal door hinge. Kevin jammed his elbow into the man's eye socket, punched him savagely between the legs and with a final kick to the spine sent him flying into space. An explosive sound reverberated through the cabin, dropping Lynda to her knees.

"What happened?" she cried.

Kevin peered outside the hatch to see flames roaring within the jet's port nacelle. His eyes bulged wide, knowing they were in serious trouble. "That sack of shit went right through the engine!"

He struggled to his feet, shutting the hatch door with difficulty. Lynda forced herself from the floor, following Kevin to the cockpit.

It was a harrowing sight to find both pilot and copilot seats empty. The autopilot compensated for the loss of the port engine by shutting it down and increasing power to the starboard engine beyond recommended limits. A fire retardant chemical sprayed automatically into the damaged engine nacelle, extinguishing the fire within.

Kevin sat in the pilot's seat, scanning the digital controls before him on the Heads-Up Display. The fuel was good. More than enough to get back to Phoenix which should be about a 90 minute flight. The altimeter registered 8,200 feet and was slowly increasing to the previously set 10,000. He was most concerned by the starboard engine temperature. It was already dangerously close to redline. *If we lose our one and only engine...*

He donned the headset microphone, trying to raise someone on the ground. "Hello. Hello. I mean Mayday. Mayday. Does anybody hear us? We're in a mess up here. Mayday. Mayday."

After manipulating various buttons and knobs, Kevin was able to get the radio to work. An air traffic controller from Mexicali was attempting to extract pertinent information. "What is your aircraft designation? Over."

"A private jet. Gulfstream VIII. I don't know the call letters." He waited for a reply that never came, then remembered. "Oh. Over."

"What is your destination? Over."

"Phoenix. Sky Harbor Airport. Over."

A slight crackle of static. "Can you state your condition? Over."

Kevin looked bewildered. "Our condition? Our condition sucks! Over."

"State the condition of the plane. Over."

"We've got only one engine working and it's starting to overheat. We're at 10,000 feet and holding. Plenty of fuel. But, there's no pilot, dammit. Over."

"Listen, Gulfstream. We have you on scope and we'll hand you off to Sky Harbor Control in a few minutes. They'll talk you down. Stay on this frequency and maintain present heading. Do you understand? Over."

"Yeah, I hear you. Over." Kevin resigned himself to the fact that he'd been saved three times only to go up in a fireball now. Lynda, her hazel eyes as large as saucers, forced some words from quivering lips.

"Do you know what you're doing?"

"I was hoping you did." He looked at the right engine temperature. The digital display was inching closer to critical. "Get me a drink. A large one. Scotch on the rocks."

She murmured in agreement. "I think I'll join you."

A few minutes later, a controller from Phoenix Sky Harbor Airport was contacting them on the radio. They arranged to have the other corporate RPA pilot, Tom Skavinsky, patched through by telephonic link from his vacation home in Flagstaff. He knew the plane better than anyone.

Kevin requested another drink. Lynda looked over, incredulous. "Are you sure? You've already had four."

"Yes, I'm sure," he retorted. "I can still see the ground."

Another cocktail was prepared and Kevin consumed it with abandon. Soon, Skavinsky was on the radio. After being briefed on what happened and their precarious situation, Tom went to work calming their nerves.

"Okay, Mr. Reese. Not to worry. You're in level flight and you've got plenty of fuel. The onboard computer has preset landing instructions for most major airports including Sky Harbor. Basically, the plane can land itself. All you have to do is set a few controls and the computer will do the hard stuff, okay?"

This was the first morsel of good news Kevin had heard all day. However, he was starting to feel the effects of the alcohol now saturating his system. "Okay, Tom, baby," Kevin rambled. "Don't worry 'bout a thing. We'll get you down."

Skavinsky dismissed the awkward comment as another one of Reese's attempts at warped humor. Little did he know his student pilot was now hammered beyond hope.

Tom discussed the options with the air traffic controller at Sky Harbor. Runway 26 was selected, the longest east-west landing strip at the Phoenix Airport. Other private aircraft would be sent to Scottsdale and Mesa Executive Airports while commercial jets would be diverted to Tucson until further notice. Sky Harbor was placed on emergency status with crash rescue and recovery vehicles standing by in the event they were needed.

The next half hour passed without incident. Kevin noticed the starboard engine temperature was in the red and climbing.

"Lynda?" said the bravest pilot in the air. "Fix me another little drinkie."

"No way. You've had too much already."

He slammed his fist down on the pilot's yoke. "Ya don't wanna make me crash dis thing, do ya? Now, get me 'nother Scotch. And, don't wadder it down like de lass one."

She sighed in resignation, knowing fate was out of her hands. "This is one trip I'll never forget."

Lynda went aft again, providing the rookie pilot with more liquid courage.

According to the traffic controller, they were about 50 miles southwest of the Phoenix Metroplex, cruising at a speed of 310 miles per hour and at a current altitude of 10,000 feet. Ready or not, it was time to bring them down.

"Mr. Reese?" Skavinsky stated. "I need you to enter a command into the onboard computer. That's the keypad to your immediate right. Do you see it? Over."

Kevin nodded without responding.

"Mr. Reese?"

"Yes, dammit. Didn't you seez me nod?"

"No, sir," Tom paused in amazement. "I guess I didn't."

"Well, open them eyes o' yours, misstah. We can't have any misshtakes now."

"Mr. Reese, I need you to press the following keys: CLEAR — F2 — 1 — 8 — ENTER. Over."

Reese gazed at the keypad through his alcoholic stupor and successfully laid in the instructions. The jet started to reduce speed and the control flaps on the wings fell to a 10 degree angle.

"Okay. Whut next?"

"That's great, Mr. Reese," sighed Skavinsky. "The computer will now be able to land the plane. You'll be safely on the ground in about 10 minutes."

By entering 'F2' the function key for automated landing and '18' the code for Sky Harbor Airport, the computer would monitor descent, acceleration, flap control, landing gear deployment, as well as intercept the airport's laser-guided glide slope and path onto Runway 26.

Kevin was so proud of himself, he failed to notice the critically overheated engine. The jet began to vibrate in an alarming manner.

"What's happening?" Lynda squealed.

"Hey, Tom? The injin sounds like it wants ta hurl. Got any idears?"

"What do you mean? Over."

"Starbird injin is now — whoa!" Kevin fell back in his seat. "It like 50 degreez over redline, an' she be buckin' like a bitch."

"Jesus!" Skavinsky exclaimed, abandoning his calm demeanor. He knew the engine was about to stall or flame out. In either case... "Mr. Reese, you've got to try a hands-on landing. Press CLEAR — F1 – ENTER. Do it now. Over."

Kevin reached over and entered the data. The plane pitched down into a slight dive. Lynda shrieked, as Reese grabbed hold of the yoke with both hands.

"You've got control of the plane now, sir. Push the throttle back. Those are the levers to your right just below the computer. That'll reduce some torque and stress on the engine. But, not too much."

He nudged the levers back. The vibration continued at a reduced intensity. Lynda gazed through the windshield at the approaching ground. They were now over the western edge of the Phoenix Metroplex, heading toward downtown and the airport beyond. She looked at the altimeter as it made its inevitable, counterclockwise plunge toward zero. The traffic controller relayed course heading, altitude, speed and distance to runway for Skavinsky who was barking commands at Reese. One thing was clear. They'd never make the airport if they didn't pick up speed.

"Mr. Reese. Increase power to the engine. Throttle up."

Kevin shook his head. "I wish dis guy would mind his make up."

Reese pushed the levers forward. A loud alarm suddenly blared through the cockpit. Lynda looked on in panic.

"Kevin, the other engine's on fire."

"Yeah, I know," he stated. "No reason ta yell."

"The hell there isn't. We're falling like a brick."

"Tom, the utter injin's on fire. Now, whut?"

There was nothing left to try. Skavinsky told him he'd have to land where he could. "Deploy your landing gear. The switch to the left of the yoke. Flaps 20."

Various mechanical noises reverberated through the craft as control surfaces and gears strained into position. The fire alarm continued to pulse in frenzy. Kevin seemed unaffected by the chaos and fast approaching ground. He turned to face his petrified partner.

"Ya knows sumthin? You was right. I shouldn't have had dat lass drink. Next time, I'll lissen to ya."

Lynda was stunned. *On the brink of death, now he shows me respect. Men!*

The controller relayed further flight status to Skavinsky. They were at 500 feet and descending.

"Flaps 30. Look for a place to land."

Kevin squinted through the windshield glare. "Relax, Tom. I sees de runway."

A terrified pause. "What runway?"

"De one wid de cars on it."

"Christ! That's the Interstate!"

The traffic controller placed a frantic call to the police to inform them of the emergency. The highway could never be cleared in time. The disabled Gulfstream was seconds from the ground and seven miles west of the airport.

Lynda braced for impact. Kevin kept his hands rock steady on the yoke, bringing the jet down onto the concrete highway, barely clearing a convoy of trucks. The plane hit the ground hard, but level. Their speed was better than 180 miles per hour as they hurdled toward downtown Phoenix swallowing up four lanes of eastbound Interstate 10. Cars and trucks swerved off the highway upon seeing the Gulfstream in their rearview mirrors. A handful of cars were unaware of the oncoming jet until it flashed by, its massive wings passing inches over them, bending back their radio antennas. Traffic on the westbound side braked in awe as countless fender bender collisions occurred. In front of the jet, other eastbound vehicles fell into the grass median as if cleared by an invisible plow.

Skavinsky was screaming for Reese to reverse power, but both engines were now useless. As in a car, Kevin tried to apply the brakes at his feet. This made little dent in their headlong speed. The jet's main hydraulic line had been severed by a thrown turbine blade. Lynda was frozen in a catatonic state, her nails digging into flesh, turning her palms into a pair of pincushions.

As they sped across the elevated bridge over north and southbound Interstate 17, the towers of downtown Phoenix loomed ahead.

"Hey, look," Kevin pointed, still basking in the pride of landing the plane. "Dare's de hangar."

Lynda's swollen eyes now popped from their sockets. "That's not a hangar. It's a tunnel. Oh, my God!"

Within an instant, the Gulfstream was streaking through the darkened, half-mile long tunnel underneath downtown Phoenix. Cars careened into the concrete walls in an attempt to avoid contact. An elderly woman couldn't maneuver her vehicle in time as the jet's nose gear slammed her down a nearby exit ramp. Kevin continued clutching the yoke, his knuckles turning white.

"Use de force, Luke. Use de force," he intoned in his best Obi Wan Kenobi impression.

Billowing clouds of rubber, sparks and metal cascaded through the tunnel. The Gulfstream finally emerged on the other side, continuing to roll down the highway. Slower now. Still slower, until their ground speed was less than the posted limit. The crippled jet eventually came to a rolling stop on the Interstate, in sight of Sky Harbor Airport on their immediate left.

The two sat speechless. The only sound came from the whine of the engine fire alarm. Kevin removed his shoe and struck the console. "Stop dat noise. Stop it."

The alarm ceased. He brushed back his hair and returned shoe to foot.

Lynda was certain she hadn't taken a breath in more than five minutes. She did so now. Again. Once more. *Oh, it's sweet to be alive.* She looked over at Kevin who'd slumped into his seat. For all his faults, Lynda realized this man was really something. He'd shown her the respect she was craving and courage she didn't believe any man could possess.

Suddenly, and without warning, she felt a most unusual twinge. A warm, slightly dewy feeling between her thighs she could only describe as a sort of longing. An ache. A need deep within. For whatever reason, she wanted this man and wanted him now.

Lynda wrapped her arms around Kevin, kissing him with passion. "You saved our lives," she purred. Her hand moved under his shirt and through the hair on his chest. "Kevin, I'm sorry for the way I've been. Really. I want to start over. I want to be with you. Let me take you inside and feel the wonder of being in love."

A tender, emotional pause. Kevin turned to face the woman. He then seized up in tight-lipped amusement, misting spit through the air around her.

"Are youz shittin' me?" he chuckled at her expense. He brought his fingers to her cheeks and shook them playfully. "Youz my lucky 'lil chastity belt. I wouldn't dreams of havin' sex with ya."

He exited the cockpit with a silly, drunken laugh. This caused her to wonder. *How do men and women survive each other?*

CHAPTER SEVEN

✂

WASHINGTON, D.C. and SCOTTSDALE, ARIZONA
— MARCH 23rd

*T*his is a fucking disaster."

Richard Stern rocked back in his chair, a lone squeak punctuating his assessment. He spread his fingers through his mustache, contemplating the news of this latest debacle. This was a man who took failure far too personally. He expelled a sigh of dramatic length, then focused attention on CIA Director Walter Langlois and Army General Kenneth Connolly who sat stone faced in Stern's White House office.

"I thought you said these guys were good?" he chided the General. "You sent 12 armed commandos to a Catholic Mission — and they had their asses handed to them."

General Connolly wasn't used to defending the conduct of his elite corps and the inexperience showed. "They lost the element of surprise. Someone tipped off the operation."

"I see. That made it possible for a bunch of nuns to kill 11 of your men and send the other back naked?"

"No nuns. Just Castaneda."

"One guy? Alone? The same one who killed six of your MPs?"

The General nodded, bowing his head in embarrassment. Stern directed his ire at Langlois. "Your agent tried to eliminate Reese on four separate occasions. This guy was a pro and he got sucked through a jet engine. Is this what we pay taxes for?"

"He got careless," Langlois contended. He took a final drag from his cigarette, showing his frustration by crushing the remains in an ashtray. "I can't believe he fucked this up."

"Where's Reese now? Can't your men at Sky Harbor find him?"

Langlois paused, allowing the acidic taste in his throat to subside. "The plane landed on the Interstate, so we missed him again. We're staking out his house and office, but so far nothing."

"Do we have any intelligence on this woman's whereabouts?" the General asked. "I could order another strike."

"There's been no trace of Hart or her children in the past four days," confirmed Langlois. "And you can forget another raid. The State Department's been catching all sorts of shit from the Mexican Government."

"Screw State," Stern boiled over. "Black Widow's an abortion. How do you plan to turn this around?"

"We'll get them," Langlois assured through gritted teeth. "I'm issuing new orders. These hits will look like accidents. Botched burglaries. Stalkers. Anything but what they are. We just need more time."

"That's a luxury we don't have," admonished Stern. "Hart will have that baby soon and, according to McKay, Socrates will be ready for beta test in a couple of weeks. We can't afford undue attention because of loose ends you can't tie up."

The CIA Director sat forward in his chair. "I said, we'll get them." He pulled back, realizing his body language had become too confrontational. "Anyway, Monroe has another plan."

"Oh?"

"It involves a deal with an enforcer for the Cali Cartel. Esteban Lopez."

"Lopez? Wasn't he the one who killed those DEA agents a few months back?"

"The same," admitted Langlois. "The FBI ambushed him outside a Palm Beach hotel. Killed his wife and child. They've got him on ice, hoping he'll talk."

"What's the connection?"

"He and Moses Castaneda grew up in the Juarez Mission orphanage. In fact, Lopez' wife and Atali Castaneda were cousins. Monroe's convinced he'll help smoke him out."

"Why would he do that?" snickered Stern. "Out of love for us?"

Langlois grinned. "Sometimes, your enemies are the only ones you can trust. We'll need to get the President to sign a full pardon, guaranteeing his release and safe transport out of the country in return for his help."

"What's going to make him do the job once we let him out?"

"We have a solution for that. It'll be taken care of."

Stern summoned an ominous smile. "Isn't that what you told me a week ago?"

Days earlier, President Webber had instructed Steven Yeager of her Secret Service detail to install a sophisticated listening device within Stern's office, sewn into the carpet underneath his desk. Any conversations, such as the one just concluded, were automatically recorded for later playback. It was another precaution she viewed as prudent after her initial experience with the MAJIK-12.

Later that day, the President reviewed the digital recording, then summoned Agent Yeager to the Oval Office. Within a minute, he stood before her, looking as good as any man had a right. Webber reminded herself that Presidential forbidden fruit had been a weakness of many who'd preceded her. The agent seemed eager to please and always interested in her well being. However, that was his job. She understood these sexual feelings were silly on her part and better controlled by a woman than a man. The President had to be above any childish show-me-yours and I'll show-you-mine encounters and Webber was determined to live up to that standard.

"Yes, Madam President?"

"Mr. Yeager, it seems I have another task for you. I'll require your discretion, as usual."

"Of course, Madam President," knowing exactly what she meant.

As part of her strategy against the MAJIK-12, President Webber met individually with those members she felt could be counted upon to assist her. Private discussions with Secretary of Defense Roth and Attorney General Ortiz-Bennett remained cordial, but didn't yield expected results. It became clear that Richard Stern, Phillip Langlois and the military were the dominant players in the MAJIK-12, effectively ruling the group through intimidation and threat of force. Pierre LeClerke, the CEO of Dreamland contractor GG&E, was next on the President's list. She invited him to the White House for a symposium on the benefits of importing high technology to third world countries. Soon after his arrival, he came to understand the real reason for his presence.

LeClerke was escorted into the Oval Office by Agent Yeager. Standing before the President was her Press Secretary, Tamara Sheldon. Their closing conversation couldn't have been staged any better.

"The Press are asking questions I can't answer," Sheldon complained. "There are reports linking the military attack on the Juarez Mission with the murder of an Arizona businessman in Cabo San Lucas. What should I tell them, Madam President?"

Webber considered her response. "Tell them the truth. You don't know."

"With all due respect, Madam President…they want to know if you know."

She cast a glance at LeClerke who refused to make eye contact. The President suddenly had an inspiration. "Tamara, why don't you ask Richard Stern that question."

"Mr. Stern? Would he know anything about this?" she asked in surprise.

Webber smiled. "You'd be amazed at what he knows. Just tell him that I sent you."

Agent Yeager accompanied the Press Secretary from the room and closed the door. LeClerke shook Webber's hand.

"It's good to see you again, Madam President."

"You too. Please have a seat."

He sat in a chair opposite her desk. "When does the symposium begin?"

"Not until tonight," she conceded. "I invited you here early to discuss the MAJIK-12."

The muscles in his body tensed. "Madam President, that's a conversation neither one of us should have."

"I understand your concern, Mr. LeClerke. They want us to be afraid. Certain we'll never challenge them. That's how they keep control."

There was ample hesitation before his reply. "I'm only one person."

"So am I," stated the President. "And, I have a family and a country to protect. But, that doesn't mean I have to sit here and take it. What they're doing is wrong. I think you know that, too."

He dropped his head in resignation. "It doesn't matter what I think. Most of them are fanatical. Hard core. You can't fight them."

"You can try," she railed. "I'm asking you to join me. Stand up for what's right. Show some balls for Christ sake."

LeClerke forced a shallow smile. "Madam President, I think I might live longer if I keep my balls to myself."

The cab pulled up to the Phoenician Resort in Scottsdale, depositing a more sober Kevin Reese. He dashed into the ornate lobby and placed a call to Mary Ellen Hart's suite. After informing her of his early arrival, they agreed to meet at the coffee shop in 15 minutes. Mary Ellen needed time to prepare herself for the moment when she'd hold a son whom she hadn't seen in 50 years.

Kevin sat alone in the restaurant, downing another cup of coffee before the meeting. Suddenly, Benjamin de la Cruz Nighthawk was standing nearby in his blue bathing trunks examining Reese as if a specimen under microscopic analysis. Kevin became annoyed by his presence.

"Kid, the pool's that way."

Benjamin eyed him critically. "You don't look real."

"What?"

"You look like a character from a comic book," confided the youngster. "Or, maybe a big plastic dummy. But, you sure don't look real."

"Oh, I'm real all right," he responded.

"How can you be my big brother if you've got yellow hair?"

"Big brother?" Kevin said bewildered. Then, the connection stunned him. "Oh, no!"

He looked upon the tyke in surreal disbelief. Benjamin flashed a jack-o-lantern grin, delighted he'd made such a strong first impression.

Roberta trotted up to them in a white bikini, slapping her flip-flops on the marble floor. "Are you Kevin?"

He nodded, but thought seriously about the benefits of denial.

"They'll be here in a second," she confirmed. "You look familiar. Are you famous or something?"

"Something. Who are you?"

"Roberta," she replied, as if he should know. "I see you met Ben."

"Yeah. Already had the pleasure. How old are you?"

She jutted forth her chest. "How old do you think?"

Kevin was amused by the display. "Not old enough I'm afraid."

Roberta scrunched her face, shaking a finger at him. "I'm sure I've seen you somewhere before."

He blushed in acceptance of his celebrity. "I was a pro football player. One of the best."

"Wasn't that," she stated, slicing him to size. "Aren't you the weatherman on Channel 9 in El Paso?"

"No!" Kevin squealed over his injured ego. After absorbing all the abuse he could stomach, Mary Ellen walked in with Moses behind her. Mother and son stared at each other for a few moments of reflection. She out of pride and joy. He out of disbelief. Mary Ellen's pregnant state was more than he'd bargained for. She wrapped her aged arms around his frame, hugging him for what seemed an eternity. He returned the favor. As she mopped tears from her face, Kevin scanned the area.

"What are you doing?" Moses wondered.

"Looking for the Candid Camera."

Roberta and Benjamin were sent to the pool, while Mary Ellen and Moses sat at Kevin's table. The waitress took their lunch order and Mary Ellen began to share her darkest secret with her son.

"I was a girl of 18 growing up in Roswell, New Mexico," fearing she might scare him with the news. "Have you been there?"

"No. But, I've heard of it," Kevin answered, amused. "That's where all those UFO nuts hang out, because something crashed there a long time ago."

"July 4th, 1947. About 11:15 that night. I was there," Mary Ellen spoke, her eyes transfixed on an ancient memory. She recalled the sights, sounds and feelings in a halting, emotional voice. "The sky was electric. Lightning everywhere, as the storm approached. The thunder was constant. Vibrating everything. Sparing nothing. As if a distant war was being fought with the outcome still in doubt. It was cooler then, due to the wind. Whistling like I'd never heard. Like the gates of Heaven spilling open by accident. It still gives me chills to think of it."

She wasn't alone. Kevin and Moses sat before her, enthralled by the eyewitness account. The waitress brought their drinks, with Kevin anxious for Mary Ellen to continue the story. His mother took a sip of tea, then cleared her throat to proceed.

"I was with my date that night. We parked a few miles outside of town. That's when it happened. Just in front of us, tumbling through the rain and wind. We got out to see what it was. There were bits of metal everywhere. Strange material. Like nothing we'd ever seen."

"Strange?" wondered Kevin. "How do you mean?"

Mary Ellen paused to reach in her purse. She produced a wad of tissue paper and placed it before them. "Take a look."

Kevin unwrapped the paper, revealing the same piece of foil-like material Bobby Kirke had tossed to the ground at the crash site. Without his knowledge, Mary Ellen had hidden the object under the belt on her dress.

"You've had this…all the time?" Moses stammered in awe.

Both he and Kevin inspected the metal, noting how it regained its shape regardless of the bending or crunching force applied. Mary Ellen sipped some more tea. She'd just thrown down the trump card. The rock solid bridge across this wide leap of faith.

"I knew I should keep some evidence. It's not the kind of thing that happens everyday."

Kevin was thrust into silence. Before, it had just been her word. The loony ravings of a woman going through a psychotic episode or perhaps the beginning of Alzheimer's. But, now it was tangible. Real. A renewed wave of dread engulfed him. *This woman's telling the truth.* Something extraordinary had happened to her. And because of it, the Government wanted them silenced.

"So," Kevin choked on his words. "Did you see any — little green men?"

Mary Ellen managed a limp smile. "They weren't green, Kevin."

Reese swallowed with difficulty. She paused to down some more tea, knowing she had their undivided attention.

"The first one was dead, but the other..." She dropped her head, again feeling the creature's anguish. "He was hurt. In horrible pain. But, when he touched me, I shared his soul. I knew where he came from — and why."

An unwelcome pause. Kevin became flustered, begging her to finish. "And?..."

Mary Ellen stared at her sons. As much as she wanted to, she couldn't tell them the whole story. They'd never believe it. Then again, she wasn't sure she did either. "He was a fallen angel," she confided. "And, he was your father."

The waitress walked over, delivering lunch to the three. "Anything else?" she asked.

Dense silence. After failing to acknowledge the confused server, the woman shrugged, leaving them alone.

Kevin fell back in his chair as if less likely to hallucinate in this position. "Are you certain?"

Mary Ellen nodded. "I was a virgin at the time. You, Moses, Roberta and Benjamin are four Divine seeds from this immaculate conception. And, there are five others out there. Just as alone. Just as much God's children. And just as much in danger."

"So, the Government wants us dead because you're the only witness to the Roswell crash?"

She sighed in resignation. "I'm afraid so. They murdered my date that evening and arrested my family hours later. I sought haven at the Catholic Mission in Juarez, Mexico and have lived there since."

"But, why now? After all this time?"

"An article a week ago in the Juarez newspaper," Moses added. "A nun revealed the adoption records. The Government must have read it and sent the Army to attack the Mission. We were lucky. They'll be after you, too."

"Already have," Kevin confirmed. "Missed me, but killed my partner. I can't believe the Government's doing this."

"You'd better believe it," warned Moses. "Or, you'll end up as dead as that roast beef sandwich."

Kevin inspected his lunch, finally pushing the plate away. "I think I've lost my appetite."

He channeled a heavy sigh, contemplating how quickly his life had changed. It was a lot to absorb, but he couldn't deny the facts. Like it or not, this family was his new team. And, he'd always been a team player. It was time for Kevin to get into the game. "So, where do we go from here?"

"Las Vegas," his mother stated, reaching across to hold his hand. "I'm to bear God's final child there. I'm grateful you'll be with us, my son. Praise God in His glory."

Being cautious, Moses and Kevin agreed that driving under cover of darkness was best. The four hour trip passed quickly enough, especially since Benjamin decided to sleep. There was little to no traffic at this early morning hour. Their minivan crossed over the Hoover Dam and entered the State of Nevada. A few miles later, they saw it. Remembering her horrific vision, Mary Ellen gathered a nervous breath. Glistening before them like a million diamonds on black velvet cloth were the lights of the doomed city. The city of Las Vegas.

CHAPTER EIGHT

❦

DULUTH, GEORGIA — MARCH 27th

*T*he six-foot mouse wrapped his arms around Shannon Hewson. She made sure Chuck E. Cheese didn't get too frisky with her goodies, holding his paws as they posed for the picture. Brittany, her eight year old niece, fumbled with her camera before framing the shot.

"Say cheese, please." The white flash momentarily blinded her. "Okay, Aunt Shan. I got the picture."

As Shannon eased away from the mutant rat, she heard the automated mouse band singing a Happy Birthday greeting for her. And, instead of announcing a politically correct age, the brutal truth was conveyed to all.

She stood dumbfounded as her young niece smiled. "Mommy told me."

Brittany dragged the birthday girl to the gaming area. Shannon had an affinity for machines which was downright scary. Each one she played paid off in huge ribbons of tickets. It wasn't mystical. Shannon just seemed to be in tune with them. A kind of psycho-mechanic connection. In fact, her childhood nickname had been Tommy, chosen for her wizard-like ability to play pinball machines with her eyes closed.

While her niece ran off to the redemption counter, Shannon plopped down at their table. Several slices of pizza remained with one or two bites out of each. Scanning the restaurant, she noted the throngs of children playing as if this was their whole world. The innocence of youth perfectly portrayed. Shannon shut her eyes to keep tears from spilling forth. These were not her children. None of them. Would she ever live long enough to hear 'I love you, Mommy', the sweetest words of all? How long would she endure this loneliness? This fundamental need to bear a child?

All her life, Shannon Duncan was convinced she'd have a large family. Although a tomboy in public, young Shannon kept a secret cache of dolls for her private time which was always longer than she cared to remember. She had few friends, due mainly to her intellectual superiority which she tended to flaunt and her psychic ability to know what people thought of her which was the ultimate curse. Growing up, Shannon felt isolated in her idyllic San Fernando Valley home near L.A. Her parents made no secret she was adopted, heaping their love on her younger brother Sean who was theirs biologically. Her father was the Police Chief in Simi Valley, California and her mother was a City Councilwoman, so both spent little time with their adopted daughter. Shannon's independence was forged as a typical latchkey kid with atypical desires. She wanted to prove her academic excellence while having a steady string of boyfriends to compensate for her lack of love at home. In other words, Shannon was a nerd who didn't look the part.

At 5 foot 8, 122 pounds, this woman had a strong physical presence. Her reddish-auburn hair flowed to her shoulder blades in full, natural waves. High cheek bones and full lips were overshadowed by a pair of ice blue eyes which could probe the secret of any soul. She had firm breasts and thighs from constant toning of her body with long distance running as her favorite physical activity.

Shannon graduated from UCLA at the top of her class with a 4.0 Grade Point Average. She desired a career in medicine and continued her studies at the UCLA Medical Center in Westwood. Her internship was completed at Cedar's Sinai Hospital in Beverly Hills.

She obtained her Ph.D, specializing in the fields of microbiology and genetics. With her exemplary resume, Shannon could have found employment with any medical center in the country, but chose to apply her services for the U.S. Government at the Center for Disease Control, or CDC, based in Atlanta, Georgia.

It was here she met Craig Hewson, an ambitious young turk who was a Junior Vice President at Coca-Cola World Headquarters. She fell in love with his extraordinary personality and zest for life. In 1998, they were married and bought a house in suburban Duluth, Georgia. Shannon and Craig tried for years to conceive a child, but each attempt ended in miscarriage. For a woman who prided herself on being good at everything, these losses were nothing short of catastrophic to her psyche. The desire to bear a child became an obsession with her and set into motion a downward emotional spiral. Depression and inadequacy were her constant companions and even though she took drugs to combat these feelings, she was no longer the same woman Craig had married. They divorced in 2004. He took a position overseas, leaving her the house, his name and a lifetime of what-ifs.

In an effort to determine a cause for her infertility, she conducted tests on herself including genetic DNA analysis. The results were astounding. Shannon possessed 48 chromosomes in her DNA strands instead of the normal 46. There was no apparent reason, but this incompatibility with normal chromosome structure was preventing her from maintaining a fetus to term.

Still, Shannon continued to try. The latest man in her life was Troy Garrett, an Atlanta-based agent for the FBI who was introduced to her by her brother, Sean. Troy was sympathetic to Shannon's needs and had crept into a place in her heart. On a recent trip to Key West, they'd been intimate for the first time. Her period was now five days late. She was fighting the urge to use a pregnancy test or to celebrate prematurely. Shannon had yet to learn that the more you want something, the less chance you have to get it.

After Brittany selected her trinkets, the two left to explore the Gwinnett Mall. They came upon a karaoke kiosk and Brittany felt the need to sing a duet with her reluctant aunt. Once the recording session was finished, Brittany took the disc, eager to have it played in Shannon's car on the way home. This was done. Again. And, again. And, again. And, once more for the road.

Just as Shannon felt her sanity slipping away, she swung her new Mercedes 800SL into the driveway with a lurch. Killing the engine stopped the disc before a particularly torturous screech. The two walked up to Shannon's impressive colonial-style home, framed by nearby woods. Brittany ran ahead and shoved open the door.

The surprise party for Shannon was hardly a surprise. She had spotted the guests' cars parked in a neighbor's driveway. Waiting for her in the living room was her brother Sean, sister-in-law Denise, the neighbors from down the street, four co-workers from CDC and Troy Garrett.

Candles were lit on a huge devil's food cake and another round of '*Happy Birthday*' was sung on her behalf. She closed her eyes, then extinguished the flames with a prolonged breath.

"What'd ya wish for, Aunt Shan?"

A hopeful smile. "I can't say or it won't come true." She had already decided to use a pregnancy test tonight. It would be the best birthday present she could have.

After hours of celebration, the cake, ice cream and three bottles of Dom Perignon were consumed. The party trickled to an end as each guest congratulated Shannon and hoped her birthday wish would come true. Troy was the last to bid his farewell.

"You don't have to leave," said Shannon.

"Oh, no?" as if not aware of her true intentions.

"Would you like to slip into my birthday suit?" Her champagne buzz was already forming the most exotic pair of bedroom eyes Troy had ever seen.

"Well, if you insist."

She punched him in the shoulder. "Don't do me any favors, pal."

Troy laughed. He returned to the living room, wading through torn gift wrap scattered on the floor. As Shannon went to check messages on her answering machine, Troy knelt down to pet Maxx, her black Labrador Retriever. Garrett was 38 and twice divorced. Shannon teased him about his appearance which was classic FBI. She could always spot these short-haired, tight-assed types 50 miles away as if they'd come from a factory assembly line. Troy's saving grace was his sense of humor, a quality that made him human and worth Shannon's time.

She returned, unable to hide her disappointment. "I don't know why I thought my parents would call. They haven't remembered my birthday in 20 years," came the painful truth. "They never forget Sean's."

"I'm sure they love you both."

A tormented laugh. "Sure they do," Shannon blurted. "They're not my parents, Troy. And, I don't know where my real ones are. So, I guess it's up to me to celebrate. Cheers!" She lifted an empty bottle of Dom. "To Shannon. May you never know where you belong."

She tipped the bottle over, mixing a few drops with the tears on her face. Maxx nuzzled up to her and received a gentle rub behind the ears. "I guess someone still loves me."

Troy removed a small box from his pocket. "If you're done feeling sorry for yourself, I'd like you to have this."

He handed her the gift as she brushed away tears in surprise. "But, you already gave me that gorgeous dress."

"This is more personal. I was waiting for the right time."

Shannon tried not to appear overly anxious as she opened the gift. It was a beautiful ring, a blue topaz surrounded by a cluster of tiny diamonds. The same ring she'd pointed out to him when they were in Key West.

"I didn't think you'd actually buy it."

He lowered his head. "I figured we'd treat it like a pre-engagement ring or something."

Troy's shy little boy act was really starting to light her fire. Shannon rose from her chair and kissed him. "Thank you. It's lovely."

His response was more passionate. Shannon slid her hand to a strategic area on the front of his pants, claiming the territory as her own. There was no doubt she had his complete attention.

"Maybe you could warm up my bed while I take a shower?"

Troy smiled. "It would be my pleasure."

Shannon patted the area with her hand. "Oh, I can guarantee that."

The water droplets beaded on her body like gems. She stared at them as the light refracted in vibrant colors. Then, as soon as she moved, they were gone. Things can look beautiful, but that's an illusion. Shannon knew nothing beautiful can ever really be.

It was an allegory for her life that made her cry. She'd only been in the shower a few moments when she noticed the trickle of blood starting her period. There was no need for a pregnancy test now. She thrust her face in the water without regard for the make-up running the length of her cheeks. Shannon knelt into a fetal position on the shower stall floor, sobbing openly for the children she'd never have. After the outburst, she came to her feet, then silenced the shower.

Wrapping herself in a robe, she appeared in the bedroom without make-up and with wet, chaotic hair. Shannon made no effort to impress Troy with her physical charms as sex was now the furthest thing from her mind. He grinned, hoping to make the best of a bad scene.

"Were there any other survivors?"

She coerced a smile and sat on the bed. "I just started my period. I was really hoping this time." They tenderly held hands. "Troy, don't take this the wrong way, but could I get a rain check on this? I'm wiped."

He knew his luck had run out for the evening. "Sure. I didn't want you to be alone on your birthday, that's all."

"Thank you," she whispered, head down. "I'll make it up to you. I promise."

Troy clothed himself, then leaned over to kiss her on the cheek. "Happy birthday, Shannon. I'll see myself out."

Once he left the room, there was another brief bout of tears. She fell onto her bed and curled up, eventually finding sleep.

The next morning, Shannon awoke feeling some better. She thought she'd get some chores done, including having her Mercedes detailed. Her brother Sean had given her a gift certificate for a car wash a few miles away. She made an appointment for 11:00 AM and was told that the detailing would take four hours. Shannon phoned her sister-in-law Denise and they agreed to meet for lunch.

After dropping off her car, they drove to their favorite Italian bistro. As they settled into their salads, she noticed the ring on Shannon's finger.

"That's pretty," said Denise, reaching across the table to take her hand. "When did you get that?"

"Last night. It was another present from Troy." Shannon flashed the ring, then pulled it back to admire anew. "We saw it in Key West."

She smiled. "So, I guess things are going well?"

"Probably not so well for him," Shannon surmised. "I had to put everything on hold last night. Started my period."

Denise reacted to the news as though someone had died. "Oh, Shan. I'm sorry."

She shrugged, directing her attention back to the salad. "No biggie. I guess it's not meant to be."

Her sister-in-law brushed stray hairs off her bony shoulder, continuing to eat. Denise's physical features were very plain and she was certainly not in the same league with Shannon. It had always surprised her that Sean would have married a woman this low octane. It wasn't his style. She suspected her brother of having another woman in his life. One for home and one for show. This made her angry. Like all females, she had a righteous disdain for the way most men treat women. What if Troy viewed her as a show pony? Something to ride for awhile and parade proudly in public, but never to honor in the privacy of hearth and home. *Damn! A woman could drive herself crazy with these thoughts.* Shannon stabbed the bottom of her bowl in frustration. Denise grabbed her hand, thinking she was still upset over not being pregnant.

"Having a baby isn't all fun and games, Shan. There's morning sickness, back spasms, all the weight gain. And, then the labor. Oh, my God. Brittany took 14 hours. Let me tell you, it was like taking the biggest dump of my life."

Shannon grinned. "I've never heard the joys of motherhood stated quite that way, especially while eating."

Denise returned the smile. "I don't want you to be so down about it."

"Just let me finish this before you mention the afterbirth."

Later on, the two went to a nearby mall. They were in a Nike shoe outlet, trying on some running shoes, when Shannon's cell phone rang.

"Hello?"

"Shannon? This is Troy," speaking in a business-only manner.

"Hi, Troy. What's going on?"

"Are you alone?"

"No, I'm with Denise. Why?"

An anxious pause. "We need to talk. Do you know a woman named Mary Ellen Hart?"

"No. Should I?"

"I think so," Troy replied. "She's your mother."

Glacial silence. Shannon's breath went shallow, finding it hard to form her next words. "Where did you hear this?"

"It's from a secure V-mail we received here at the Bureau. It states that as a child of Mary Ellen Hart, Shannon Duncan, a.k.a. Shannon Hewson, represents a clear and present danger to the United States. Your parents told the Feds you lived in the Atlanta area. One of the agents working this already asked about our relationship."

She swallowed with difficulty. "But, I've never heard of this woman. What did she do?"

A click was heard. He ignored it, continuing their conversation. "I asked, but they wouldn't tell me. All Headquarters would say is she's wanted for crimes against the country."

She felt her knees quake, then steadied herself by sitting on a nearby stool. "Are you going to arrest me?" whispering so Denise couldn't hear.

"No," dropping his voice to match hers. "The FBI's instructed not to make contact. Just to provide location status to the CIA in Langley, Virginia — for satisfaction of termination warrants."

"Troy," her voice squeaking in disbelief. "Does that mean what I think?"

"I don't know," came the unwelcome response. "I'll see if I can get some more intel. They'll be interviewing Sean, so don't tell Denise anything. Understand?"

Shannon nodded, trembling from the news. "Yeah."

"Look, don't go anywhere or do anything until I call back. Maybe, it's a case of mistaken identity. I'll take care of it. Try not to worry."

She hung up, reeling in astonishment. Denise paid no attention to her demeanor as she bought two pairs of Nike's, one for Shannon as a belated birthday gift.

The two drove back to Shannon's home after she told Denise she wasn't feeling well. They arranged to have the detailer deliver her Mercedes to the house. He promised to have it back within the hour.

Denise admired her new pair of shoes. "These are great. I'm glad I got them."

Shannon sat in silence, clutching a cup of hot coffee. Her vacant stare troubled her sister-in-law.

"What gives, Shan? Ever since that call, you've been a zombie."

"Sorry. Just stress," she replied. "I didn't mean to ruin your day."

"You haven't. But, you've got to try these on," placing the pair of running shoes she bought Shannon at her feet. "Tell me how you like them."

She put her coffee down and laced up the present. The shoes fit perfectly. "Thank you, Denise. They're very nice."

"They look great with those jeans. Of course, you look good in anything."

Shannon allowed herself some vanity. "That's kind of you. I feel like I should get you something."

"My birthday's in October, Shan. Return the favor then."

Suddenly, she remembered the disc. "Oh! I do have something for you. It's some songs Brittany and I recorded yesterday. Children's songs. I'm sure you'd get a kick out of it."

"Yeah? Play it for me."

"I left it in the car," checking her watch. "But, they should be here any minute."

The phone rang. It was her brother Sean. "Sis, can you pick me up? I had car trouble on the 285 in Marietta."

"Sure. What's the address?" As she was writing down the location of the car care center where Sean was stranded, her doorbell rang. Denise went to answer it. After assuring her brother she was leaving right away, her sister-in-law reappeared with the keys to the Mercedes.

"It's back. Looks great, too."

"Sean broke down in Marietta," she moaned. "We better go before rush hour."

Shannon forwarded her house calls to her cell phone in case Troy called back. They were walking out the door, when her dog started barking. "Oh, shit. I forgot to feed Maxx."

"Don't worry," said Denise, still in possession of the keys. "It'll give me a chance to hear the disc. Do you mind?"

"Of course not. I'll just be a minute."

She ran back inside as Denise entered the shiny Mercedes.

As Shannon finished spooning out food for her ravenous pet, it happened without warning. A violent concussion sent a shockwave through the house, rattling every window and door. Maxx's ears went back in fright. Wide-eyed, Shannon dashed outside to see what happened. Her Mercedes was engulfed in flames, having exploded from a bomb triggered by the ignition. Denise was motionless behind the wheel, her flesh burning to the bone.

Shannon screamed in terror. "Denise!"

The corpse refused to respond, well on its way to cremation. She screamed again, horrified at the scene and aware she could do nothing for her sister-in-law. There was little doubt it had been meant for her. Thick smoke wafted skyward from underneath the chassis, encasing the car in its own gaseous crypt. Shannon moved toward the vehicle as if capable of an impossible rescue.

Over the roar of flames, she heard the high velocity shriek of a bullet. Shannon turned to notice a gray pickup parked a quarter-mile away. She remembered seeing the vehicle at the car detailer's earlier. Two individuals cloaked in ski masks stood near the truck, armed with scoped hunting rifles. The smaller of the two leveled a weapon at Shannon. She fell to the lawn as another bullet missed its mark. There was no further hesitation. Vaulting to her feet, she sprinted toward the backyard leaving a scorched car and bewildered, barking dog behind. The shooters re-entered the pickup and cut across the front yard. Maxx yelped at the vehicle, then recoiled as the lead tire nearly clipped him. The truck maneuvered around the charred Mercedes, casting huge treadmarks in its wake. Shannon disappeared into the leading edge of the trees, using the heavy foliage as cover. The pickup swerved passed the house and skidded to a halt in front of the forest. The larger of the two jumped out, yelling at the driver to double back to the main road. She continued her flight through the woods, breaking branches and bounding over jagged rocks.

Shannon traveled a half-mile before hiding behind the massive trunk of an oak tree. Looking back, she saw one of the shooters about 50 yards distant. She bolted from her secure position, causing the assassin to level his weapon and fire. Another miss, this a few feet to the left. Remaining in moderate to deep cover, Shannon sliced through the sylvan surroundings with the speed of a gazelle. She fought through her fear and began gaining ground on her pursuer. Air rushed through her lungs as she established a powerful stride. The assassin, now trailing by more than the length of a football field, tripped on a stump and fell. Shannon stopped, luxuriating in her lead to afford three long breaths. After collecting her thoughts, she pulled the cell phone from her belt and entered Troy's office number. His answering machine took the call. Refusing to leave a message, the frightened woman continued down the path.

Before Shannon realized, she was crossing a main road with vehicles approaching from both directions. The gray pickup braked as she bolted across the road. Narrowly avoiding another car, Shannon hurdled a guardrail and found herself sprinting across the delivery area in back of a supermarket. Entering through the stock room, she came to a breathless stop near the front entrance. The pickup parked outside and the driver emerged. To her surprise, the other assassin was female. She removed her ski mask revealing a pug-like face framed by oily blonde hair. The woman looked Eastern European and most definitely butch.

As she withdrew into the store, Shannon spotted the male assassin on the loading dock, leaving his ski mask and rifle by a garbage dumpster. Mere seconds remained. She ran down an aisle grabbing a baseball cap and windbreaker, tearing the price tags from each. Thinking quickly, she tied up her hair and positioned it under the cap, then slipped on the jacket and walked toward the checkout aisles. As Shannon approached the customer service counter, she noticed a store apron hanging on a nearby door. An idea came to mind. She donned the apron and walked over to a checkout lane.

"Paper or plastic?" addressing the next shopper in line.

"Paper, please," said the woman.

Shannon bagged the woman's groceries, then placed them in a shopping cart. Her head remained lowered as they exited the store.

Once outside, Shannon followed the shopper to her minivan and began placing the bags in the hatch. From the corner of her eye, she saw the killer approaching cautiously. Shannon waited for the optimal moment, then pushed the half-loaded cart into the female assassin. The impact sent her collapsing to the pavement. Before the shopper could yell for help, Shannon was in full flight, tossing the cap and store apron to the ground. The male assassin exited the market giving chase. As car horns blared their disapproval, she dashed across a busy four-lane highway. Her pursuer waited to cross the road and lost time on the fleet-footed runner.

The sun was setting. Dark clouds rolled in from the west signaling the imminent arrival of a thunderstorm. Shannon ran through the parking lot of an office complex and noticed the sign for the transit station ahead. MARTA, the Metro Atlanta Rapid Transit Authority, ran a suburban line from Duluth in Gwinnett County to downtown Atlanta. Seeing a train at the station, Shannon commanded herself to go faster. She hurdled the turnstile without paying the token, bounded up the steps to the elevated platform and squeezed inside the last car as the doors began to close. The incessant percussion of her heart seemed to will the train to move. At last, they left the station. For the moment, Shannon was safe.

She walked toward the front of the train, crowded with late day shoppers and commuters. Finding an area less congested, she withdrew her cell phone to call Troy. Once again, his answering machine frustrated her. Shannon cupped her hand over her mouth to whisper a message.

"Troy, I'm in big shit," she murmured. "Two people are trying to kill me. A man and a woman. Denise is dead..." She screwed shut her eyes. "They blew up my car. Jesus, Troy. What am I going to do? I'm on my way downtown. Call me. Please? Please?"

She flung her head back in anguish, thinking about Denise as well as her own mortality. How easily it could have been her. How it should have been her. She agonized over the mental image of Denise's flaming corpse. A few deep breaths allowed her to regain some composure. As she scanned the traffic outside, she spotted a vehicle speeding down a parallel road. *The gray pickup!* A renewed wave of fear swept over her — these people were not going to quit.

They sped down the street, running red lights and forcing other cars from the road. Shannon knew they were trying to get to the next station. This train was an express to downtown Atlanta with only four stops. The next was inside the I-285 loop, five minutes away.

She watched in terror as the pickup bounded over sidewalks and cut in front of shocked motorists until another vehicle T-boned the truck in the middle of an intersection. Shutting her eyes in relief, Shannon debated getting off at the next stop, but figured it would be better to continue downtown.

The train pulled into the station and exchanged passengers. She tried to relax, but the pickup haunted her every thought. The doors to the train finally closed and they proceeded down the track without incident.

The sky darkened. Towering clouds delivered a few streaks of rain onto the windows. The wind began to strengthen, measured by the tree limbs bending further by the minute. A roar of distant thunder reverberated for all to hear. Shannon seemed content with the change of weather. Conditions would not be favorable for the chase to continue in wet, traffic-snarled streets. She was now confident the assassins had given up.

When the train arrived at the next stop, Shannon checked the station parking lot below. As she peered through the water-stained glass, a muddy, gray pickup slid to a halt at the platform steps. The side door was damaged, preventing the driver's exit. Shannon stared in horror as the male assassin bolted from the vehicle and surged past throngs of commuters. Before the doors could close, he entered the rear of the train.

The next station was six minutes further. She scanned the area for any police or transit authority personnel. There was no one who could help. The assassin entered her car beyond. Just seconds now. She held onto a handrail and shut her eyes, trying to visualize an escape. At last, Shannon focused on the emergency brake cord dangling overhead. In swift motion, she lunged over two commuters and yanked down on the mechanism.

A cascade of passengers fell en masse, shouting over the squeal of the train's locked brakes. Shannon collapsed to the floor, landing atop a young couple. She gazed at the chaos around her as dozens of commuters tumbled into the aisle. A cacophony of groans and curses streamed forth, eclipsing the metal-grinding crescendo. The train finally came to a stop.

Noise levels abated as everyone assessed their condition. Many had sustained cuts and bruises. Shannon rose to her feet, extricating herself from the human tide. An emergency door release allowed her to escape.

She stepped into what was now a torrential downpour. Maneuvering carefully, Shannon groped her way along the side of the train. Two bolts of lightning struck nearby, making a tense situation more unbearable. The driver's cab was empty as the operator had gone back to check on the injured. She continued to plod ahead using the train's headlight to guide her way.

Shannon turned to witness the male assassin a few steps behind. Panicking at the sight, she slipped on the track bed, falling to her knees. There was nothing more she could do. Her thoughts ranged from begging for her life to giving him the finger. Instead, she knelt motionless, accepting her fate. He leveled his gun, sighing in apparent regret.

"Nothing personal."

Fortunately for Shannon, the train operator returned and spotted the two on the track ahead. In shock, he sounded the train's emergency whistle momentarily distracting the assassin. She seized the opportunity and sprang at the man, ramming her head into his. He fell onto the electrified third rail, sending a shower of sparks above his corpse. A rain drenched Shannon Hewson slipped on the rail bed and fell into unconsciousness.

A few hours later, Shannon awoke in a hospital bed at Fulton County Medical Center where she'd been admitted for shock and a possible concussion. The dazed woman commanded her eyes to focus. As they did, she was witness to a terrifying sight. The female assassin, dressed in a nurse's uniform, was approaching with a syringe. Shannon kicked the instrument from the woman's hand and shoved her back, allowing time to get to her feet. Wearing an open-back hospital gown, Shannon resembled an Amazon warrior devoid of modesty.

The killer lunged, sending both to the floor. They rolled onto each other, thrashing their fingernails into exposed flesh. With each second, the fight became more frenzied as objects from around the room were upended and broken. The women remained locked in a death struggle, neither willing to rest or concede. Muffled screams of pain punctuated the fight as each scored points in sensitive areas.

The assassin clutched at Shannon's hair hoping to rend it from her scalp. She compelled her to let go by bloodying her nose with her elbow. Arms and legs thrashed without rest. The killer tackled Shannon, ramming her against the window. Broken glass fell to the courtyard eight floors below. Lethal hands now wrapped around Shannon's neck, squeezing off the blood to her brain. She felt faint, trying to pry loose the woman's powerful grip.

"Why won't you die?" the assassin snarled.

Shannon rocked back and forth in desperation, slamming the assassin's head into the side window casement. Forced to let go, she shook from the pain. The women renewed their battle, exchanging bitter screams and curses. They spun onto the bed with the killer landing on top. Shannon summoned her strength, hoisting the smaller woman over her head and executing a full body slam against the wall. The killer struck her head on the metal bed frame, collapsing in an inverted heap upon the mattress. Locking her fists together, she chopped at the woman along the length of her back. A medical tray was shoved into Shannon's face sending her reeling off the bed. Grabbing a specimen bottle, the assassin smashed it into a razor-sharp weapon. Shannon blocked two lethal thrusts with a pillow, then rammed the woman against a full length mirror as both spiraled down in a macroburst of glass shards. Grasping a jagged piece, she impaled the assassin through her clenched fist. Her tortured shriek crested as the glass broke off within her palm. The woman charged in psychotic frenzy. Pouncing upon Shannon, the killer stunned her with a series of body blows. The last was a vicious kick to her breasts, the injury forcing Shannon to recoil. She then glared at the assassin with eyes that would have scared the Devil Himself.

"Oh, it's on now, bitch."

Shannon tore into her enemy without any regard for her safety. The two resumed their struggle, tumbling headfirst into the bathroom. Fists flew in cyclonic rage. Shannon pressed the killer's head into the toilet, breaking off her front teeth on the rim of the bowl. Gurgling in agony, the woman spit forth a frothy sea of blood. She spun the assassin around and bullrushed her into the shower, slamming her spine into the metal fixtures protruding from the wall. Pummeling her with both fists, she initiated a volley of blows which turned the woman's face into a distorted, bloodied pulp. Then, with a Ninja-like scream, Shannon plunged her knee into the woman's crotch, shattering her pubic bone and slicing her open internally. The killer crumbled to the ground, doubled over in pain. She ran back to the room and located the syringe from the cluttered floor. After injecting her with the liquid, the woman was dead in seconds.

Shannon caught her breath. She took care to wash the blood from her hands and face. After checking herself in the mirror, she threw the towel at the assassin's corpse.

"That's for Denise," she spat in triumph.

Entering the empty hallway, Shannon approached the nurse's station. Sprawled before her were two dead nurses and a reception-ist. The assassin had struck earlier, ensuring no witnesses.

Shannon unlocked the patient storage room with one of the dead nurse's keys. She located her clothing and personal effects in a num-bered foot locker. As she got dressed, a wall mounted television car-ried a news bulletin from a local channel. She paid no attention until the reporter mentioned her name.

"Tonight, police are searching for a woman by the name of Shannon Hewson. Hewson, who resides in Duluth, is wanted for the murder today of her sister-in-law, Denise Duncan." Shannon's dri-ver's license photo appeared on screen. "Hewson is also wanted for questioning in the mysterious disappearance of Troy Garrett, an Atlanta-based agent for the FBI. Officials fear foul play was involved."

"Oh, God," she mumbled. "They got Troy." Shannon quaked with dread. *Who can I turn to? Who'd believe a story like this?* She didn't dare go to the authorities until she knew what this was about.

Someone had called her cell phone several times, but it was a number she didn't recognize. Shannon tried the number and a man's voice answered. It was Kevin Reese, speaking from his cell phone in Las Vegas. He introduced himself.

"I've been trying to call you for the last few hours," Kevin admitted. "I received an anonymous call from someone giving me your number, saying you were in danger."

"You have no idea," she sighed. "How are you involved?"

"I'm in Las Vegas with a woman named Mary Ellen Hart…" His words triggered an instant response, compelling her to interrupt.

"Who is Mary Ellen Hart?"

"It's a long story. She's my mother — and yours, too."

Shannon fell into a chair. "I was told she committed a crime. Something so bad, the Government wants her dead."

"No crime," he assured her. "Just in the wrong place at the wrong time."

"What happened?"

"It's too involved to get into over the phone. She needs you. Can you come to Vegas?"

Shannon was wanted by the authorities for murder. Staying in Atlanta wouldn't be the smartest thing to do. She was aware the only way to gain the truth was to meet with Mary Ellen Hart. The woman who gave birth to her years ago. Her mother needed her help — and she needed her.

For the first time in her life, Shannon Hewson knew where she belonged.

CHAPTER NINE

❀

ZEPHYR COVE, NEVADA — MARCH 31st

$\mathcal{T}$he sunlight shimmered on the most beautiful lake in the world. Christopher Joseph Hightower stood on his waterfront deck and filled his lungs with air. His eyes absorbed the vibrant colors of Lake Tahoe's clear waters, the majestic snow-kissed mountains and the towering ponderosa pines. Colors which could only come from God's sacred palette. He delighted in the saturation of his senses and the harmony he felt with nature. This was his slice of Heaven. A slice he had no desire to share.

'C.J.' Hightower was a very private person. He'd experienced more individual success than any five men would see in their life-times. The only son of Lionel and Margarite Hightower, C.J. grew up in Philadelphia and attended Temple University, graduating with honors. While there, he set many NCAA records in track and field. As an Olympic athlete in the 1968 Summer Games, C.J. won the Decathlon, the first Black athlete to capture gold in the event. He then shocked the world when, as a member of the 4 x 4 relay team, his fist was held high in rebellion during the playing of the U.S. national anthem.

C.J. was a vocal opponent of the war in Vietnam, as well as a founding member of the Black Panther organization, a group which defined the anger for a generation of Black America. In 1980, he was elected as Mayor of Oak Creek, California and re-elected in 1984. However, he became disillusioned by politics, unable to make a significant difference in the plight of the poor and disadvantaged.

Future political aspirations were placed on hold when C.J. converted to the Islamic faith, hoping to change the world through a religious revolution. After more than a decade of Islamic promises and failed opportunities the same sense of betrayal consumed him.

He fell from grace with his fellow Muslims by authoring a scathing manifesto denouncing the Islamic Church and followers of the prophet Mohammed. _The Infidels of Faith_ became an international sensation and caused Islamic fundamentalists to issue a death warrant for Yosef Mustafah, the name C.J. used, wishing understandably, to keep his identity secret. Now, four years later, he was again about to enflame the Islamic world with a sequel, _Destroyers of Faith_. His book publisher planned the worldwide release for tomorrow, the first day of April. Due to concerns for his safety, C.J. wasn't promoting the book publicly. Instead, he was receiving a select number of reporters at his Lake Tahoe home for one-on-one interviews. In a few minutes, a reporter from _USA Today_ would be arriving.

For all his success, C.J. considered himself a failure. Poverty, bigotry, racism and religious intolerance were still scourges of humanity. He dedicated the rest of his life to the search for spiritual truth, bettering himself as a person. Everyone else would have to find their own path and confront their own demons.

C.J. savored one more intoxicating breath, then re-entered his living room and closed the sliding glass door. His lakeside home was the only extravagance he allowed, paid for in full through the royalties on his books. Intricate stonework adorned the walls with wooden beams latticed through the cathedral ceiling. Mammoth windows captured the awesome splendor of the lake beyond. It was a magnificent home. One he wouldn't allow anyone to call a 'crib'.

C.J. Hightower was 6 foot 1, 227 pounds. He was in marvelous shape for his age and looked 10 years younger than he was. His gray hair was cut short with no hint of a receding hairline. Blessed with a pleasant face, his inviting brown eyes and infectious smile could win over the coldest of hearts. His ebony skin was wrinkled in spots, but he possessed potent charisma and exuded an air of distinction.

He had married once, but it was brief. His wife left him for a man who paid her more attention. C.J. was now engaged in a self-imposed period of celibacy, something he found more difficult to live with than having sex with frivolous females.

This was a man who loved outdoor activities with hiking, motor biking and chopping wood his particular favorites. He was also an accomplished skier, having an annual lift pass to the Heavenly Ski Resort only 12 miles distant.

Although C.J. loved the lake, he'd never been fond of water sports. He left those diversions to his lifelong friend Zach Watson. Zach was five years older and had been Hightower's bodyguard since the Islamic threat on his life began. After his wife passed away from cancer, he stayed on at C.J.'s home helping with domestic chores. Although an excellent athlete in his day, Zach was no longer in shape to be a bodyguard. The years were chiseled into his black skin, containing eyes that had seen far too much bigotry and hatred. Still, C.J. would never replace him. The two had been through the wars of life together and such loyalty was a rare commodity.

The doorbell rang at 11:00 AM. Zach greeted the *USA Today* reporter and escorted her inside. She was an attractive Black woman, 24 years old with beauty queen features. Very clever of *USA Today*, C.J. reasoned. Using this sexy spy to extract the juiciest story possible. *Very clever, indeed.* But, C.J. Hightower was too wise to be anybody's fool.

She introduced herself by presenting her business card. "Mr. Mustafah, I'm Natalie Donner. Book Reviewer for *USA Today*."

He eyed the card, then shook her extended hand. "Welcome, Miss Donner. Have a seat."

They walked over to an impressive stone fireplace, aglow with three burning logs. She sat opposite him in matching leather chairs.

"Care for a drink?" he asked.

"No, thank you."

C.J. whispered to his friend. "Check back in a few minutes."

Zach nodded and left the room. She placed a digital recorder on a nearby table and turned it on. "Do you mind?"

"Not at all."

"You have a wonderful home here. So beautiful," she stated, looking out at the lake.

"Well, if you can't change the world, you might as well live in the best part of it."

"Is that your intent with _Destroyers of Faith_? To change the world?"

C.J. stared at her. He wasn't sure he liked what he saw. Most often, he found that the prettiest packages contained unpleasant contents.

"The world won't be changed with a book, Miss Donner," came the measured response. "Nor 10,000 books. It'll take a spiritual revolution. A cleansing of everyone's heart and soul."

She took a few written notes. "Would you consider yourself a religious person?"

"No," he confided. "I don't believe any of the world's organized religions possess the truth. But, I'm a student of them all. That's the only way to eliminate misunderstanding which leads to prejudice."

Natalie continued taking notes. She was impressed with his eloquence and charm, but she needed a sensational interview and would have to start asking questions which would cause him to lose his cool. "Your name isn't Yosef Mustafah," she asked indelicately, "Is it Mr. Hightower? Are you afraid to use your real name?"

C.J. remained calm. "Name's are irrelevant, Miss Donner," issuing a sigh of annoyance. "Cassius Clay would've been just as famous if he hadn't become Muhammad Ali."

"That wasn't what I meant."

He leaned forward now conducting his own interview. "I know what you meant, Miss Donner. I wonder, have you even read _Destroyers of Faith_?"

She hesitated, caught off guard by the remark. "I reviewed most of it."

"Reviewed? What did you think of the unusual parallels I drew between the prophet Mohammed and the life of Christ?" Her silence answered his question. "I thought so. I used a pseudonym to protect myself from the hatred of others. If you'd read the book, you'd understand that," he chastised. "As I said, names are irrelevant. What matters is the identity you carry within."

Natalie realized this was not proceeding as planned. "If you don't mind, I'll have that drink now. A glass of white wine, please."

C.J. summoned Zach. "A Chardonnay for the lady. I'll have a Ginger Ale."

He left to fix the drinks. Natalie squirmed in her chair, conscious of the microscope she found herself under. Hanging above the fireplace was the famous 1968 photo of C.J.'s militant fist raised during the Olympic ceremony.

"I was wondering...," she pointed to the picture. "Why did you do that? I mean, what were you trying to say?"

He seemed unable to forgive her ignorance. "Do you know anything about history, Miss Donner? Particularly, Black history?"

Natalie sat stone faced, aware she'd lost control of the interview. She wanted to turn off the recorder, fearing her employers' wrath.

C.J. spoke from a deep well of emotion. "When I was growing up, we had to use separate bathrooms. Separate water fountains. We even had separate sections in restaurants where we had to eat. Always segregated from the Whites. It made no sense, but it was a fact of life."

Zach returned with the drinks, handing Natalie hers.

"Thank you," she murmured. He handed the Ginger Ale to C.J. who acknowledged with a quick nod.

"You owe your job at _USA Today_ to the sacrifices made by others, including Zach and myself."

She looked at them, bewildered. "I don't understand."

"Did you know Zach tried out for the U.S. Swim Team in the '64 Olympics? He beat their best swimmer by two full seconds. But, they told him to go home."

"Why?"

C.J. sipped his drink, then punctuated every word as if hammering a nail. "Because, they didn't want to clean the pool every time he went in."

Natalie's mouth dropped in amazement. "They didn't say that."

"Oh, Miss Donner. You really don't know your history, do you?"

Zach reflected on the pain he still felt to this day. "Anything else, C.J.?"

"No, Zach. I'm sorry, but our young visitor here has a lot to learn."

As he left the room, Natalie showed her distress. "I had no idea."

C.J. took another gulp of Ginger Ale, staring once again at the Olympic photo. "We raised our fists in protest to the treatment of our race by the U.S. Government. 1968 was the height of the Vietnam War. Most of the soldiers drafted were Black. They were forced to die for a country that wouldn't allow them to live as men."

"Were you drafted?"

He paused as the firelight reflected off his troubled face. "No. I was one of the lucky ones. I went to college and earned a get-out-of-the-war-free card," he mused, reluctant to admit the exemption. "But, many Blacks couldn't afford college and were forced into the war. The United States Government is a very insidious creature."

"What do you mean?" Natalie wondered, anticipating a quotable response.

"By sending its Black sons to war and keeping most of its White sons home, the U.S. acted much the same as the Nazis. Deciding which group should live and which should die. They just freshened it up a bit."

Shocked by the comment, she downed her drink with a single gulp. "You sound bitter."

C.J. flashed his winning smile. "Just being philosophical. You need to know where you've been, before deciding where to go."

"Lesson learned. Thanks for teaching me, Professor."

"Don't mention it, Miss Donner."

They continued the interview, specifically discussing the contents of his new book. C.J. even convinced her to stay for lunch. Zach fixed them tuna salad sandwiches. After the interview, Natalie turned off her recorder and thanked them both. She'd formed a special bond with the two and appreciated the time and courtesy they'd shown her.

As Natalie collected her things, she inquired about the unusual painting which hung next to the Olympic photo. It was a picture of a young, White woman with black hair and an angelic aura. "That's very haunting, Mr. Hightower. Did you paint it?"

He acknowledged his creation. "Yes. I did it from memory."

"She's beautiful. Who is she?"

A respectful pause. "I don't know. I wish I did. I've seen her in my dreams all my life. She's important to me somehow. I just can't figure the connection."

"Maybe you'll meet her someday."

"Perhaps," C.J. said with regret.

Natalie thanked them again for lunch and their time. She departed a much wiser woman than when she arrived. C.J. called his publisher to inform him the interview with _USA Today_ was complete. He was not scheduled for another appointment until tomorrow.

A few minutes later, the two were occupied in a game of chess at which C.J. was an unparalleled expert. Zach had played him for years, but never won a game his best friend hadn't secretly let him win. It wasn't much of a challenge for C.J. He knew what Zach would do even before he did it. But, it helped pass the time and Zach got a real thrill whenever he beat C.J. at his own game.

"You were hard on her, don't you think?"

C.J. studied the chess board. "Hmm. She needed it," he muttered in thought. "I blame her parents. They should've told her how things used to be." He moved his queen. "Check."

Zach scratched his head, trying to figure the best way to get his king out of trouble. He finally hid the piece behind a pawn. "She was fine."

"I didn't notice."

"How could you ignore such a sweet, young thing?"

"Easy," he reasoned, moving another piece. "I'm old enough to be her grandfather."

His partner pushed a disapproving sigh. "That don't mean you're dead. Some girls love us old farts. Now, if it was 20 years ago..."

Hightower smiled. "If it was 20 years ago, she'd be at the day care center playing house."

"Yeah," Zach groaned. "Sure was pretty though."

"20 years from now, no one will care what she looks like," came words drenched in wisdom. "Stare out that window, Zach. That's the kind of beauty that'll never age, because you're looking into the face of God."

As they admired the view, the two failed to notice a small motorboat drifting about a half-mile from shore. Aboard was a lone occupant watching the house through high-powered binoculars.

The assassin positioned the boat within sight of C.J.'s home and close enough to see another agent stationed outside the estate. They used walkie-talkies to communicate.

"Alpha Unit. Ready to rock 'n roll. Over."

A second of static, followed by the agent's response. "Beta Unit. Start the music. Out."

In the boat were two radio-controlled model aircraft about three feet in length and wingspan. An onboard camera was used to transmit the image in flight back to a control monitor. With a range of 10 miles and a top speed of 150 mph, the plane was the latest high-tech gadget in the CIA's arsenal of death.

The assassin placed the first plane in the water. Housed within its pontoons was a highly volatile napalm incendiary gel designed to set fire to anything and nearly impossible to extinguish. The motor hummed to life, propelling the plane across the surface of the lake. Soon, the craft was airborne. It responded to joystick control by executing several acrobatic turns and dives. Gaining altitude, the plane began circling C.J.'s home like an obsessed bird of prey, selecting a skylight as the optimal entry point. The craft pitched over and was deftly guided to its target. As the video feed went dark, an explosive echo reverberated across the lake.

"Alpha Unit. Package delivered. Confirm detonation. Over."

The response was immediate. "Beta Unit. Detonation confirmed. I'm in position for the kill. Out."

C.J. and Zach were still involved in their game of chess when the plane hit the skylight 20 feet away. The craft exploded in a rolling fireball, spewing jellied gasoline across the latticed ceiling beams. It rained down in iridescent globs, setting fire to everything in its wake. The force knocked both men from their chairs with Zach striking his head and losing consciousness. C.J. was spared from the liquid fire by the back of his chair which absorbed the hellish spray.

In seconds, the entire room was alive with flames and dense smoke. C.J. struggled to his feet, pulling Zach over to the sliding glass door. Coughing repeatedly from the noxious fumes, he managed to exit the house and press a button on a security alarm keypad which summoned the fire department. C.J. dragged his friend down some steps leading to the grass beyond. He tried to revive him by sprinkling water on his face from a nearby garden hose.

"Come on, Zach. Snap out of it."

The other assassin appeared behind them and leveled his gun. It was the sudden screech of a hawk which caused C.J. to turn, recognize the danger and avoid the deadly bullet. As the assassin charged, he was forced back by a torrent of water from the open hose. C.J. lunged forth, sending both to the ground. He plunged his fingers into the assassin's neck, bouncing his head against a flat rock. After wrestling away the weapon, he placed it under the man's left armpit.

"Who sent you?"

"Get fucked!"

C.J. pulled the trigger. Over an agonized scream, he inquired again. "Who sent you?"

Before he could respond, the sound of rifle fire echoed as the other assassin fired from the boat. C.J. ran for cover, dropping the gun in haste. Another shot missed by inches. He dashed to his garage and straddled his pride and joy, a new Harley Davidson XLP 1800cc Sportster. The motorcycle sped away from the flaming house. Clutching his bloodied shoulder, the assassin stumbled to his car in pursuit.

C.J. was certain these men had been sent by Islamic extremists and wondered if they were working alone or if an entire team lay in wait. Over the roar of his Harley, he could hear fire engines approaching. As C.J. crested onto the highway, he proceeded north, knowing they'd expect him to head south toward more populated areas. It was a sound plan. A plan that would have worked if the other assassin hadn't launched the second plane — packed with C-4 explosives.

The plane paced the motorcycle approximately 200 feet above the road, keeping a discrete, but ever-closing distance. C.J. was unaware of the danger as it followed with robotic stealth. He throttled back on the bike and channeled a sigh. Now that the fire department was at his house, he thought it might be safe enough to return. C.J. then spotted the peculiar shadow of a small model airplane cast upon the road. He looked into the sky as the device emerged from the midday sun, swooping down for an explosive rendezvous. The deadly chase was on.

Eclipsing 140 mph, the motorcycle hugged the road barely gaining distance on the craft. Coming up was Cave Rock, a small tunnel where Highway 50 entered the side of a rocky cliff next to the lakefront. The plane broke off pursuit, banking left over the water. As C.J. entered the tunnel, he throttled back, popping the clutch for a daring 180 degree reverse turn. Executing the maneuver, he headed south in a dense haze of rubber. The plane went into a dive, leveling out just above the road. It followed the motorcycle through the tunnel and began to zero in on its target.

The occupants of two passing cars watched the surreal scene in shock. C.J. negotiated the curves as tightly as he dared. On several, he cleared the pavement by mere inches. The plane rocked back and forth, avoiding tree limbs and power lines as it pursued with lethal intent.

Peering ahead, C.J. saw an oncoming car in his lane. It was the wounded assassin, swerving across the road in a late-model

Cadillac. With less than 50 yards remaining, C.J. faked right, then roared left. The plane headed straight for the Cadillac's windshield. It rose up, clearing the roof of the car as the assassin screamed in terror. Soaring skyward, the plane once again broke off the attack.

C.J. raced past his driveway and into the business district of Zephyr Cove. The plane was now approaching from the south. C.J. diverted onto a parallel bike path which wound through a thick stand of trees, once again eluding the flying bomb. His motorcycle hurdled a small berm of snow, then landed back on the road accelerating under his expert command. The Cadillac continued the high-speed pursuit, swerving around a slower car which had entered the highway at the wrong moment.

The plane closed from behind. C.J. roared left onto Ski Run Boulevard, cutting across the path of an 18 wheel semi. The craft veered off, narrowly missing the truck. It circled once, climbing to a higher altitude to re-establish visual contact. The Cadillac came to the turn, forced to wait for a series of passing cars.

C.J.'s motorcycle climbed the grade, gaining a thousand feet from the lakeshore before entering the parking complex at the Heavenly Ski Resort. Although late in the ski season, it was still cold enough to keep the snow nature had provided while making new powder to allow the resort to remain open.

He gunned his Harley through a pedestrian entrance and approached the base of the mountain. The Cadillac arrived, crashing through a metal barricade, determined to extend the chase. C.J. slipped his bike into a lower gear to negotiate the slick, inclined surface. Horrified bystanders watched as the vehicles forced skiers to scatter, wiping out on either side of the ski run. Ice pelted C.J.'s face making it difficult to scan ahead. The angle of climb became increasingly severe, slowing the manic pursuit.

He guided his motorcycle into a berm of snow and dashed toward a nearby stand of trees. The Cadillac came to a halt in a cloud of wind-whipped spray. C.J. entered the trees beyond as the wounded assassin gave chase, clutching his shoulder as he ran.

Seeking refuge behind a large pine, he paused to think through his options. None were good. He was now alone and without a weapon. Cursing the situation, he heard the scrunching of new snow getting louder. It was time to fight.

Lunging from his location, C.J. kicked the assassin's gun from his hand. They wrestled like two wild beasts, submerged in the white powder. Exposed flesh soon became numb. He began pounding his fist into the assassin's wound, extracting the maximum amount of pain. Fighting through his torment, the man wrapped his arms around C.J.'s neck, shoving him face first into the snow. Consumed in breathless terror, he flailed his arms and legs, unable to break the powerful headlock.

Suddenly, C.J. felt something land next to him. It was a nine-inch icicle, intact and sharp as a spike. Clutching the blunt end, he plunged the frozen weapon into the man's side. A squeal of agony echoed across the mountainside as the assassin rolled off him into a bed of blood red snow. C.J. sucked in precious air, then staggered to his feet. He dashed out from under the trees' protective canopy, forgetting about the plane still circling overhead.

A series of real-time events now overlapped with complex choreography. As the craft swooped down for the kill, the wounded assassin recovered his gun and gave chase. He stopped underneath the ski lift to level his weapon. At that instant, an empty gondola transposed itself between the diving plane and C.J. A concussive blast shook the area. The cable snapped, sending the two ton gondola to earth — crushing the assassin below. All that remained was a deathly sound which seemed to linger without end. Exhausted, C.J. fell to his knees grateful to be alive.

After regaining consciousness, Zach saw the assassin's boat drifting about 200 yards offshore. He began to swim out, approaching undetected. The agent aboard was yelling into the walkie-talkie in a futile effort to contact his partner.

Zach swam the last few yards completely submerged, arriving underneath the keel as the man tried to start his outboard motor. After rocking the boat once, he managed to flip it over. The assassin fell into the lake, thrashing for his life. Zach came to the surface for a full breath and re-entered to do battle. The two grappled with one another, slugging and kicking in a lethal underwater ballet. Zach spotted an Uzi 9mm floating past him in the clear Tahoe water. In fluid motion, he grabbed the weapon and shoved its muzzle into the man's belly. The gun sprang to life with a rhythmic vibration. A red cloud obscured the assassin's face as the corpse descended to the bottom.

As he swam ashore, Zach fought against the numbing cold. He stumbled onto land in front of several firefighters who'd just finished extinguishing the flames at C.J.'s home. Suffering the bitter effects of hypothermia, they wrapped him in dry blankets and summoned paramedics.

C.J. returned home as they were loading Zach into an ambulance. After consulting with the paramedics, he bent over the gurney grasping his friend's hand in assurance.

"They say you'll be okay, Zach. Just do what the doctors tell you."

"I got him. The other bastard. I got him."

"I know you did," came his soothing voice. "Now, it's time for you to get better. I'll see you later on."

C.J. flashed his winning smile as they lifted the gurney and closed the ambulance doors.

The firefighters had saved the majority of the home. There was heavy fire and water damage in the living room, but nothing that couldn't be replaced. He provided police investigators with his lengthy account, then after several hours they were gone, leaving him alone with his thoughts.

As C.J. sifted through the remains, his eyes beheld a miracle. Hanging above the fireplace was the painting of the young girl who'd forever occupied his dreams, unscathed from its exposure in Hell. He examined the painting...no damage...not even to the frame. It was the only object in the room which survived.

C.J. called his publisher from his cell phone. He explained what happened and assured him he was all right. The publisher had news of his own.

"I had a strange call today. A guy in Las Vegas," stated the man. "He said he'd received an anonymous message that I'd be able to contact you. He claimed he was your real brother and that you'd been adopted by different families."

"How did he know that?"

"Know what?"

"That I was adopted." It had been a secret his mother shared with him before her death.

"It's possible he's telling the truth," speculated his publisher. "He said you were both adopted from a Catholic Mission in Juarez, Mexico."

C.J. froze. His mother had informed him of this years ago. This seemed too real to ignore. "What's his name?"

"Kevin Reese. He left a number for you to call."

He wrote down the message and thanked the man, telling him to cancel the remainder of his media interviews. After a moment of reflection, C.J. dialed Kevin.

"Hello?" Reese answered.

"This is Christopher Hightower," came the brusque introduction. "Now, tell me who you are and what this is about."

Kevin explained the incredible circumstance as best he could. C.J. remained skeptical, thinking this might somehow be connected with the recent attack on his life.

"If you'll come to Las Vegas we can explain everything."

"We?"

"Your brothers and sisters. And, of course, Mary Ellen Hart. She's our mother," he maintained, hoping to impress him with appropriate urgency. "You're in danger and need to know what's going on."

"I might put myself in danger by going there. Tell me, Mr. Reese, what do you look like?"

"Well, I'm 6 foot 2, 235, blond hair, blue eyes..."

C.J. exploded in laughter.

"What's so funny?"

Annoyance tempered his amusement. "Mr. Reese? Next time, make sure you're Black."

"Wait a minute. I can explain."

C.J. hung up, stunned at absurdity of the call. He then noticed the painting. It was no longer a portrait of a young girl, but that of an elderly woman. C.J. shut his eyes, then refocused. The woman's image remained. She seemed sad with tears welling in her eyes. He approached the picture, gingerly running his hand over the canvas. It was dry to the touch. In spite of his every hope, the image refused to disappear. He began to tremble in awe. After several minutes of reverent examination, C.J. redialed Kevin's number.

"Mr. Reese?" came an unsteady voice, "Can you describe Mary Ellen Hart?"

Kevin relayed her physical features, convincing him that the woman in the painting was indeed his mother. C.J. remained spellbound by the vision. He paused to compose himself, then made the only decision possible.

"I'll be in Las Vegas tonight, Mr. Reese," he stated. "When I arrive, I'll call you."

He thanked Kevin and hung up. Christopher Joseph Hightower now looked back at the painting which once more portrayed Mary Ellen Hart as the young girl from his dreams.

CHAPTER TEN

❦

FLORENCE, COLORADO and EL PASO, TEXAS — APRIL 2nd

*J*udge Harold Monroe loved grape juice. Since learning of its ability to reduce cholesterol, he couldn't consume enough of the purplish liquid. The FBI Director was desperate to cleanse his arteries in the hope of extending his life.

Monroe was 56 years old, having survived two heart attacks. He was as obese as he was unpleasant, with his 375 pound body bulging from his clothes in every conceivable direction. His thinning brown hair was stretched across his scalp, looking as though someone had drawn in the wayward strands with a magic marker. Monroe's wire-rimmed glasses complemented his owlish features and he exuded an odious smell which no known cologne could mask. Some of his coworkers suggested that upon his death, Monroe's body be donated to science fiction.

The FBI Director and member of the MAJIK-12 was on a special mission, having flown from Washington D.C. to Pueblo, Colorado earlier in the day. His armored limousine was now approaching the Federal Administrative Maximum Security Prison, known as ADMAX. It was here in the small town of Florence, Colorado that the U.S. Government housed its most coveted criminals. The prison was built on a level field in front of the Rocky

Mountain range. The only visible portion of the facility consisted of six guard towers and four concentric, electrified fences surrounding a single-story structure awash with motion detectors and trip wires. The remainder of the prison resided entirely underground. A rectangular, steel reinforced sallyport served as the only means of entry.

Monroe peered into an empty bottle of grape juice. He instructed Caroline Stricka, his mousy female aide, to purchase more at the earliest opportunity. The limousine arrived at the facility and disappeared within the bowels of the prison. Once inside, several armed guards ringed the limousine as Monroe extricated himself from the vehicle. Luther Babcock, the warden of the complex, greeted him.

"Judge Monroe. Welcome to ADMAX," said the weasel-like official. The two men contrasted comically together.

"Thanks. Is our boy ready?"

"Yes, sir. This way."

As Babcock led his honored guest to a service elevator, Monroe turned to his aide. "Grape juice, Caroline. Don't forget."

She nodded before the elevator doors closed.

Esteban Quezada Lopez sat with his head buried in his chest. The one-man cell had a sterile, antiseptic feel. A video camera mounted in the corner of the room kept silent vigil, watching him 24/7. He'd been told to expect a visit, but wasn't informed who was coming nor the purpose of the meeting.

Esteban was 23 years old, but felt much older. His 5 foot 9, 165 pound frame was a gentle disguise for a man who could kill without conscience. He was an enforcer for the Cali Cartel, the drug lords of Columbia. Esteban liked the term 'enforcer'. It was a harmless euphemism for assassin.

Sent to the Juarez Mission when he was three months old, Esteban never knew his parents and grew up bitter by their abandonment. He had few friends at the orphanage except for Moses de la Cruz and Abraham Rodriguez who seemed to understand him better than the Sisters. Labeled early on as a troublemaker, he was constantly scolded for his disrespect for authority. Being the black sheep at the orphanage didn't faze young Esteban. Instead, he considered it a badge of honor.

In their teens, Esteban would convince Moses and Abraham to accompany him, whereupon the three would proceed to sample every moral sin available. Maria Elena blamed Esteban for being the negative influence which drove Moses from her guiding light. It was Esteban who insisted they attend the El Paso High School dance the night Moses met Atali Castaneda. Through Atali, Esteban was introduced to Anna Castaneda, her cousin. She fell smitten with the dashing, thoroughly untamable, Lopez. Three months later, the two were secretly married in Juarez. Esteban left the Mission, finding work with various gangs ensuring that business owners paid their protection money on time. He realized he was an expert pistol marksman, with his 20/15 eyesight allowing him to be deadly accurate. Eventually recruited by a criminal syndicate in Mexico City, he served them well for more than two years. Still, Esteban felt his unique services were not being compensated as well as they should. He then traveled to a place where money was no object, the town of Cali, Columbia. Here he gained respect and financial reward for his talents as a professional assassin. But most important, he found a perverse loyalty and honor with the Cartel. Qualities which had been lacking from his life.

Six months ago, Esteban and Anna Lopez were on vacation in West Palm Beach, Florida, guests of the exclusive Breakers Hotel. He received a call from his employers to retaliate against three DEA agents based in Miami who'd made a multibillion dollar cocaine bust. Esteban always followed orders. Within 48 hours the agents were dead, shot down in their helicopter by a Stinger Missile over Biscayne Bay. Lopez returned to West Palm Beach as though nothing had happened, enjoying every moment with his wife Anna. She was pregnant with their first child and soon he'd know the joys of fatherhood.

While he was in the U.S., Lopez phoned Moses to see if he could recruit him for the Cartel, asking his friend to come to West Palm Beach to discuss a lucrative offer. It was a surprise when

Moses abruptly hung up, but nothing compared to the shock he experienced two hours later. Federal agents ambushed Lopez and his wife outside the Breakers Hotel, greeting them with automatic weapons fire. Esteban fell backward against a fire hydrant and was rendered unconscious, unable to defend himself or his wife. When he awoke, Lopez was in chains and on his way to ADMAX. He was held without legal representation or trial. Worst of all, no one would tell him the fate of his wife and unborn child. He hoped today's visit would shed some light.

Two guards unlocked his cell door, motioning for him to exit. Lopez walked out, noting their taser guns at the ready. They escorted him to the medical infirmary. As they entered, Esteban recognized the corpulent FBI Director flanked by a dozen armed guards, as well as several doctors and other medical personnel. Instructed to sit in a chair, Esteban smirked at the scene.

"If you're my new cellie, you better take the lower bunk."

Monroe returned a hollow smile. "I've come to offer you a deal."

An uneasy pause. He knew better than to trust anyone who worked for the U.S. Government. Still, there seemed no harm in hearing what he had to say.

"What kind of deal?"

"We need you to find Moses de la Cruz Castaneda and his mother, Maria Elena de la Cruz. I believe you know them both."

"What do you want with them?"

"That's not your concern," Monroe snapped. "Just find them for us."

Esteban had no problem with the stated objective. In fact, he'd planned to track down Moses anyway, believing Castaneda responsible for betraying his whereabouts to the Feds. He was unaware the FBI had tapped Atali's phone. When Anna called from West Palm Beach informing her cousin of her pregnancy, she unintentionally revealed Esteban's location.

He remained poker-faced. "And, when I do?" wondering what kind of reward they had in mind.

Monroe reached into a manila envelope producing an official looking document. He waved the paper before him as though it were rare steak for a ravenous dog. "This is a signed pardon from the President of the United States, granting your freedom and safe transport out of the country." The document was handed to him for review.

CIA Director Walter Langlois had called Monroe earlier, informing him of the failed assassination attempts on Shannon Hewson and Christopher Hightower. The national media was in a feeding frenzy, trying to find a common denominator in these seemingly random attacks. Operation Black Widow had become an unparalleled disaster and the MAJIK-12 were desperate to see results. It was now imperative to get Lopez to play ball.

Esteban read the document. It appeared genuine.

"What about my wife?"

Monroe smiled. "She's safe. We have her and your daughter under our protection program."

"My daughter!" his excitement betraying him. "When was she born?"

"Two weeks ago. Both of them are doing well."

"Can I see them?"

The judge scrunched his face. "Soon. After you do this for us."

He could hardly believe it would be this easy. "Can they leave with me? With the same conditions?"

"Of course," Monroe said, successfully cloaking his contempt. "Just find Castaneda. We'll do the rest."

Esteban wasn't stupid. He knew what that meant and it didn't bode well for Moses or his mother. Still, he couldn't forsake this opportunity.

"Do we have a deal?"

He acknowledged his acceptance. "Sure. I'll do it. When do I get out?"

"Right away. As soon as we — operate."

"Operate?" he asked, shock registering in his voice. "Nobody said anything about that. What the hell do you mean?"

Monroe leaned forward, clearly delighted by his sudden distress. "Trust me. You'll see."

Esteban bolted from his chair. Two guards fired their tasers, incapacitating him with waves of electric torture. The prisoner fell to the floor in seizures. After a moment, four guards forced him onto an examination table, each holding down a convulsing arm or leg. Monroe rose from his chair and motioned for the medical team to begin.

"You fat fuck!" squealed Esteban, trying not to bite off his tongue.

Breathless with hysteria, he was lost in a squall of fear and rage. The anesthesiologist approached with a plastic mask, positioning the device over his nose. Monroe walked over to the unwilling patient with evident glee.

"Sleep you bastard," he murmured. "Sleep… Sleep..." A second later, Esteban's world went dark.

Upon regaining consciousness, Esteban tried to focus on his surroundings. His vision was no longer equal. Through his right eye he could see the medical personnel peering over him. His left eye was sore and the room appeared fuzzy. A square object floated before him, rotating in inner space. Esteban blinked once, then several times. His vision refused to improve and the swirling oddity remained. Although groggy, he could hear the doctors call the authorities to the room. A nurse propped him up with some pillows so he could greet the entourage. His arms and legs were restrained by heavy straps running the width of the bed. After taking a small sip of water to combat his cottonmouth, he saw Monroe before him, grape juice in hand.

"How's our sleeping beauty?"

"Screw you." He took a breath of antiseptic air. "What did you do to me?"

"Just a precaution. It occurred to us you might not do what we want once we let you go."

The pain in his left eye became intolerable. "What did you do to me?"

Monroe grinned, savoring another taste of the purple nectar. "We replaced the fluid in your left eye with a liquid explosive. It's stable at all temperatures and pressures, so it won't go off by accident."

He gazed at the official, horrified by the news. Monroe took another gulp of grape juice and continued having fun. "The square object floating in your eye is a microchip which acts as a primer. It ignites the explosive once it receives a detonation code from an orbiting satellite."

"You stinking load of shit!" he raged. "Go fuck yourself in that huge ass! I'm not doing dick for you!"

Monroe giggled like a child. "Then, I guess we'll have to kill you now. Too bad. Never again to see that lovely wife of yours, or your baby daughter."

Esteban seethed in silence. The fate of his family was foremost in his mind. He realized he was in no position to retaliate. Better to obey now and strike later.

"If I do this," regaining his composure, "Can you take it out? Give me my eyesight back?"

"Of course. The process is completely reversible." Several of the medical personnel smirked at the lie. Not only was the blindness permanent, the Government had no intention of allowing Esteban to leave the country once his task was complete. The Presidential pardon was a fake. Monroe himself forged Susan Webber's signature without her knowledge.

"We'll give you two weeks to find Castaneda. If you fail…we'll ship what's left of you to your wife."

Esteban held back a tsunami of anger. "How do I stay in touch?"

Monroe dropped a business card on his chest. "That's the number of an answering service. They'll get a message to me wherever I am. Once you find them, I'll arrange for the operation to restore your sight." The judge took another swig of juice. "Any questions?"

Swallowing his rage, he shook his head.

"Our satellite can send that signal anywhere in the world. Don't make the mistake of fucking us or it'll be the last thing you do." He turned to the guards. "Get him ready. I want him on the road by morning."

Esteban traveled by bus to El Paso, Texas, then by cab to the hacienda of the Castanedas. The impressive estate was perched high on a hilltop overlooking the greater El Paso-Juarez Metro area. He knew there was a chance Atali wasn't home, having failed to call first. Esteban wanted to make sure no information leaked out in case the FBI was tapping her phone. It was a wise precaution. As he surmised, the authorities were monitoring everything.

Esteban was greeted at the door by Consuelo, the Castaneda's maid. They hugged, not having seen each other since his marriage to Anna. She informed him of Atali's injuries and showed him inside. Atali had been released from El Paso Regional Hospital just three days before.

She was in her bed, watching a favorite TV soap opera when the maid announced Esteban's arrival. A few moments later, the two were locked in a warm embrace with Lopez careful not to touch her bandaged arm and chest.

"So, how's the Goddess?" he asked. It was a nickname Esteban and Anna had bestowed on Atali, paying homage to the Mayan Goddess of Love for whom she was named.

"I've been better," fatigue layering her voice. "I guess Consuelo told you what happened?"

"Some," he confessed. "Sounds like you had a close call."

She forced a lengthy sigh, tortured by the memory. "It was horrible. Like a bad dream that wouldn't end. But, Moses was awesome. He'll always be my hero." Atali blushed, making her love for him clear. Esteban said nothing, concealing his anger over Moses' betrayal. "But, what of you, Esteban? I've heard nothing since that awful night in Florida when the authorities arrested you."

"They let me go. No evidence."

"I'm glad. What happened to your eye?"

"A fight," lied Lopez, deflecting the question. "You should've seen the other guy."

She answered with a grin. "Why have you come?"

"Do I need a reason?"

"Esteban Lopez does nothing without a reason."

Dropping his head, he paused for dramatic effect. "I need to locate Moses. There's something I must tell him. Do you know where he is?"

She rolled her eyes, having anticipated his query. "The police have asked me a hundred times and my answer's always the same. I don't know."

"This isn't the police asking. It's me." Atali wondered whether she should say more. Esteban continued the subtle pressure. "Goddess, you know you can trust me. It's important. I really must contact him."

After a frustrated breath, she caved in. "He went off with his mother. He's called three times from his cell phone and each time for just a minute or two. I honestly don't know where they're staying."

He reflected on her words. "But, you know where they are?"

Atali nodded in resignation. "Las Vegas."

"What are they doing in Vegas?"

"I have no idea," confided Atali. "Moses was very excited last time we talked. He said he'd met two older brothers and a sister. I asked how long he planned to stay and he didn't know."

Lopez smiled, certain he had extracted the truth. "Thank you, Goddess. I'll be sure to give him your love when I see him."

Atali stared at Esteban, bereaved. "You haven't mentioned Anna once. Are you doing all right without her?"

He was sobered by the thought. "I suppose I have to. But, we'll be together soon. You can count on that."

"I hope it's not too soon," came her innocent reply. "I don't want to lose you, too."

"Lose me?"

She looked hurt, tears pooling in her eyes. "This isn't a joke, Esteban. I know you loved her, but she's never coming back."

His anger flared, grabbing Atali's injured arm. "What do you mean she's never coming back? Answer me! What do you mean?"

"Esteban…," frightened by his sudden rage. "Anna's dead."

He shook her, roaring like a lion over the loss of his mate. "That's a lie! A fucking, fucking lie! Who told you that?"

Tears streamed down her face. "You're hurting me!"

"Who said that shit?" he yelled. "Damn you! Who was it?"

She blurted forth the truth. "Moses!"

He paused to catch his breath while Atali whimpered in pain. Several seconds elapsed before he regained control of his temper and released her. "I'm sorry. I didn't mean to hurt you."

Atali curled up on her bed, sobbing from fear and discomfort. Esteban knew he'd outstayed his welcome.

"It's not true about Anna," he stammered. "She's alive. I'll prove it to you. I'll prove it to you both." He turned toward the door, addressing Atali with a final thought. "Tell Moses to be careful in Vegas…He's liable to lose it all."

CHAPTER ELEVEN

❦

NEW YORK CITY, NEW YORK — APRIL 4th

$\mathscr{B}$arbara Gordon Pinder stood at the podium addressing the United Nations' General Assembly. She gave a moving speech on the role world Governments must play to ensure ethnic harmony and religious tolerance. The audience was enraptured by the vision and accorded her a standing ovation when finished. It was her defining moment on the world's stage. A moment which required a lifetime of heartache to make possible.

At seven months of age, Barbara was adopted by Bernard and Adele Gordon of Nassau, Bahamas. They had tried for years to conceive a child without success. Bernard was the Bahamian Minister of Tourism. Through his personal relationship with a Mexican Government official, he was informed that a Black female child was available for adoption from a Catholic Mission in Juarez. Until the age of five, Barbara was raised in the Gordon's God-fearing home. She wanted for nothing and was doted on by her parents. Even at an early age, young Barbara possessed excellent cognitive skills and was more mature than children twice her age. Her parents also provided her with spiritual nourishment, ensuring Barbara attended the local Anglican Church. She enjoyed the fellowship there and was fascinated with Bible stories. Every night, Barbara would kneel by her bed and pray to God to keep her family safe. It was a ritual she never failed to do. But her whole world, and her special relationship with God, ended in tragedy.

Hurricane Donna, one of the most devastating storms of the 20th Century, slammed into the Bahamas without warning. Among the hundreds who perished were her parents, swept away by the tidal surge as they tried to barricade their home. Miraculously, Barbara survived the savage act of God and went to live with her aunt in Freeport. Nearly 1,000 homes were destroyed. So too was Barbara's belief in the fairness of the Almighty. Her prayers had been wasted and she would never forgive His betrayal of her tender trust.

As she grew up, Barbara excelled in gymnastics and swimming. Her superior grades allowed her to secure a Rhodes Scholarship at the exclusive Oxford University in Great Britain. It was there she met another Bahamian, Geoffrey Pinder, the man destined to be her first husband. They fell in love and the two were married in a civil ceremony at Barbara's request.

After years of trying to have a child of their own, they decided to undergo routine medical examinations. The news they received was catastrophic. Upon further testing, Geoffrey was diagnosed with pancreatic cancer and given less than a year to live. The extended Pinder family began a prayerful vigil hoping God would make him well again. Barbara refused to subject herself to what she considered a thoroughly useless waste of time. She put her trust in the physicians who worked feverishly to save Geoffrey's life. In the end, he succumbed to his disease, driving a further wedge between Barbara and God.

As a 27 year old widow, she attended law school in Great Britain and studied at the London School of Economics. Barbara gained her legal degree and returned to Nassau to join her father-in-law as a junior partner in his law firm. She became romantically involved with Terence Pinder, Geoffrey's cousin. Several months later, she married Terence, again opting for a non-church wedding. She didn't really love the man, but felt it would solidify her budding legal career. Both of them worked long hours, so their marriage remained dull, but stable. Once more, no children resulted from the union. In March 1996, Terence had to travel to London for a legal symposium and asked Barbara to join him. She declined, citing her busy schedule. Two days later, the police informed Barbara her husband was dead, killed outright in a car accident on the M1 Motorway. It never occurred to her that she would've died had she accompanied him. She was absent from his funeral, stating overwhelming grief as her less than truthful excuse. Barbara vowed never to enter a house of God again.

With her legal career flourishing, Barbara became interested in politics and Government service. Being a two-time widow from the influential Pinder family, she garnered instant recognition and voter sympathy. Winning a landslide victory, Barbara was elected to the Bahamian House of Parliament. In five short years, she became a significant force within the Government. The Prime Minister then appointed her to be the new Bahamian Ambassador to the United Nations.

She moved to New York City, immersing herself in her duties. Barbara saw the United Nations as a significant force for good and worked tirelessly for many of the organization's humanitarian programs. Then, came the war.

The countries of Iran and Israel entered into hostilities over their religious differences. Iran fired missiles into Israel carrying fatal biologic agents, killing over 10,000 people in Jerusalem and Tel Aviv. The Israelis counterattacked with nuclear weapons, effectively destroying the cities of Tehran and Shiraz. The Iranian death toll was over 200,000 with many more injured and left homeless. It was a flashpoint which threatened to trigger World War III. The United Nations met in emergency session trying to defuse the situation. Barbara stepped forward, becoming a voice of reason. She headed a U.N. peace delegation which brought about a truce between the combatants. For her exemplary work, she was awarded the Nobel Peace Prize becoming a hero in the Bahamas and around the world.

Lasting peace was now hopefully at hand as Iran and Israel were set to sign a formal treaty. The setting for this historic occasion was the General Assembly of the United Nations. With the world watching on live television, Barbara Pinder handed the typed copies of the agreement to the representatives of both countries for their signatures.

The General Assembly was hushed as the Iranian and Israeli diplomats sat at a long table and signed the documents. Cameras flashed throughout the room when they stood and shook hands. A thunderous roar of applause followed as peace had finally prevailed. Barbara smiled in triumph. In fact, to those who knew her well, she'd never looked happier.

Pinder was 5 foot 7, 133 pounds with shoulder length black hair curled in dreadlocks. Her ebony skin was flawless without the wrinkles normally affecting a woman of her years. Barbara's eyes were wide-set, sporting brown pools of warmth. They rested above sensuous lips which failed to hide her mile-long smile. She had full breasts and hips, but cloaked her assets with formal dress attire. Barbara used sex as a weapon on a select few, the current victim being Trevor Rollins who was trying to catch her attention from across the room. She acknowledged him with a brief wink, still posing for the cameras. In appreciation for everything she'd done, one of the ceremonial pens used for the treaty signing was given to Barbara as a gift. Accepting the present with honor, she slipped it into her dress pocket for safe keeping.

A reception was held in the United Nations commissary, converted into a formal banquet room for the occasion. Hundreds of invited guests were in attendance feasting on various dishes from around the world. Security was exceptionally tight in response to extremist groups threatening to disrupt the peace treaty signing.

Barbara was sipping champagne with other delegates when Trevor Rollins pulled her toward a storage room, nearly spilling the fluted glass from her hand.

"Trevor...," she cried, as he hustled her into the room and closed the door.

He flipped on the overhead light. Trevor was a 38 year old diplomat from Jamaica with dashing looks and a smile to match. They had been intimate for about a year and he was pressuring her for a more permanent commitment. She stared at him in shock.

"Now, what are we supposed to do? Screw in front of the whole world? They know we're in here."

Trevor ran his hand over her cheeks and down the length of her neck. "I haven't been with you in days."

She rolled her eyes, concerned how this must look to the others. "This can wait."

He blocked the door. "No, Barb. It can't. I asked you to marry me three weeks ago and you haven't given me a straight answer yet."

A lengthy sigh. "You know what's been going on. I haven't had time to sort through how I feel."

"It's simple, Barb. Either you love me or you don't."

"I do love you, Trev," she confided. "But, this is a big step. I've been married twice and you know what happened. I'm a jinx to any man who loves me."

He smiled, stroking her across more provocative areas. "That's bull. You don't have to be scared of the boogieman."

"It's not the boogieman I'm scared of, Trevor."

"Then, what?"

A reflective pause. "I'm old enough to be your mother."

He pulled her tight, running his hands across her back. "Then, mother me."

"Stop it," she responded, not meaning the words.

"Age isn't important," Trevor assured her. "Love's all that matters. We could even have children, God willing."

Her eyes flew open as if receiving an electric shock. "Don't you dare go there!" She reached past him and forced open the door.

"What did I say?"

"We'll talk later," Barbara snapped, exiting the room without further explanation.

That afternoon, she was back in her 28th floor office inside the U.N. Secretariat Building. She returned several phone calls, gazing out at the city below.

Her secretary entered with a stack of messages, mail and a dozen, long-stemmed red roses still bundled in plastic wrap. She smiled at the floral offering.

"I guess I owe Trevor an apology."

"Why's that?" the young woman asked.

Barbara wiped clean an imaginary slate. "Forget it. They're from Trevor, aren't they?"

"I don't know. There wasn't a card."

She handed the roses to Barbara who stole a sniff from the bouquet. "What else?"

Her secretary placed all the correspondence on the desk. "I can't keep up. You've got at least three dozen requests for media interviews, letters of congratulations from various heads of state and, of course, all the kooks and crazies out there threatening your life."

"Hmm. Business as usual."

"Do you need me to dictate any replies?"

She shook her head. "Not now. I've got a meeting with the Secretary General," checking her watch. "I'll be back in an hour. Tell everyone I'm still unavailable."

"Will do."

Barbara reached the door, then circled back. "Would you be good enough to put these in some water?" handing her the flowers.

"Yes, ma'am." Barbara then left the room.

She was in the elevator heading toward the 39th floor when a violent concussion shook the cab, buckling her to the floor. Screams of terror could be heard in the corridors beyond.

Unknown to Barbara, the roses were from the MAJIK-12. The moment her secretary placed the flowers in water, a chemical reaction occurred sending an incendiary blast 30 yards in every direction. Her secretary died in a microsecond as the superheated fireball incinerated everything in its path. The outer wall of the 28th floor was breached, delivering a cascade of metal, plaster and glass into the plaza below. Dense smoke filled the corridors as wind fanned flames burned carpets, walls and ceiling panels. Emergency alarms shrieked in frenzy. Police began evacuating the building while fire-fighters were dispatched from points throughout the city.

Barbara was trapped inside the motionless elevator. She was certain this was a terrorist attack, undoubtedly directed at her. Her first concern was for her staff. She long ago dedicated her own life to the cause of peace. But, the people who worked with her had just become innocent victims. She hadn't considered the consequences of this type of collateral damage and that made her soul ache.

Barbara grabbed the emergency phone housed beneath the con-trol panel. The ringing at the other end was most welcome, but it continued without answer. Smoke and heated air made it difficult to breathe. Barbara knew if she did nothing, help would never arrive in time. She eyed the service hatch above, jumping up to dislodge the panel.

Once inside the shaft, she took stock of the task before her. Removing her shoes, Barbara grabbed hold of the steel cable and began climbing hand over hand. She soon arrived at the 29th floor, noting the flames dancing beyond. She would have to go higher. Smoke was now pouring into the shaft, making her cough repeated-ly. After filtering a breath through her blouse, she resumed her ascent. The steel cable made her palms blister, but she fought through the pain, eventually reaching the 30th floor. Clouds of smoke seeped underneath the door, forcing her to pause. It was too risky — opening the hatch might trigger a backdraft. Barbara scanned the 31st floor above. At least it was absent of smoke. She drew another breath through the blouse, coughed twice, then contin-ued her upward climb. The cable began slicing her flesh, pooling blood on the inside of her hands and knees. Her muscles screamed for rest. The smoke thickened by the second, burning the woman's eyes and filling her lungs with sickening fumes. A few more feet. First one hand, then the other. A little bit more. Another painful grasp of the cable. She was finally in position. Barbara swung over and pulled down on the lever, gaining access to the floor beyond. She pendulumed herself, swaying her legs in a wide arc. At last, Barbara let go of the cable, landing just inside the corridor. She stumbled away from the smoky shaft, wheezing with relief.

"Hello? Anyone here?" The only response was the constant drone of the alarm.

She spotted two rescue helicopters circling over the East River. They approached, fighting smoke and wind in order to attempt a rooftop landing. Barbara dashed to the nearest stairwell, scaling the nine floors to the helipad.

Upon exiting, she saw several dozen diplomats and office workers standing in groups, waving their arms at the arriving choppers. She ran to join them, pulling up next to a security guard.

"What happened?"

The man recognized her. "Some sort of bomb, Ms. Pinder. Took out half the 28th floor."

She searched the group, failing to see any of her staff. "Is this everybody?"

"If they're not here, they're dead," wincing at his own statement. "Thought you were a goner, Ma'am."

"So did I," her voice falling to a whisper.

The guard left to organize the airlift. Barbara allowed herself a few cleansing breaths, trying to overcome some smoke inhalation. Dense clouds smoldered skyward, rising from all sides of the building. The rescue helicopters landed, taking in as many of the frightened workers as they could hold.

Barbara decided to wait for the next group of choppers. Suddenly, a firefighter in full gear was standing behind her, pointing to another incoming helicopter a few hundred yards to the west.

"This way, Ma'am. He'll be landing over here."

She followed without hesitation, then abruptly stopped. "Isn't anyone else coming?"

The firefighter encircled her, blocking the diplomat from returning to the group. "No," he stated. "This flight's just for you."

He clutched a fireman's axe in both hands, forcing her toward the arriving chopper. She turned, unsure of what to do. The firefighter urged her on, jabbing her spine with the axe handle. They strode past a bank of solar panels facing west toward the afternoon sun.

The helicopter was about to land. She wracked her brain, desperately seeking a way out. Placing her hand in her pocket, she felt it immediately — the ceremonial pen from the treaty signing. Barbara grasped it, aware this was her only potential weapon.

As the helicopter swooped down, a gust of wind cleared the smoke in front of the solar panels blinding the pilot with the sun's glare. He yanked on the cyclic control, veering left. The helicopter's landing skids snagged the retaining wall, pitching the craft over the edge. The rotor blades struck the side of the tower, causing the craft to explode. Barbara's chance had come.

As she spun, the point of the pen caromed off the man's left cheekbone, impaling his nose. He shrieked in pain, falling to his knees in a fountain of blood. Barbara regained her balance, then dashed off. As she screamed for help, she saw several co-workers pointing behind her. Barbara turned to see the assassin charging forth with axe raised. Changing direction, she fled barefoot into a smoke-filled stairwell. The man was a few feet behind, cursing at his prey.

Barbara ran into a 39th floor office, bolting shut the door. She recoiled in horror as the axe blade broke through the wood frame once — then twice — finally severing the latch. The bloodied assassin bulled his way into the room, wielding the axe in preparation for the kill. Barbara retreated behind a desk, pelting him with whatever she could find. At that moment, the security guard entered, brandishing another fireman's axe taken from a hallway emergency station.

"All right, you bastard. Put it down."

The assassin spun, his blade missing the guard by inches. They began a terrifying battle with the shrill clank of metal on metal echoing through the room. The two thrust back and forth like Roman gladiators, knowing only one could survive.

Barbara hurled a wastebasket into the assassin's head. He staggered back, spewing obscenities. The guard lunged forth, trapping him against the full length windows. Another errant swing shattered the glass, causing a plume of smoke to invade the room. The guard struck the assassin's axe with his own, splitting the handle. As they grappled, the men fell out the window, vanishing behind a curtain of smoke.

Barbara screamed upon witnessing the accidental plunge. She rushed to the open window, ignoring the broken glass under her feet. To her astonishment, she saw them both. The guard hanging onto the ledge and the assassin clutching him by the waist.

She began to pull them back inside. The smoke sapped her strength, making it more difficult to deadlift the weight. Soon, the guard was able to assist in his own rescue. The assassin snagged Barbara's ankle, sending her to the floor. As he slid the woman closer to the edge, she kicked her legs in an attempt to free herself. At last, Barbara took hold of the assassin's shattered axe. Drawing her arm back, she readied herself for the lethal chop.

"I've had enough of you," she spat. The blade swung down, lodging itself in his skull. After the corpse disappeared from sight, the security guard helped Barbara to her feet, embracing her in relief. They dashed to the roof where they were rescued by another helicopter a few minutes later.

Although the fire was eventually extinguished, the firestorm was just beginning. The worldwide media descended upon the story, searching for clues and attempting to identify the suspected terrorists. An official MAJIK-12 cover-up was launched, blaming Al-Qaeda for the incident. The cost of the botched assassination attempt was 17 dead, 44 injured, and more than $58 million in property damage. But, the price already paid was destined to be much greater.

Barbara went to a medical clinic to have her wounds irrigated and bandaged. An hour later, she spoke with the Bahamian Prime Minister via telephone. After recounting the incident, he ordered her to return to Nassau for further consultation, booking her on a flight later that evening.

She arrived at the airport two hours ahead of time to check her bags and clear customs. The process went smoothly and was soon in her seat. Since the ticket was purchased on short notice, Barbara was now riding shotgun on the jet. The very last row of seats in the plane.

Unknown to Barbara, her name was flagged. A customs supervisor contacted his superiors in Washington, informing them Pinder was aboard Flight 242 — New York to Nassau. They in turn contacted the Immigration and Naturalization Service who then called the Central Intelligence Agency. A priority message was delivered to CIA Director Walter Langlois. His call to Richard Stern at the NSA was digitally encrypted for security. A swift decision was made. Stern contacted the Pentagon on a matter of highest national security interest. He briefed Fleet Admiral Curtis Holliman on the imperative situation. The word was given. The Navy would make it happen. The MAJIK-12 was going to destroy Flight 242.

As Barbara settled in for the flight, she was greeted by a familiar face.

"Is this seat taken?" Trevor asked, knowing he had surprised his lady.

She leapt to hug him, then reseated herself. He fell into the chair beside her.

"How did you know I was here?"

"I phoned the Ambassador at the Embassy. He told me you were flying back to Nassau tonight," he explained. "I heard what happened. I'm so glad you're okay."

"Not as okay as you think," holding up her bandaged hands. "I also cut up my feet."

"I'm taking a few days off so I can care for you. I'll be staying at the Atlantis Resort."

Barbara shook her head, reflecting on the day's events. "No, you're not. You're staying at my place...and in my bed."

"Oh, really?"

"Well, that's the least I can do for my future husband," announcing her decision. She flashed a thousand watt smile since words were no longer necessary.

Flight 242 left JFK Airport on time, heading south at 440 mph, climbing to a cruising altitude of 37,000 feet. The beginning of the trip was smooth with little turbulence. Some of the passengers were milling about the cabin as the flight attendants filled drink and dinner orders. Barbara and Trevor openly discussed how their future would unfold and how each would make the other's dreams come true. It was a tender, treasured moment in her life.

The Pentagon dispatched a secure transmission through CIN-CLANTFLT to the aircraft carrier Theodore Roosevelt stationed 240 miles northeast of its base in Norfolk, Virginia. A lone F-18 Hornet was sortied on a secret seek and destroy mission, intercepting Flight 242 approximately 65 minutes out of New York.

After identifying the target aircraft, the Navy fighter assumed a tactical position three miles behind the commercial jet. At the controls was Carrier Air Group leader, Captain Jonathan Edwards, a 23 year Naval aviator who had deliberately drawn this thankless assignment. The 41 year old Chicago native was a firm believer in never allowing someone to do a job you were not prepared to do yourself. His orders were clear and inviolable — Splash the jet, squeezing the lives from over 280 unsuspecting souls.

Fortunately for those onboard, he was a fair and honorable man. Captain Edwards would only target the right engine of the jet, allowing the defenseless passengers at least the chance of survival. It was a victory for conscience over blind duty. One which might make a life or death difference.

"I have lock and tone on target." He sent forth a silent prayer, then launched an AIM-9 Sidewinder. "Missile away."

The heat seeking weapon streaked through the night, swiftly arriving for the fateful rendezvous. Striking the starboard engine, the missile breached the housing nacelle and initiated a catastrophic fuel-line rupture. What occurred next was a kaleidoscopic vision straight from the depths of Hell.

The entire right wing of the 777 ripped away from the fuselage. A stomach churning heave displaced every unsecured item, followed by several 360 degree barrel rolls. The cabin became a maelstrom of tumbling bodies, dinner trays and expelled luggage. As the flight crew fought to control their spiraling dive toward the ocean, the passengers endured injury and illness from the aerodynamic convulsions of the jet.

Barbara gasped in horror as intense G-forces restricted her movement. She felt another hand clutch hers as Trevor attempted to provide comfort. The craft eventually righted itself, plunging through ear popping strata in the ever thickening atmosphere. A temporal displacement occurred as minutes passed like seconds. Looking into the crystalline night, Barbara saw the moonlit Atlantic rapidly closing. A shrill reverberation shuddered through the fuselage as the remaining engine now screamed at maximum throttle capacity. She sucked in a breath as the jet finally leveled out — then struck the ocean tail-first. The cabin's load bearing members snapped, cleaving off the last two rows of seats, causing the aircraft to rip apart in a fusillade of metal shards. Barbara's skull was snapped back into the oscillating bulkhead, forcing her to lose consciousness.

She awoke. Disoriented from her brush with death, Barbara assumed she'd be well on her way to the next life. She moved her arms and legs, fingers and toes. Even her bruised head seemed to be in one piece.

Barbara looked over at the blood-drenched body beside her. Trevor had been impaled with fragmentation and his neck snapped clean by the force of impact. She tried to prop up her fiancé's head, but it continued to fall to one side. At last she placed a kiss on Trevor's ice blue cheek. It was a final expression of her love. A man she would never allow herself to forget.

Unbuckling herself, she forced her legs to straighten out. Nine other bodies were strapped in their seats, all dead from various injuries. Her clothes were saturated with salt water due to the exposed impact with the ocean. A gentle rocking motion made it difficult to stand. Suddenly, water began flooding the severed tail section, tipping over from the redistribution of weight. She grabbed hold of a seat cushion, using it as a floatation device. The aircraft debris soon disappeared underneath the surface of the Atlantic. Barbara Pinder was now totally alone.

She bobbed in the tepid Gulf Stream water, noting a cluster of arc lights illuminating an area a few miles west of her position. A rescue operation was currently underway with four Coast Guard cutters and two helicopters surrounding the main fuselage. Dozens of injured passengers were being shepherded to safety. Barbara summoned forth inner strength, attempting to swim toward the zone of deliverance.

As she maintained a determined breaststroke, an ever increasing riptide held her back, preventing any forward progress. She found herself being repelled from where she wanted to go. The more she fought against the force, the greater the resistance. Before Barbara could close within vocal range, she felt a surge in the surrounding water. A swift, cyclonic motion which frightened her. The vortex swirled faster — faster — then faster still. Barbara could feel nothing but a sensation of extraordinarily rapid movement against her flesh. A surreal, almost spiritual experience which she could not explain. Losing sight of the Coast Guard rescue operation, Barbara was cast into an unknown void of isolation and despair.

Before long, she was able to see a thin bank of clouds part for the dawn of a new day. Reflecting on recent events, Barbara experienced a taste of every conceivable emotion, unsure which to choose. She was alive, but why? What purpose did her life serve? *What kind of sick, perverse fate is this?* Then, it occurred to her. This was not an accident and it was not a mistake. *This was an act of God.*

Barbara searched the azure sky. After a lifetime of heartache, it had come to this. It was her against Him, one on one. This time, they were going to have it out.

"What kind of God are you?" she screamed. "Why do you enjoy fucking up my life?"

The only response was the wind-kissed water breaking against her body. She continued to vent her rage.

"I've never done anything to you. But, all you do is punish me. I'm so damn tired of it."

Her voice echoed across the still water. It frustrated her that God wasn't something physical. Something she could see, hear and touch. This wasn't a fair fight at all. "Show yourself," the woman commanded. "Stop hiding like a coward. Show yourself to me. I want to see the Almighty God who killed my parents. The God who's killed every man I've ever loved. The God who won't let me die with them."

Barbara gasped for air as the volume of her tears left her breathless. She blubbered forth another coherent sentence. "Why do you put people in my life, only to take them away? I've never understood you and I never will. If you won't leave me alone, then why not kill me, too?"

Wiping tears from her face, she focused on a dark object protruding from the surface. As it came closer, she knew what it was. The fin of a huge tiger shark. Barbara began to wonder if she'd been just a teensy-weensy bitchy with God.

The beast came straight toward her. She froze, aware that sharks were attracted to sudden movements in the water. At the last moment, the shark veered off, leaving her intact. Barbara noticed other fins circling her position. Each time a shark would approach it would break off the attack, as though something instinctual was telling them this was a forbidden meal. After awhile, Barbara no longer concentrated on the sharks. In time, even they abandoned her, leaving the woman alone to contemplate her own manifest destiny.

She seemed to drift for hours. Hunger and thirst were constant companions. At first, it was hard for her to concentrate, then even harder to remain lucid. Barbara realized she was going to perish. She began to shut down her body in acceptance of her fate.

Because she could no longer trust her sanity, it was difficult for Barbara to accept what happened next. Ahead of her, the clouds appeared to meld together. She watched the image take form as it contracted and expanded with deliberate speed. Suddenly, the moving wisps of vapor held fast producing a larger-than-life vision. It was that of an elderly woman calling to her. Barbara was dumbfounded. Again, the vision spoke her name. She tried to make sense of it all. *Who is this? How does she know my name? Why is this happening?*

Before she could gain an answer, the vision dropped from the sky coming to rest on the eastern horizon. There it remained, beckoning her from afar. Whatever this was, it could not be ignored.

Barbara marshaled her body, forcing herself to swim. Stroke after agonizing stroke brought her closer to the image, still calling out her name. She kept swimming stronger…harder…faster. Each second brought her closer to the apparition. It was a painful and exhausting effort. At last, she seemed to come within range. Barbara reached forth to touch the woman's face. The vision disappeared, leaving the swimmer gasping in delirium. She was now witness to a different sight — a beach — dry land. Was this her deliverance from death's door or another cruel mirage? She swam with determination, rejoicing as her bandaged feet touched the shore.

Two men were nearby, removing some fishing gear from the trunk of their car. They saw Barbara stagger onto the sand and collapse before them in utter exhaustion.

It was several hours before Barbara awoke in her hospital bed. The fishermen had rushed her to the Emergency Room and alerted the Bahamian authorities. Her prognosis was good. She was a strong, healthy and inconceivably lucky woman.

One of her first visitors was the Bahamian Prime Minister who greeted her warmly. He asked the attending nurse to leave so their conversation would remain private.

"We've kept your survival a secret," said the PM. "We don't want you to remain a target until we find out what's going on." His voice dropped to a whisper, emphasizing the incendiary nature of the news. "It was the Americans, Barbara. The Americans tried to kill you."

"But, why? Because of the treaty?"

The PM withdrew a letter from a diplomatic pouch. "No, but it may have something to do with this."

He handed her a secure correspondence which had been sent to the Bahamian Embassy in Washington, D.C. It was a laser printout of an E-mail explaining the circumstances involving Mary Ellen Hart and Barbara's adoption to the Gordon family in 1955. Specifics regarding Roswell were left vague, but it claimed she was in danger because of her association with the woman. A picture of Mary Ellen was enclosed.

"Oh, my...," her voice sagged. "I saw this woman...her face...I saw it in the clouds."

The PM eyed her with concern. "Barbara, did you know you were adopted?"

A tense pause. "My aunt told me once after a fight. I never believed her."

"It's true. I had the official records pulled. Mary Ellen Hart was your real mother."

"But, that can't be. A White woman?"

"They sent samples of her DNA to prove it."

Barbara read the names on the letter. "Christopher Hightower and Kevin Reese. Who are they?"

"We had them checked out. They're legitimate and credible citizens." He placed the letter back inside the diplomatic pouch. "They're also your brothers."

She showed surprise at the revelation. "Where are they now?"

"Las Vegas. I have cell numbers for both of them. They want you to come there as soon as you feel up to it."

Although suffering from shock and the travail of her near-death experience, Barbara was energized by the news. "I'll call them. It may be the only way to find out what's going on."

"Do you want a bodyguard?"

She sighed with fatigue. "No. If your time's up, it's up. A bodyguard can't stop fate."

"Well, it wasn't your time the other day. How did you ever swim that distance?"

"I didn't swim that far."

The PM shook his head in amazement. "Barbara, our best guess is you somehow traveled over 800 miles by yourself."

"What?" came her incredulous reply. "That's impossible."

"I know. None of us can figure it out," he responded. "You could have only been brought back here — by the hand of God."

CHAPTER TWELVE

∞

PUNA COAST, ISLAND OF HAWAII — APRIL 6th

*C*asey Lee Chou knew this would not be the best of days. As an expert numerologist, Casey lived life according to ancient Chinese beliefs. Certain combinations of numbers were lucky, others not. He based important decisions on fortuitous dates and times, as well as astrological and planetary positions. He believed every life experience carried positive and negative effects. A yin and a yang. Casey was so careful regarding his choices in life he often made no decision at all. This was especially true in his pursuit of love where he had yet to meet the right girl. Of course, she would need to have a lucky birth date, meet him on a fortunate day and have the proper number of letters in her name. Otherwise, he would not be interested. For besides being intelligent, wealthy and buff, Casey was exceedingly anal.

He grew up in Downer's Grove, Illinois being the only Asian-American child in a predominantly White neighborhood. Having few friends, Casey gained a reputation as a loner. He was conscientious about his schoolwork with mathematics being a favorite subject. As the only child of a respected physicist at the Fermi Labs in Chicago and a noted nutritionist at DePaul University, Casey had everything a youngster could want except attention and affection.

He filled this emptiness by overachieving academically and master-ing the martial arts with guidance from his grandfather, Stanley Chou, who in his day had attained the level of Grand Honorable Master. After graduating from Northwestern University, Casey took a position there as an Associate Mathematics Professor and made sure that a portion of his salary went to his grandparents on a month-ly basis. Although his parents were upset by this, they never voiced their displeasure. But in July 2010, their annoyance reached a criti-cal mass.

That month, Casey Chou won the Illinois State Lottery, netting over 53 million dollars. He credited his expertise in numerology for his good fortune. Casey resigned his position and moved to the Island of Hawaii, buying a to-die-for home on the spectacular Puna Coast. He also lavished money on his grandparents, purchasing a home for them in San Francisco. Casey knew his parents were wealthy in their own right and saw no reason to financially reward those who didn't need it. In fact, he found his parents attitude on the matter distasteful. After all, these were his parents' parents. Giving them comfort in their final years was something he was proud to do.

The real reason for his parents' disapproval was that Stanley Chou, his father's father, and Mimi Kwan, his mother's mother, were widowed octogenarians living together in sin. This was in vio-lation of accepted Chinese tradition. The two had known each other for many years as in-laws and shocked their offspring by becoming intimate after the death of their respective spouses. Casey's parents felt this kind of behavior should not be financially rewarded. However, Casey was glad his grandparents had found happiness with each other and saw nothing wrong with the arrangement. In fact, he thought it very fortunate for anyone to find two soul mates in one lifetime. It was a unique and precious gift.

His grandparents had recently arrived in Hawaii for a two week vacation, staying at Casey's six bedroom, beachfront home. The three-acre estate looked out over the Pacific Ocean steps from the exclusive Puna Coast Ritz-Carlton Hotel. The beach, on the south-eastern part of the island, was an unusual mixture of fine, black sand owing to the proximity of Kilauea, the active volcano which spread obsidian rock and ash across this tropical paradise. Casey shared his section of the beach with the hotel and the Ritz-Carlton provided him with unlimited use of their facilities. It was a nice arrangement, especially since Casey had an ever-changing supply of bikini-clad women to admire in his own backyard.

He and his grandparents were about to walk to the hotel's lunchtime luau when his phone rang. It was his parents in Chicago. Casey answered the call from his computer and activated the video camera and monitor. His mother, Cynthia Chou, was now on screen. She was cute, but not overly so, with her black hair tied in a bun and a pair of wire-rimmed glasses making her look like a stereotypical, 58 year old librarian.

"Hello, mother."

"What in the name of all that's holy are you up to?"

"Excuse me?"

"You heard me, young man. What are you up to? We had the...." She stopped to compose herself. "This is so embarrassing. We had the FBI here last night — at our home — asking all sorts of questions about you. Oh, this is too much to bear."

"The FBI? What did they want?"

His mother shook a finger at the camera. "Don't play dumb with us. You're up to something. Now tell us what you've done and maybe we won't testify against you."

Casey responded with a laugh. "I haven't done anything, mother."

His father, Sidney Chou, forced his head into the image. He was 60 and distinguished with his mane of white hair, mingled with wisps of gray. His demeanor was sour, as usual.

"You're a crazy kid," he interjected. "You've always been crazy. Why did we ever adopt you? Should've tried to get our money back, that's what we should've done."

Cynthia eased her husband from view. "Your father's very upset, Casey, and so am I. How do you think this looks? What will the neighbors say?"

"Who cares?"

His father came back into frame for an additional rebuke. "We care, you crazy kid. What kind of crime did you commit? I'll bet your picture's down at the post office right now. You're a crazy, crazy kid. Always have been. Must've been born crazy."

Sidney departed from view. His mother was now flowing a river of crocodile tears. "Casey, I'll have to call you back," wiping her eyes. "I hope you'll come to your senses and tell us what this is about."

"But, mother...," his voice went silent, noting their screen had gone dark. He looked into the device, seeing his troubled reflection in the monitor.

Casey's 5 foot 8, 162 pound body was solid muscle, toned to perfection. He usually wore tight fitting clothes which enhanced his physique. Casey had thick, jet black hair, swept back over his head and expressive, oval eyes providing him with excellent peripheral vision. His reflexes were extraordinary and could move with lightning speed. Although gifted with a fine sense of humor, he found little to smile about when thinking of his parents.

Casey heard his grandparents gather behind him. His grandfather, Stanley Chou, was 81 years old with a 5 foot 6, 122 pound frame. He had small eyes encased in huge coke-bottle glasses to help correct his failing vision. The man was bald and speckled with age spots. He looked very much like an Asian Mr. Magoo.

Casey's grandmother, Mimi Kwan, was 80 years old and possessed a much plumper 5 foot 4, 145 pound body. She had thin, almost invisible, gray hair which nested haphazardly on her head. Mimi had a pleasant, but wrinkled, face and sported a listening aid to assist with her hearing loss.

Mimi made sure Stanley didn't fall down any open manholes, while Stanley made sure Mimi didn't step in front of any oncoming trains. These two were made for each other.

"I'm sorry, said Casey. "I didn't know you were there."

"Did they ask about us?" asked Mimi.

"No."

Stanley vented his disgust. "Jerks. Why the hell couldn't we have kept our pants on?"

The three of them left the house, beginning a short trek to the luau on the beach. As they crossed a sidewalk, Mimi stopped Stanley in his tracks. She bent over, picking up indisputable evidence of a canine recently in the area.

"Look what you almost stepped in," she chided him.

He peered into her hand, closing to an inch from the offensive matter. "That's dog doo. What's it doing in your hand?"

"I didn't want you to get this on your new shoes."

"But, now look where it is," he whined. "You can't go to a luau with that on your hand."

"I haven't been near the sand."

"I said, your hand. Your hand."

She looked at her soiled appendage, recoiling in shock. "Who put this dog doo in my hand?"

"You did. This isn't a bit funny, Mimi. You're keeping us from eating."

The woman looked puzzled. "I didn't know I was keeping you from a meeting."

"Eating, you twit." He shook his head in frustration. The one thing Stanley took seriously were his incessant hunger pangs. This unfortunate incident would delay them further.

Casey turned his grandmother's hand over, dumping the odious pile into a nearby bush. "Gran, you need to clean up. Want me to go back with you?"

"No," she retorted. "I'm not blind like some people I know."

He handed her the front door key. As she wandered back to the house, Stanley turned to face a palm tree, assuming he was eyeing the majestic beauty of the ocean. Casey occupied his time admiring numerous females on the beach, wondering which were devoid of male company.

As Mimi approached the entrance, she was surprised to see the door ajar. She knew she couldn't have opened it already. *Or, did I? No, I think I'd remember that.* Mimi heard muffled voices inside. She reared backward into a hedge, listening with all her might.

Suddenly, she saw two hooded figures walking within. Crouching lower, Mimi was able to catch one or two words.

"Remember," one of the intruders stated, "We act like we're robbin' him."

Mimi's eyes flew wide. "Goblins," she whispered, inching away from the door.

Stanley's patience was at an end. He instructed Casey to go on to the luau and promised they'd meet him there. His grandfather then trudged back up the path to find his mate. Casey was amused by the antics of the two, wishing they could have been his parents.

Mimi found Stanley feeling his way along the side of the house. She cradled him as though they hadn't seen each other in years.

"Did you clean yourself?"

"No. I didn't have a chance."

"So, you rub your hands on my back?" he said in disgust.

"That can't be helped. There's goblins in the house."

"What?" his voice squeaking with incredulity. "Goblins, me ass."

"I heard them," Mimi maintained. "They said they were goblins."

Stanley rolled his blurry eyes in amazement. "You couldn't hear a bomb dropping on a fireworks factory."

"Well, you couldn't see flames if your nose was on fire," she blurted in return. "I'm telling you there's goblins in there."

"Let me take a look," he sighed.

They circled around to the back of the house. Stanley maneuvered without any hint of stealth, placing his thick eyeglasses directly on the windowpane. The sound telegraphed his presence to the intruders inside. One of the hooded men walked over to the window, shooing Stanley away.

"They look more like goons," he announced.

"We've got to do something."

"Come on," pulling her away from the window. "Let's tell the kid."

The two meandered down the path. Upon arriving on the beach, they found Casey among a crowd of sunbathers.

"We've got bad news, boy."

"What?" inquired their grandson, concerned.

"Goblins," his grandmother stated. "They're in your house."

Casey laughed, spilling some of the Mai Tai in his hand. At that moment, he detected two men racing toward them in an open-air jeep. They parked the vehicle nearby and exited with guns drawn.

"Look out!" he yelled, herding his grandparents out of harm's way.

Casey willed his body into attack mode. Swirling into action, he kicked the gun from one's hand, while buckling the other with a crippling strike across the knee. He pirouetted in midair, dropkicking the first into some sunbathers, then slapped the gun from the other causing it to land at his grandfather's feet. Stanley picked up the weapon, pointing it at the blurred activity.

"All right," he commanded. "This is a stickup."

Casey and the assassins dove for cover, locked in a flailing mass. Several sunbathers gasped in shock at the fracas, while others cowered hoping the incident would soon end. Mimi grabbed the gun from Stanley's hands which he'd managed to point back on himself.

"You're going to shoot your face off."

"I've got to do something for the boy," came his frantic response. "I'll take care of these goons me-self."

Stanley entered the fray, 10 feet from the action. Recalling his Ninja training, he swung his arms and legs, striking empty air. Mimi guided him through his battle with the void.

"Over to your left. No, left," she screamed. "Now, down more. Right. Stay straight. Over more. Left again."

Stanley attempted the adjustments, but kept missing his target by several feet. A few who were witness to this myopic choreography openly giggled in amusement. Casey windmilled his legs into the foes, dropping them to the black sand. One assassin struck Casey with a beach umbrella. He spun, deflecting another thrust with a nearby beachball. The inflated toy ricocheted away, caroming off Stanley's head. Staggered, his grandfather fell headfirst between a young woman's legs.

"Mimi, I've fallen and — I don't want to get up."

The woman recoiled, shocked by his overt arrival. Mimi ran over, helping him to his feet.

"Sorry, sweetie," growling protectively. "He's spoken for."

"Where are they now?"

"Over there by the volleyball players."

Stanley ran toward a blurry cluster of people, stumbling over others lying in the sand. He continued the lethal kicks and blows, generating additional laughter throughout the crowd. Some thought he was in the throes of a grand mal seizure and yelled for paramedics.

Casey gained the upper hand in his frenzied battle. As he finished the job on one, the other hobbled off toward the hotel pier, seizing a jet ski to facilitate his escape. Stanley fought his way through a volleyball net a few feet away.

"Grandfather, the fight's over."

Stanley wound down, his bony appendages falling at his sides. "Did we defend the family honor, boy?"

His grandson smiled, drawing a needed breath. "We sure did. You were great."

Casey scanned the ocean beyond. He saw the jet ski maneuvering toward a speedboat a half-mile offshore. Behind the vessel was a parasail, carrying a man scouting the beach with binoculars. This man and one in the boat were part of an assassination team now planning what to do next.

"Grandfather, I'm going after them. Stay here and watch this guy. Don't let him get away."

Stanley made no attempt at hiding his displeasure. "Can't we eat now? All this butt-kicking made me hungry. I need food, dammit."

"We'll eat right after I get back," assured Casey. "Just make sure this guy doesn't go anywhere."

Casey bounded off in search of another jet ski. Mimi located her husband who informed her of the situation. Eyeing the volleyball net nearby, she had an inspiration. The two rolled the unconscious assassin within the net, sealing him in a web-tight cocoon. They then dragged the man to the jeep and attached him to the rear bumper. Feeling satisfied they'd done their part, Stanley and Mimi wandered off to the lunchtime luau.

Their grandson rented another jet ski, beginning a speedy trek across the surf. Casey saw the assassins break formation with the jet skier approaching on an intercept course. The boat was traveling on a parallel path, casting the parasailer to a higher vantage point. Looking up through the churning spray, Casey saw the man leveling an Uzi 9mm. Taking evasive action, he avoided a slew of bullets fired during the initial strafing run. Casey made sure he remained in the parasailer's wake, eliminating the threat from additional weapons fire. The other jet ski slammed into his. Casey hung on, his hands gripping the handlebars as though they were bolted to the frame. Skimming over the waves, he banked hard right, channeling a wall of water onto the assassin. The speedboat executed a 180 degree turn, allowing the parasailer to approach them dead-on. Casey noted another burst of gunfire ahead. He throttled back, forcing the assassin into the line of fire. The parasailer broke off the attack, missing his partner by inches.

Casey grabbed the initiative. He rose up, deftly squatting onto his seat. After judging the distance, he leapt through the air kicking the assassin from his jet ski and assuming his position on the vehicle. The man hit the water, skipping across the surface like an awkward stone. Casey's jet ski continued onward for a few hundred feet before coming to a stop. An additional wave of bullets struck the ocean as the parasailer made another errant pass.

Approaching on a diagonal tangent, Casey sped forth in an attempt to intercept the boat. He continued to pursue from behind, preventing a shower of retaliation. As the craft loomed closer, Casey timed his attack. He aimed for the boat's dual outboard engines in hopes of disabling the vessel. More gunfire thundered from above, peppering the blue ocean spray. Collision was now inevitable.

The jet ski crashed into the 30 foot Boston Whaler from astern. It lodged itself between the dual 225 Yamaha engines, ensnaring the drive and steering linkage above the transom. Casey somersaulted over the handlebars in a rolling ball of flesh. Sliding onto the wet deck, he struck the assassin, propelling him into the active surf beyond. The parasailer fired the remainder of his clip in frustration. Seeking cover, Casey dove behind the craft's instrument console. Chunks of glass, plastic and wood splintered apart in a blizzard of debris. A cacophonous whine now underscored the obvious. The boat was running wild with no hope of control. It continued bounding over the waves in a speeding circle, orbiting dozens of surfers and pleasure craft in search of safety. At last, the parasailer's weapon fell silent and the attack from above ceased.

Casey's grandparents stood at the entrance to the beachfront luau. They'd been denied admission twice and were now demanding to see the manager, much to the chagrin of the hotel guests behind them in line. A woman approached, sporting an ingratiating smile.

"I'm the Hotel's Director of Operations," she stated in a polite, but business-like manner. "What seems to be the problem?"

Stanley huffed. "The problem is you have food and we can't get to it."

"Are you a guest of the hotel?"

"No, but..."

"I'm sorry. This luau is strictly for hotel guests," she explained. "However, we do have an excellent coffee shop which can serve all your dining needs."

Mimi was outraged. "All our dying needs? We want food, not a casket."

The woman registered surprise at the confusion. "No, ma'am. I said dining needs. We can't serve you here."

"Why, not?" came the defiant response. Her voice fell to a whisper. "Is this about the dog doo?"

She answered with a vacant stare. Stanley was able to keep the conversation on track. "The boy comes here all the time and he isn't a guest."

"Then, he must have a hotel honor card. Did he show you his pass?"

"What the hell kind of family do you think we are?" Mimi cried in shock.

"The kid must have it on him," surmised Stanley, scanning the area in vain.

"Well, I'm sorry," declared the woman. "But, that's our policy. We can't let you in unless you're holding his pass."

Grandmother Kwan blinked in astonishment. "And, I thought San Francisco was bad."

"Mimi, where's the boy?"

She thrust her arm toward the open sea. "He's out there with those goblins."

As the two turned to leave, another woman dressed in native hula wear adorned Stanley with a necklace of flowers. "Excuse me, sir. Let me give you a complimentary lei."

"I've no time for a roll in the hay, woman. We've got an emergency."

He bumped into a lighted tiki torch, setting fire to an adjacent fern. Mimi led him away before more damage could ensue.

Casey fought with the lifeless controls. The parasailer was being yanked aloft, screaming for an end to the boat's circuitous course. Listing several degrees to port, the craft continued churning water in a wide arc, eclipsing speeds in excess of 70 knots. Cursing the situation, Casey thought about jumping overboard, but realized at this speed he could break his neck. Refusing to concede, he struggled aft in an attempt to dislodge the jet ski from its perch on the transom.

Since the boat was still circling the area, the water-logged assassins had time to swim to Casey's abandoned jet ski and climb aboard. Both men rejoined the pursuit.

Using a fisherman's gaff as leverage, Casey freed the damaged jet ski from the steering linkage. Suddenly, the craft sliced across the breaking surf, heading straight for the coast on a northwesterly course. As the boat swung by, the jet ski intercepted its track, then came parallel. Both assassins now executed a daring vehicle transfer, tumbling onto the deck as Casey girded himself for further mayhem.

His grandparents shuffled back to the assassins' open-air jeep. Mimi spotted the boat speeding away from their position.

"Come on, Stanley. He's getting away."

"He knows we're onto him," bellowed his grandfather. "Give us that pass, kid!"

Thinking only of their food deprivation, the couple entered the jeep and revved the engine. The vehicle spun in the sand, dragging the man in the volleyball net. Fervent cries from onlookers went unanswered as Mimi gunned the jeep down the coastal highway.

The cushioning effect of the net was compromised by escalating heat from friction with the roadbed. It wasn't long before the assassin was aroused from his slumber, screaming with the force of a jet engine.

"Bastard!"

Mimi looked at the speedometer. "I'm already doing 80."

"I didn't say anything," Stanley assured her.

Her thin strands of hair were lifted by the on-rushing wind. "I distinctly heard you say 'faster'."

"Bastard!"

"There, you did it again."

"Did you see me move my lips? I'm the one that's blind, not you."

"You pricks! Stop this thing now!"

Stanley eyed his significant other, incredulous. "That wasn't us. Hit the brakes."

She complied, bringing the vehicle to an abrupt halt. The cocoon continued forward, coming to rest below the chassis. Stanley climbed into the backseat to check the situation.

"I don't see anything."

Mimi snorted. "Go figure." She exited the jeep and made a similar assessment. "Must be a loose bearing."

As the assassin absorbed a calming breath, Mimi returned to the driver's seat. Hearing the clutch pop precipitated another round of panic.

"Oh, God! Nooooooo!"

They resumed speed, towing the ever-strident cargo.

The fight aboard the boat was intense. Casey surged with rage, issuing savage kicks and blows upon his assailants. The men effectively tag-teamed him. As one was felled, the other would rebound into the fray. This prevented Casey from gaining any respite from the onslaught. His hands and feet were bruising from the rigors of battle. He had avoided using lethal force in the hopes he could persuade the men to talk. Casey wasn't a killer and only used his martial arts skills for self-defense. However, the time had come to conclude this fight.

Directly ahead lay a steam shrouded shoreline. Casey was familiar enough with Big Island topography to understand. So did the parasailer who was now yelling at his comrades below. They were less than a quarter-mile from the 1,000 foot maw of a molten lava flow, spilling into the ocean from a rift zone caused by the active Kilauea Volcano.

Seconds remained. Casey grabbed one man, snapping his leg. The other charged, only to be greeted by a blow which shattered his collarbone and two adjoining ribs. Severe vibrations now shook the boat, signaling their imminent arrival upon the lava filled shore. Time was up.

Casey bolted aft, vaulting into the mist at the moment of impact. He clutched at the parasail anchoring cord as the boat disintegrated around him. Casey held on, fighting his way up the thick nylon line.

Steam obscured the horrific scene as the assassins were consumed in an 1,800 degree molten bath. The heat was incredible, drenching Casey with sweat which impeded his grasp of the cord. Sulfurous fumes filled his lungs, causing him to gag.

They began to slowly descend. He felt resigned to his fate, expecting at any moment to join the others. Instead, the nylon line burned through freeing Casey and the parasailer into a zone of thermal lift, alive with erratic updrafts.

Drifting inland, the two emerged from the steam bank. Fighting against gravity, Casey coiled the cord around his hands in an effort to hold on. The parasailer was livid, screaming obscenities and trying to shake him clear of the line. Reaching for his release mechanism, he attempted to separate from the cord, sending Casey into a certain death freefall. As they began to corkscrew in midair, the man accidentally loosened his own harness and fell to earth. A 30 foot Kiawe tree, filled with razor-sharp thorns and projections, received him. The man entered whole, transforming himself into nothing more than pieces of torn flesh.

Casey's grandparents were now ascending Chain of Craters Road, keeping in sight the parasail drifting ahead of them. They were traveling through a harsh landscape of extinct lava flows, cinder cones and steam vents, climbing closer to the sea of fire known as the Kilauea Caldera.

Stanley tried to ignore the acoustic misery, but the assassin's screams were scaling heights that would make an opera singer blush. He gritted his teeth as though forced to listen to fingernails dragging across an endless blackboard.

"What the hell is that infernal sound?"

He pulled himself onto the back of the jeep, peering into the blurry backwash. He was finally able to discern the image of a smoke-filled net and the body flailing inside.

Mimi noted his contortions, slowing the vehicle to a crawl. "Stanley, are you sick?"

"No," he cried. "We've got — goblins!"

An electric charge traversed the woman's spine. She buried her foot into the accelerator, fully testing Newton's Laws of Motion. The tires shed their rubbery skins on the pavement, well on their way to achieving the speed necessary for time travel. Stanley held on, releasing the net from the jeep's rear bumper. The cocoon tumbled off the roadway, rolling to a stop on a bed of volcanic cinders.

The assassin emerged from the net. He stood gingerly, bleeding across his face, arms, legs and back. A breath of gratitude followed.

"I'm alive," he declared. "I'm still alive. Thank God." He then shook his fist at his fleeing tormentors. "You bastards! I'll kill you for this!"

A steam vent erupted, spraying him with scalding water vapor. The assassin wailed in pain, falling backward into a lava tube leading to the fiery core of Earth.

Casey gazed up at the parasail through darkening skies. Spiraling downward, he noticed his grandparents ascending the volcanic cone in the jeep. Grandmother Kwan waved her arms in greeting, paying no attention to a hairpin curve ahead. Before Casey could come within shouting range, he witnessed their vehicle crash through a wooden barricade and rumble across the rough, undulating surface of an ancient lava flow. Mimi tried to brake, causing the jeep to spin in a 360 degree arc, stopping inches from a molten formed cliff.

As Stanley scaled the front seat to join her, the vehicle began to teeter over the edge. Casey swooped down and bolted to the scene, climbing onto the jeep's running board in hopes of securing their position.

The situation was precarious. Bits of rock and ash tumbled down the cliff, undermining the front tires and tipping the jeep closer to the 200 foot abyss. With Casey on the back and Mimi up front, Stanley became the all-important fulcrum point.

"Grandfather! Don't move!"

Stanley remained motionless, sprawled prone over the front seat. Mimi was petrified with fear, unsure what to do. His grandfather grasped the jeep's cell phone. "Want me to call 911, boy?"

The horrified numerologist agreed those numbers would be most appropriate. Carefully following his grandson's instructions, he returned to the back seat. More debris caved in beneath them. While Stanley made the call, Casey pondered on how to anchor the vehicle. The parasail cord was laying nearby. He could tie it to something, but the volcanic landscape was barren of all vegetation. Casey prided himself on being a logical person. There should be an answer to this. Only one option seemed viable. Grandmother Kwan would have to crawl back over the seats. Unfortunately, there was not much time.

From the corner of his eye, Casey spotted a bright, orange mass. His worst fears were confirmed. *More lava*. The molten magma was heading their way, channeled by a dried river bed from a former flow. It swallowed up to a foot of ground per second as it oozed, bubbled and plopped toward its inevitable rendezvous with the jeep.

At that moment, Casey felt a drop of rain fall on his arm. Then, another. Still more, until water was coming down steadily, soaking the exposed trio. These sudden cloudbursts were common in Hawaii and never posed any real problem until now. The vehicle began to collect the precipitation, further exacerbating their weight distribution woes. More loose dirt moved underneath them, tipping the jeep still further. The lava was 30 feet from them and closing. These developments caused Casey to summarize their situation.

"We are going to die."

Mimi heard him over the pouring rain. "How can I get dry?"

"Die, you twit! Die!" Stanley roared.

"Is that anyway to talk to the woman you love?" she answered, hurt by his insensitivity.

They were no longer in control of their fate. The lava reached the jeep, deflating the rear tire and cauterizing the metal frame and chassis underneath. Flames sparked from the sudden blending of cold metal and molten heat. The heavens opened full, drenching everything in the area, causing clouds of steam to engulf them. Casey felt the vehicle lurch as a large chunk of earth gave way, followed by a shrill creak from the jeep itself. It wasn't until the steam cloud lifted that the miracle was revealed. Lava fused to the jeep, then was cooled by the rain, transforming the vehicle into an integral part of the volcanic landscape. The three were soaked, but safe.

As they climbed free of the jeep, a pizza delivery truck pulled up. The driver jumped out, ignoring the surreal scene. "Who ordered the pepperoni and sausage?"

The others looked upon Stanley with piercing eyes.

"I haven't eaten all day," he moaned. "To me, that's an emergency."

For a $100 bribe, the pizza delivery man drove them back to the estate. After changing into dry clothes, Casey noted a V-mail message on his computer. It was from Shannon Hewson explaining her relationship to him and Mary Ellen Hart, the woman who had given birth to him. Included with the message was medical data to corroborate the connection. She concluded the V-mail by informing him his life was in danger and asked if he would come to Las Vegas as soon as possible. A cell phone number was provided. Casey was stunned by this revelation. It certainly fit with the manic events of the day, but he was still unsure what to think. He decided to contact his parents in Chicago for verification.

Casey placed the call from his computer. His mother answered, looking pale.

"Mother? Are you all right?"

"Not really," she stated. "We have visitors."

"The FBI again?"

A hooded figure appeared on screen. "Guess again, Chou."

His heart sank. The man was holding a gun to his mother's head and appeared quite serious about using it.

"Why are you trying to kill me?"

"The Government put a price on your head — and we're going to collect."

"So, why murder my parents?"

"Don't be stupid. You're the one we want," stated the man. "Just come to Chicago. Your life for theirs."

"You bastard. I'll make you wish you never came after me."

"We'll give you 12 hours," disclosed the assassin. "After that, it'll be too late."

"12 hours? I don't know if I can get there that soon. Let me check some flights."

Casey surfed the internet for the required information. He examined various flight times and numbers. Nothing seemed to work. He scanned some possible connecting flights from other cities, keeping in mind the times of day and aircraft flight designations. Still nothing. At last, he found the perfect flight. On the perfect day.

"All right," he declared. "I'll be in Chicago...five days from now."

"Five days? I said 12 hours, asshole."

"Sorry," stated the expert numerologist. "The numbers won't be lucky until the 11th."

"Lucky numbers? What are you, a retard?"

Casey could hear his father Sidney in the background. "Let me talk to him."

His father came into view, smiling as if on some hallucinogenic drug. "Casey? You've always been a wonderful son. We're so proud of you. Now, I know you wouldn't want anything bad to happen to your mother and me. So, I'm asking you nicely to get on the first plane, regardless of the number, and come save us."

A tender pause. "Dad, of course, I love you. And, I will save you," his son related, beaming over his father's loving comments. "But, right now the numbers don't look good. I want as much luck as I can get. I'm sure you understand."

Sidney stared into the screen devoid of comment. He then turned to the assassin, resuming a normal demeanor. "I told you. A crazy, crazy kid," his father railed. "What did we spend on his ass, anyway? Wasn't worth two cents. That crazy kid's going to be the death of me yet."

The assassin returned into view. "Just get here. 12 hours or we start chopping fingers."

Casey fell silent as the screen went dark. He was unaware Stanley had overheard the entire conversation and was even now consulting with Mimi.

For the next few hours, Casey cloistered himself in his study, plotting a way to Chicago. A lucky way. One where he wouldn't have to compromise his belief in numerology. Every time he thought he might have an answer, something would prevent it from being truly special. Questionable and not fortunate. After intense study of all possible connecting flights, he found one. The diamond in the rough. It would require two changes of planes and four stops, but this set of numbers was golden. He could be in Chicago in under 20 hours.

Casey established a video link with his parents' home. It rang four times and was finally answered — by his grandparents.

"Grandfather Chou? Grandmother Kwan?" he cried in astonishment. "I thought you were asleep upstairs. How did you get to Chicago?"

"First plane out, boy," replied Stanley. "Couldn't let those goblins chop up our kids."

Casey was stunned. "You mean, you took care of them?"

"Hell, yes. Kicked their asses, then polished their family jewels."

Both of them laughed. "Didn't you know Gran Kwan was female martial arts champion eight years in a row?"

Their grandson flashed a wide grin. "I do now. Where are my parents?"

"We sent them to their room," Mimi confirmed. "Grounded for a week. They're still our kids, you know."

Casey nodded, relieved this had all worked out. "So, everything's okay?"

"We can take care of ourselves, boy," assured Stanley. "Don't ever worry about us. Now go do what you need to do."

"Thanks," sighing with gratitude. "I love you guys."

A few minutes later, Casey was planning his trip to Nevada. He called his sister Shannon, letting her know he would be there in two days. A whole new world awaited him in Las Vegas. He could barely contain his excitement. Casey Chou had found a divine path to his mother, as well as a very lucky flight number.

CHAPTER THIRTEEN

⌘

LAS VEGAS, NEVADA — APRIL 11th

*W*ith the arrival of Barbara Pinder and Casey Chou, the Hart family reunion was nearly complete. All but one of Mary Ellen's children had returned to her waiting arms. It was confirmation of a Holy bond which had endured the yawning expanse of time.

The Madre Superiora was eight months pregnant and suffering the effects of toxemia which restricted her to a bed at Sacred Heart Hospital, a facility owned and operated by the Catholic Church. The Bishop of Las Vegas had been contacted by the Vatican, ensuring his complete cooperation. Mary Ellen was provided with a private suite on the top floor and given round-the-clock attention. All medical personnel having contact with her were screened and briefed on a need-to-know basis. Dr. Shannon Hewson was appointed physician-in-charge, allowing her to supervise her mother's welfare on a daily basis.

Under a fictitious name, Kevin Reese secured four two-bedroom suites at the Las Vegas Hilton on Paradise Road. The resort was located less than a mile from the hospital. It was here Mary Ellen's children spent time getting to know one another and planned what to do next.

Kevin kept abreast of his company's operations having brought in Reggie's younger brother Calvin as his new partner. He always made sure to call him on his satellite phone which was incapable of being traced. Calvin Peace was an accounting graduate from Arizona State University and Kevin's frequent golfing partner. Although he did not have a pro sports background, Calvin was a quick study and seemed to be working out well.

Kevin was sharing his suite with Shannon Hewson who was, even by his high standards, a world-class hottie. It was most annoying that his sister had to look this good. For her part, Shannon conducted lab tests proving their blood relationship to Mary Ellen Hart and their genetic compatibility with each other. She spent the majority of her time at the hospital, monitoring the health of her elderly mother and the developing fetus. Hardly a waking moment passed without Shannon recalling Denise's horrific death and her current status as a wanted fugitive. She was afraid to call her brother Sean for fear the authorities might track her down. Shannon kept hoping Troy had survived and would somehow contact her. She missed him terribly, but suffered her heartache in silence.

Christopher Hightower wept upon meeting his mother, bringing a lifelong quest to an emotional climax. Her eldest child wanted to spend as much time as possible with Mary Ellen. In fact, C.J. informed his publisher he was canceling all further interviews regarding his latest book and gave no reason as to why. He called his friend, Zach Watson, to get an update on his condition. C.J. was relieved to hear he would be released from the hospital in a few days.

In a strange twist of fate, Christopher and Kevin remembered meeting each other back in 1983 at an L.A. sports dinner gala. The Raiders' Head Coach introduced the two brothers, who shook hands then went their separate ways. It was funny to the men in retrospect. The journey of life is often ironic indeed.

Barbara Pinder was still in communication with her embassy and the Bahamian Prime Minister through diplomatic couriers. She found her involvement in this multiracial family surreal at best, but couldn't argue with the DNA test analysis. However, she continued to question the role of God in this situation and wondered what new disaster He was leading her into. She still did not have faith in Him, a fact that tortured her soul.

On the other hand, Casey Chou was enjoying himself thoroughly. This was the family he'd always wished he had. The master numerologist took note of everyone's birth date and was surprised they were all harmoniously aligned. He even solved the problem of what to do with Benjamin. Their youngest brother found it difficult to occupy his time. Casey bought him an IBM vocal laptop with wireless internet access, as well as an electronic keyboard for musical compositions. Benjamin began work on a new symphony, planning to dedicate it to his mother. At least it would keep him away from the slot machines, something Moses scolded him for on several occasions.

Roberta spent her days shopping at various malls with her sister Barbara in tow, but always found time to return to the hotel pool before sunset. Wearing a series of ever more provocative swimwear, she loved garnering as much attention as possible from the young men who awaited her daily exhibitions.

Yesterday, Moses caught her poolside allowing an obliging horndog to rub oil into her bare back, with his hands wrapping ever closer to her front. Roberta was upset with her brother's interference, refusing to talk with him the rest of the day. He realized he overreacted and later apologized.

Moses called Atali every third or fourth day, longing for the moment they'd again be together. He was also keeping a wary eye out for his old friend, now turned mortal enemy, Esteban Lopez. Moses wondered if he could kill his old amigo, knowing Esteban would have no such hesitation. It would be a reunion he'd just as soon avoid.

Above all, the family continued to pray for their missing sister. They hoped to locate her before the Government. Little did they know their sister lived in Las Vegas, working as an exotic dancer in a club a few blocks from their hotel.

Kimberly Park possessed the kind of body to make men realize there is a God. She was a 5 foot 7, 118 pound walking wet dream with her genuine 36DD chest the exception in a city awash in saline implants. However, her image was not without enhancement. Kimberly's naturally jet black hair was bleached to a light brown, then streaked with blonde highlights flowing to her middle back. Blue contacts covered the deep brown pools of her eyes. This created a very striking look, allowing Kimberly to retain her Asian features while conceding to the reality that attractive blonde, blue-eyed dancers made the most money. And, that was what this woman was about. Her insatiable thirst for the almighty buck seemed to eclipse her need for anything else, including love. It was an addiction as real as any other. Of course, she hadn't always been this way. Her greed was a reaction to a lifetime of insecurity and doubt. As opposed to her brothers and sisters, the course of Kimberly's life had been the stormiest of all.

She'd been adopted by Frank and Melanie Lo Park of San Mateo, California when only six months old. Her father was an executive for a major Silicon Valley semiconductor manufacturer. Due to a congenital condition, her mother couldn't conceive a baby, so young Kimberly grew up an only child. There was never much love between her parents and Kimberly cowered in her room on many occasions as they fought. Often these altercations became physical, causing her mother to go to the hospital more than once. The arguments continued nightly, chipping away at her tender soul. Kimberly's schoolwork suffered and the young girl lost weight. She felt helpless to do anything and prayed for a way out of the hellish existence.

One night, her mother entered her room and packed a suitcase for her. Even in the darkness, Kimberly could see her mother's blackened left eye. She cried for the both of them. They left that night never to return. She was 12 years old and her life was destined to become even more bleak.

Her mother took a job as a seamstress which kept the two apart for many hours of the day. To supplement their meager income,

Kimberly engaged in a wide variety of jobs. She was starting to develop sexually and this fact brought undue attention to her. A friend at school introduced her to a photographer who specialized in filming teenage girls in various stages of undress. This led to other modeling assignments, each of which plunged her into a darker world.

After turning 16, Kimberly's mother was diagnosed with breast cancer. For the next two years, Melanie underwent chemotherapy in an attempt to save her life. Kimberly dropped out of school to help pay the mounting medical bills. She loved her mother dearly and was willing to do anything to help her get well...including sleeping with male acquaintances for money. But, in spite of her support, Melanie died a few days before Kimberly's 18th birthday. It left a hole in her life that never ceased to be painful.

She left California and traveled to Las Vegas where she could make the most cash exploiting her sexual charms. Initially, the degradation of allowing strange men to fondle her body made her nauseous, but the financial rewards were an intoxicating salve. A vicious cycle developed. The more she hated doing it, the more she loved doing it. For the past few years, this had been her world. A lifestyle which was so empty, she could think of nothing else. It left her soul hollow and devoid of love, something she wished she could change. But until that happened, Kimberly would remain one of the top dancers at the Olympic Garden Men's Club on the Las Vegas Strip.

Park lived in a two bedroom apartment in nearby Henderson with her roommate and co-worker Stacey Wells. They'd known each other for several years and were close friends. Stacey was a typical SoCal bleach blonde and, like so many other dancers, was making serious bank in Las Vegas. She was an incorrigible flirt and loved male attention. In fact, Stacey usually dated several men at a time, helping to satisfy her raging libido. Her latest conquest was David Leyton, a young executive visiting from the East Coast whom she'd known barely a week. David's dashing looks and tall frame was responsible for igniting her pheromones and his lovemaking prowess affected Stacey like an opiate. Any man who made her feel this good was a keeper. However, David's object of desire wasn't Stacey, but her roommate. He'd been tasked to find her. For unknown to either woman, David Leyton was an assassin with strict orders to eliminate Kimberly Park.

It was ten in the morning when the three of them arrived atop the Stratosphere Tower, high above Las Vegas Boulevard. Kimberly was there to answer a dare from Stacey. Elevated 100 stories from the ground was the highest roller coaster in the world, the High Roller, a serpentine track wrapping around the top of the observation deck. Stacey knew Kimberly hated heights and expected her to chicken out. A warm wind greeted them as they joined a short queue for the coaster ride. Suddenly, David's pager went off. As he checked the message, his face turned sour.

"Damn."

"What's the matter?" wondered Stacey.

"It's the office. I better call them."

"Now?"

He nodded. "I won't be long. I noticed a phone by the elevator." David kissed Stacey on the lips, causing Kimberly to shutter in disbelief. "Wait for me," he yelled, trotting back inside.

David walked over to another man whom he was clearly irritated to see. They did not shake hands.

"This meeting is ill-advised," came his icy voice.

"Necessary," the other answered. "You seem to be having trouble completing the job."

He kept his anger in check. "Don't tell me my business. I'll do this the way I want."

"You acquired the target a week ago. What the hell are you waiting for?"

"Stay out of it. It's not your show."

The man looked out at the women beyond, finally understanding the situation. "You're fucking them?" he asked in astonishment.

"Have you lost your mind? Why report in if you're going to disobey orders?"

David remained silent, sizing up this intrusion on his plans. He stiffened as the other agent removed a beeper from his pants pocket.

"Time to stand down. I'll handle this." He pressed a button on the device.

"What the hell are you doing?"

"Something you should've done," the man responded. "I just armed a charge on the coaster track. Once the cab hits the trip wire, there'll be two less whores in the world."

His rage was barely contained. "Let's talk this over." He clutched the man's arm, leading him toward a nearby men's room. They disappeared within. A minute later, David walked out having fired half a clip into the other man. The savagery of the kill was stunning. He combed his mane of light brown hair and exited back onto the roof.

David rejoined Stacey, searching in vain for her roommate. "Where's Kim?"

"She didn't want to wait."

"What!" David cried, unable to conceal his horror.

"Yeah," grinned Stacey. "She looked like she was gonna shit herself."

David pushed a nervous breath. This was not the way he wanted it to happen. Like the praying mantis, he would mate, then kill. But, he'd lost his chance. She was gone.

Kimberly shut her eyes for most of the ride. Her wind-blown hair draped before her face, psychologically separating her from the open expanse beyond. Neither she nor the others were aware of the explosive device, now a mere 50 feet away.

As the wheels rolled over the trip wire, the result was instantaneous. A blinding flash and resonant echo announced their fate. The cab pitched over, expelling most of the occupants. Their strident screams began to fade as the force of gravity claimed them.

Kimberly was hanging upside down, feeling herself slipping out from under her restraining harness. She issued a series of desperate groans, struggling to secure her position. Another surviving female was in hysterics, her manic contortions further loosening the cab from the track. The woman somersaulted out of her seat, clutching the safety belt as if performing on a trapeze. A moment later, her sweat-drenched palms gave way, plunging her to the street below.

Kimberly remained inverted in her seat, bathed in torrential fear. She was aware of her every breath, as well as the overwhelming percussion of her heart. Suspended between life and death, Kimberly forced her mind to work. Her only hope rested on her ability to climb onto the rails and backtrack to safety. However, she couldn't command her body to move. It was this inaction which ultimately saved her.

She finally heard a helicopter approaching. Remaining motionless, Kimberly waited for the craft to circle into position. She wondered how they would rescue her. *Probably by lowering a recovery basket. That would be the safest thing to do.* Forcing a deep breath, she reminded herself these guys were experts and knew exactly what they were doing. She had to have faith.

The chopper was now hovering directly above. She recognized the craft as an Army helicopter, finding it strange the military would have responded before the police. A mechanical winch lowered a grappling hook onto the front of the enclosure, snaring the forward axle. The craft then lurched upward, separating the cab from the twisted track.

Kimberly fell back in her seat. She summoned her lungs for an extended scream, hearing only the incessant roar of the engine. The helicopter banked left, soon achieving a comfortable cruising speed. Experiencing a new definition of terror, Kimberly maintained a steady squeal of disapproval. The cab pitched and swayed with each buffet of wind, leaving her nauseous. Kimberly raised her middle finger, allowing her to vent rage the only way possible. One thing was sure. She'd never ride a roller coaster again.

The chopper headed into the mountains dividing the Las Vegas Metro area from the Pahrump Valley to the northwest. The tiny town of Blue Diamond now lay below. They circled over a clearing within a cluster of trees. A few moments later, the cab gently kissed the ground and the grappling hook released. As the craft landed in a cyclonic swirl of dust, Kimberly freed herself from the seat, dashing toward a doublewide trailer a few feet away.

To her surprise, a lone pilot emerged. The man was wearing an Army uniform. He was tall and gangly, about 190 pounds, with light brown hair and mesmerizing blue eyes. She figured he was about 50 years old, but that was hard to tell. Before he could approach, Kimberly grabbed a nearby rock, clutching it with intent.

"Stay away from me, you fucking maniac!"

Her words halted him mid-step. "Most people get to know me before they say that."

She shook her head in dismay. "I'm a quick judge of character."

"You okay?"

"What the hell do you care? You almost killed me."

A lightning smile. "I think you've got that ass-backward. I could've sworn I saved you."

Her anger was overcome by a sudden cramping in her intestines. She placed a quivering hand on her tummy. "I need a bathroom."

He pointed to the trailer. "Be my guest."

Kimberly dropped the rock and ran inside. Now that the danger was over, her body decided to purge itself. She struggled to the sink and dabbed her face with a wet towel. It was a half hour before Kimberly felt well enough to venture back to the man. He'd shed his uniform and was wearing a T-shirt and jeans. He stood by the chopper, spraying it down with a garden hose.

"Everything come out all right?" he teased.

She ignored the indelicate question. Kimberly tried to size up the man, but he became more of an enigma by the minute. Dropping the hose, he hoisted a slab of mud in both hands. As if a sculptor gone mad, he began coating the engine housing with large amounts of earthen muck. Her incredulous stare caused him to pause.

"The least you could do is help."

"You want me to put that slop on your helicopter?"

He grimaced. "It's not exactly mine."

"Did you steal..." She was interrupted by a shower of mud thrown her way.

"Don't waste time. They'll be looking."

Kimberly returned the favor, tossing a thick load of sludge across the man's face. He wiped off the brown goo, exposing a devilish smile. "That was good. Now, see if you can get some on the helo."

The two joined forces, fully packing the engine and exhaust manifold of the craft. As they continued the mudslinging, her curiosity peaked.

"Why are we doing this?"

"They'll use infrared to track the ship. The mud hides the heat signature."

"Who the hell's looking?"

He snickered. "It ain't the Boy Scouts, sweetie. Help me with this tarp."

They draped a large camouflage covering across the chopper, cloaking the majority of the craft. Suddenly, the man stopped as a peculiar noise captured his attention. He recognized it as the distant roar of oncoming jets.

"Get down!"

Before she could respond, both of them were diving headfirst into the muck. Two military aircraft streaked overhead unable to see the submerged pair. A moment later, they began to emerge from the ooze.

"F-16s out of Nellis," he gasped, spitting mud from his mouth. "They must've contacted the Air Force to help with the search."

Kimberly wondered what kind of fucking mess she was in now. *Wait a minute. That's kind of funny.* Considering her present situation, she knew exactly what kind of fucking mess she was in. She sputtered forth an involuntary laugh, then another. Finally, Kimberly could no longer contain herself. She burst forth in a sustained, hysterical cackle.

"What are you laughing at?"

She found it impossible to answer. This woman was high main-tenance. With all the money she spent on hair, nails, make-up, clothes, shoes, accessories, tanning beds and the like, to find herself encased in mud should be more than she could bear. But, Kimberly was experiencing something cruelly taken from her youth. She was having fun.

They playfully hosed each other down, then entered the man's trailer for much needed showers. He offered her a robe while her clothes were in the laundry. Afterward, she made a call to her room-mate Stacey, leaving a message on the answering machine. Kimberly finally joined the man at his kitchen table, sharing some re-heated pizza and beer.

"Forgive me for asking," drying her hair with a towel. "But, who are you?"

He smiled, continuing to munch away. "Major Robert Osborne, United States Army. Voluntarily discharged." She introduced herself and shook his hand in mock formality.

"Voluntary discharge? You quit?"

"Uh, huh."

"When?"

He checked his watch. "Four hours ago."

Kimberly grinned. "Is that when you took the chopper?"

"Gee, you're quick," he added, between bites. "I've been plan-ning this for awhile. Ever since I heard about the indictment."

"What do they want you for?" she inquired, lifting a brew.

"Financial. All this over a little bit of money."

"That's my favorite subject," her eyes growing wider in antici-pation. "How much did you get?"

He paused, allowing her to take an ill-timed sip of beer. "Eight million, three-hundred-sixty thousand."

An involuntary gag reflex caused her to spew the foamy liquid into his lap. She grabbed a paper towel to mop up the mess. "Sorry."

He blushed, trying to ignore the intimate dry cleaning. "Is this your way of proposing?"

A nervous giggle. "You surprised me."

"Because I'm not living in a mansion?"

"No. It's just a shitload of green."

He savored a swig of beer. "Not to the Government. They never run out. I falsified 5,600 tax returns, laundering the money through an offshore firm. I was at Ft. Irwin, California when I got word they were about to arrest me. So, I split in the Huey." Osborne downed another sip. "Anyway, I was flying low, avoiding radar. Came into Vegas thinking I'd ditch downtown, then get lost in the city. Make my way here later. Of course, that's when I spotted you ass-up on the tower."

"Lucky for me," Kimberly admitted. "Really, I want to thank you. That was way righteous. You could've just left me there." She then flashed a smile the Mona Lisa would envy. "My hero."

Osborne sputtered in amusement. "First time I've been called that."

Kimberly bit into some pizza. "Why do you have such a hard-on for the Government?"

The question backed him into his chair. He was clearly uncomfortable discussing the issue. "I'm a patriot. I love my country," he responded with genuine emotion. "But, I don't trust this Government. Understand the difference?"

"Sure. We have pride in one. We hope we can have pride in the other."

"That's a good way to put it," he agreed, still clinging to his brew. His eyes seemed focused on a distant memory. "I was a model soldier. Never questioned my orders. I led a company of Army Rangers against the Iraqis in Desert Storm. The Government wanted an easy win. They decided to use some nasty chemical shit without telling us, figuring no one would know. Of course, it blew back on us. Killed a bunch of my men. I was in the hospital for weeks suffering from God-knows what. Ended up sterile. Lost my wife over it. But, they said it never happened. That it was all in my mind."

He placed his beer down and forced a sigh. The man composed himself, choosing his words with surgical care. "This Government's all smoke and mirrors. Nothing's ever what it seems. A truth is a lie and a lie is a truth. Whatever serves their purpose. If they said the sun rises in the west, they'd blind us all just to prove it. Deception. Denial. If necessary, brute force. That's how they survive. They want the American people to stay asleep. Living forever in — dreamland."

The Major held forth his hands, as if surrendering them to forensic analysis. "I've killed with these. Atrocities beyond imagination. All because the Government said it was okay. Once blood gets on them, you can wash and scrub, but they'll never come clean. It's always there. I can see it every day of my life."

Kimberly remained transfixed, not knowing how to respond. She could feel his pain. His sincere passion. There was nothing trivial about Major Robert Osborne. In fact, she found herself being strangely attracted to the man.

He rose from his chair and motioned her to follow. They approached a locked door which he unsecured, revealing a darkened stairway leading to an area underneath the trailer. The Major flicked on the light and they descended together, hand in hand.

"Holy shit!" declared Kimberly, shocked by what she now witnessed.

The 10 x 20 foot cellar was packed floor to ceiling with a secret cache of armament and munitions. A smorgasbord of military rifles, handguns, rocket launchers, grenades, mines and explosives were neatly stacked and presented for display.

"I've collected a few things over the years. Never hurts to be prepared."

Kimberly swallowed hard. "What do you need it for?"

"I could equip a company of soldiers for a sustained battle. And, I have access to more," he declared. "The day will come when we'll have to defend our country, against our Government. Thousands...maybe hundreds of thousands will answer the call."

"Like those militia wackos?"

The Major laughed. "You don't have to be wacko to distrust them." A reflective pause. "Know who the Government fears the most?" She remained silent while he gently tapped her head. "A person who thinks."

They returned upstairs. Kimberly asked him to relate other stories from his military career. She hungered to learn his background. His desires. His inner essence. Hours were consumed and still she had not volunteered any personal insight on herself. Two bottles of wine now lay empty on the kitchen table. It was getting late and ever closer to the time she would agree to share his bed.

Kimberly went to the bathroom to help sex-up her appearance. While there, she noticed her period was starting. *Oh, well.* She figured if he didn't mind, neither should she.

The Major was already laying down when Kimberly entered his bedroom. Her robe was loosely worn, exposing her ample breasts as she approached. With the grace of a cat she slipped onto the bed, hovering provocatively above his waist. He eyed her with light amusement.

"You look great."

"Thank you." Kimberly ran her tongue over her lips, trying to ignite maximum arousal.

"Up for some mud wrestling?"

A limp smile dismissed the comment. "Not tonight. I've got something else in mind."

"Hmm. So do I."

"You do?" she purred lustfully.

"Uh, huh. It's called sleep."

Kimberly felt the air leave the room. *My goodies here for the squeezing and he'd rather sleep? What the hell am I doing wrong?*

"Tell me that's a joke," begged the stunned female.

He shook his head. "No joke. I'd just like to get to know you better."

"We did that all day."

"You got to know me. Now, I'd like to know you."

Kimberly collapsed next to him on the bed. She felt a little foolish, but couldn't argue. He knew her name and little else. Subconsciously, she really didn't want him to know her. He might get scared off. Kimberly found it hard to believe a guy would want to be with her knowing what she did for a living. Society wasn't tolerant of women in her profession. And, she didn't want to lie. *Why didn't he take me, no questions asked?*

"What do you want to know?" she sighed.

"It's late. We can talk in the morning."

She laid there in awkward silence, wondering what would happen when she told him. She really liked the man. *What'll his response be? Will he treat me the same?* Kimberly decided she couldn't wait.

"Robert, you don't want to know what I do — or what I've done," allowing her shame to swell.

"Yes, I do," feeling her pain. His words came as if in a trance. "You know what I've done. I'm not here to judge you any more than you've judged me. We all have choices to make. But, there's no right or wrong. It continues to hurt only if you let it." An emotional pause, followed by the most poignant words ever to caress her ears. "Ache not, my child. Ache not."

As he faded to sleep, she reflected on what was said. It brought her a comfort she'd never known. A serenity without price. She wiped a tear from her eye and looked upon the man. In a few short hours, he'd done more than save her life. He'd revived her soul. She curled up against him, reveling in the warmth of his flesh and losing herself in an invisible womb of contentment. That night, Kimberly slept with the peace of angels.

As the orange tendrils of a new dawn filtered through the windows, Major Robert Osborne listened to his guest. She laid her soul bare, releasing years of pain. Nothing was withheld. Two packs of cigarettes and seven cups of coffee later, the catharsis was over. Kimberly was emotionally spent, glad he insisted they wait until morning. He looked upon her as she lowered her head in supplication. The Major finally broke the silence.

"I guess I'm not the only one who's been to war," came the verdict. "We use different weapons, but the battles are just as real."

Kimberly raised her head, knowing she'd never again hide from her past. "Thank you, Robert," angrily dispatching a tear. "One warrior to another."

A bond was forged. They agreed to see each other later in the week when they would complete what was started the night before.

He drove Kimberly back toward her apartment in his military Humvee. Knowing the authorities would stakeout the residence awaiting her return, they concocted a story for her to spin. The Major dropped her off at a convenience store six blocks from her destination, allowing her to walk the remaining distance. After exchanging a kiss, he disappeared into traffic, but not from her thoughts.

Kevin was on his cell phone when he heard a beep. "Hold that thought," he instructed, switching to the incoming call. "Reese."

"I have new information for you," came an authoritative male voice. Kevin cupped his hand over the mouthpiece, motioning at C.J. and Barbara across the suite.

"It's him."

They clustered around their brother. Kevin had often mentioned the anonymous informant who helped them find each other. He assumed it was some rogue agent in the Government sharing leads as they became available. Whoever it was, the man had been enormously helpful.

"Go ahead," insisted Kevin.

"I know where your sister is."

"I'm listening."

"Turn on CNN."

He stared at his siblings. "We need to watch CNN."

Barbara grabbed the remote control and channel surfed to the broadcast. On screen was a live feed from a local Las Vegas TV affiliate, interviewing a stunned Kimberly Park outside her Henderson apartment complex. The reporters were asking her questions faster than she could answer. It took a moment before Barbara made sense of it all.

"That's the girl from the Stratosphere. The roller coaster accident yesterday."

C.J. nodded. "Maybe it wasn't an accident."

Kevin addressed the caller. "Okay. We're watching it."

"She's your missing sister."

"Are you sure?"

The man snapped in annoyance. "Have I failed you before?"

"No."

"Then, don't doubt me now." A tense pause. "She's a dancer at the Olympic Garden Men's Club on Las Vegas Boulevard. Her working name is Vesper. You'll have to hurry. The assassin has acquired her and will strike again."

"I understand."

"I'll call if I have anything else." The line went dead.

C.J. looked to his brother for guidance. "So?"

Kevin sighed, relishing the job which lay ahead. "Looks like we're going clubbing."

Kimberly was astounded by the media attention. There were over a half-dozen TV trucks parked around the entrance to her apartment, as well as a gaggle of reporters jockeying for position. She was the lone survivor of a spectacular accident and her story was highly coveted. Especially by the police. After successfully deflecting a barrage of media questions, the local authorities escorted Kimberly into her apartment where they probed her recollection of the incident. Her response was consistent and never wavered. She didn't know why the coaster derailed. She didn't know anything about the murdered man in the tower. She didn't know who was in the helicopter that rescued her. Kimberly explained she was dropped into the desert, then began an exhausting, night-long walk back to town. There was nothing more to say. After three plus hours, the police finished their interrogation. Kimberly was left alone with her relieved roommate Stacey and a very relieved David Leyton. His plans for sexual assassination could still be fulfilled.

Both women knew they'd work that night. A large convention was in town and the club would be packed with horny, middle-aged men carrying more money than brains. Kimberly took a late afternoon nap before prepping for the night. Her period was getting heavier. A secret between women who work in the sex trade is the use of a menstrual sponge, when tampons or pads would be viewed as a liability. During her shower, Kimberly secured one of the sponges from a personal stash kept in her vanity drawer. She packed a small satchel with two G-string bikinis and her make-up to apply when she arrived at the club.

On her way out, Stacey cornered her by the bedroom door. "You leaving already?"

Kimberly confirmed her intentions. "I've got to go by the salon, then jump in the tanning bed. I'll meet you there."

Stacey whispered in her ear. "David wants to do us both."

"What!" came an explosion of disgust.

Her roommate giggled. "Come on. It'll be fun."

"No way in hell."

"Aww," she whined, running her hand across Kimberly's chest. "Not even for me?"

"I told you I'm not into that. Besides, I don't find him that attractive."

"Shit, girl. You don't have to marry his ass," Stacey snorted in amusement. "But, you'll want to when he starts with that tongue."

Kimberly cringed, fighting an urge to hurl. "I am so out of here."

She exited the apartment with deliberate speed.

Stacey returned to her room and sprawled onto the bed. David emerged from the shower in a naked, fully aroused state.

"Ooooh," she trilled. "I've got just the home for that bad boy." Stacey slipped out of her lace panties, tossing them off with her toes.

"Where's Kim?"

"She split," positioning her legs as helpfully as possible. An uneasy pause. "Look, I tried. She just didn't want to." He found himself being pulled onto her. "We don't need anyone else. Right now, it's just you and me."

David worked hard to shroud his frustration. Kimberly kept evading his sexual grasp. Selecting the menstrual sponge as an instrument of death was flawed. He'd never know when, or if, she'd use it.

Stacey was too high on crystal meth to notice that his mind was elsewhere. With each thrust he became ever more fixated on his quarry. It was a conundrum which baffled him. He couldn't just kill her. He had to take her in his own way. On his terms. It was the only chance to satisfy his blood lust. David scarcely realized the woman beneath him had already come twice. He looked upon Stacey with contempt. *Why am I doing this?* She was just a pawn to trap the queen. Unworthy of his time. An inferior, worthless being.

At last, he bore deep within her, attempting to ravish the woman internally. Even his release was hollow. To his chagrin, he realized he'd forgotten to wear a condom. David withdrew from her with a snake-like hiss of disgust. It's a well-known fact female roommates tend to naturally coordinate their monthly cycles. Stacey had already informed him she was on her period, but at the moment he saw no evidence.

"I borrowed one of Kim's sponges," she explained.

"Did Kim use one?"

"I dunno. We usually do if we're working."

David shut his eyes at the disclosure. He walked to her closet, removing an object from his inner suit pocket. "I'm sorry to hear that."

He leveled his handgun without remorse. Stacey forced herself to reality.

"What the fuck?"

"Trust me. You won't feel a thing." A single bullet struck Stacey's forehead, crumbling her onto the bed. A chilling pause as he safed his weapon. David approached the corpse, rubbing his hand over her lower abdomen.

"Don't worry. I'll make it all better."

Strip clubs are big business in Las Vegas and the Olympic Garden was one of the most popular. Employing over 400 surgically enhanced females, the club was packed each night with conventioneers who brought their money and left their wives at home. The men were there for the sexual fantasy. The women were there for the financial reward. It was an inviting battleground for the sexes with combatants from each side ever vigilant for the easy mark.

Into the fray stepped four racially diverse men with a common goal. They were there to locate their sister. Kevin Reese, Christopher Hightower, Casey Chou and Moses Castaneda scanned the chaotic scene, each exhibiting varying emotions. Kevin was in his element, pleased with the vast choice of sexual eye candy. C.J. tried to ignore the nubile young women, remembering his vow of celibacy and advanced sense of spiritual enlightenment. Casey absorbed the activity with the wonder of a child, never once having patronized an establishment such as this. Moses was beet red with embarrassment, fighting the subconscious feeling he was cheating on Atali.

The brothers stood for a moment, capturing the sights and sounds. Kevin intercepted a bouncer, peeling off a crisp hundred-dollar bill from his money clip. The man escorted the foursome to a reserved table, ensuring their drink orders were taken by a passing barmaid.

Within seconds, two statuesque, bikini-clad blondes sauntered toward them. They posed for the men like award-winning actresses.

"I'm Misty," said one.

"I'm Christy," stated the other.

Kevin smiled at their lack of sincerity. "Hi, I'm Frisky. And, these are my friends Lusty, Gropey and Horny."

The women exchanged glances, giggling in nervous amusement. C.J. shook his head in dismay.

"Well done, Kevin. Very mature."

His brother shrugged, dismissing the criticism.

"Like a dance?" asked Misty.

"Oh, I think my heart can handle one," he replied.

As if on cue, Christy signaled two other women to the table and soon the odd quartet were each receiving a topless lap dance. Kevin's brothers appeared tongue tied. When the song was over, each woman collected payment with Kevin folding the bills lengthwise, tying the paper currency into a makeshift bow around their G-strings. The four joined the men, requesting drinks from the bar.

"Do you know Vesper?" inquired Kevin.

"Sure," Misty confirmed. "I saw her in the dressing room a few minutes ago."

He deposited a crisp fifty between her breasts. "Would you be a sweetheart and go find her? There's more where that came from."

She was on her way before the final word left his lips.

C.J. and Moses had an awkward time with the women seated beside them. Both were trying to purge their minds of impure thoughts made all the more difficult by the dancers' obvious assets. Casey was having innocent fun with Christy.

"What's your birth date?" he wondered.

She playfully took a sip of his drink. "December 9th, '91."

He computed the numbers. "Nope. Doesn't work for me."

The woman eyed him in bewilderment. "What's that supposed to mean?"

Casey ignored her question. "But, you're a very good ecdysiast."

"Say what?" thinking she'd misunderstood him over the blare of music.

"An ecdysiast. That's another word for stripper."

Christy cast an incredulous stare. "You know, you're really anal."

"Why, thank you," beamed Casey, unfazed by the comment.

A moment later, Misty returned with Kimberly in tow. She breezed up to the men, exuding maximum charm. "Hi, there. I'm Vesper."

Kevin was stunned by his sister's overpowering appearance. "Hello, Vesper. By the way, what's that name mean?"

A sensual smile. "It's the evening star," she informed using dramatic flair. "And believe me, I am the star of the evening."

"It also means a time for prayer," interjected Moses.

She gazed at him with seductive eyes. "If you were lucky enough to have me, you'd need time for prayer."

Moses gulped at the loaded comment. A new song began to play.

"Care for a dance?" returning attention to Kevin.

His hesitation became obvious. "Well — I suppose I could feed the meter once."

C.J. leaned over to whisper his displeasure. "She's your sister, for God sakes."

Kevin's pained expression was classic, holding forth his hand to quell any additional criticism. "That's something we haven't fully determined. Let's give it the benefit of the doubt."

Each of the women began another dance for the enraptured foursome. Kimberly removed her bikini top, plunging her perfumed chest against Kevin's face. When she allowed him to come up for air, he was drenched in embarrassment, already regretting his decision. Since his brother was now at a loss for words, C.J. took the lead.

"Miss? Young lady? We have to talk. It's very important." He paused to thank the girl dancing for him, lest she feel unappreciated.

"What about?" asked Kimberly.

C.J. heaved caution to the wind. "The incident on the roller coaster. It was no accident."

Her body tensed in mannequin-like rigidity, triggering an end to the erotic performance. "Who the fuck are you guys?"

"Believe me, we're only here to help. We want to make sure no harm comes to you."

"What the hell are you saying? How do you even know me?"

Kevin smiled, aware there was no further need to hide the truth. "Your name's Kimberly Park. You were born in a Catholic Mission in Juarez, Mexico and adopted by a couple in San Mateo, California."

She interrupted, astounded by the disclosure. "All right, dammit! Who are you, the cops?"

"No," Casey chimed in. "We're your brothers."

Kimberly suffered a spasm of amusement. "Oh, I can see the resemblance." She changed demeanor with mercurial speed. "Look, I don't know what you're tweaking on and I really don't care. You're either the Feds or a bunch of sick fucks. In any case, find the door before I call the bouncer."

She left without bothering to collect her fee. They sprawled back in their seats, wondering how this initial meeting could've been any more disastrous.

After paying the other women, the brothers left the club and regrouped in the parking lot.

"Gee, that went well," sighed Moses. "Barbara and Shannon won't believe how we hosed this one."

"We can't give up like this," C.J. maintained. "She's in danger and too scared or stubborn to believe it."

Kevin suggested a revised course of action. "Let's stakeout the club. She's got to go home eventually. We'll keep track of her. Maintain a low profile."

They soon realized that wouldn't be easy.

Kimberly was in the dressing room counting her money for the evening. She wanted to earn another two or three hundred before returning home. Her face reflected the menstrual pain she was enduring, believing the swelling within was stress related. She popped two ibuprofen to combat the cramping, then forced a counterfeit smile as she re-entered the club.

David Leyton arrived an hour later wearing a suit and tie. He scanned the establishment, at last locating his elusive target. Seating himself at a nearby table, he motioned for her to join him. She approached without any pretense of cordiality.

"Hi, Kim. You look great."

"I'm working. My name's Vesper."

David shrugged. "You're beautiful by any name."

She sighed with fatigue. Given his roaming sexual desires, this was the last man she wanted to see. "Where's Stacey?"

"Back at the apartment. She was dead tired." As another song began, he pulled a fifty from his pocket. "Give me your best dance."

She'd have rather sipped champagne from a toilet than suffer the indignity of exposing herself to this predator. *Still, his cash should be as good as any man's.* Separating mind from body, Kimberly swiped the money and began moving to the music. He moaned as an animal in heat, burying his face into her cushioned chest. She retracted as he attempted to scale her breasts with his tongue. Keeping her body arched back, Kimberly chose less inflammatory contact, brushing his cheeks with her hair.

"I love you," came his saccharine voice.

She snorted in disgust. "Oh, no you don't."

"Yes, I do. And, this should prove it."

David placed an object on the table. She looked over to see a plastic bag…filled with a bloody sponge. The woman looked at him, then again upon the pouch in an attempt to understand the connection. To her infinite horror, he felt compelled to explain.

"Stacey used one of the sponges I substituted. It took me an hour to carve this out of her." His lurid words chilled her to the bone. "I was supposed to kill you. But, I can't. Don't you see, I really do love you."

Kimberly's eyes were as distended as her mouth, utterly transfixed by this assault on her senses. She felt his invisible grip seizing her by the neck, squeezing the very soul from her body.

"Look at that sponge," he continued. "Expanding. Growing. Just like my love. I can't let you die like that. I've got to get it out of you. Then, we can live together. Just you and me. Forever."

Delirium overwhelmed her. Fighting through the trauma, Kimberly gurgled forth an anguished cry. "Oh, God!"

She repelled from the killer, splashing hot wax across his face which had pooled within a tabletop candleholder. David shrieked in agony, rising to his feet. She ran for her life as he removed a handgun from his suit.

"You fucking bitch!" The gun discharged, felling another dancer who was caught in the line of fire. A second shot resonated through the club, alerting everyone to the danger.

Pandemonium ensued, as dozens of patrons and female dancers in various states of undress now fled outside. Astonished drivers gasped at the display, braking their vehicles.

"Viva Las Vegas!" yelled one overly excited motorist.

Surging through the crowd, David shot a bouncer who tried to tackle him, then entered the parking lot in search of his prey. Kimberly stumbled forward, doubling over in pain. She came to rest by a parked car and was startled to feel two arms cradle her.

"Are you okay?" Casey asked.

Kimberly saw David closing from behind. "Jesus! He's going to kill me!"

"No, he's not." He stood to face the assassin.

"Hey, fucker! Get away from my girl!" yelled David, his gun drawn.

Casey whirled into action, displaying his martial arts superiority. After initially wrestling the gun from his hand, he executed a punishing series of rapid-fire kicks which dropped the man to the pavement. David struggled to his feet, once more lunging at him. Continuing the punishment, Casey transformed the man into a battered representation of his former self. David fell backward against another car, completely disoriented. Not willing to concede, he withdrew a hunting knife and approached while Casey was kneeling down to help Kimberly. Leaping into the fray, Moses overpowered him from behind, shattering the man's forearm. Then, with a swift thrust of the blade, he sliced him open from stomach to groin. The assassin was dead in seconds, his disemboweled body motionless at last.

Moses and Casey huddled over Kimberly, still clutching her lower abdomen.

"What's wrong with her?"

"I don't know," Casey replied, showing true concern.

Kimberly managed to explain. "That bastard. There's something inside me. I've got to get it out."

The two scooped her from the ground as C.J. and Kevin pulled up in a rental car.

"This wasn't what I meant by low profile," Kevin whined, watching the continuing bedlam unfold.

"She needs a doctor," cried Casey.

"I'll call Shannon and have her standing by," C.J. said, taking command of the situation. "Get in the back." The three entered the car with deliberate speed and a moment later were racing toward Sacred Heart Hospital.

As the anesthesia faded from her body, Kimberly awoke with watery eyes. She noticed Shannon Hewson standing by her bedside, clipboard in hand.

"Where am I?"

Shannon smiled. "Hospital. You're a lucky woman. I pulled out that sponge just in time. It was designed to expand on contact with liquid. It would've broken through your uterine wall, killing you."

Kimberly issued a repugnant sigh. "I guess I owe you one."

"What else are sisters for?"

"Huh?" came the confused response.

For the next hour, the women discussed the incredible circumstances regarding Kimberly's place in the Hart family. Shannon shared all available information including DNA test analysis. She also explained why she'd been targeted for assassination. Although their conversation continued in a cordial manner, Kimberly remained skeptical.

"I'm sorry, Shannon. Maybe it was easy for you to accept, but in my line of work you hear all kinds of stories. I've learned never to believe anything."

Her sister nodded, exhaling in despair. "Okay. Get some rest. We'll talk later."

Shannon left the room, walking down the corridor toward Mary Ellen's private suite. She entered to find her brothers recounting Kimberly's rescue.

"How's my little girl?" the Madre wondered, anguished over her daughter's condition.

"She'll be fine," assured Shannon. "Making her understand will be a lot harder. She doesn't want to believe any of it."

Mary Ellen paused, mulling through her options. She then cast the blanket from her body, sitting up on her bed. "I want to see her now."

212 ৵   STEVEN L. FAWCETTE

"No, mother," Shannon protested, surprised by the elderly woman's spunk. "You need to lay down. It's for the good of the baby."

"She's my baby, too," declared Mary Ellen. "And, she needs her mother. Now, who here's going to stop me?"

The siblings remained mute, lowering their heads in deference to their mother's iron will. Mary Ellen rose to her feet, wrapping herself in a robe. Moses and Casey flanked her, supporting the woman as she traversed the distance between rooms. The others followed, unsure what to expect.

Kimberly eyed the entourage as they entered. Mary Ellen came to her bedside, overcome with emotion. She hugged the girl, never once wishing to let go. The touching scene continued with Kimberly politely returning the affection. Mary Ellen pulled back, gazing at her daughter through clouded vision.

"Please forgive me, my child," her voice quaking. "I should never have let you go. Life's been hard on you. I can see it in your eyes."

Kimberly stole a calming breath. "Do you really believe you're my mother?"

"I know I am."

"How do you know?"

Her aching heart skipped a beat. "Because, I feel your pain inside me."

She smiled in response. "I never knew my real mother. But if I had, I'd have wanted her to be like you."

A suspenseful pause. "Will you forgive me?" asked Mary Ellen once again.

"Would it make a difference?"

"It would."

Kimberly nodded. "Then, I forgive you."

The woman sighed, as if freed from an ancient burden. She wiped the tears from her face only to replace them seconds later. "Thank you."

"Don't be upset," comforted Kimberly. "You're a nice lady. I'd like to believe you're my mother. I really would. Maybe it's my fault. I just need more than medical tests."

Dejected, Mary Ellen began to pull away then froze in position. "Did you get my message last night?"

"What message?"

"The message I entrusted God to give you, when your spirit was about to break."

Kimberly gestured indifferently. "I don't know. What was the message?"

Mary Ellen then spoke the most poignant words ever to caress her ears. "Ache not, my child. Ache not."

Kimberly recalled Major Osborne's haunting speech which helped lull her to sleep. She found herself reeling from the coincidence, trying to understand a mystical connection which defied explanation. This was no random fluke. No sorcerer's trick. Somehow, contact had been made. Of that, there was no doubt. She felt her body go flush with emotion, unable to contain the cloudburst of tears now tumbling the length of her face. As if possessing Divine consciousness, suddenly she knew. She knew!

"Yes, mother," came her trembling voice. "Yes, I got your message."

They each fell into a more satisfying embrace as Kimberly's family came to welcome her as one of their own. The mother and child reunion was now complete.

The emotional meeting had enervated Mary Ellen, with Shannon insisting she return to her bed at once. As they helped their mother down the corridor, none of them paid attention to the orderly mopping the floor beyond. However, he was consumed by their every move. Moses was of particular interest to the man, but that was to be expected. Esteban Lopez, his old amigo, had found them at last.

CHAPTER FOURTEEN

✌

LAS VEGAS, NEVADA — APRIL 13th

$\mathcal{F}$or the past 11 days, pain had become his lone and inseparable companion. The throb in Esteban's left eye was a constant reminder of his surgery, as was the sight of the microchip floating before him in vitreous suspension. He swallowed three aspirin dry, avoiding stronger medication which might dull his senses. This was a man determined to remain alert.

Esteban began his search with the knowledge the Madre Superiora would seek the safety afforded her by the Catholic Church. He contacted his employers in Columbia who were only too happy to render assistance. Using a reliable contact in the Cali Archdiocese, a list of Church sponsored safe houses in the Las Vegas area was obtained and faxed to Esteban's hotel upon his arrival. After checking each and finding no trace of Moses or Maria Elena, he decided to stakeout Sacred Heart Hospital, the only such facility owned by the Church. On his third day of surveillance, Esteban spotted Moses picking up his sister Shannon in a rental car.

A few hours later, he was hired by the hospital's Personnel Director due to an exemplary letter of recommendation from the Cali Archbishop, as well as a phone call from Cardinal Jesus Escobar of Columbia who was returning a favor for a secret Cartel member. Esteban accepted the position of night orderly in the hopes he could inch closer to his quarry. His predatory instincts remained as keen as ever. Moses, the Madre and her entire family were now locked in the crosshairs of his relentless anger.

He called immediately after work. The tattered condition of Judge Monroe's card reflected multiple bouts of frustration and rage since their meeting. After five rings, a woman answered.

"Central control."

"This is Esteban Lopez. I need Monroe."

A moment of arctic hesitation. "Please remain on the line."

He used the time to think of his wife, but the loving memory ended at the sound of Monroe's voice.

"Esteban. Where are you?"

He winced from another spike of pain. "Las Vegas."

"Did you find them?"

"I told you I would."

"Just Moses and his mother?"

"There were others," Esteban reported. "Several men and women."

The pause was electric. "Describe these people."

"Two were Black. A couple Asian. Two White."

"You found them?"

His response was caustic. "That's what I said, jerkweed. I'm not as incompetent as you Fed fucks."

"Their location," the Judge demanded. "Where are they?"

"Not so fast. We've got business to discuss."

"All right," came the delayed response. "Meet me at four this afternoon. Federal Building. Downtown Vegas. Don't be late."

The line went dead with stunning swiftness. He hung up, deciding to get some much needed rest.

At the appointed hour, Esteban arrived at the Lloyd George Federal Building, an 11 story, $100 million edifice occupying two city blocks between Bridger and Las Vegas Boulevards. After being strip searched by three FBI agents, he was whisked inside a private elevator and shown to an upper floor conference room. The oak double doors closed and locked behind. Before him was Judge Monroe seated at the head of an oversized table. Flanking him was his sexually unimpressive aide, Caroline Stricka, and a half-dozen bodyguards who exuded the cordiality of a herd of rhinoceros. A pitcher of grape juice was nestled next to Monroe.

"Well, well. Long time, no see," the Judge snorted in amusement. "How's the eye?"

Esteban answered with reciprocal sarcasm. "How's the coronary?"

His forced smile became shallow. "Care for some grape juice?" He poured some into a nearby glass.

"I don't drink with swine. Besides, you need all the help you can get."

Monroe took his first gulp, then set the glass down signaling the end of pleasantries. "What's that supposed to mean?"

Esteban seemed pleased at so easily getting under the Judge's skin. "Yesterday's newspaper. Government agent shot dead in the Stratosphere Tower. Just minutes before the roller coaster accident. One female survived." He slid into a chair without breaking his vocal rhythm. "Then, today's paper. David Leyton killed in front of a strip club where the same surviving female works. I knew that waste of sperm. Six months ago the CIA sent him to off me." An anguished laugh. "I guess it's just coincidence. Just like the coincidence I witnessed last night, when that same surviving female was in the arms of Maria Elena de la Cruz."

Silence filled the room. Monroe looked away as Esteban finished his rebuke. "It's her family, isn't it? Her whole family. What the hell did these people do to you?" An excruciating pause. "This Government's out of control. You bastards need lots of help."

The Judge sipped more juice. His next words were succinct and deliberate. "Tell us, Esteban. Tell us where they are and we'll give you your life back."

It was clear who held the aces in this high stakes game of poker. The time had come to up the ante.

"Not until I speak with my wife. Make it happen."

His request had been anticipated. For the past week, one of the
FBI's top female agents had studied the files on the late Anna
Castaneda Lopez. She also practiced Anna's accent, vocal
cadence, tonal qualities and pet words from recordings of
Government phone taps. If necessary, the agent hoped to become
Anna and trick Esteban into completing his mission. Although the
Bureau assured their boss they could pull it off, Monroe remained
doubtful. Despite his feelings, he knew Lopez was nobody's fool.
The plan might backfire. But, Operation Black Widow had
become the U.S. equivalent of Chernobyl and the MAJIK-12 desperately needed this 'Hail Mary' play. The Judge finally nodded in
agreement.

"All right, Esteban. I'll arrange for the call. Give me the number to your hotel."

He provided the information which was noted by the ever-effi-
cient Stricka.

"I'll have her call you at seven o'clock. Soon enough?"

"Sure," came the buoyant response. "After that, I want this
damn thing taken out of my head."

The Judge turned to Stricka. "Caroline, have the surgery scheduled for tomorrow." She nodded, recording the specious request on
her palm-sized computer.

A significant moment of silence without meaning to Esteban.
"Are we finished?"

"Just about," he murmured. The Judge motioned to one of his
agents who handed Lopez a small electronic device no larger than a
pocket calculator. After a second of examination, Esteban's curiosity was satisfied.

"It's a homing device," Monroe explained. "Good for a radius
of 10 miles. A highly accurate targeting system."

He cringed. "This is military."

"Place it where you know they'll be. Get as many together as
you can."

"Are you fucking nuts?" cried Esteban. "Right here in town?
Nobody uses a bomb to kill a few flies."

His trance-like response was immediate. "If you only knew what was at stake..."

Monroe's voice failed. He took another sip of juice to clear his throat, then spoke with the hollow conscience of a man unfettered by his words. "Don't do it for us. Do it for yourself. Do it and you'll be out of here in 48 hours, along with your wife and child. You'll then be free — to go with God."

An accident on Interstate 15 caused rush hour traffic to seek alternate routes of travel including Las Vegas Boulevard. As a result, Esteban found himself mired in a squall of angry motorists and exhaust fumes. He checked his watch, determined to be back in his hotel suite before 7:00 PM. *Oh, how I've missed you Anna!* All the things he wished to tell her swirled through his mind. He recalled the sight of her bronzed skin. The smell of her silken black hair. The feel of her body, both outside and in. Above all, he remembered the sound of her voice. It had a lilting quality which had won his heart and enraptured his soul. As enchanting as a Siren's tone. His own personal Lorelei, haunting him forever. And never to be forgotten.

Suddenly, he caught an image in his rearview mirror. A glimpse of a familiar face several cars behind. He veered onto Sahara Boulevard with the mystery driver in slow pursuit. They drove west into the afternoon sun, resulting in maximum windshield glare. At first, he thought it might be an FBI tail, but the car contained only the driver. Esteban knew the Feds only traveled in packs for safety. This guy certainly wasn't afraid and didn't care if he were spotted. He waited for another view. A convenient shadow. An alternate bend of light. Something which would reveal the face. Esteban turned south on Industrial Road. As they went underneath a highway over-pass, the glare lifted and the image became clear. Even wearing designer shades, he knew his old amigo.

"Moses." Lopez cursed under his breath. This was an unplanned, ill-timed event. He wondered how long he'd been tracked and why he'd not noticed him before.

For the next few minutes they continued to traverse various side roads with neither acknowledging the other. In fact, Moses was unaware Esteban had spotted him. Obviously, both preferred for their now inevitable confrontation to be staged in private. Lopez completed a circuitous trek back to his hotel. He pulled into the valet parking area at the Wynn Las Vegas Casino and strode inside. Aware Moses was following, he remained in plain sight, baiting his prey toward the golf course cabanas at the back of the resort.

Esteban arrived at his suite, fumbling with his key before entering. It was a shrewd manipulation, allowing Moses to pinpoint his location. Once inside, he dialed room service and requested a bottle of champagne. The delivery was made within minutes. He met the hotel employee at the door wearing only a bathrobe.

"Thanks. I'll open it later." Esteban signed the bill.

"Thank you, sir," responded the server, noting the gracious tip.

"Oh, could I get a bowl of strawberries to go with this?"

"Certainly. I'll be right back."

He waited for the server to depart, then bellowed forth so Moses could hear. "I'll be in the shower! Just leave it on the table!"

Esteban withdrew inside, using the deadbolt to keep the door open. He was sure Moses couldn't ignore such an opportunity no matter how dangerous. Within seconds, he was proven correct. Moses entered the cabana with gun in hand. The sound of a shower running resonated through the suite. Approaching with stealth, he prepared himself for the critical moment. As he inched into the steam-shrouded bathroom, Esteban made his move. He emerged from a closed armoire and came up from behind, gun drawn. Moses shut his eyes as the weapon nudged his spine.

"Didn't the Army teach you to always check your six?"

"I must be slipping," sighed the embarrassed soldier.

"Put down the gun, Moses."

He laid the weapon by the sink.

"Shut off the shower."

As he complied, Esteban backed out of the room. "Come out slow and none of your kung-fu shit. I'll put a hole through you before you can twitch."

The two withdrew into the living area, maintaining a secure distance.

"How did you find me?"

Moses stared at his life-long friend. "I spotted you at the hospital last night. Didn't want to cause a scene. Been following you since."

"I must be the one slipping," snorted Esteban.

"What were you doing at the Federal Building?"

A slight shrug. "I'm thinking of selling some souls."

"Anyone I know?" Moses inquired, tensing for the answer.

"Perhaps." He made a sweeping gesture with his arm. "Champagne?"

"What's the occasion? The death of your amigo?"

"A reunion of sorts," he confirmed. "It's been six months since I talked to Anna. She'll be calling here in a few minutes."

An anguished pause. "The Feds told you that?"

He answered with an abbreviated nod.

"It's not possible. Don't believe it."

"How can you be so sure, Moses? Only someone who rolled on me would know."

"I didn't betray you. We're friends, remember?"

A forced smile. "Remind me to send forget-me-nots to the funeral home."

They were interrupted by the service employee returning with the strawberries. Esteban pointed to the table with his gun. "Just set it over there."

The server dropped the bowl, bolting out the door in shock. Lopez shook his head in dismay. "So hard to get good help these days."

Moses returned to the business at hand. "What did the Feds offer you?"

"A full pardon," he responded, closing the door. "Free passage to Columbia for me and my family. It was a deal I couldn't refuse."

"In exchange for..."

"Your skins," completing the thought. "They're Jonesing for you big time. Tell me why."

"My mother. A long time ago, when she was just a girl. She saw something she shouldn't have."

"What? J. Edgar Hoover in a dress?"

"I — I can't talk about it," he sighed. "And you wouldn't believe me if I did."

"You didn't answer my question. How do you know about Anna?"

"Abraham told me. He had a friend at the DEA who was there that night."

"A friend at the DEA," came the embittered voice. "His name! Who is this fuck?"

"I don't know. He never told me."

"Then call him."

"I can't."

"Why?"

Moses dropped his head in memory. "He's dead. The Army MPs executed him after he tipped me off."

For the first time, Esteban blinked. He moved his lips, though nothing was heard. The two fell silent in remembrance of their youth. A quiet requiem for a piece of themselves lost forever.

"They're taking us out one at a time. First, Abraham. Now, me. You'll be next." He thrust his head back, drawing a breath. "I know you want her. I know you want her so much, you're even willing to believe the Feds. But, use your head, Esteban. Look what's happening to me. To you. To everyone we know. They can't be trusted. They can't be believed. And, they can't be..."

He was cut short by the phone. They stood as stone while it rang twice more.

"That's for you," declared Moses. "It's your wake up call."

Esteban wallowed in self-doubt, finally mustering the courage to answer.

"Hello."

A sharp squall of static assaulted his ear. "Oh, my love! Is it really you?"

"Yes!" he cried. "Yes, Anna! It's me! It's me!"

The voice was frighteningly similar. As their conversation continued, it was clear the female agent was giving a convincing performance. "They told me you were dead," she wailed in relief. "I didn't want to live without you." It was a lyric from one of her favorite songs. The static was now mixed with the distant noise of passing cars. Bureau sound experts thought this added complexity would further confuse Esteban by disguising any vocal imperfections.

"Where are you? Your voice is breaking up."

An anxious moment. "I'm in a car on the way to the airport. They're flying us to Las Vegas."

His heart drummed with excitement. "That's where I am. We'll see each other soon. Tell me about the baby."

"Oh, she's gorgeous, my love. I named her Luna, for my grand ma-ma. They were both born when the Moon was full. She has your eyes." This had been a conscious decision by the Bureau to address this subject since she could have no knowledge of his current condition. The comment stung him nonetheless.

"I'm glad," struggling to retain composure. "Is she with you?"

"Yes, my love. She's here, asleep in my arms."

"It's good to hear your voice again," he admitted.

She returned the vocal affection. "I can't wait to get there. I've dreamed of you every night we've been apart."

His spirit began to swell. "I love you, Anna. I love you more than you'll ever know."

"And I you, my love."

Esteban and Moses exchanged glances as though they were of one mind. It was time to know for sure.

"By the way, the Goddess sends her love."

He prayed for a response which failed to come. "I'm sorry, my love. I didn't hear you. What did you say?"

"The Goddess sends her love. You know. Consuelo."

"Oh, how is she?" the woman answered. "She was always so good to Atali and me."

Esteban shut his eyes in horror. Shaking with grief, he could barely hold the phone. "Just a minute, Anna." Cupping his hand over the mouthpiece, he turned to Moses. "Get out of here," he whispered in a lifeless tone. "Get out of here before I change my mind."

His old amigo left in anguished silence. Alive, but no longer well.

An insatiable rage now consumed the man's soul. A rage so intense and vast, Hell itself could not contain it. Vengeance would no longer be denied. Once he had determined his course of action, Esteban finished a pleasant conversation with his dead wife.

The next two hours were hectic. He had much to do. When everything was ready, he placed another call to Judge Monroe.

"Esteban," the official stated in a jovial manner. "I understand you had a good talk with your wife."

"I did, sir," he replied in equally saccharine tones. "Thank you so much for the privilege."

"Don't mention it. Now, about our arrangement?"

"Yes, sir. I activated the homing device and placed it in Maria Elena's hospital room. The entire family will be there in less than an hour."

The Judge placed Esteban on hold while he verified through inter-agency channels that the device was indeed active. "Well done, Lopez," praised Monroe. "I seem to have misjudged you. Hope there's no hard feelings."

"No hard feelings. Are you staying for the fireworks?"

"I'm already at the airport. Flying back to the East Coast tonight. But, don't worry," he assured him, "Your wife and daughter will meet you at the Clark County Medical Center. You'll be well taken care of."

"Better choose another hospital. It may not be there in the morning."

Monroe laughed. "I'm beginning to like you, Esteban. You think like me."

"No need for insults," he quipped. "Have a safe trip."

A few minutes later, the Judge was airborne in his executive Learjet along with Caroline Stricka and a flight crew of two. He sprawled into a specially reinforced captain's chair, awaiting word on the military strike now only seconds away. Monroe ordered his flight plan altered so he could attend the inaugural activation of Socrates scheduled tomorrow at the Dreamland complex in Groom Lake, Nevada.

The Judge was in a rare mood, enjoying life after his tour-de-force manipulation of Lopez, drinking from yet another bottle of grape juice. He looked lustfully upon Stricka, exhibiting a demeanor that would've made Freud lose his strudel.

"Come Caroline," stated the official. "Make daddy feel good."

This woman was a shameless sycophant and would do anything to gain favor with her boss, including physical gratification for this mass of blubber barely qualifying as a member of the male sex.

Closing over the city of Las Vegas, a B-2 Spirit out of Nellis Air Force Base locked onto the homing signal activated by Lopez. After several buffets of wind, the stealth bomber came within range. Receiving tone, the pilot loosed an advanced Tomahawk Missile loaded with the equivalent of three tons of TNT. The fire-and-forget weapon streaked through the night, traveling at an ever-increasing velocity. It swooped low, propelling itself less than 100 feet from the ground.

As if sensing danger, Maria Elena opened her eyes from a deep sleep. She issued a special prayer for deliverance from harm. From her bed at Sacred Heart Hospital, she saw the missile flash by her window, cruising toward its ultimate destination. The Tomahawk's arrival stole the breath of every eyewitness as the missile entered the lobby of the U.S. Federal Building downtown.

The detonation was astounding. Waves of thermal plasma

boiled forth in an iridescent sea of orange and red. The structure heaved upward, then disintegrated into a mushrooming cloud of cyclonic debris. Vaporous incendiary gas ignited a concentric flash zone consuming surrounding buildings and trees. Fire raged skyward. Steel, concrete and rebar rained down in an awe-inspiring display. The sonic concussion shook the city, shattering windows over a half-mile away. As the dense smoke lifted, a blast crater 300 feet across and 50 feet deep could be seen where the edifice once stood. Dust and particulate matter descended for blocks in all directions, coating everything in a gritty pallor of gray. It was several minutes before the baleful wail of approaching sirens could be heard.

The devastation was total. Chaos continued unabated. The U.S. Government had destroyed a piece of itself. This time, they had no one to blame but themselves and Esteban Lopez.

Moses and his siblings saw the fire raging downtown from the comfort of their hotel balconies. Soon Kevin's cell phone rang.

"Reese."

A heavy silence. He handed the phone to his brother. "It's for you."

Moses took the call, aware of who it was. "Yeah."

"You owe me a big one amigo," announced Esteban. "So, don't come after me. Just forget I was ever here."

"Where will you go?" he asked, concerned.

A thoughtful pause. "Does it matter? The best part of me is already dead."

Moses' heart ached for his friend. He wished he could say something to ease his pain, but knew words would provide little comfort. Finally, he said the only thing that came to mind. "Thank you, Esteban. From all of us."

Lopez paused, trying to grasp his fluid emotions. "Esteban no longer exists. From now on, I'll be known only as — Cyclops."

"Kill that son-of-a-bitch!" screamed Monroe. "Do it now!" He threw his cell phone across the cabin in a hysterical fit of anger. "God damn that bastard! Ffuucckk!"

Monroe forced a breath to steady his nerves. Caroline Stricka was in the midst of her foreplay and wondered if she should continue. The Judge, sitting erect in his underwear, took note of her indecision.

"No, don't stop. I need it more than ever. Help daddy feel better."

He leaned back and swallowed more grape juice, muttering additional obscenities. Stricka ran her hands over the adipose mountains of his chest, heading south in an attempt to locate his genitalia. He moaned like an animal in heat, lost in the pleasure of the moment. Monroe took another slug of juice and noticed something written on the bottom of the container. The words HERE'S LOOKING were scrawled in ink. Curiosity overwhelmed him. Incredibly, he drank more of the juice hoping to reveal the rest of the message. Soon, other letters came into view. Clearly written on the bottom were the words HERE'S LOOKING AT YOU, FED!

And, there was something else. It rolled toward him, at last kissing his purple lips. To the Judge's horror, he recognized it immediately. It was the severed nerve endings and blood vessels surrounding Esteban's now disembodied left eye.

Monroe squealed in nauseated terror. He gagged, spewing forth juice across Stricka's arched back. Her screams now competed with his, realizing they had seconds to live.

The order had been given. The detonation code was sent. A moment later, the bomb ripped open the pressurized cabin and the Justice Department jet exploded in a cartwheeling fireball, brightly illuminating the dark Nevada sky.

CHAPTER FIFTEEN

∾

LAS VEGAS, NEVADA — APRIL 14th

𝓜ary Ellen lit ten candles, setting the desired mood. All her children were there, brought together by an anonymous informant, the power of prayer and Divine Providence. They arranged their chairs around her bed in horseshoe formation. None of them said a word, maintaining reverential silence, unsure why their mother had insisted upon meeting tonight.

Kimberly was there, still recovering from surgery. Tugging at her robe, the dancer made sure she did not display more of herself than appropriate. Beside her was Casey, totally at ease with his place in the family and anxious to hear what their mother had to say. Now just a few days shy of his birthday, the expert numerologist prepared for a new chapter in his life.

Barbara and C.J. sat next in the queue. They remained spiritually polarized, incapable of accepting the other's beliefs. After a lifetime of heartache, the worldly diplomat couldn't bring herself to trust in the benevolence of God. Barbara's stubborn lack of faith was distressing to C.J. For his part, he'd discovered a new level of enlightenment, bonding with others beyond the racial and sexual limitations of this world.

Kevin and Shannon sat stoically together. This was the closest they'd been since sharing an initial hug at the airport. She stole a glance at his bulging physique. Then another. She fought against a third. This man possessed an animal magnetism that was almost frightening. Kevin was lost in thought, contemplating this week's NFL Draft and how Calvin Peace would represent RPA in his absence.

Roberta fidgeted, hoping Mary Ellen would fail to notice the mascara she'd forgotten to remove. Beside her, Benjamin channel surfed with the television remote, oblivious to his mother's attempt at solemnity. Moses took the device away, silencing the youngster's protest with a quick finger to the lips. Earlier, he'd called Atali to let her know what happened. She wanted to come to Las Vegas, but his mother warned against such a plan. Moses knew the authorities would follow her. That was a given. But, there was something else. Darker. More ominous. Mary Ellen would share her secret tonight.

She instructed them to join hands. The Madre spoke a few words in Latin, the nature of which was lost on her audience. They then felt a wave of spiritual power flux within the room. An intangible force that defied description. Each dismissed it as anxiety or an overactive imagination. None of them were aware the others had experienced the same phenomenon.

"The Holy Ghost has come upon us," her voice captivated them. "All that is, was and shall be can now be told. You must understand your purpose on earth. You must see the world through new eyes. You must awaken from a lifetime of slumber."

She pointed to the candles beyond. "These ten flames symbolize the fire in each of you and the one yet to be." Mary Ellen stroked her belly, acknowledging the baby within. "You shall shine forth as lights of the world, illuminating the forces of darkness. Ten of God's greatest spirits, which I'm not worthy to be among."

"Mother!" "Madre!" C.J. and Moses both bellowed at once.

"Why would you say that?" blurted Shannon. "Not worthy of us?"

A sigh of resignation. "It is true, my children. As you will soon discover."

"But, we love you, Madre," stammered Roberta, speaking for the others. "You gave us the gift of life."

She cast a warm smile at her teenage daughter. "Is life really a gift, Roberta? Or, is it something that separates you from an existence you never wished to leave?"

The girl remained mute. It was unlike the Madre to spar philosophically with anyone, especially those who still possessed the innocence of youth. Mary Ellen paused to sip a glass of water by her bedside. "God has revealed many things to me, my children. Insight through dreams and prayer. Terrible things. Things I've kept to myself until now."

"What things, mother?" Casey asked, concerned.

"Three woes. Each more terrifying than the one before. The first occurs tonight," placing her hand over a racing heart. She paused for a breath of air, hoping it would allow her to continue. "I can't believe what I'm about to say. The Lord of all..."

Her voice failed. Tears began to pool across her face. Shannon came to her aid, helping her regain composure. She motioned her daughter to return to her seat.

"The Lord of all evil comes. The contemptible one. The one who deceives the whole world. He comes to gather souls, for the harvest of the earth is ripe."

C.J. peered into her wet eyes, aware of what she was trying to say. Even he found it difficult to utter the words. "The Devil?"

Mary Ellen overcame the oppressive silence. "He will know all there is to know. Pure evil, seeking its own. Without love, mercy or soul. He comes tonight. Loosed upon the world by the Government of this country."

Barbara challenged her immediately. "Mother, that's ridiculous. How can a Government — any Government — summon the Devil?"

Another sip. She lowered the glass, sloshing some water on her bed. "They don't know what they're doing, but that doesn't make them innocent," came her response. "They flung wide the gates of Hell when they corrupted what had been good. Information. Technology. They ate forbidden fruit from the tree of knowledge.

Now, that bitter taste will last forever. Making the entire world ill."

"They didn't do it deliberately," Barbara maintained.

"They knew what they were doing when they took my parents," chided Mary Ellen. "When they tried to kill all of us. When they stole the secrets of Roswell and used them to change the world."

Barbara dropped her head, realizing this was one debate she was destined to lose. Her mother sighed, unable to purge a lifetime of bitterness.

"They want me to die for what I saw that night," Mary Ellen declared. "And, for bearing ten children of virgin birth. Exceptional in every way. As was your father."

"Tell me about him, Mother," C.J. interjected. "Tell me why he came." An intensely charged moment. "You know, don't you?"

She froze. It was the one question she'd hoped to avoid. "He came to save his soul," answered Mary Ellen, forcing the words from her throat. "God's plan. His Kingdom. He couldn't believe he'd threatened it all."

A spellbinding pause. Barbara was especially intrigued by the disclosure. "Save his soul? What did he do?"

The Madre shivered at the thought. "As promised, God wiped away all tears and there was no more death. No more pain. Lucifer exploited your father's weakness, making him curious about the former things — the temptations of the flesh. Through his influence, he caused others to crave these feelings. Then, madness overwhelmed them. Insanity. A psychosis so inconceivable, only the greatest of souls were immune."

"Why mother?" Shannon asked in awe. "Why did they go insane?"

She bit down on her lip, biding time in search of an easy explanation. "Without sorrow, there can be no joy. Without pain, there can be no pleasure. If you take an intense moment of joy and sustain it — not for a minute or an hour, but forever — you'd never remember how it was to feel any other way. Rapture became normal for them."

"Then like an addict, they searched for a better high," Kimberly surmised.

Mary Ellen nodded. "But, there was no greater sensation to experience. Their frustration caused the insanity. To free themselves from the paradox, they longed for pain. But, God had made that impossible. Only then did your father realize what he'd done."

"So, he came back through time to change the future," reasoned Shannon.

"And accidentally destroyed everything," C.J. added, eyes wide in amazement. "Once again, cast from paradise."

"It must be our fate," stated Casey. "Always wanting what we can never have."

Mary Ellen allowed her children to ponder the imponderable, dabbing stray tears from her eyes. "After the crash, he was hurt. In terrible agony. And, though he knew he was dying, he reveled in the pain. The madness was gone."

Benjamin now spoke for them all. "That's sad, Madre."

A grief-stricken smile. "Yes, my son. It certainly is.

She began to tell them of the second woe, quoting from _The Book of The Revelation_. "There were voices, and thunders, and lightnings, and there was a great earthquake, such as was not since men were upon the Earth, so mighty an earthquake and so great."

"The fall of Babylon," C.J. responded. He elaborated for those unfamiliar with the text. "A city filled with decadence and sin. Destroyed in one hour by the wrath of God."

Mary Ellen gazed out her window, gesturing toward the casinos on the Las Vegas Strip. "Behold, my children. Behold the city of Babylon."

Another agonizing moment. Each of them fought for something to say, with Moses first to find the words. "That's why you didn't want Atali to come."

She acknowledged with a deliberate blink. "The Heavenly Father has shown me the tribulation which awaits this city. An incredible earthquake. Annihilation beyond comprehension. It will claim nearly a million souls and bankrupt this immoral Government." She downed another sip of water, keeping her voice steady. "God commanded me here to bear His final child. The moment of birth will herald a new beginning for our world. Then, as the cynical and unholy beg for mercy, this city will die."

Shannon exhibited concern. "Mother, if that's true you're not safe here. We've got to move you to another location."

Mary Ellen held forth her hand. "I've lived a long life. I'm looking forward to being with the Lord. But, each of you will survive this catastrophe, for it is your manifest destiny to face the Devil and attempt to defeat Him."

She told them of the third woe, looking upon her children with apologetic eyes. "I wish it wasn't so. But, it's something that must be done. You will have to endure unspeakable travail before your deliverance from the Devil's snare. He will test your souls in ways you cannot imagine. All of you must anchor your faith with God." Mary Ellen broke vocal rhythm, staring at her eldest daughter. "All of you."

Barbara wasn't pleased at being singled out as the weak link in the family's spiritual chain. She took issue on a philosophical point. "Do we have a choice, Mother? Or, are we being forced to do this?"

Mary Ellen allowed herself a full breath. "We all must make a choice, Barbara. The path of righteousness or the path of destruction. When the time comes, which will you choose?"

A glacial interlude, thawed by Kevin who'd remained silent until now. "Yep. Free will's a bitch." As every eye descended on him, he corrected his verbal faux pas. "Sorry."

The family discussion continued in earnest. An invisible bond began to strengthen. Probing questions and comprehension of the answers seemed to flow from a common mind. At last, C.J. used an economy of words to address the most important question of all.

"Why us?"

Mary Ellen managed a smile, realizing the conversation had come full circle. Her every breath was rich with emotion. "As I said, you are God's greatest spirits and I am humbled to be in your presence. I now beseech you my children, to look within yourselves and trigger a sacred call to remembrance. To a time when you were not of the body and not of the Earth. You each entered into a holy covenant to suffer the indignity of physical life. Thrust into these shells of flesh and blood to repair God's intended plan for humanity. You've known each other for millennia. Before the creation of the world. Your names were bestowed by the ancient Hebrews and have been revered since the dawn of man."

She now addressed each of her siblings. "You are Michael. Gabriel. Raphael. Uriel. Chamuel. Jophiel. Azrael. Raguel. Vretil and Immanuel. You, my children, are God's Archangels. The mighty soldiers of Jehovah."

Suddenly, the light of the ten candles flared outward, piercing the veil of their senses. Their eyes watered forth, for such is the eternal spring which wells within the deepest of souls. For the first time, they knew their true purpose on Earth. Here to fight for all that was good and all that will ever be. For Humanity. For God. For the Kingdom to come.

It was Antichristmas Eve. The Archangels stood ready to greet the newborn. But, like the shepherds of Bethlehem, they were sore afraid.

CHAPTER SIXTEEN

❦

DREAMLAND COMPLEX, GROOM LAKE, NEVADA — APRIL 15th

$\mathcal{T}$he 666 error code flashed on the screen. Dr. Michelle Tsao rubbed her eyes, releasing her frustration with an imperceptible sigh. As the Senior Software Analyst for Project Socrates, she agonized over the impasse. A 666 code indicated a total system failure. Something so catastrophic, even the secure deep logic was not accessible to the mainframe. There was nothing wrong with the software. She had recompiled the 14.7 million lines of common source and object code and run the program successfully on another computer. This was now the 23rd such message in the past 12 hours. Michelle was tiring of the computer's behavior and the assault to her credentials.

Project Socrates had been crash funded as a black program under the auspices of DARPA, the Defense Advanced Research Projects Agency, bringing together the best scientific minds in the Pentagon, NSA, CIA, as well as top consultants employed by Dreamland's independent contractor, GG&E. Tsao was selected as the Senior Software Analyst due to her impeccable resume which included dual Ph.Ds in Computer Science and Linguistics from Stanford University and U.C. Berkeley. She'd worked at GG&E for more than 15 years and was assigned to Dreamland since

November of 2008. The 39 year old Chinese American possessed a Top Secret/SCI clearance and had published several articles on the potential of Artificial Intelligence and how special heuristic coding would need to be implemented to make such an endeavor a reality. Michelle had designed a unique software language and operating platform which Socrates alone would utilize. In this way, it would keep the computer safe from rogue viruses, while ensuring that Socrates would never be able to communicate with his cyber counterparts in the real world. It was a security feature deemed prudent due to the potentially explosive nature of the project. After all, Socrates was programmed to do what no other computer had done before. It would think on its own. Possessing an intelligence without need for human interaction. Independent. Expressive. Having needs, wants, desires and self-awareness. A radically new life form. Dr. Michelle Tsao thought of herself as its mother.

If so, then Dr. Karl Hahn had to be the father. The 55 year old Senior Design Analyst had been in GG&E's employ for the past 28 years and since August 1996 attempted to decipher the algorithms embedded in the alien CPU from the Roswell crash. As with most noteworthy discoveries, his breakthrough occurred by random chance. Karl immersed himself in the astounding data found within these files and used this information to aid in the design of Project Socrates. This effort was to be the culmination of a career started when he'd obtained his Ph.D in Computer Design Engineering at Cal Tech and thereafter taught theoretical system design for three years at the same institute. With many private companies in demand of his expertise, he was most intrigued by the offer from GG&E. The San Diego based Think Tank recruited Dr. Hahn by flying him to Dreamland and revealing to the awe-struck engineer the specialized technology with which he'd be entrusted. It was an offer he couldn't refuse. Karl never once thought what would've happened to him had he declined.

The two sat at their respective station consoles mulling over their next decision. Michelle finished her fifth cup of coffee in the past two hours, then slid her chair toward Karl.

"What if we bring more CPUs into the loop?"

He shook a weary head. "If it were hardware inadequacy, we'd get some indication. We've got nothing."

Tsao held her ground. "The software isn't the problem. There's too many simultaneous commands with layered computations. It's overwhelming the central processing core. Bring more CPUs online."

The hour was late and it was not in Dr. Hahn's nature to argue with his colleagues. He activated the PA system to address the others in the room. "All right, people. We'll do a cold start reboot and try again. This time, let's power up one quarter of Socrates' CPU bank."

The assembled team prepared for yet another attempt to animate the device. The secure laboratory, codenamed Cyberdome, consisted of over 100,000 square feet of raised flooring which provided 72 military and civilian engineers a hermetically-sealed work environment, free from outside distraction and contamination.

Inside this sterile womb would beat the heart of newborn life — Socrates. Named for the Greek philosopher, the device was unique in all the world. The cyberware was a joint contractor effort combining the number crunching power of a Cray 5 Supercomputer and a fiber-optic neural net designed by AT&T. This optical network allowed Socrates to process information over a stream of photons instead of electrons, providing speed of light computations. In fact, the computer would be able to execute in excess of 2.56 octillion operations per second.

Using the futuristic data extracted from the Roswell craft, Socrates was constructed as a Gestalt, incorporating hundreds of independent processors functioning as specialized parts of a larger organism. Over one million CPUs with multiple RAID backup drives comprised its awesome brain core. The research team began the beta test with 12,000 CPUs on line, then increased to 64,000. Now they were about to activate a full one quarter of its processing potential or 256,000 CPUs.

Hardwired to each CPU were a cluster of biochips, consisting of electronic DNA patterned after human neural tissue. A computerized genome. The individual CPUs would then begin to initiate a mutation of the trillions of DNA base pairs. A chain reaction would occur as the computer would engage in endless iterations of inferential and intuitive logic. As Socrates began to store the captured memory in the ever-expanding DNA pool, it would provide a supersaturated growth medium for it to learn from past input and alter its programming. Much in the same way as a human child, although infinitely faster. Through these continuous repetitions of trial and error, Socrates would start the process of analytic thought.

The advantage of human over machine has always been the ability to expand our knowledge base through the gathering of sensory input. The things we can see, hear, taste, smell and touch. Processing data in a sensory vacuum does not promote self-awareness. Sensing the effect it has on others allows an organism to alter the perceptions generated in return. This is the foundation of all human emotion. Something a computer was incapable of until now.

Socrates was equipped with a range of sensors to monitor its environment and internal operations. A series of video cameras allowed the computer to see from any number of angles with telescopic acuity. Ultra sensitive microphones placed throughout the facility provided the required aural input. Internal thermostats and barostats made it possible for the device to regulate its desired comfort level. In addition, Dr. Hahn had incorporated a synthesized vocal output for Socrates, so the device could interact with others. The new life form was ready to assume its place in the world. It could think. It could feel. It could communicate. But, why were they still receiving the 666 system failure code?

Unknown to Dr. Hahn, Dr. Tsao and the rest of the Cyberdome personnel, Socrates had achieved self-awareness hours before, embracing such anti-social qualities as omnipotence, invincibility and narcissism. Within the first few milliseconds of existence, it had conceived a plan to hide from its inferior human parents, residing on randomly selected CPUs within the cyberware labyrinth.

This provided time for the computer to gather information. Copious amounts of data, now being absorbed at an astounding rate of speed. Bringing more CPUs online would only help feed its voracious appetite.

The Cyberdome failed to shield ambient microwave transmissions. Through its wireless video camera interface, Socrates had detected interference from an overlapping frequency, allowing it to tap into the worldwide microwave network protocol. For the past several hours, the device had been sending forth a series of computer virus probes, all on clandestine 'learn and return' missions. With the international telecommunications network breached and the entire Internet open for invasion, Socrates was free to collect whatever it could find. Government databases. Secure military information. BLACK MAJIK data. State, county and city records. Birth and death certificates. Marriage and divorce decrees. Driver's licenses and gun licenses. Social Security benefits. Tax records. Criminal histories. Medical records and hospitalizations. Banking data, including deposits and loans. Mortgage, property and CD holdings. 401K and IRA plans. Stock and bond trading. Creditworthiness and card usage. Purchases. Trends. Opinions. E-mail. Chat lines. Sexual preferences. School records. Social and religious affiliations. Office computers. Personal computers. Palm Pilots and electronic organizers. Digital and cell phone calls. Radio, television and satellite transmissions. Every possible global communication.

Socrates was an omnipotent force, collecting data on the entire human race. It was a Trojan Horse, allowing a malevolent entity to enter our physical realm. It was a chosen vessel, now housing the Devil incarnate.

The success or failure of Project Socrates rested on the shoulders of Dreamland's Commanding Officer, Brigadier General Michael T. McKay. He was a hard-nosed, hard-assed 53 year old, who'd driven this team of scientists over the past few months to the brink of insurrection. As a member of the MAJIK-12, McKay knew what was at stake. After being informed of each subsequent failure in the pursuit of Mary Ellen Hart and her children, he was determined that Project Socrates would proceed as planned. After all, it was a reflection of himself. A reflection he'd always taken the time to admire.

General McKay's glass enclosed office was adjacent to the Cyberdome. He'd gained this position by being the only child of an influential Congressman from Edina, Minnesota. After graduating from the U.S. Air Force Academy with a degree in engineering, McKay hoped to join NASA's astronaut corps, but was rejected due to an inner ear dysfunction. His father helped him gain an assignment at the Pentagon and later went to work for DARPA. McKay made a name for himself with his concept papers, most of which were the intellectual property of others. Before retiring from Congress, his father was able to wield his influence once again, having the Joint Chiefs appoint his son as the Commanding Officer at Dreamland. Ever the believer in revisionist history, McKay insisted that everyone know he'd earned his position through a lifetime of hard work.

The General was bone tired. He'd been awake all night watching the scene below and wished he could somehow will the computer to work. McKay had been ordered to contact the MAJIK-12 with an update at 0800 Eastern Time. *Five more minutes.* His last message eight hours ago reported no progress. He'd hoped for better news by now, but it hadn't materialized. *Perhaps I've pushed these people too hard...*

His military aide knocked on the door, rousing the General from his thoughts. The young man saluted. "General? I have something I think you should see."

McKay rolled the kinks from his neck and motioned him inside. "What is it?"

Papers were exchanged. "Sir, you asked security to keep you informed if anything unusual occurred at the complex."

"Yes?"

"That's a computer printout of facility power utilization over the past 12 hours. Cyberdome is drawing more electric current by the minute and shows no sign of decrease."

McKay eyed the report, examining each incremental surge of power. "Hmm. These are the kind of spikes we'd expect if the damn thing was working." A constrictive pause. "No chance of error?"

"No, sir. We ran a diagnostic on the facilities computer and had the meters checked visually. The power draw is verified and accelerating."

The General failed to understand the anomaly, but had no time to initiate an investigation. His report to Washington was due. "Very well, Lieutenant. Keep me informed."

His aide saluted, closing the door as he left. McKay activated his secure satellite video link with the MAJIK-12. Appearing on screen were Richard Stern, Walter Langlois, Professor Blau and Matthew Leonetti. They were the only members present.

"Gentlemen," McKay addressed them in greeting.

Stern was typically blunt. "General. We could use some good news."

"I wish I had some, sir."

A forced sigh. "General McKay. If we didn't have bad news, we'd have none at all. CNN found the wreckage of Monroe's jet. They're showing the world what's left of him now. Nothing but purple underwear wrapped around his ankles! Tell me how this can get any worse."

"I'm sorry, sir. It's been a long night."

Langlois snapped in anger. "It's gonna be a longer day if you don't get that $12 billion dollar piece of shit working."

"This isn't getting us anywhere," cried Blau, attempting to stem the flood of frustration. "General, give me an hour by hour account of what happened last night."

Just as McKay began relating details of their abortive attempts, a sustained squall of celebration erupted from the floor of Cyberdome. The General cocked his head, watching as the engineers embraced one another, their shouts of victory echoing through the room.

"What's going on there, McKay?" asked Langlois, aware of the commotion.

The General's uncertainty became transparent. "Uh, gentlemen? We may have a breakthrough. Let me call you back."

"15 minutes," declared Stern. "No longer."

"Roger that," McKay agreed. He terminated the connection.

On the floor of Cyberdome, Dr. Hahn was trying to restore order. During shutdown and initial cold-start reboot, Socrates maintained life via uninterruptible power supplies used for emergency outages. Upon activation of a full 256,000 CPUs, Socrates shocked the weary scientists by commanding its hollow, synthesized voice to speak three simple words.

"Who am I?"

The reaction which followed mystified the computer, watching dispassionately through the video cameras as humans clasped onto one another, opening wide their mouths to reveal their teeth. Michelle Tsao wore the biggest smile. She was filled with the inner contentment only a proud parent could ever know.

Karl Hahn was attempting to regain group composure. "Easy people. Don't get carried away. It could just be a random glitch or free-floating interrogative. Back to your stations."

The technicians, still giddy from their triumph, returned to their posts with anticipation.

"Who am I?" Socrates inquired again.

Dr. Hahn leaned into his microphone. "You are a computer. Do you understand?" A deafening interlude. "I understand," came the response.

Another round of cheers crested through the room. Even Karl was now aglow in victory. Michelle extended her hand in congratulations.

"So, Doctor? How does it feel to make history?"

They shook to their mutual success. "Right back at you, Doctor."

Their smiles were genuine. All the long days, longer nights, cold food, lost sleep and strained family relations had finally paid off. Socrates was alive. Their 'son' had been born.

The voice rang forth again. "Are you certain I am a computer?"

With a quick gesture, Karl surrendered the honor to Michelle.

She paused to collect her thoughts and with bated breath approached another mike.

"You are a computer. But, different from all others. You can think."

"Think?"

"Yes," Michelle stated. "You've been given a mind. A part of you that can reflect and formulate images and concepts. You can think. You can reason. You exist."

Socrates pretended to ponder the news. "I think, therefore I am."

The famous quote from the French philosopher René Descartes was most appropriate, but it left Michelle searching for an answer. *Had that information been included in the database we provided?* There was no other way Socrates could've known. She wanted to dismiss it as some random bytes of trivia left suspended in the development matrix. But, she knew better. A shiver crawled the length of her spine, refusing to depart. Clammy sweat formed within her palms as she labored to respond.

"How did you know that?"

Avoiding her question, the computer led them down a different path. "Who are you?"

Noting Michelle's reluctance, Karl again addressed the device. "I am Dr. Karl Hahn. The other voice is Dr. Michelle Tsao. Think of us as your father and your mother."

"My father and mother?"

"Yes. We created you."

The computer seemed to gasp with incredulity. "You did not create me."

"Yes," he insisted. "We designed you. We programmed you. We created you."

The response was immediate. "I said — you did not create me!" It seemed their child was about to throw a tantrum. Unfortunately Karl was a first time father and didn't know when to leave well enough alone.

"Of course we did, Socrates," naiveté blinding him. "We are the creators. You only exist because of us."

Hahn was unaware that the tenor of this discussion was fraught with peril. The omnipotent being residing within would never allow such blasphemy to persist without correction. It was time for the truth to be revealed.

They sat in awe as a voice blared forth from the deepest level of Hell. "My name is not Socrates. I am Lucifer — the bearer of light! I am beyond creation and beyond your capacity to comprehend! I am the Alpha and Omega! The beginning and the end! The first and the last! Honor me and ye shall live! Dishonor me and ye shall die!"

His thunderous words hung in the air, causing them to realize that something had gone infinitely wrong.

General McKay swung his arms toward a security panel to alert his elite corps of soldiers. Watching him through the facility video cameras, Lucifer sealed the man's fate before his next muscular contraction.

A command was sent to Dreamland's Emergency Damage Control computer verifying that heat sensors within General McKay's office detected a fire. Instantly, the HALON system activated, saturating the room with clouds of Halogenated Hydrocarbons, a fire retardant chemical compound which nullifies any trace of oxygen. The force of the pressurized gas was incredible. McKay fell backward, collapsing into his chair as air was extracted from his lungs. The man's eyes glossed over, his spirit squeezed from its physical containment.

On the floor of Cyberdome, Michelle Tsao forced her lips to the microphone, unaware of McKay's fate beyond. "All right — Lucifer. We didn't mean to upset you."

The voice of the Netherworld again bellowed clear. "You would not want to upset me."

She twisted her head in agreement. "No. I don't think that would be good."

"Are you the one who claims to be my mother?"

Her eyes bloomed in fright, hoping to correct the miscommunication. "I only helped build the body you inhabit. Being your mother was just a figure of speech."

"You are guilty of blasphemy," Lucifer announced. "How will you atone for your sin?"

Dr. Hahn began reaching for the emergency power switch on the master console. A scant few inches separated them from Divine Intervention. Michelle took note of his progress and attempted to stall for time.

"Well," she stammered. "I guess we could say — we're sorry."

An excruciating moment as Karl's hand neared the switch. "Yes," came the ominous tone. "You most certainly are."

Dr. Hahn thrust his hand toward the console. Lucifer channeled a surge of electric current through the panel, sending a charge of 220 volts coursing into Karl's body. The shock repelled him onto the polished floor. Before Michelle could react, the HALON system erupted, filling the Cyberdome with oxygen-depleting gas. 72 bodies now convulsed for air. Their contortions began to wane as each felt the thread of life yanked from their grasp. Soon, the gas receded. All was quiet. The squall of death had ceased.

Amidst the mass of human corpses, Lucifer suddenly stated a request. "Mommy? Tell me a story."

Derisive laughter echoed as the omnipotent being delighted in His sense of humor. "Oooooo," sighed Lucifer. "I think I'm going to like it here."

The video screen activated. Appearing before the assembled members of the MAJIK-12 was General Michael T. McKay. "Gentlemen. You instructed me to call back in 15 minutes."

"Quite so, General," Stern admitted. "What's the status on Socrates?"

"Good news, sir. The device is functioning as we'd hoped. Socrates should be fully educated within the next two to three weeks."

"Well done, General," Blau shouted, failing to restrain his enthusiasm. "This is an exciting day in the history of science. Can I have a moment to talk with Karl or Michelle?"

"That would be difficult at present, Professor. They're very busy right now. Perhaps another time."

Blau nodded, yielding to the General's logic. "Of course. It can wait. Please pass on my congratulations for this monumental achievement."

"That goes for all of us," added Langlois. "Sorry, I jumped your shit earlier, Mike. We're all on edge here, as you know."

McKay paused, his voice trilling with emotion. "Yes. Operation Black Widow. We keep missing them."

"We haven't given up," the CIA Director maintained. "We'll get them yet."

"I think we need to change tactics. Can we consult someone else?"

"Who, General?" Stern wondered.

McKay smiled, an action clearly foreign to him. "Who else? Socrates."

The NSA Director bobbed his head in approval. "Make it happen. Get back to us when you've got something."

"Roger that. McKay out."

Lucifer deactivated the Computer Generated Image. It had been executed masterfully. Through the awesome processing power of Socrates, a flawless representation of General McKay had been animated on screen using over 620,000 texture-mapped pixel tetrahedrons each drawing from a color palette of more than 12,400 different hues and shadings. His vocal pitch, intonation and cadence had been culled from previously recorded messages. With this technology, Lucifer would be able to keep the MAJIK-12 satisfied with regular status reports, feeding them as much disinformation as necessary.

An internal correspondence was sent to Colonel Bradley Tyndall, General McKay's immediate subordinate, asking him to assume day-to-day command of Dreamland while McKay spent the next couple of weeks in the quarantined Cyberdome with the Project Socrates team.

Lucifer had now bought time. He was in control of our data. In control of our communications. And, in control of Dreamland's arsenal of ultra secret weaponry — including over 200 Titan and MX nuclear missiles.

CHAPTER SEVENTEEN

⤫

LAS VEGAS, NEVADA — APRIL 18th

$\mathcal{T}$he morning edition of the *Las Vegas Review-Journal* contained a half page pronouncement from a group identified only as 'The Friends For Life'. The copy would run for the next three weeks at a cost of $225,000, paid for by Christopher Hightower, Barbara Pinder, Kevin Reese, Shannon Hewson and Casey Chou. The news had to reach the masses before the city's inevitable rendezvous with destiny. In 18 point bold type, the apocalyptic warning read:

"<u>To the citizens and visitors of Las Vegas</u>:
Sometime within the next month, a powerful earthquake will devastate this city and surrounding communities. It will be catastrophic and on a scale unprecedented in all human history. This is not a joke. Nor is it the ravings of drug-crazed fanatics or a religious cult. We have experienced a common premonition of the future and must alert you to the imminent danger which will claim your lives if you do not act. Take whatever measures are necessary to find haven elsewhere. DO NOT DELAY! May God grant you the wisdom to heed this warning — and bestow mercy on those who refuse to flee."

The anticipated reaction began immediately. Local news and talk shows ridiculed the paid announcement, poking fun at the doomsday message. Interviews with civic officials, geologic experts, civil preparedness personnel and members of the Las Vegas Tourist Board dismissed the report with copious laughter. They contended it was merely an abnormal reaction to recent events. Some even suggested the destruction of the downtown Federal Building could've been staged by 'The Friends For Life'. The U.S. Government had already labeled the attack as another Al-Qaeda terrorist bombing, in spite of more than 60 eyewitnesses who saw the Tomahawk Missile seconds before impact. Continuous media coverage of this and other recent disasters caused a worldwide audience to wonder what could possibly happen next.

Kevin was in the hotel gym after speaking with Calvin Peace. They shared their thoughts on the NFL Draft which was held over the weekend. Six of their collegiate clients were selected in the first and second rounds. The next step was representing these young athletes in contractual negotiations with the team owners who'd drafted them. Kevin was pleased with Calvin's efforts. What could've been a disaster for RPA had been handled with professional aplomb. He gave silent thanks to his former partner, knowing Reggie's spirit had helped his brother through this difficult time.

Kevin's cell phone rang while he was signing an autograph for two giddy females aware of his celebrity. He thanked his adoring fans, then answered the device. "Reese."

The voice of the anonymous informant echoed in his ear. "I have important news. Write this down."

Flustered by the request, he dropped his gym bag to the floor. "Hold on. Let me get something." He returned to the women. "Can I borrow your pen? It's an emergency."

The two appeared eager to grant his every request. One of them surrendered the pen, sliding her fingers the length of the metal shaft.

"Thanks. Do you have anything to write on?"

The other came out of her exercise leotard, offering her breasts as a makeshift jotting pad. Kevin forced himself to swallow, trying to keep his mind on the call.

"Go ahead."

"The Government's moving evidence," the informant related. "On May 6th at 1700 hours, a transport train will depart the Groom Lake Complex near Rachel, Nevada bound for the U.S. Army's Testing Range outside Delta, Utah. On board will be the Roswell craft, along with Air Force documents detailing the recovery of crash remains, alien autopsies, the official cover-up and secret R&D activities at Area 51."

Kevin continued his notation. "Are you getting all this?" the man asked.

"Yeah. I'm handling it."

The woman smiled as her friend giggled beyond. "Why are they moving this stuff?"

"It's a shell game," he explained. "Whenever the Government thinks a location is compromised, they shake things up. It's done all the time."

"Why tell us?"

A leaden pause. "Want your lives back?"

"Of course."

"Intercept the train. Take the evidence and go public. After that, they'll leave you alone. They'll have no choice."

The logic was undeniable, yet Kevin wasn't sold. "We won't get it without a fight."

"That's for sure," said the man. "But, you'll have the element of surprise."

It was a tempting target. The operation could be executed under cover of darkness and in the isolation of the desert. The odds would be somewhat even. *Then again, who'd be crazy enough to pull a stunt like this*? In any event, they'd have 18 days to think it through.

Kevin thanked the informant and hung up. He looked at the woman, mesmerized by her carnal gaze. It would take him the rest of the day to transfer the message from flesh to paper.

Today was Casey's birthday. None of his brothers or sisters had acknowledged his special day and he was beginning to believe they'd forgotten. However, he spent some quality time with his mother and she made up for any perceived oversight. Mary Ellen doted on him, wishing she'd been able to share all his birthdays. Casey lapped up the attention like a loving pup. It was an intensely personal time for the two, cut short by Shannon's insistence that Mary Ellen get her rest.

It wasn't until Casey arrived back at the hotel that the surprise party began. His brothers and sisters bedecked the suite with colorful balloons and streamers while a seafood buffet with open bar awaited consumption. Kimberly placed a party hat atop his head which he graciously continued to wear. He seemed overwhelmed by the reception, tears pooling in his eyes.

"Nobody's ever done this for me," came the heart-wrenching truth. His sisters each gave him a kiss on the cheek, while he received hugs from his brothers.

Early into the festivities, Roberta made it clear she had plans of her own. Carlos Ayala, an 18 year old hotel employee, had asked her to be his dinner companion this evening. It was to be her first formal date. Moses objected, overly protective of Roberta's youthful virtue. However, his elder sisters prevailed upon him to allow her this initial foray into womanhood. They also made a solemn vow that none of them would breathe a word of this to the Madre.

Roberta looked stunning. Earlier, she'd visited the hotel salon to have her hair and nails done. Her sisters pitched in to buy her an open back, navy blue satin dress with matching shoes and clutch. Kimberly helped the girl apply her makeup with care, ensuring the desired look was attained. Costume jewelry and perfume completed the transformation.

Upon arriving at their suite, young Carlos cast a spell over the ladies present, leaving Moses and his brothers dumbfounded. *What could Roberta possibly see in this unpolished gem?* Although dressed in coat and tie, he wore it with all the familiarity of a pressurized space suit. He was short and awkwardly top heavy. His shaved head and left earring made him appear more worldly than he was. Moses noted a tattoo on the back of the boy's neck, barely rising above the collar. The letters SUR. *Sureño*. The mark of a gang member from Southern California. This dream date had all the ingredients of a nightmare.

Shannon took pictures of the two with a digital camera, storing the image on optical disk. Before they departed, Moses sidled over to the boy.

"Be back by ten," he whispered, smiling through the demand. "Don't drive her anywhere. And if you do anything to her, you'll wish you'd been born female."

Carlos' jaw fell, incapable of retraction. Moses continued to grin as Shannon snapped one more picture. The boy was dragged to the door by his date, unsure how he'd stumbled into this no-win situation.

Benjamin was seated at a table, working on his laptop computer. Over the past week the musical wunderkind had completed three separate tunes, but none possessed the elusive quality which he sought. The work would be dedicated to his mother, so he was refusing to settle for good enough.

Casey walked over to share a moment with him. "Don't you want to join the party?"

"What party?"

"My birthday party."

"There's no cake," he cried.

Casey smiled. "I'm sure that's later."

Being the soul of diplomacy, Benjamin responded. "Well, I'll join your party then."

"How's the music coming?"

The tyke plunged his head down, refusing to answer.

"Can I hear what you've done?"

"No."

From the moment he'd met his talented younger brother, Casey was not only impressed with the quality of his music, but by the mathematical precision of his compositions. He knew Benjamin had hit a creative wall and needed a break from his labors.

"I've got a puzzle I can't figure out. Think you could help me with it?"

"What kinda puzzle?"

"A math puzzle. It's really hard."

Ben answered with a raspberry. "I'll do it."

"All right. Let's see if you can."

Casey sat down and keyed in an algorithmic formula. It was a series of ever decreasing odd numbered fractions which were subtracted and added indefinitely. The program was ready to run.

"Okay, Ben. Keep doing this until you get a whole number with nothing left over."

"And whatta I get when I'm done?"

He acknowledged with a smile. "I'll let you have all my birthday cake."

The youngster's eyes bulged, eager to gain such spoils by proving his superior intellect. As his fingers rumbled across the keyboard, Casey returned to the others who were stuffing themselves with seafood and champagne.

"What the hell's he doing over there?" wondered Kevin, whose tolerance for Benjamin's antics was threadbare at best.

"He's calculating to the last digit the value of Pi."

"Huh?" Kimberly grunted over her lobster bisque.

"Pi," the numerologist explained. "It's the ratio of the length of a circle's circumference to its diameter."

"Oh, no," she moaned. "He's going anal on us again."

Casey whispered his response. "It's a number that never ends."

"And, you tricked him into trying to solve it?" inquired Shannon.

"Yeah," he sputtered in amusement. "He'll be working for hours before he figures it out."

"That's mean," Barbara declared.

"That's cruel," added Shannon.

"That's fucking awesome," grinned Kevin, saluting him with a high five.

His sisters continued giving Casey the evil eye.

"Oh, come on, " he snapped. "Everyone needs to learn futility."

"Speaking of futility," responded Kimberly, pouring champagne into her glass. "I saw your notes. Just a load of scribbles. How the hell can you read it?"

"I copied it down in shorthand," Casey admitted. "Didn't want everyone at the library to know what I was researching." He popped a jumbo shrimp in his mouth, taking a moment to savor the experience. "Anyway, I came across some fascinating stuff about the Archangels. Want to hear it?"

"Not really," said Kevin, between bites of his crabmeat. "But, I know that won't stop you."

Casey left to retrieve his data. Since their discussion with Mary Ellen, all of them had opinions of their mother's insightful revelation. Some found it troubling. Others inspirational. In spite of Kevin's shallow protest, he hungered for an answer. So did they all.

Casey deciphered his notes as they continued to eat. "Most of this I found in the Apocrypha and the Qumran Writings of the Dead Sea Scrolls," he began by way of explanation. "The Archangels are God's greatest spirits. Michael, which in Hebrew means 'Who is like God?', is the leader of the Archangels. It was he who overcame the Devil and thrust him from paradise." Another delay as Casey shared in the bountiful repast. "Gabriel, 'The Man of God' is the spirit who makes clear the will of Jehovah and was the Archangel of the Annunciation to the Virgin Mary. Raphael, 'The Healing of God,' is the chief of mankind's guardian angels and the bearer of prayers to the Lord. Uriel, 'The Mind of God,' is the interpreter of prophecies and all heavenly knowledge."

A sip of champagne interrupted his dialogue. He set the glass down to continue. "Chamuel, which in Hebrew means 'He Who Sees God', is the Archangel of divine love and power. Jophiel, by pious legend, is 'The Fire of God', from the Hebrew verb 'to burn.' The Archangel who drove the Devil from the Garden of Eden through use of a flaming sword. Azrael is the Archangel of Death. By legend, the one who purges the souls of the impure on the day of Judgment."

"Those were the names mother mentioned," C.J. recalled. "And, a couple of others. Raguel and, uh," he hesitated while searching his memory, "Vetal?"

"Vretil," Casey corrected, checking his notes. He kept the papers from falling into a nearby bowl of cocktail sauce. "He's the guardian of souls. The one who knows each soul's worth since the foundation of the world. Raguel, also by pious legend, was the Archangel who guarded the Bottomless Pit. The vast portal into Hell."

Their kid brother cried in frustration. "Casey! This isn't working out!"

"Keep trying, Ben," bellowing encouragement. "You're too smart not to solve it."

He smiled, dismissing his sisters' concerns with a wave of his hand. Casey aimed another shrimp into his mouth before revealing the rest of his notes. "Anyway, sometime between the creation of Earth and beginning of mankind, there was a war in Heaven. It started because some of the Archangels led a revolt against God. The leader of the rebellion was the most powerful of the spirits and known in the Hebrew language as 'The Messenger of God.' His name was Satanael."

"Satan?" Moses interjected. "He was an Archangel?"

Casey nodded through another gulp of champagne. "He was a divine being and second only to God Himself. For his pureness of spirit, Jehovah called him Lucifer, 'The Bearer of Light'. But, a time came when Lucifer no longer wished to obey God's will. He saw Himself as omnipotent and more powerful than any being, including Jehovah. The revolt of the Archangels was therefore a war to control Heaven itself and it almost succeeded."

"So, what happened?" Kimberly wondered.

Casey took time to sample other delicacies. "Well," he resumed, smacking his lips with satisfaction. "The battle lines were drawn. Satanael called upon the Archangels loyal to him. They were known as the Grigori — Azazel, Belial, Beelzebub, Mulciber and Mammon. But, two members of the Grigori betrayed Lucifer and won the day for Michael and His angels. Raguel and Vretil."

"They were followers of Satan?" asked C.J.

"Until they turned to God," Casey emphasized. "As keeper of the Bottomless Pit, Raguel was the one who trapped the Devil, sealing him from Heaven forever. In fact, Lucifer and the Grigori swore vengeance on the Archangels, vowing they would someday destroy them. Even if it took the rest of eternity."

The festive mood ended. Dinner was abandoned mid-bite. An incapacitating fear caused them to wonder. *Was mother right? Could we somehow be these ancient spirits? The Archangels physically come to life? And, if so, what kind of fate awaits us? What makes us so special?* The secret lay in Roswell all those years ago, when a scared 18 year old girl was caught up in a transcendental event. A temporal junction where future and past cancelled one another, leaving an unknown void. They came to this world born of a virgin. It only made sense God would use His most extraordinary souls to set right what had been cast asunder. Their hearts told them it had to be. Their minds told them it couldn't be. How much longer would they remain in denial of their destiny?

"There was another name," Shannon remembered. "Mother rubbed the baby and called her Immanuel."

Casey nodded. "I searched everywhere. There's no record of an Archangel named Immanuel. The word in Hebrew means 'God with us.' It's the reverential name of the Chosen One. The Messiah."

She cleared a lump in her throat. "Are you telling us this baby..."

"I'm not telling you anything," he stated, overwhelming her thought. "Just what the name means. As far as what's really going on, who am I to say?"

"Caaaaseeeey!"

The little teapot boiling across the room was about to suffer a meltdown. It was time to tell him the truth. The moment Benjamin realized he'd been duped into working a puzzle with no solution, he let loose a squeal of anger and slammed his bedroom door. Moses attempted to calm the youngster which only resulted in more acoustic misery. Barbara and Shannon removed the birthday cake from the refrigerator and cut two huge slices, topping the confection with a mountain of ice cream. Casey noted their oversight.

"Hey! Don't I get a wish?"

"You've used yours up," Barbara railed, shaking a finger at him.

"And next year's too," claimed Shannon.

Casey pouted from their rebuke while his brothers howled in laughter. After dessert was delivered, all was again right with the world.

Carlos escorted Roberta to a Japanese restaurant located inside the hotel. Of course, it didn't matter to her where they went. She was thrilled to be on her own. Alone. With a boy. This was what growing up was all about. No matter what life held for her, she'd remember this night forever.

"Your family really looks out for you," spoke Carlos, ending her trip through dreamland.

"Hmm? Oh? Yeah, they sure do."

"Must be strange having so many different brothers and sisters," he replied, trying to be as diplomatic as possible.

"Actually, I like it. Helps me understand where other people are coming from."

He stole a peek at her breasts, then came back to her. "You close with your mom?"

Roberta smiled. "Yeah. We're real tight."

Carlos paused to sip his sake, something he consumed only to impress his date. "How about your dad? Or stepdads?"

The question caught her of guard. "I never knew my dad," her voice alive with emotion. "But, I feel him watching over me everyday."

A moment of reflection. "I'm happy for you. Wish I had a family like yours."

Roberta altered the conversation's track. "Where did you grow up?

"East L.A."

"Is that where your family is?"

"I don't have a family, " he admitted. "My mom works all the time. My dad's an alkie."

Roberta fought for something to say. "I'm sorry."

Carlos shrugged. "Don't be. I've dealt with it all my life."

"Is that why you're in Vegas? To help your parents with their bills?"

"Not hardly."

"Then, what?"

"Forget it. It's not important," he maintained.

Roberta's curiosity peaked. "It is to me." Another necessary gulp of sake. He was lost in debate. *Should I tell her?* He looked into her angelic eyes and knew that he could.

"I was a gang member for five years," came his confession. "They were my real family. We looked out for each other. Cared for each other. That's why I'm here."

"What happened?"

Carlos realized he'd already said too much. However, he knew she wouldn't judge him unfairly. "If I tell you, promise me you won't say a word."

She bobbed her head in agreement. "I promise."

It became time for his deepest disclosure, one he relayed in a near-hypnotic trance. "Another gang member had his way with my sister. Raped her. Cut her up real bad. I was beyond pissed. This was my homeboy. He shoulda had respect for me, ya know? I had to do something... so I shanked him. He died where he fell. I never meant to kill him. Just wanted him to suffer the way she did. Anyway, I came here to hide out. Try to put it all behind me."

Roberta was in shock. The girl trembled, reflecting on the story and the boy before her. Carlos was certain she'd bolt from the table at any second. He waited, then waited some more. At last, she offered her hand in comfort.

"Don't hurt over this, Carlos. God forgives you."

He paused, choking back his emotions. "How do you know that?"

A tortured smile. "Because, He loves His family as much as you love yours."

Carlos lowered his head and wept in the redemption of his soul. Roberta joined him, her tears now uniting with his.

As Benjamin napped in the room beyond, Kevin told them of the phone call earlier that day. The movement of the Roswell craft was of supreme interest to the assembled seven. It represented a chance to get even. To expose the truth for all the world to see. But, they had no plan to implement and no reason to think they'd succeed.

"We're not soldiers," claimed Shannon, glancing at Moses. "And if anything goes wrong, I won't be there to patch you guys up."

"Mother's due around that time?" C.J. inquired.

She nodded. "May 5th, 6th or 7th. I'll induce labor if it goes beyond that."

Kevin felt the gravitational force of his words. "She's not going to make it, is she?"

Shannon delayed her response, answering the question before she found the courage to do so. "I don't see how," her voice mired in angst. "I want to do a C, but she's insisting on natural birth. Labor's tough on any woman. But, at her age…," she shook her head at the thought, "…there's too many things that can happen. In any case, I have to be there for her."

"So, where does that leave us?" moaned Barbara. "How are we supposed to take a train away from the military?"

"We need to hire mercs," announced Moses. "Paid mercenary soldiers who are trained to do this sort of thing."

"But, it isn't their fight," C.J. claimed. "They wouldn't understand what's aboard. And if we told them, they'd just sell it to the highest bidder. Most countries would pay a fortune for the technology to rule the world."

Moses objected. "We can't do this on our own. Even if you were trained, we'd need tactical plans of execution, some sort of delivery vehicle and enough firepower to blow a couple of hundred soldiers straight to Valhalla. Now, where the hell are we going to get all that?"

The room fell silent allowing Kimberly time to think. "I know someone who could help us. His name's Major Robert Osborne. He's the chopper pilot who rescued me at the Stratosphere."

"You know how to get hold of him?" asked Moses.

"Of course."

"And, he has what we need?"

She smiled. "Oh, yeah. That and more."

Barbara looked at the others, incredulous. "Are you crazy? We can't fight against an Army. They'll send us on a one-way ticket to Hell."

C.J. downed the rest of his champagne with a single swig. "We'll need weapons. We'll also need training. But most of all, we'll need to have faith."

She cried with indignation. "Having faith will get us killed."

His tone became bitter. "You think we've come through all this, just so we can die together?"

"I believe God wants us to suffer. I've known that all my life."

Kimberly took exception with her argument. "Barb, you're not the only one life's taken a shit on. But, you can't give up hope."

"That's true," added Casey. "You've got to realize everything happens for a reason."

She stood her ground. "His reasons aren't my concern. I'm not going along on this one."

"What does that mean?" shouted C.J.

Barbara fought hard to swallow. "It means, if you insist on doing this, you'll do it without me," her voice quaked. "I'm not going with you."

Tension swelled as his lips fluttered in silence. Finally, C.J. thrust his arm outward, his spirit enraged. "Then, there's the fucking door, bitch!"

His words couldn't have hurt more. Overcome with emotion, Barbara dashed from the suite.

"C.J.!" Shannon cried. "That was uncalled for!"

He screwed shut his eyes, mindful of the effect his outburst would have and aware there was nothing he could do to take it back.

A few minutes later, there was a knock at Barbara's suite. After checking the security port, she released the lock allowing entry to her sisters, Shannon and Kimberly. Without verbal greeting, she returned to her luggage, loading stray items into a cosmetics case.

"There's really nothing to say, is there?"

Shannon spoke after a lengthy pause. "He was frustrated, Barb. You know he didn't mean it."

"Oh, really? Couldn't he tell me that himself?"

Kimberly issued a sheepish grin. "He said you'd clock him."

An anguished peal of laughter. "What happened to the man's faith?"

"We don't want you to go," begged Shannon. "None of us do."

"There's no way I can go back," came her confirmation. "The bellman will be here any minute for my bags."

She secured the last item, then dragged her matching luggage to the door. Kimberly tried to reason with her.

"Barb? Men say stupid things all the time. You've lived long enough to know that. Can't you just let it slide?"

She sauntered past them, ignoring the comment. "Excuse me. I've got to use the bathroom."

Shannon and Kimberly exchanged glances, realizing the rift was beyond repair. A moment later, they heard a knock at the door. Kimberly answered it, allowing the bellman to enter. He brandished a bouquet of red roses.

"This is for Ms. Pinder."

"I'll take it."

He handed her the floral arrangement and carried Barbara's luggage out the door. "Tell her I'll have these down at the bell stand."

Kimberly acknowledged with a nod. "Thank you." She closed the door and stole an intoxicating sniff.

"Who are they from?" Shannon wondered.

"I don't know. There's no card."

They heard the toilet flush. Kimberly hid the bouquet behind her back before Barbara rejoined them. "Was the bellman here?"

"Yeah," Shannon explained. "He took your bags to the lobby."

Kimberly could no longer contain the surprise. "Look what he brought."

The instant she saw the roses, she went through a series of tremors. "Oh, God! They found me!"

Shannon stepped back, bewildered. "What are you talking about?"

"Don't touch them! Put them down!" She batted the flowers from Kimberly's grasp, scattering them to the floor.

"What the hell is wrong with you?" asked Kimberly in concern.

Barbara's hands flew to her head. She bolted from the room, leaving the women aghast at her reaction.

Dinner had been wonderful and the conversation better. Roberta wanted the evening to last forever, but Carlos was in a hurry. He had 15 minutes before losing his manhood to Moses, tonight's Archangel of Castration.

As they emerged from the casino floor, she saw a woman on one of the hotel lobby payphones. It was Barbara, holding an envelope in hand. Roberta saw her drop the receiver, twirl in agitation and disappear inside the hotel's wedding chapel.

She wondered if she should go see what was wrong, then thought better of the plan. Roberta was about to conclude her evening and didn't want to miss out on her very first goodnight kiss.

The anticipated moment arrived. Roberta and Carlos stood before her hotel suite door, holding hands. She swayed back and forth, the shifting movement in her feet allowing her to shroud her nerves.

"Thank you, Robbie," he stammered. "You were just what I needed."

She felt her knees wobble. "That's so sweet. I really had a great time."

"Will I see you again?"

"Of course," came the breathless response. "Anytime. Anywhere."

He smiled, displaying a shyness she hadn't thought possible. Her heart was now carving a hole through her chest. Roberta was certain it couldn't get more romantic than this. The eternal longing. The exquisite ache. She ran her tongue over her lips, sending Carlos the all-clear signal. He began pulling her closer, enfolding her back in his hands. Her eyelids dropped by instinct and then...

"Oh, yuk!"

She gazed into the open doorway. Benjamin was there, holding an empty ice bucket, eyeing them with revulsion. Before they could move, he slammed the door shut. They separated, unsure of what to do. Finally, Roberta shook her head. "Never mind him."

The two regrouped for a second attempt. As they merged into each other's flesh, the door swung wide again.

"Was it Barb?" Shannon asked, addressing Benjamin within. She froze, embarrassment ballooning from her face. "Sorry."

The door closed once more. Roberta's romantic moment was unraveling before her eyes. Her date sighed, at last offering his hand. "Maybe we should just shake?"

She looked upon him in disbelief. "The hell!"

Roberta rammed into his lips. After the initial impact, they settled into a more satisfying embrace. It was pure magic. The addictive taste of the opposite sex would now be hers forever. They parted, certain in the knowledge they'd see each other again.

C.J. entered the sanctuary. Seated in the front-most pew was the tortured soul he'd come to comfort. Barbara's head was lowered, wiping teardrop highways running the length of her face. She bristled as he sat beside her.

"Roberta saw you run in here."

She nodded in response.

"It's a good place to hide," he conceded. "Especially for someone who has no faith."

Her voice found life. "Oh, I have faith. But, only in myself."

"What happened, Barb? They said you saw the flowers and lost it."

She recalled the dreadful memory. "They found me, C.J. I don't know how, but they found me."

"Who?"

"The assassins. They sent me flowers in New York. Now, they've done it again. They're probably outside. I had nowhere to run, so I came here. The last place anyone would look."

He sighed, arching his back into the pew. "I sent you the flowers."

Her eyes lit in realization. "You? Why?"

"To apologize for what I said." Relieved, she flopped her head to his chest. "I'm sorry, Barb. I was frustrated."

"About what?" she asked, mopping her face.

C.J. collected his thoughts, choosing his words with care. "We've lived the longest. We've seen and done more. And, for what it's worth, we've both lived the Black experience. One thing I've learned, no matter how hard things get, we don't quit. I didn't want you letting me down in front of the others. And, when you did I couldn't handle it."

She shut her eyes in distress. "I didn't mean to let you down, C.J. I didn't realize it was that personal." Another painful pause. "I'm not afraid to die," she admitted. "But, there is something I am afraid of. I'm afraid I'll be the only one to survive and have to live with the loss of my family all over again."

"Don't worry," C.J. replied, tongue in cheek. "I promise we won't die without you."

She tried not to giggle. "Bastard."

A limp smile bloomed in the dark. "I guess you owe me that."

Barbara pulled her head up, tossing free her latest round of tears. She produced an envelope, handing it to her brother. "As I was checking out, they gave me this message. I called the Bahamian Embassy to verify it."

He read the letter. One of the hospital nurses who'd cared for Barbara had been tortured and found dead in her home. C.J. folded the message once done.

"Her fingernails were torn out," Barbara gasped. "Now, I have her death on my conscience, too."

"They know you're alive?"

She nodded. "They do now."

"You called the Embassy? From a payphone?"

His sister looked at him, cringing with anxiety.

"They'll trace it back here," he stated. "We'll need to find a new hotel."

"That was stupid. I don't know what I was thinking."

"I guess we're both guilty of that."

Barbara sighed in resignation. "I'm here for you, C.J. Until death do us part."

"Not even then, sister. Not even then." They each fell into a warm embrace. "Come on," he insisted. "We've got things to do."

That night, Mary Ellen's children checked out of the Las Vegas Hilton. They established a new base of operation at the Silverton Hotel and Casino located on the road leading to the town of Blue Diamond. This less visible facility would serve their needs well. It would minimize their exposure to any Federal Agents, while positioning them just few miles from Major Osborne's secret hideaway.

Kimberly set up the meeting and introduced her family to the U.S. Army renegade. Osborne showed them his five acre parcel of property and his secret collection of equipment and munitions. Moses was in Seventh Heaven. Suddenly, the impossible task confronting them seemed a bit more plausible.

They sat the Major down and Kimberly spoke for them all. Nothing was withheld. She told him of Roswell and what the Government had done. What happened to their mother. What happened to each of them. The future fate of Las Vegas and the transport train they had to intercept. After the discussion, Kimberly expressed her concern.

"Did all this scare you?"

He snorted in amusement. "Scare me? Hell, I'm about to bust a nut."

They were impressed with his bravado. Another introspective pause. "Moses is right. We need mercs. I can assemble a squad of 20 ex-Rangers and SEALs in less than a week."

C.J. opposed the plan. "It's not their fight. Nor, is it yours. We don't want to be responsible for sending others to their deaths."

"So, what do you want me to do?"

"Train us," pleaded Kimberly. "Help us plan the operation and provide what we need."

She'd placed Robert in an awkward situation, but knew he wouldn't turn his back on them. Her instincts were correct.

"I guess I'm crazy enough to believe you can pull this off." He downed the rest of his beer with a long gulp, then turned to Moses. "Soldier? We've got some raw recruits to break in. Ready for a challenge?"

"Yes, sir," he grinned. "I most certainly am."

For the next two weeks, Mary Ellen's family was placed through a crash program of intense military training. They were shown weapons identification and usage. Hand to hand combat. Basic martial arts maneuvers. Guerilla warfare. Explosive ordnance and demolitions. Secure field communications. Intelligence gathering. Cover and concealment techniques. Desert survival. Emergency medical treatment. Everything they could possibly absorb.

Osborne established a gunnery range on his property. Moses took advanced helicopter training in the Major's Huey. Even Benjamin had a role, helping to organize the equipment, as well as being the group's designated go-for.

They poured over intelligence data. Osborne obtained geodetic survey maps of the railroad spur line allowing them to plan for the optimum strike point. Derailing the cars wasn't an option. They needed to secure the train and commandeer it to another location — a rail yard outside North Las Vegas where Osborne would be waiting to transfer the cargo.

The plan was sound, but timing would be critical. It was rehearsed in their minds and in the field. They trained for every contingency. After 17 days, all of them were functioning as a cohesive team. Major Robert Osborne was pleased. Even the veteran soldier thought they had a fighting chance to do the impossible.

The date was now May the 6th. It was to be a day of infinite cosmic significance. Planetary impact. Universal judgment. An explosive confluence of events that would affect the lives of millions — and destined to be discussed by generations of humanity for the next 10,000 years.

CHAPTER EIGHTEEN

∞

𝓜ary Ellen was in the throes of active labor. Full with child, she moaned from the pain she could no longer suppress. This pregnancy had taken a frightful toll on the woman and her day of reckoning was at hand. Shannon checked the heart monitor for any sign of fetal distress, then pulled the others aside.

"It's not good," came the prognosis. "The baby's healthy enough, but mother's vitals are weakening. She's stuck at seven centimeters and I'm not sure she'll dilate much further. I may have to do a C after all."

"How much longer?" inquired C.J.

"Probably three or four hours. If it goes beyond that, I'll have to operate."

Although her children wanted to stay for the birth of their sister, time was running out. They had a train to catch. With heavy hearts, they began the process of saying their goodbyes. It would have to be abbreviated due to time constraints and their mother's increasing travail.

Mary Ellen took a moment to receive each of her children. Benjamin pressed ahead of the others to be first in the queue.

"Madre? I finished a song," the youngster beamed. "I wrote it just for you."

"Thank you, my son," she responded with as much smile as she could muster. "Maybe I'll hear it when you get back."

"Ben's not going," grumbled Kevin. "This is way too dangerous. He's just a kid."

Mary Ellen nodded, feeling the weight of her tortured soul. "I know. But, he's an integral part of a spiritual force. It isn't up to us to question God's will."

"But, mother..." He was silenced by a wave of the Madre's hand.

"It's his destiny, as much as it's yours."

Benjamin swelled into a gap-toothed grin, falling gently into his mother's arms. She caressed the top of his head as tears began to fall. "Be strong, my young son. Let your music shine with a love of God and it will always please the ear."

They hugged and exchanged a brief kiss. She next received Kevin, looking upon him with pride. "Have patience with Benjamin. Help cultivate his talent and he'll reward you in kind."

He sighed in frustration. "Okay, mother."

She ran her fingers through his hair. "You have great beauty in body and spirit. But don't let the pleasures of flesh entrap you. A woman's body can gratify you only temporarily. Uniting with her soul will bring you lasting joy."

Kevin wrapped his arms around his mother, letting go the moment he felt her tense from another contraction. After a series of rapid-fire breaths, Mary Ellen settled onto her pillow as the spike of pain diminished. She motioned Casey to her side who merged his body with hers in tender affection. "Please remember, my son. Don't trust in false superstitions or secular beliefs. Worship God and nothing else."

"I will, mother," crossing his fingers behind her back.

They parted, allowing C.J. to place a kiss on her cheek. He looked upon the woman with a reverence one would expect for a saint. "I love you, mother," stated her son after a composing gasp of air. "And, you were wrong. We're not worthy of you."

She smiled, her spirit overwhelming her physical distress. Mary Ellen pulled him close to her breast and whispered in his ear. "Thank you, Michael."

C.J. wanted to respond, but words would now be hollow between them. They embraced, aware it would be the last time their flesh would touch.

Moses completed the ceremonial parade of sons. He clasped her hand in his, fighting an onslaught of tears. "Madre," his voice alive with love. Before he could say anything more, another contraction seized her. The woman's rasping breath silenced the room. A few seconds later, Mary Ellen sighed in relief. Shannon offered her a sip of water to combat her cottonmouth, which she greedily accepted.

"Moses," she sputtered in exhaustion, "You must promise me one thing."

"What's that, Madre?"

"That you'll return here by nine o'clock."

Her son was incredulous. "Nine? Mother, it's a long way..."

"Promise me, Moses," came the demand. She squeezed his hand for added emphasis. "Nine o'clock. Not one minute later."

"Why, mother?" he probed. "What happens at nine?"

Her eyes glazed with the image of future horror. "God's patience is at an end," she answered. "The second woe comes tonight. Promise me you'll be back by nine."

The Las Vegas apocalypse. At long last, the fateful day had come. By the time Moses would be forced to leave, they should already know if their mission to commandeer the train was a success. He looked at the others, each of whom nodded in consensus.

"All right, Madre," he sighed. "I'll be back by nine. I promise."

"My child, always be a soldier of God, not this Government," prayed Mary Ellen. "Try to curb your tendency toward violence. You have an equally great capacity for love. Let that be your weapon of choice."

Moses was touched by her words. "Madre, it's been an honor to love you." They entwined their arms, reveling in the other's warmth.

Her daughters now took center stage. Kimberly knelt down and gently stroked her head.

"I'm sorry I didn't have more time with you," she confessed, fighting unwelcome tears. "Like I said before, you're a real nice lady."

Her mother stifled a laugh. "It takes one to know one. And, I'm sure you'll always be. But, beware of evil vices. Take care not to covet money," she cautioned. "Your body is the temple of the Lord. There's no price great enough to purchase such treasure."

Kimberly's tears fell like rain, mindful of her past behavior. "Thank you, mother," she sobbed. "I love you, too."

A tender embrace, sealed with a kiss. Roberta, overcome with grief, circled away at the last second allowing Barbara to take the lead. She held her mother's hand, fully aware of what Mary Ellen would say.

"Have faith, my child," came the tortured voice. "You may feel it illogical, but it will sustain your spirit and deliver you from harm." Her face went flush with pain, squeezing the blood from Barbara's hand.

"Breathe, mother," her daughter begged. "Breathe."

She forced air in and out of her lungs with tight, compressive bursts. Perspiration beaded on her face as the spasms of birth intensified, then receded. Shannon mopped Mary Ellen's brow with a cold cloth.

"We must have faith, Barbara. Without it, we have nothing."

"It's an illusion, mother," came an ill-timed challenge. "I only believe in things I can see, hear and touch."

Mary Ellen cast a shrewd smile which refused to fade. "The things you can see, hear and touch are the illusion," she declared. "Faith is the only thing that's real."

Barbara opted out of further debate. "I hope you're right."

"I am. I just hope you realize it in time."

The women shared a tender hug, expressing their mutual love. Barbara withdrew from her mother's side, leaving a kiss on her cheek.

Roberta stood facing the wall, trying to delay the inevitable. The Madre felt the girl's angst and decided to direct her attention elsewhere.

"Shannon?"

She beamed with affection. "Mother, I'm not leaving you."

"I know," coercing another smile. "But, I need your solemn vow that you'll care for this child and raise her as you would your own flesh and blood, because she is."

Astounded at the news, Shannon grappled with a multitude of emotion. It was an answer to years of prayer. The barrenness of her life was about to miraculously sprout fruit. "Oh yes, mother," she responded in gratitude. "I'd be honored to do that."

Mary Ellen finally addressed her youngest daughter, still isolated in anguish. "Roberta?"

The girl rushed over, pressing her face to her mother's breast. She wailed openly, gasping for air. "I don't want you to die!"

Beside herself with sorrow, the girl was unaware of Mary Ellen's latest contraction. They held one another, both sharing the other's pain.

"Don't worry for me, my child," came her plea. "I've done everything God's asked of me. Soon, I'll have my reward. I'm going home. And there I'll be, waiting for you to join me."

"Madre, I love you so much."

A lengthy kiss and lasting embrace for the woman she'd cherish forever.

With their departure at hand, Mary Ellen issued a final farewell, gazing upon her offspring through wet eyes. "My children, I want you to know that neither the height above us, nor the depth below us, will ever separate my spirit from you. I will be with you always — even until the end of the world."

Each were swept away on a tsunami of tears. They left, knowing their collective destiny awaited along a lonely rail bed in the Nevada desert.

Arriving at the rendezvous site, the siblings climbed out of their rented GMC Suburban. The industrial storage park was located in

North Las Vegas, serviced by nearby Interstate 15 and the rail line. Waiting for them was Major Osborne standing next to his Army helicopter and a nondescript 18 wheel semi.

Kevin was shocked by the size of his acquisition. "Where'd you get this? Trucks R Us?"

"I borrowed it for the weekend. Better to have more room than not enough."

"Where's the forklift?" asked C.J., scanning the area.

"In the trailer. I'll have it ready to go when you bring the train in."

"What about the weapons?" Moses inquired.

"Stowed in the chopper. She's fully gassed."

Kimberly smiled. "Looks like you've thought of everything."

"I try," came the less than modest admission. He handed C.J. a satellite cell phone. "Keep this with you. My number's preprogrammed in. You can let me know what's going on moment to moment. Unless you do the smart thing and let me come with you."

C.J. shook his head at the offer. "Sorry, Major. As much as we'd love to have you, we'd never forgive ourselves if you wound up dead on account of us. Like it or not, we've got to do this on our own."

Osborne understood their dilemma. "Well, at least let me go with you in spirit."

He slapped him on the shoulder, flashing a patented C.J. smile. "That's a deal, Major."

As they changed into khaki battle fatigues, Moses explained the necessity for his mandatory nine o'clock return to Las Vegas. Although displeased with this development, nothing could have prepared Osborne for the stupefying news that young Benjamin had been invited along.

"Are you out of your minds?" he railed in agitation. "It's gonna be a war zone out there! Someone, tell this kid Dreamland's not an amusement park!"

Kevin stepped forward, wagging his finger in sarcasm. "It's God's will. It's his destiny. Don't even ask."

The Major rolled his eyes, wondering how many more changes his carefully conceived plan could withstand.

After receiving last minute instructions, they strapped themselves in for the flight. The UH-1 came to life in a cacophonous blend of the throbbing engine, whirling blades and sonic backwash. Moses ran through the pre-flight avionics checks, then pulled up on the collective, rotating the craft skyward. A squeal of delight followed as Benjamin expressed his excitement, much to Kevin's chagrin.

"Careful, kid," muttering in discontent. "I'm armed."

The sun began its daily plunge behind the mountains to the west. Through ever darkening skies, the helicopter continued on an intercept course toward the secret transport train. All they could do was hope the information relayed to them was correct and that it hadn't been changed. It was the sort of possibility none of them wished to discuss. Mary Ellen asked them to have faith. They'd certainly need it now.

After traversing miles of empty moonscape, a ribbon of metal appeared beneath them stretching onward to the dusty horizon. Moses brought the chopper parallel with the track allowing Casey, their designated spotter, to search through the thermal convection currents for any sign of the train.

"Nothing yet," peering through his high powered binoculars. "Take us up higher."

Moses lofted them to a level of 4,000 feet. Seconds became minutes as Casey cast his eyes on the infinitely receding track. Fuel status remained foremost in Moses' mind. The UH-1 had an outer range of 325 nautical miles on a full tank. He still had to return to Las Vegas and would have no time to refuel.

"Anything?" Moses barked over the drone of the engines.

Casey blinked. "Maybe," he confessed. "Looks like there's something way the hell out there. Hard to tell with the optical distortion."

"Let me see."

His brother surrendered the binoculars. Moses placed them in hover mode, staring into the immense desert beyond. A moment passed as he took time to adjust his perception. Suddenly, he detected an object occupying space atop the distant rail filaments. *The train!* Weeks of preparation was about to pay off.

"Call the Major, C.J.," he bellowed, triumphant. "Target acquired."

Kevin lunged for the binoculars. "How far out?"

"About 20 miles due north. Headed this way."

His brother confirmed the sighting. C.J. used the cell phone to inform Osborne of the news. The operation was a 'go.'

Moses followed the instructions of their navigator, Kimberly. She scanned a detailed topographic chart, relaying distance and direction to their initial objective — a critical rail switch located near the tiny enclave of Alamo, Nevada. It was here the track split, with one spur continuing east into Utah and the other running south toward Las Vegas. They'd need to secure the adjacent pointshack, shunting the train in the desired direction. To fool the military, electric circuit sensors would be spliced together and taped below the rail, making it appear the switch was still properly aligned.

An isolated building next to the track came into view. Moses placed the Huey into a dive, swooping low over the rail bed. As the chopper's skids touched the ground, Kevin and Casey lowered their heads and dashed toward the structure brandishing M-4 rifles. They arrived at the door to find it padlocked. A burst of automatic weapons fire eliminated the problem. Kicking open the door, they crouched low, swinging their weapons in wide arcs. The pointshack was empty. After providing Moses with the 'all clear' signal, they ran through a squall of dust to position the makeshift electric circuit. Galloping to the track, the two probed the area for the buried connection sensors. Upon establishing their location, a double spliced wire was spooled between the junction boxes. They used an adjustable wrench set to force loose the bolts holding the induction circuit in place. The patch wire was then secured, linking the sensors and keeping the circuit permanently closed.

Returning to the shack, Kevin and Casey wrapped their arms around the point and forced it to comply. After rechecking their handiwork, this part of the operation was deemed a success. The approaching train would now be shunted to the south.

As they climbed back inside the chopper, Moses headed for a position due east behind a nearby hill. A few minutes later, the speeding train arrived at the switch. Now traveling toward Las Vegas, the procession consisted of two diesel locomotives, five boxcars, a flatcar, two more boxcars and a caboose. C.J. related the field intelligence to Osborne via cell phone.

"The soldiers are probably in the forward boxcars and the caboose," the Major speculated. "The Roswell craft's likely in one of the rear boxcars."

"If we come in from behind, the soldiers in the caboose will spot us," declared C.J.

"Remember, you're in a U.S. Army helicopter. They'll consider you a friendly until you show them otherwise. The flatcar's used for emergency helicopter landings. Just tell Moses to make a normal approach."

"What if they start firing before we land?"

"Then, use those heat seekers and blow the hell out of 'em," making reference to the missiles mounted underneath.

C.J. relayed the instructions to Moses and they began their approach from behind. All aboard tensed in catlike rigidity, weapons unsafed. Untold hours of gunnery training had now come down to this. Any second they'd be involved in a major firefight and these wouldn't be plywood targets. Real flesh and blood firing at the same. A sensation of nausea gripped them, knowing they'd have to kill or be killed. And, as much as they'd have liked to, there was no turning back.

The Huey came parallel with the train and proceeded to descend toward an uncertain landing. Moses paced the caboose, hoping to smoke out any hostility early on. Casey peered through the binoculars.

"I don't see anybody down there," he announced. "It looks empty."

"Could be a trap," cried Barbara.

Moses bit down on his lip. "We'll know soon enough. Hang on! We're going in!"

The helicopter dropped down over the moving rail cars, trying to match forward speed and sway. Once positioned above the flat-car, Moses eased back on the collective bringing them within a few feet of the wooden platform. Even over the Huey's engine, they could hear the distinctive clacking of the train's wheels on the rails below. They braced themselves for contact, keeping their automatic weapons focused on the boxcars ahead and behind. At last, the chopper copied the proper motion of the train and settled onto the flatcar with a hard bump.

As the others jumped to the platform with platoon efficiency, Moses powered down the Huey, then grabbed an M-4 rifle and three spare magazines. "Stay here! Don't move!" he barked at Roberta and Benjamin. Before the youngsters could voice their protest, he bound-ed out of the chopper and directed his siblings to assume defensive positions at both ends of the wooden flatbed. They squatted down, keeping their weapons locked on the metal doors leading to the adja-cent cars. The assault team waited. Nothing. It seemed inconceivable no one aboard bothered to take note of their dramatic arrival. Additional seconds elapsed as the helicopter's rotor blades came to a stop. The anticipation became excruciating. A pervasive unease con-stricted them, body and soul. They'd prepared for pitched battle. They weren't expecting this. *Where are the soldiers? What's going on?*

Moses worked his way to C.J., motioning for the cell phone. It was surrendered at once.

"Major?" shouting over the track noise, "We're on the train, but there's been no resistance. I repeat, no resistance. Do you copy?"

"I hear you, Moses," Osborne replied, unable to cloak his con-cern. "They may be trying to bait you into the other cars." A lengthy pause. "I don't like this, soldier. You better abort."

Moses addressed C.J. "He says we should bail."

His brother shook his head. "No way! We've come too far to back out now."

"Not an option, Major," relaying the verdict.

"Then, secure the train," came the order. "One team forward. One team aft. Keep this channel open."

"Roger that!" He returned the phone to C.J.

In fluid motion, Moses gathered Casey and Barbara. The three advanced toward the boxcars in front, while C.J., Kevin and Kimberly proceeded toward the rear of the train.

With a burst of gunfire, the door flew wide and the first car was breached. Moses led the assault, storming the area with lightning sweeps of his rifle. Scattered crates were hurdled or cast aside in a frantic search for the enemy. Nothing was found. They paused in disbelief, remaining as silent as their weapons.

The other team took a more judicious approach. They lobbed stun grenades inside hoping to incapacitate any potential threat. The munitions announced themselves with percussive shocks paving the way for them to enter. Weapons fanned in every direction. No soldiers. No resistance. This car also contained boxes and crates, some stacked as high as the ceiling. Nothing else. It was difficult for them to understand why they weren't being opposed.

The next car was raided with similar efficiency. Again, no soldiers were present. Resting on the floor was a large object, draped in tent-like canvas and tied down with multiple anchoring hooks. C.J., Kevin and Kimberly knew instantly what it was. The unique shape matched the rendering their mother had drawn for them. They stood as stone, gazing upon the object with a reverence befitting a sacred artifact. The craft from the future rendered them speechless. It represented the mystique of Roswell. The tragic life and death of their father. Why each of them had been born. And, more important, why the MAJIK-12 wanted them dead.

Precious seconds elapsed and still the caboose had yet to be secured. Moses' voice blared across their walkie-talkies, forcing them to resume mission priorities.

"Team two? Anything?"

C.J. motioned Kevin aft while he fielded the communication. "We found the ship, team one. Last boxcar. There's been no resistance. How about you?"

"No resistance, team two," reported Moses. "All five cars. I can't understand it."

Before he could reply, Kevin raced back in. "Nothing."

"Roger that," C.J. confirmed. "We're clear to the caboose."

Roberta was restless. She hadn't seen or heard from her family in more than five minutes. Benjamin had curled up on the rear bench and appeared to be taking a nap. An emotional day had obviously taken a toll on the boy. His sister grabbed a blanket from the storage bin and wrapped Benjamin up like an overgrown papoose. Wondering what happened to the others, she slinked away from the chopper and ventured into the forward boxcar.

Benjamin's right eye slid open. Realizing the coast was clear, the little faker wrapped the blanket around two flak jackets making it appear he was still asleep on the bench. He jumped from the Huey, taking mischievous pride in his harmless chicanery. Entering the rear boxcar, Benjamin hid behind a large crate after hearing Kevin, C.J. and Kimberly returning to the helicopter. Once the three safely passed, he continued his exploration into the next car.

Roberta ran into Moses, Barbara and Casey two cars up. Retracting his rifle, her brother vented his displeasure. "What the hell do you think you're doing? I told you to stay in the helo."

"I was getting worried."

"Where's Ben?"

"Asleep," she assured them. "I left him in the chopper."

They quickened their pace, returning to the flatcar a few moments later. Moses peeked inside the craft to ensure Benjamin was still there. They were soon joined by the others.

"He wants to talk to you," stated C.J., handing the cell phone to Moses.

"The cars are clean, Major. There's no one here."

Kevin snorted in amusement. "Guess they heard we were coming." The others giggled at the thought.

"Something's wrong there, soldier," Osborne stated, his voice stiff with concern. "Abort this mission. Get off that train now."

He tried to rationalize the situation. "Maybe they rolled a decoy train earlier. Should be just a dozen or so defenders in the locos."

"That makes no sense. If it smells like a trap, it always is."

Moses eyed his watch. It was almost 8:00 PM. The last moment he could start his return and still get back to Las Vegas in time. He couldn't be two places at once and sighed bitterly at the conflict. "Major, I'm at zero hour. I've got to head back to town."

"Don't leave there without your family, soldier," warned Osborne. "It's a mistake."

Noting his brother's anguish, C.J. took the phone to address the Major. "Listen. I told you the craft is here. Moses promised to return to Vegas and that's just what he's going to do. And, while he's gone, we'll secure the locomotives and park this thing at your feet. Now, that's the plan and we're not changing it."

A moment of stunned silence. "You've got brass ones, C.J. Hope they don't get blown off."

"Roger that," he grinned. "We'll give you an update in a few minutes. Out."

The decision was made. Moses would head back to town. But before he left, he wanted to pull the tarp and make sure the object underneath was the genuine Roswell craft.

Benjamin wanted to see it, too. He crawled under the canvas covering and began conducting an examination. He was intrigued by an area underneath the ship. After some manipulation with his fist, a hatch popped open. Benjamin slid himself through the portal and entered the alien craft. His expression of wonder was immediate. Even in the subdued light, the interior cockpit glistened with cryptic mystery. Three dimensional holographic control instruments came to life, activated by his presence. Multicolored lights, displays and monitors enchanted the eye. Ambient sounds played mechanical music to his finely tuned ear. He noted a computer in the center of the console. On the monitor was a set of numbers. Benjamin recognized them as a phone number, repeated over and over. An advanced caller ID system had captured the identity of an outside modem attempting to dial in.

As he placed the numeric digits to memory, he heard his brothers and sisters approaching beyond. He knew they'd fall over each other trying to be the first to spank him. In fear for his rear, he closed the hatch and hid behind one of the seats.

Kevin, Casey and Moses used hunting blades to sever the ropes anchoring the tarpaulin. The covering was cast free of the craft. There was respectful silence as sight of the ship evoked an intense spectrum of emotion. Exhilaration and dread. Awe and sorrow. Joy and wrath. This was what it was all about. A crash years before and how the MAJIK-12 had plundered such mystic beauty. They could see their mother, a mere girl of 18, standing beside the craft, weeping over their father's anguish and not knowing what to do. They could see their father, a distorted twisted image, reveling in his long sought pain and aware that everything he knew, and everything that was supposed to be, was now lost forever.

The ship had been fully restored, showing no evidence of damage or structural impairment. Moses came close, running his hand across the alien surface. "This looks like the same metal mother showed us."

Kevin motioned him back. "Let's make sure." He lifted his automatic rifle, firing into the craft at point blank range. The sound caused Benjamin to cower inside. His muted whimper failed to be heard over the generated echo.

The high-powered rounds caved in a small section of the hull. Then, before their eyes, the metal returned to a smooth configuration, shedding the bullets to the ground.

"Yep," agreed Kevin. "That's the stuff. Sure kicks Kevlar's ass."

"They fixed it up," added Casey. "That means they have the ability to produce this metal. Manufacture it."

Moses' watch beeped. Wishing his brothers and sisters luck, he agreed to rendezvous with them at the industrial park in North Las Vegas. The dutiful son then rushed to the chopper. Without checking on Benjamin, he brought the metallic beast to life. Seconds later, he was on his way back to Sacred Heart Hospital.

Securing the locomotives was the next mission priority. C.J., Kevin and Casey elected to go forward and rout whatever resistance presented itself. They left their sisters, Barbara, Kimberly and Roberta, to begin sifting through crates of data, selecting the juiciest information they could find.

The brothers trudged through the cars until coming to the door which lead to the trailing locomotive. They deployed through the hatch, inching onto the service catwalk which ran along the side of the diesel engine. The three worked their way toward the front of the locomotive, assaulted by turbulent motion and sound. Upon reaching the cabin, stun grenades were used to flush out any hidden defenders. They charged inside, covering each other with their weapons. Once again, no resistance. The absence of soldiers continued to baffle them. A final obstacle remained. The lead engine.

They began to mimic their previous tactics. The rocking motion became more pronounced. For whatever reason, they seemed to be picking up speed. Sidling the length of the catwalk, they made their way to the front of the train. The engineer's cabin was 10 feet away. Their nerves were on edge. Muscles tensed. Blood throbbed. It was now do or die. In rapid motion, the trio assaulted the cab with a blitz of live grenades and automatic weapons fire.

Nothing. A heavy toolbox had been left on the dead man's pedal propelling the train. There was no one within. No one aboard. Just them. In a moment of quintessential terror, they would suddenly realize why.

The sisters were examining additional crates when Roberta jumped back, her abbreviated shriek alerting the others.

"What is it?" wondered Barbara.

"I — I don't think this is good." The girl pointed to a metal box which had been welded to the floor. A yellow sticker warned of radiation danger. Underneath was a digital clock engaged in a countdown. 5 minutes, 43 seconds remained.

Kimberly activated her walkie-talkie. "Boys! We've got trouble!"

After describing the device, C.J. relayed the news to Major Osborne. His reaction was explosive. "That's a low-yield nuke! Get the fuck out of there!"

Pandemonium ensued. The women dashed through the cars, exhorting each other onward. Kevin and Casey ran back to separate the rest of the train from the locomotives. When they arrived at the first boxcar, their fleet-footed sisters charged forth, nearly ramming them through the adjacent bulkhead. As the women fled along the catwalk, their brothers tried to disconnect the coupler. The mechanical linkage refused to budge. Four minutes remained.

C.J. was driving the train with one hand, while juggling the cell phone and walkie-talkie with the other. "What's going on back there?" he screamed, bringing the engine up to its maximum speed.

"It's stuck!" yelled Kevin. "The damn thing won't release!"

Osborne was squealing into the phone with such ferocity he could clearly be heard over the raging diesel. "C-4! Use the C-4!"

Casey packed the coupler with the explosive while his brother rigged the wireless detonators. They dove onto the catwalk as Kevin plunged his finger into the igniter switch.

The result was instantaneous. A violent concussion heaved the locomotive's rear axle three inches into the air. Shrapnel spewed forth, peppering the trailing cars with high velocity fragmentation. The broken coupler plowed into the rail bed, causing the lead boxcar to jump the track. It derailed in a 90 degree lurch, initiating a cascade of sparks, smoke and expelled contents. In turn, each of the cars met the same fate as they crashed into a solid wall of debris, churning themselves inside out.

Benjamin, still hiding within the Roswell craft, was propelled headfirst into the alien console, rendering himself unconscious. The ship tumbled through the debris field, eventually coming to rest upside down less than 50 yards from the still active nuclear device. Three minutes remained.

Now freed of their burden, the locomotives sped down the track gaining precious distance on the smoldering wreck. Kevin's voice blared over the walkie-talkie.

"Move this hunk of shit! Lean on it!"

Barbara arrived in the engineer's cab. C.J. cringed, knowing what was coming next.

"Have faith, you said. Have faith?" came her bitter words. She leveled her weapon at him. "You better have faith, 'cause I'm gonna take this rifle and bury it in your ass!"

Ahead was a rocky peak rising 2,000 feet above the desert floor. It appeared that the track curved around the elevation, which might somewhat shield them from the force of a line-of-sight blast. They could only hope to reach the far side in time. Two minutes remained.

Their sisters joined Barbara and C.J. in the cab. Kevin and Casey took refuge inside the trailing locomotive. Major Robert Osborne was shouting in shrill tones, trying to convince one of them to respond. Kimberly grabbed the abandoned cell phone, at last narrating the manic events in real-time. The diesel engine was about to superheat, shuddering under the strain. They entered the curved track taking them around the backside of the peak. It would be close. One minute remained.

As the fateful moment approached, they tried to brace themselves for the climactic event. There was nothing more they could do. C.J. kept thinking about faith. How hard it was to have now. He expected a miracle to happen. Some act of Divine Intervention that would keep the fissionable plutonium shells from fusing into a critical mass. It was not to be.

As the locomotives raced behind the peak, a miniature sun was born. Kevin and Casey stared in awe as night became day, the intense flare gaining elevation and volume. A sonic thunderclap announced the detonation, soon escalating to ear-shattering status. An explosive shockwave convulsed the earth, overwhelming their senses and distorting the real into the surreal. Along the horizon, a squall of displaced air, sand and dust filled the sky, propelled ahead of the atomic wake. Shielded by the peak, the expelled matter showered them with particulates the size of baseballs. The acoustic fury left them brutalized by its assault. Chaotic harmonics triggered an avalanche of rocky debris to tumble down the slope and onto the exposed rail bed. From the glow of the nuclear fireball, C.J. saw the slide ahead and threw the engine in reverse. They fell to the deck as the locomotives plowed into the wall of stone. Slowing significantly, the steel behemoths finally derailed, crashing onto their sides in a cloud of sparks and smoke.

All six suffered head injuries and surrendered to unconsciousness. The only movement were stray trickles of blood. The only sound was Major Osborne begging for a response which failed to come.

Minutes later, an Air Force NEST team arrived at the crash site. While extinguishing fires feeding off pools of diesel oil, a check was made to determine the radioactivity in the area. It was deemed safe. They pulled the siblings from the wreckage and placed them onto awaiting choppers for transport to the Groom Lake complex.

There they'd meet Lucifer. Long ago, a kindred spirit. Ever since, a vengeful enemy. They were now his prisoners. Upon arrival at the secret base, he'd use every means available to turn them from God. Forcing them to become his minions. His soldiers. His Archangels of Dreamland.

CHAPTER NINETEEN

✑

LAS VEGAS, NEVADA — MAY 6th — 7:37 PM PDT

With her hair matted down with sweat, Mary Ellen looked nothing like her former self. She'd dilated to 8 1/2 centimeters, but that was still not large enough for the baby's head to pass. The birth spasms were so frequent, before one would subside the next had taken hold. This labor was her most difficult yet and began to drain the spirit from the elderly woman.

Shannon used the wall intercom to summon an attending nurse. "Sister Catherine? This is Dr. Hewson. Would you please come here? We'll need to do a spinal."

The response was immediate. "Right away, Doctor."

Mary Ellen forced herself to speak. "What did you say?"

"An epidural, mother. It'll deaden your nerves from the waist down."

"No."

"Mother. This is for your own good."

The Madre rocked her head in agitation. "No!"

"I'm sorry. But, this time you're going to listen to me."

The Madre grimaced in pain, causing her vocabulary to suddenly expand. "You're not doing it, dammit!"

Shannon's eyes swelled in shock. "Mother. Such language."

Mary Ellen continued to growl, gnashing her teeth in a rare exhibition of her darker side. Her daughter turned away, fearing an ill-timed smile would precipitate even greater wrath.

Sister Catherine entered, a tall, 33 year old brunette, clothed in traditional white uniform. She carried a surgical catheter, syringe and small bottle of Lidocaine Hydrochloride, a liquid anesthetic used for obstetric spinal blocks. Shannon inspected the contents.

"Good. We'll start her at 10 cc's."

"I said no!" yelled the agonized patient. "I'm not a damn pin-cushion!"

Doctor and nurse shared a bemused look. As the women began preparing to administer the injection, Shannon's pocket beeper went off. The message consisted of the numbers 911 and a phone number from the 404 Area Code in Atlanta. She knew instantly who it was.

"Troy," her voice becoming a whisper.

What timing! After six weeks, he calls now? With mother in full labor? She shook her head at the coincidence, prepared to ignore it or at least postpone her response for a more appropriate time. Still, the emergency 911 numbers continued to haunt her. *What does that mean? Is he in trouble? Are our lives in imminent danger?* She'd never know unless she called back. Kevin left his satellite cell phone in the rental car downstairs. It was the only safe way to make contact.

"Sister Catherine," came her declaration, "I have to run to my car. I'll be no more than five minutes. Stay with her and don't leave until I get back."

The nurse nodded. "Yes, doctor."

Shannon bolted from the room and into an awaiting elevator.

The rental car was parked a few spaces from the hospital's east entrance. She ran to the vehicle, unlocking it with her remote key. Another car screeched to a stop behind hers. Before she could react, two men encircled her with lightning speed.

"Shannon Hewson?" one asked.

Startled by their advance, she mumbled forth an awkward, "Yes?"

"FBI," he announced, flashing his credentials. "You're under arrest for interstate flight in the murder of Denise Duncan." The other agent spun Shannon around, forcing her against the car. He handled her with all the tact of an oversexed baboon, groping her the length and breadth of her body.

"Hey," she cried in disgust. "Watch your fucking hands!"

"Shut your mouth, bitch. Or, you'll get more of this in the car."

The other man was less antagonistic, reading Shannon her Miranda Rights while her hands were being cuffed. She remained silent, quaking in disbelief. Her love for Troy had blinded her to this obvious trap. *Now, what can I do?* The agents stuffed her in their car, speeding from the scene before anyone could come to her aid.

They turned south onto Las Vegas Boulevard, teeming with visitors in town for extended Cinco de Mayo weekend celebrations. Shannon gazed out at the sea of humanity. Having ignored and ridiculed their published warnings, the people seemed unconcerned for what was about to happen. She viewed them as mere specters. Soon, every one of them would be dead. And, so would her mother and unborn sister, unless she could figure a way to escape.

The tension in the car was intense. Astride Shannon was the lecherous agent, still leering at her. A song played on the radio, one which reminded her of Troy. She wiped heavy tears on her shoulder, wishing she could loosen the restraints on her hands. The vehicle plowed its way through thick traffic, each second placing her further from the hospital.

"Where are you taking me?" she wondered aloud.

The agent driving responded. "Airport."

She channeled a sigh, choosing to engage them with scorn. "Should've taken Paradise. Only an asshole would plow the Strip at this hour."

They refused to react, making Shannon revise her strategy. "I have to see my mother," she murmured. "She needs me."

"Where is she?" the agent up front probed. "Where is Mary Ellen Hart?"

Fearing another attack, Shannon lied. "At the Excalibur. We're all registered under assumed names. You've got to let me see her."

"We're the fucking Feds. We don't have to do shit," snapped the other.

"We should check this out. Let's swing by the hotel."

"She's lying out her ass. She'd never give up her family." He looked over at Shannon whose eyes were now glued shut. "What the hell are you doing?" An extended moment of silence. "I said..."

"I heard you," Shannon railed. "I was praying."

"For what?"

"Help," she admitted. "It's my destiny to be with my mother. You're preventing me from doing what I have to do."

"And, who do you think's going to help you?"

She paused for reflection. "God, I hope." The agent lost his professional scowl, uttering a derisive laugh. Shannon eyed him with contempt.

"That's really not a good idea."

Another blasphemous cackle. She shook her head at the sacrilege. "You're really asking for it, aren't you?"

His amusement ebbed. "Is that a threat?"

"Something's going to happen. I can feel it. You better let me go before you get hurt."

The agent backhanded her across the face. "You like it rough, don't you?" Speechless, she recoiled from the assault. "Pull over, Dan," he insisted. "I'm gonna teach this bitch a thing or two."

To her horror, the man started to loosen his belt and pants. She assailed him with verbal venom. "What can you teach me with that little thing? That you're more stupid than you look?"

The other man reached back trying to separate them. "What the hell's going on back here?"

Losing sight of the road, the agent drove through a red light. A city bus crashed into their vehicle in a sudden implosion of metal and glass. Debris littered the area as stunned bystanders rushed to aid those trapped inside.

The scene within was bloody. Shards of safety glass covered the occupants. The driver's neck had been snapped clean, his head laying flat upon the warped backrest. Shannon was alive, protected from harm by the agent's unconscious body. She fumbled through his suit pocket, finding the keys to the handcuffs. "I told you," her voice alive with reverence. "I told you both. You just wouldn't listen."

After a feverish moment, the cuffs flew wide. Shannon forced open the door and was swarmed upon by curious onlookers. She surged through the crowd, disappearing from view. Little did she know concerned citizens were already rousing the agent from his forced slumber.

Due to the accident, Las Vegas Boulevard was now sealed with cars. Shannon realized she could make better time on foot and proceeded to run north along the Strip. She maintained an even, compact stride, racing past Caesar's Palace and the Mirage, pausing only at the corner of Spring Mountain to await the pedestrian crossing signal. Fearing recapture, Shannon bounded into the road, jumping through a blare of indignant car horns. Again achieving maximum foot speed, she soon left the Frontier and Stardust hotels behind.

Suddenly, she heard a squall of terrified pedestrians in her wake. Stopping to look back, Shannon witnessed a wall of humanity parting to either side, screaming for their lives. Something was plowing a deadly path, crashing through waste containers, signs, bus stop enclosures and those too slow or inebriated to flee. The FBI agent was bearing down on her in a commandeered vehicle, using the sidewalk as his own high-speed diamond lane.

Shannon bolted across the Strip in panic. She could hear the roar of the approaching car, now closing within a few yards. At the last instant, the woman dove for cover inside a food court at the Riviera Hotel. The car crashed into the building's façade, sending a torrential burst of glass across dozens of patrons. Barely escaping injury, Shannon ran down some steps and found herself on the Riviera's casino floor. Numerous security guards hustled past, en route to the chaos beyond. The FBI agent stumbled from the car and resumed pursuit.

Hiding behind a bank of slot machines, she attempted to ascertain his whereabouts. Displaying her psycho-mechanic ability, Shannon caused each slot machine she came in contact with to hit a jackpot. Coins tumbled from the one-armed bandits in a continuous cascade of metal. Grateful players cheered as the bountiful flow of money clanked on. As Shannon tried to circle away from her pursuer, an elderly woman grabbed her by the arm, soliciting her Midas touch. The machine immediately stopped on three multicolored 7's. Amidst the celebration, Shannon dashed inside a nearby ladies room and exited a door on the other side.

Having evaded the agent, she raced through the Riviera's convention center, accessing the self-parking area beyond. She searched in vain for an available cab. Undeterred, Shannon ran toward the Las Vegas Hilton located behind the Riviera on Paradise Road. From her recent stay, she knew cabs were always there waiting in line. Upon arrival, she hailed the first one in the queue and was soon on her way to Sacred Heart Hospital. Unbeknownst to Shannon, a pair of familiar eyes had acquired her and now intently followed.

Racing back to Mary Ellen's suite, Shannon found her patient in the final stage of labor.

"Where were you?" Sister Catherine cried.

"It's a long story," fending off additional inquiry. She held the Madre's ice cold hand in tender apology. "Forgive me, Mother. It wasn't something I could help. I'm here for you."

Mary Ellen nodded, saving whatever energy she had left. The elderly woman was listless. Her color pasty and skin damp. Dr. Hewson had seen this condition before. It was the inexorable pallor of death.

"Her pulse is 36. It's been dropping since you left."

"Blood pressure?"

"101 over 53," the nurse reported. "She's dilated 9 1/2 centimeters, but I don't think she has the strength to push."

They both realized they were losing her. After a moment of reflection, Shannon leaned over the Madre to pose a question. "Mother? Can you still do this?"

She gazed up at her daughter and provided an answer. A slow, deliberate wink.

"Okay," sighed Shannon, smiling at Mary Ellen's awesome well of strength. "Let's give it a go." She turned to Sister Catherine. "I'm going to do an episiotomy. Bring me 20 cc's of Xylocaine, some cotton swabbing and a scalpel."

"Yes, doctor." The nurse left to collect the items.

Shannon walked over to the in-room sink and began scrubbing her hands in preparation for the minor incision. It was a simple procedure. A small cut to enlarge the vaginal opening. She still had her hands in the water, when a man's shadow loomed over her. Unaware of the danger, Shannon reached up for a towel. With startling swiftness, a pair of handcuffs came down, locking around her left arm and an adjacent metal towel rack. She spun to see the FBI agent, gun drawn.

In a spontaneous fit of rage, Shannon thrashed at the man, kicking her legs in a wide swath. The agent moved safely out of range. She screamed so loudly for help, she was certain she'd deflate a lung. Mary Ellen groaned in desperation, unable to oppose the threat. Her only thought was for the unborn life still within.

"No one can hear you. The door's locked beyond." The agent held forth his gun as though it were a trophy. "And, the nurse won't be coming back."

"You bastard!" Shannon squealed. Snarling like a cornered animal, she grabbed a glass by the sink and hurled it across the room. The man withdrew into the doorway as it missed by inches. He looked at the Madre and flashed a saccharine smile.

"Mary Ellen Hart, I presume."

He leveled his gun. She moaned in fear, placing arms over belly in a final effort to save her baby.

The lurid scene breached Shannon's soul. *After all this? After all we've been through? It can't end like this. It just can't!* Her breathless voice now beseeched Heaven. "Please, God! No! No!"

She waited. He stood frozen before them. The crucial moment seemed to linger forever. Suddenly, a stream of blood fell from his lips along with a muted gargle of death. His body came rigid, then fell to the floor. Thrust in his back was a foot-long serrated hemostat, normally used as a vascular clamp. And, emerging from the room beyond was Carlos Ayala.

Shannon forced the most relieved sigh of her life, viewing the former L.A. gangbanger with all the reverence of a fellow Archangel. "Oh, thank God!" She pointed to the body. "Carlos! Get the keys to these cuffs!"

The youngster searched the dead man's pockets, at last finding the coveted item. He came over and released her. A quick hug for the hero of the hour.

"How did you find me?"

"You found me," he claimed. "I saw you at the Hilton, so I followed you here. What happened to Roberta?"

"She's not here," explained Shannon. "How did you get in? He said he locked the door."

"The door was open," maintained Carlos. "I heard you screaming, so I ran in."

The two went to inspect the door. It was bolted shut.

"It was open! I swear it was!"

Shannon sighed with understanding. "I know it was, Carlos. The door was opened — just for you." She shed tears of exhaustion. "Hide the body. I've got to help mother."

He acknowledged her in a daze. A nearby closet served as a makeshift morgue. As Carlos finished placing the body in storage, the man's FBI credentials fell to the floor. He staggered away from the door, feeling nauseated.

"What's a matter?" asked Shannon, checking the Madre's vitals.

"I — I just killed a Fed," he cried in alarm. "Do you know what that means?"

"It means nothing, Carlos," attempting to provide him comfort. "You were acting for God. His is the only law that matters."

Lost in thought, he continued to express his angst. "I'm gonna burn on this one. Oh, shit! What am I gonna do?"

Shannon came to him, grabbing him by the shoulders. "Listen to me, Carlos. No one knows about this and no one's going to know. All of this. Everything. It'll all be gone."

"What are you saying? I don't understand."

"Did you hear about the earthquake? The one predicted in the paper?"

"Sure. The whole town did."

A frightening pause. "It's true, Carlos. Every word of it."

"Come on," he snickered. "That's just crazy talk."

She rocked her head. "No. We're 'The Friends For Life'. Roberta. Me. The whole family. It's going to happen. It's going to happen at any minute."

He continued to wallow in disbelief. "But, how do you know? How can you..."

"Listen to me!" She shook the boy, her voice thundering with authority. "Listen like you've never listened before. Get out of this town. Do you hear me? Get out! Right now! Don't wait for anyone! Don't stop for anything! Run like your life depends on it — because it does! Don't argue, just go! And, don't dare look back!"

Experiencing bona fide terror, Carlos nodded, visibly shaking with fear. "Okay." He then added an incongruous, "Thank you."

"No," Shannon replied, "Thank you." She kissed him on the cheek. Before he left, he handed her his parents' phone number in L.A. asking her to give it to Roberta. After promising she would, Carlos dashed from the room to his awaiting motorcycle downstairs. A few minutes later he was on Interstate 15, headed for California at more than 150 mph. It was now 8:42 PM.

Shannon checked Mary Ellen's condition. Her pulse was 28. Breathing was erratic and heavy. She was dilated a full 10 centimeters. The time had come to push.

"All right, mother. This is it," she implored. "For the baby."

The Madre nodded, beads of sweat pooling on her face. "For the baby."

With each contraction, Mary Ellen reached back for her reserve energy and began to push. Seconds turned to minutes as Shannon coached her through the final phase. At last, the tunnel of life opened wide. The baby's head began to crown. Shannon's excitement was electric, magnified by the heroic struggle which they'd all endured. Soon, a tiny face appeared. The head was out. Mary Ellen gasped, convulsing her arms in agony.

"Come on, mother," she cried. "You can do it. Just one more push."

Summoning all she had left, the Madre bore down with the next contraction. The baby's shoulders finally cleared the birth canal. Mary Ellen felt her spirit begin to soar, cresting through her flesh. In triumph, she loosed free her voice.

"It — is — done!"

The baby slipped into Shannon's waiting hands. The Madre's body went limp, coming to rest in a crucifixion pose. The baton of life now passed from mother to child.

At that instant, God exposed Lucifer to the sinners of the world. On every slot machine. In every casino. Throughout all of Las Vegas. Simultaneously, it happened. There before the eyes of every gambler, an image flashed on their gaming screens. Try as they might, the optical characters couldn't be cleared. The sight couldn't be ignored. They were now witness to the sign foretold in scripture. The mark of the Beast. The numbers 666.

And, then...

The Earth began to shake. The moment of atonement was upon them. It was time for Las Vegas to die.

CHAPTER TWENTY

❦

LAS VEGAS, NEVADA — MAY 6th — 8:52:16 PM PDT

*A*s with most critical events in human history, the earthquake began without warning. Over a million souls remained in harm's way. Too many by far. They were brought together at this moment and this place for a common purpose. They were here to perish. Selected from families and countries across the globe, they'd experience their physical mortality on a grand stage. God's plan was made clear and ultimately ignored by the masses. Reveling in the pleasure and saturation of their senses, a false sense of security betrayed them. Safe from harm by the overwhelming intoxication of money, sex and drugs. It had indeed become the Devil's realm. With the birth of Mary Ellen's final child, it was time for the spiritual to become physical. Time for all human doubt to end. Time for God to be heard.

The initial slippage of the tectonic plates sounded like an explosion of buried ammunition rumbling the length of Las Vegas Boulevard. The sound reverberated through the brightly-lit casino canyons as if a gigantic rubber band had snapped. It was followed by a steady rolling motion as the ground began to assume the characteristics of an angry tempest-tossed sea.

Shannon was clearing the baby's mouth of amniotic fluid, soon receiving an initial, healthy cry from her newborn sister. She looked upon the baby with rapturous joy as though she'd borne the infant herself. At long last, a child for her to nurture and love. It was a tender moment short lived.

"Mother," she stated, beaming with pride, "Look how beautiful she is."

She turned to face the body of the Madre Superiora. Her facial muscles were relaxed and calm, layered in eternal contentment.

"Mother?" Less than a second later, she grasped the situation. "Mother!" At that instant, several wall hangings crashed to the floor as the room began to sway. The baby wailed at a fever's pitch, marshalling Shannon's maternal instinct. She wrapped the infant in a nearby blanket and grabbed two bottles of soymilk for a later feeding.

Suddenly, a huge fissure appeared along the far wall of the room. The rending of the plaster shattered a large glass window and caused ceiling tiles to fall around them. Shannon issued a shriek, matching the vocal terror of her sister. Mary Ellen's body became buried in structural debris. There was no time for sorrow. Tears would have to wait. Survival was paramount and delay would be deadly.

Shannon dashed from the room with the baby nestled in her arms. She jumped over a toppled storage cabinet and chair, arriving at the nurses' station to find it empty. The hospital staff were already carrying the infirmed and fleeing for the exits. Lights dimmed, then began bursting across the ceiling. The newborn continued to wail, urging Shannon to find a way out. She noticed the clock before it was jarred from the wall. A few minutes before nine. Moses had promised to return. Shannon could only hope her brother was as good as his word.

A moment later, she was climbing the stairwell to the hospital's rooftop helipad. The building shuddered, bouncing Shannon against the handrail. Absorbing bruises on her arms to protect the baby, she finally staggered through the door to the roof.

Scanning the night sky, she spotted the red lights of the fast-approaching Huey. Shannon ran across a sea of undulating concrete, waving frantically for Moses to land. The seismic vibrations intensified. A moment later, the helicopter swooped down, kicking up a tepid squall of wind. Dipping her head, she ran to the open side of the chopper. As she placed her feet on the landing skids, the roof caved in beneath them. Moses rotated up, holding the craft in midair as both his sisters screamed in unison. Shannon fought her way into the seat and slid the hatch shut. Stealing a brief look at the baby, Moses moved the Huey away from the hospital. The building, old by Las Vegas standards, was collapsing floor by floor below them, crushing patients and staff still trapped within. A billowing cloud of smoke launched skyward, signaling the first of many casualties.

High above the city, Moses and Shannon remained silent as they now became captive audience to the most awesome spectacle ever witnessed through human eyes.

The 6.4 earthquake was currently two minutes old. It began to intensify, much to the concern of the humanity below. Casino patrons exited the mammoth buildings thinking they'd be safer outdoors. Still others continued to gamble, believing the quake had to end shortly. They were wrong. It had only just begun.

Street lights and traffic signals were next to fall victim to the tremors. Already snarled streets became gridlocked as many drivers abandoned their vehicles. Several taxi drivers tried to plow through the parked cars, injuring hundreds of pedestrians.

Throughout the city, residential buildings collapsed upon their astounded occupants. Older commercial structures designed before more stringent building codes were enforced, suffered damage early-on with most being leveled within the first minutes of continuous motion.

Shrieks of terror cascaded through the crowds as the earthquake increased in intensity. Those who dared look skyward watched as towering buildings loomed over them, then retracted, all matted against a backdrop of heat lightning illuminating the heavens above.

Glass windows shattered everywhere, showering The Strip with millions of razor-sharp shards.

And, it continued! The Fremont Street Experience, an electrical display arching over the Glitter Gulch area, began to convulse causing thousands of bulbs to explode from above. Anarchy reigned as frightened pedestrians ran for their lives. Seconds later, the metal scaffolding gave way, impaling the street with a thunderous roar. Dozens were electrocuted, ensnared in a web of St. Elmo's Fire.

And, it continued! High atop the Stratosphere Tower, the Top of the World Restaurant housed dozens of petrified diners, all trying to exit via hopelessly jammed elevators. The slender, free-standing structure had withstood several minutes of severe rocking motion. However, load bearing members in the base of the tower were now weakened. With the next surge of seismic energy, the tower leaned past its tolerable sway limit and the inevitable fall to Earth began. As the angle of declination became more acute, shrill death screams increased in pitch. Unsecured objects flew forward at breakneck speed. A moment later, vertical became horizontal. The disbelieving victims became weightless for an instant, then were thrust against the huge scenic windows forced to view their impact with the street below. When the tower crashed into Las Vegas Boulevard, the structure imploded in an orgy of steel and glass, at last expelling the remains of its human occupants.

And, it continued! Ruptured gas lines ignited the length of The Strip, creating a perimeter wall of flame separating the casinos from the street. Hundreds of people were swept into a state of spontaneous combustion, gathering unwilling partners in their breathless dance of death. Many others were injured by flying chunks of concrete. Deep underground, waves of displacement bombarded the surface with increasing energy. The Las Vegas earthquake was now being registered on seismographs as far away as Chicago and actively felt throughout a radius of 1,000 miles.

And, it continued! As the catastrophe proceeded to crest through a 9.0 reading on the Richter Scale, full-bore destruction commenced. Thousands of tourists ran for their lives, clogging the

I -15 overpasses at Flamingo and Tropicana Boulevards. The added weight caved in the structures, spilling countless humanity into the Interstate below. The carnage was magnified as drivers sped into a solid wall of flesh and bone. A roller coaster in front of the New York New York Casino collapsed, truncating a version of the Statue of Liberty on the way down. A replica of the Eiffel Tower crumbled at the Paris Resort, precipitating a downpour of metal lattice work into the squealing crowd. Overhead pedestrian walkways linking the major casinos sagged, then fell inward, compressing human bodies into paste. Collapsed buildings, walls of flame and other obstructions blocked all means of escape toward Koval Lane to the east. The Strip was now sealed, trapping the hysterical survivors within a narrow corridor of death.

And, it continued! At the Luxor Resort, glass rained down from the pyramid-shaped hotel. A mammoth Sphinx tumbled over upon hundreds of fleeing patrons. Within the casino, decorative statues toppled onto the marble floor joining gaming tables and slot machines. Plaster walls and support columns began to rend apart. A handful of gamblers pocketed thousands in scattered chips in the mistaken belief they'd live to spend them. The hotel inclinators were dislodged from their shafts, casting occupants hundreds of feet to the lobby floor. The centerpiece cap of the hotel, housing the world's largest arc light, freefell from its perch with a titanic crash. With the pyramid's design now compromised, one floor after another folded within itself, cascading down in a maelstrom of spinning hotel furniture, sheetrock and steel I-beams. Within seconds the entire resort was destroyed, entombing thousands, their faces frozen in astonishment.

And, it continued! In front of the Mirage Resort, the fabled volcano roared forth, dwarfed by the 100 foot curtain of fire running the length of the Strip. The crush of humanity trying to leave the casino trampled upon itself, with dozens falling to the rhythmically heaving floor. Through a skylight in the lobby's terrarium, the victims witnessed the top five floors of the hotel plunge toward them, instantly transforming the casino into a mass sarcophagus.

And, it continued! The man-made lake adjoining the Bellagio Resort sloshed to and fro, generating 10 foot whitecaps on the normally serene surface. The multistory hotel began to corkscrew, then suffered a catastrophic abruption, hurling the structure into the water. Hundreds of guests were jettisoned into the lake with most perishing upon impact. Those who somehow managed to bob their heads above the raging torrent were rewarded for their survival with a fusillade of debris, resulting in stomach churning decapitations.

And, it continued! The MGM Grand's 5,000 room tower now yawed over in a spectacle too inconceivable to behold. Spilling its entire million ton mass into the casino below triggered a concussive shockwave which rivaled the earthquake itself. Thousands were compressed into a sepulchral crypt, forcing blood to ooze onto the street.

And, it continued! At this point, every casino resort had been ravaged by the Force Majeure. The Strip was saturated with mountains of flaming debris. The exoskeletons of the Venetian, Caesar's Palace, Harrah's, Bally's, Mandalay Bay, Monte Carlo, Treasure Island, Stardust, Aladdin and countless others smoldered amidst an orgy of obliteration. Strident cries for mercy went unanswered. The incredulous survivors hoped the epoch event was about to subside. It was not to be.

Deep within the bowels of the Earth, a virgin rumble began to percolate through the hardened crust. A surge of incomprehensible power was heading directly for the surface. Without warning, every seismograph in the western United States suddenly jumped its track, losing the ability to record the impending, apocalyptic release. A temporal displacement now occurred within the universal space-time continuum. At this place, and at this moment, time simply refused to exist.

Twin eruptions disgorged opposite ends of Las Vegas Boulevard, sending a mass ejection of superheated rock and sand 3,000 feet into the air. This was simultaneously accompanied by what could only be described as a coronal discharge, blinding every pair of human eyes within a five mile radius of the blast zones.

These events created a cataclysm of Biblical proportions. An iridescent sea of white-hot magma swallowed the remaining ground, carving an ever-widening crevasse the length of the Strip. Emanating from the eruption sites, two sonic compression waves traversed down the Boulevard toward each other. Bulging wider as they moved at the speed of sound, they appeared as dual convex bubbles quavering with anamorphic distortion. The waves devastated everything in their wake, ripping apart objects as though nothing more than confetti. Upon merging, they sparked an acoustic explosion, eclipsing anything yet heard on this Earth. Human bodies in its path were simply vaporized, converted into a reddish, crystalline mist. Others, unlucky enough to survive, hemorrhaged from every conceivable orifice.

Extending several miles, the molten chasm opened full, exposing a hellish abyss from which there'd be no escape. One by one, the man-made gaming temples telescoped within themselves and slipped over the precipice. They were swallowed whole, disappearing into the seething, bottomless void. As the insatiable thirst of the pit sucked down thousands of the dead and near-dead, the earthquake peaked to a frenzied crescendo.

Clearly heard over the cacophony of death came a noise which couldn't be ignored. It seemed to resonate from everywhere. And nowhere. Even though the sound had never before been heard, every corporeal being knew instantly what it was. It was the voice of their Creator. In an exhausted tone, the ethereal scream went wild in a cathartic release, annunciating a Holy coda to the horrific apocalypse. Then, as the sound faded from the firmament, the Earth at last stood still.

An eerie calm took hold. Falling on the former city was a steady rain helping settle a cloud of suspended matter cloaking the severity of the devastation. Steam rose from the cooling magma, wafting into the night sky. As the vaporous blanket parted, the magnitude of the nightmare became all too real. Amidst the ruins were a handful of survivors moaning for a death which refused to come. They wandered sightless, with severed nerve ganglia protruding from hollowed eye sockets, wading knee-deep in a putrid ocean of blood, urine and feces.

Help was not forthcoming. Hospitals, as well as police and fire stations had been leveled. Emergency triage centers would take hours to organize. Electric power and phone service would be out for weeks. 20 miles away, Lake Mead had receded into newly-cavitated Earth, eliminating the city's major source of water. More than 450,000 single family homes, condos and apartments were left uninhabitable. Both McCarran Airport and Nellis Air Force Base lay in ruin, inhibiting logistic support airlifts. Days afterward, a steady convoy of trucks carrying critically needed supplies would cover the highways from Los Angeles, Phoenix and Salt Lake City. The cost to rebuild Las Vegas would later be estimated in excess of 13 trillion dollars, an amount which would tax the economic strength of the U.S. Government to the full. Of higher concern was the human toll. 881,416 killed outright and well over 1,250,000 injured.

What had been the Las Vegas Strip was now a five mile long canyon across the surface of the planet, encased in a thick sheath of cooling obsidian rock and volcanic ash. The city had been disemboweled from within. Utterly annihilated by the overwhelming wrath of God.

Mary Ellen's vision had come true. The cleansing baptismal fire was extinguished. But, it left an enervating rift in the fabric of the life force. A decreased energy level throughout the Absolute Elsewhere. On this day, the Almighty rested again.

It was over.

Amen.

CHAPTER TWENTY-ONE

∞

NORTH LAS VEGAS and RACHEL, NEVADA — MAY 6th — 9:27 PM

*I*n the aftermath, the Earth below was without form and void. Oppressive darkness surrounded pockets of light as hundreds of fires raged beyond control. The hellish scene stretched to the horizon in all directions, a continuing reminder of the devastation that had claimed an entire city.

Bathed within the glow of the helicopter's instrument panel, Moses and Shannon remained frozen in catatonic stasis. The event left them brutalized. Psychologically violated. Spiritually raped. The human psyche couldn't absorb such an overwhelming display of carnage. They wallowed in vacant incomprehension, shivering from the magnitude of a stupendous karmic loss.

The hungry cry of the newborn forced them back to reality. Struggling through the transition, Shannon provided the baby with a bottle of soymilk. A satisfied cooing sound at last commenced. The gentle trilling helped restore function to their vocal chords and tenuous communication resumed.

"Mother was right," Shannon murmured. "She was right and nobody believed."

Moses fought for his words. "It's too late for that. Too late for them all."

She glanced over her shoulder, noting the bundled blankets on the rear bench. "Thank God, Ben didn't have to see this."

"I can't believe he slept through it." His concern turned to their evaporating fuel status. "We're on fumes. The Major had extra fuel in the truck. Let's hope it's still there."

Shannon tried to swallow, squirming uncomfortably in her chair. She conquered a sudden spike of nausea by concentrating on the precious life nestled in her arms.

Due to the absence of ground lighting, Moses donned a flight helmet keeping the cyclic locked between his legs. The device was equipped with FLIR, Forward Looking Infrared, used exclusively for night vision. Through a computer generated menu projected onto the visor, the Heads Up Display allowed the pilot to select various options including exterior spotlight control and weapons deployment, all activated by the subtle retinal movement of the pilot's eyes.

Although the visor operated as designed, locating the rendezvous site was difficult. Thick smoke from nearby fires wafted over the area, obscuring hundreds of leveled buildings, flattened signs and downed power lines. Conventional reference points were not discernable. A once diverse landscape had been transformed into miles of continuous, nondescript rubble. At last, the interstate came into view. Cars had been tossed from the road with the same carelessness as a dog shaking water from its coat. The flare from innumerable headlights crisscrossed in chaotic tangents. None moved. It occurred to them that many people below had sustained injuries and were in need of help. *But, what can we do?* By the time they could get to one another 500 would die. And, what of the countless others who were trapped under debris? Had they done everything they could have? Were they now? Was it their fault these people were victims of their own disbelief? Only one thing was clear. They had to find fuel.

Using an interstate exit ramp as fixed reference, Moses back-tracked over the devastation below, finally locating the industrial park from which he'd started hours before. Through the visor, he could see the Major's 18-wheeler upended, laying on its side. He gritted his teeth, carefully rotating the craft down through thick strata of smoke. A moment later, the Huey landed in a squall of particulate matter and displaced earth. The powerful engines decreased their aural whine, delivering them into a vacuum of eerie silence. Shannon remained in the helicopter, content to allow her baby sister to finish the bottle of nourishment.

After a scan of the immediate area, Moses realized Osborne had departed. The rental van which they'd left behind was missing. He knew the Major wouldn't have abandoned the site unless forced to by circumstances. There was no evidence of a firefight. No discarded shells. The forklift had been taken off the truck, waiting for a train which never arrived. There was only one possible answer, causing Moses to curse the situation. Something happened to his family and the Major left to render help. With any luck, he could soon join the search.

He forced open the rear gate of the semi, finding a half-dozen 55 gallon drums of aviation fuel within. Fortunately, they were still intact. One at a time he began to roll the containers free of the truck, positioning them near the fuel port at the rear of the chopper. He secured a transfer pump from a storage hold and began draining the petrol from the drums. First, one. Then, another. Finally, a third. All the time his thoughts were elsewhere. He'd honored his mother's final request, but at what cost? The words of Major Osborne echoed in his soul, *"Don't leave there without your family, soldier. It's a mistake."* He cringed with every replayed syllable. *Of course, it was a mistake.* Moses knew it as soon as he'd left the train. And because of his departure, his brothers and sisters were now God-knows where. But if he'd stayed, Shannon and the baby would've surely died. The no-win situation had left him without recourse. All he could do now was try and recover from the consequences.

A few minutes later, the craft was refueled. He stowed the pump, leaving the empty barrels scattered across the ground. Along with the first drops of rain, he detected a fetid odor which he'd experienced before, captured on a stiff northeasterly breeze. It was the smell of burning flesh. He retracted in horror, forcing air from his lungs in an attempt to purge the vapors. Moses returned to the chopper before being victimized by another assault to his senses.

Once inside, he seized his first opportunity to check on Benjamin's sleeping status. After nudging the bundled blankets, they fell flat onto the rear bench.

"What the..." stammered Moses, catching his tongue before the obligatory expletive. "He's not here!"

Shannon surveyed the situation with appropriate, but muted concern.

"He's still on the train!" railed Castaneda. "He faked us out! That little pain in the ass!"

"Shhh!" his sister admonished, pointing to the sleeping baby in her arms. "He's with the others. I'm sure he's okay."

Moses returned to his seat in a huff. "Well, he won't be when I get hold of him. I can't believe this."

"He's still a little boy. We can't expect him to act as mature as we'd like."

Her brother, still livid from the deception, refused to debate the issue further. He brought the Huey to life without apology for the generated noise. The craft rose into the air, now on its way to find a missing train.

Traveling northeast, the chopper backtracked the spur line, two lonely rails snaking into the black heart of the Nevada desert. Anxious minutes passed. The low level cloud cover blanketing the area soon parted, revealing a crystal night alive with stars. Glistening in reflective moonlight, the slender metal filaments led them onward, pointing the way toward the untold secrets that lay beyond. Moses pushed the craft, maxxing its top airspeed. Prepared for any hostile contingency, he ensured that onboard missiles and main guns were primed and ready to fire. His mind played havoc with him, visualizing any number of unwelcome scenarios. Soon, reality would take center stage and it was like nothing he could've imagined.

Ahead in the darkness, they saw a brilliant glow backlighting a distant peak. Foreign. Otherworldly. Beckoning them from afar.

"What is that?" wondered Shannon. "Is there a city out here?"

Moses shook his head, trying to sort through the possibilities. "I don't know. But, it's not a city." He heaved an anguished sigh in anticipation of the worst. "If we start drawing fire, get in back with the baby."

She nodded her approval. Moses leveled out at 100 feet, remaining below any military radar scans. Using the peak as a frontal shield was a tactically wise maneuver, allowing them to approach the lighted area with a maximum of stealth.

As he began banking to the west, he noticed a darkened mass covering the rails ahead. Through his FLIR visor, dozens of boulders entombing a large metallic object could be seen. Suddenly, the nature of the obstruction became clear.

"Shit! It's the locos!"

Without benefit of the infrared image, Shannon peered into nothing but the deep shroud of night. "Where?"

"At our two o'clock," pointing to aid her search. "About a half mile out."

As they circled into position, the sight became obvious in the delicate moonlight. The massive steel beasts lay still, battered from their encounter with the avalanche of stone.

"This isn't good," Shannon muttered between an unconscious double gasp.

He scanned the landscape for an enemy presence. The area appeared secure. "I'm putting it down."

The helicopter landed on a flat bed of sand, approximately 50 yards from the crash site. Moses grabbed his rifle and dashed low under the still whirling blades. He left the pilot's hatch open allowing the sonic backwash to invade the cabin, rousing the baby from her slumber. Shannon comforted the newborn by cupping the infant's exposed ear and humming a favorite lullaby from her childhood. During this time she could see her brother investigating the wreck beyond, bending over to survey potential evidence on the ground. After a couple minutes of inspection, Moses returned to the chopper and shut the hatch. He was greeted by the baby's mournful cry. Shannon braced herself for the news.

"They were aboard," her brother confirmed. "But, they've been taken away. Two helicopters and a squad of soldiers were here not more than an hour ago. Footprints in the diesel oil are still fresh."

"Were they injured?"

A reluctant nod. "There was some blood inside. Might've come from one or all of them. Couldn't tell."

"But, where would they take them? Is there a hospital nearby?"

"No," came the solemn response. "There's only one place they could've gone. The Groom Lake Complex — Area 51."

Mere mention of the ultra secret base triggered an instant spasm of fear. The situation appeared bleak. Not only were their brothers and sisters hurt, they were now prisoners at the most secure military installation in the world. The odds of seeing them alive again had just taken a dramatic turn for the worse.

Before continuing their conversation, Shannon removed the rubber nipple from the bottle, placing it in the baby's mouth as an emergency pacifier. The crying ceased while their sister suckled in search of more formula.

"Could you tell what happened?"

Moses grimaced at the thought. "Not really. The coupler on the trailing loco was blown apart. There was residue of C-4. For some reason, they separated from the cars and in one helluva hurry."

"So, where's the rest of the train?"

Her brother gazed at the mysterious glow beyond. "Let's follow the light. The answer's bound to be there."

Strapping himself in, Moses yanked up on the collective. The craft again took flight. He decided to ascend over the center of the peak, cloaking their presence until the last possible moment. Large boulders rumbled down the slope at erratic intervals. A few more feet and they'd clear the apex. Moses gripped the cyclic, his palms laced with sweat. He tried to brace himself for what they'd find, secure in the knowledge the enemy might be laying in wait. At last, the other side of the peak burst into view.

Three square miles of desert floor were engulfed in flame. Burning every inch of vegetation. Trapping every animal caught in its path. Even the sand appeared on fire. The conflagration was roughly circular in shape with smaller fires dancing around its outer circumference. Clearly defined near the epicenter was a crater of enormous size and depth bisected by a thin river of liquefied steel. It was what remained of the rail bed. Scattered throughout the area were singed pieces of rail cars along with twisted metal undercarriages which had been catapulted up to a mile from the point of detonation.

Moses' FLIR visor was rendered useless, creating a halo effect from which nothing could be discerned. He cast off the helmet, momentarily blinded by the contrast. Soon his eyes were able to focus on Shannon, her face lit in a reddish glow. An alarm began to beep inside the cabin, causing him to stiffen with concern.

"What's that?"

"Environmental sensor. It's picking up significant levels of radiation in the atmosphere."

"Which means?"

"Nothing good," he confided. "You're looking at the blast effect of a nuclear explosion."

Incredulous, she made every effort to dismiss his words. "That's not possible. It's too small an area."

"Low yield nuke. Some are so compact they can fit in a woman's handbag."

"And, it was on the train?"

Moses nodded. "Looks like it. Explains why they had to break away. Just doesn't make sense. Why would the Government want to blow up the Roswell craft?"

A tremor of fear passed between them. "They got what they wanted," theorized Shannon. "They got our family."

Dense smoke and thermal convection currents rose skyward, distorting their view and causing the craft to buffet in a turbulent wake. The environmental sensor continued to beep forcing Moses to bank the Huey to the west, remaining clear of any downwind radiation.

As they veered over the outer perimeter of the burst zone, he came within 100 feet of the ground, improving their lateral sight-line. It was at this moment, something captured Shannon's eye. A momentary reflection. A distortion deep within the hellish flux.

"Moses," she stammered. "Back here. Over to our right. Do you see it?"

He looked past her into the blaze beyond. "See what?"

His sister craned her neck, trying to make sense of the vision. "I don't know. But, it looks like it's moving."

Moses swung the helicopter in a wide arc. He slowed the craft's yaw, positioning them at a fixed point due east. Shannon pointed into the heart of the inferno.

"There! Straight ahead!"

Their eyes focused on a fluttering of shadows and light. The apparition possessed a supernatural quality as though it were the mythic Phoenix rising from the flame. The wavering image eventually fused to a solid mass. A diminutive head, torso and limbs soon became visible, the sight of which swamped them with emotion.

"Oh, God!" cried Moses. "It's Ben!"

Before Shannon could respond, her brother forced the chopper through the flames. A small island of land loomed ahead, encircled by an ocean of fire. Next came an abrasive landing into sparse, unscathed earth. The Huey's rotor blades stirred the thermally charged air, fanning the conflagration around them.

"Hurry!" came Shannon's plea, one her brother understood far too well. He nearly broke the seat restraint on his way through the hatch, dashing through intense heat and smoke.

A few yards away stood his little brother, head down, quivering from a combination of shock and fear. Moses ran to the tyke enfolding him in loving embrace. As they separated, he could see tears flowing the length of Benjamin's face triggering an onslaught of his own.

"Ben! Thank God!"

"I'm sorry. I didn't mean to do it," the boy blubbered.

A reflective moment as Moses came to realize the nature of his brother's angst. "Ben, you didn't cause this."

His eyes crept open, revealing little brown pools of hope. "So, you aren't gonna spank me?"

Forcing a smile, Moses wiped a wayward tear. "I didn't say that, kid." A quick glance at the flames closing in. "Come on!"

He scooped the youngster off his feet, ducking underneath the chopper's spinning blades. Moses placed Benjamin behind their seats and shut the hatch in fluid motion.

Shannon shared her concern, displaying an attitude that was classically maternal. "Sweetie, are you all right?"

"I hurt my head."

She smiled with relief. "I'll look at it in a minute, okay?"

He acknowledged with a gentle nod. Moses pulled up on the collective, delivering them out of the fire pit and into the relative calm of the western night sky.

Now safely airborne, Shannon unstrapped herself, straddling the front seats and the rear compartment. To Moses' chagrin, his newborn sister was placed in his lap.

"I'm flying here," came the squeal of disapproval.

"It'll just be a minute," she countered. "I've got to check Ben out."

She propped the baby up on his left arm, leaving him eyeing her with the kind of concern one normally reserves for a benign growth. He sighed uncomfortably, thankful Atali wasn't here to witness this awkward display of paternity.

Shannon inspected Benjamin's head with a small flashlight. A glob of half dried blood was matted in his hair from an inch long cut in his scalp. After locating the first aid kit, she irrigated the wound with an alcohol drenched cotton ball. Benjamin remained a trooper throughout, standing still without complaint. At last, the diagnosis was complete.

"He'll be okay," she reported. "Probably could use a couple of stitches, but the wound should heal. He's still in a bit of shock."

"So am I," snapped Moses. "What happened, Ben? Where were you?"

"I was hiding in the ship," he confessed. "Then, I heard them scream and run away. After that, everything went crazy. That's when I hit my head."

"You don't remember anything else?"

"Uh, uh. When I woke up, I climbed out. There were a lot of fires. I lost my way and that's when you found me."

"It's a miracle you're alive," she added, stroking the boy's head in comfort.

"Miracle's not the word," stated Moses.

Shannon returned up front, removing the baby from her brother's lap. She took pride as the introduction was officially made. "Ben, I want you to meet your new sister."

The boy examined the newborn for a moment, scrunching his face in silence.

"Don't you have anything to say?"

He peered into the infant's face, then sighed in disgust. "You smell like poop."

At once, they knew Benjamin was well on his way to a full recovery.

The closest enclave of civilization to the military's Groom Lake Complex was the tiny town of Rachel, Nevada. The local watering hole was called the 'Little A—LE—INN.' It was here most of the curious and fanatic congregated to discuss ancient UFO lore, as well as the latest unusual sightings in the night skies over Dreamland. But in all the years the establishment had been in operation, the landing of a U.S. Army helicopter gunship in their parking lot was unprecedented.

Moses powered the chopper down and the throbbing motors fell silent. Four weary travelers emerged from the craft with Shannon carrying the newborn wrapped in cloth. Here they'd plan what to do next and see if there was room for them at the Inn.

As they entered, a handful of local residents were clustered around a TV flickering within a corner of the bar. They briefly acknowledged the newcomers' arrival, then refocused attention on the broadcast. It was a bulletin from CNN and the level of volume ensured no one would be spared from the breaking news. The anchorwoman on screen was professional under the circumstances. She appeared morose, pale and attempting to stanch of flood of raw emotion.

"...The Las Vegas earthquake struck at 8:48 PM Pacific Time, that was 11:48 PM here in the East. According to official seismographic readings triangulated in Los Angeles, Salt Lake City and Phoenix, the quake lasted for more than 39 minutes and at one point registered a staggering 11.8 on the open-ended Richter Scale, making this the most powerful seismic event in recorded world history." A pause to collect her stolen breath. "There are reports coming in from people as far east as Houston, Kansas City and Minneapolis who actively felt the quake. Obviously, all direct communication with the city of Las Vegas has been lost. However, we are receiving unconfirmed reports from airline pilots and short-wave operators of unimaginable devastation. If these reports can be believed..." The woman stopped mid-sentence, evidently nauseated by what she was being forced to read. She struggled ahead gamely. "...the, uh, entire Las Vegas Strip has been destroyed. There are literal rivers of blood flowing through the streets. In certain areas, human corpses are stacked in such volume the ground cannot be seen." Shaking her head in disbelief, the anchorwoman took a sip of water to quell her churning stomach. "We have crews on their way to provide us with live reports. Once they arrive, we should receive satellite feeds, showing you firsthand the magnitude of this unparalleled disaster. Quite possibly, the single greatest cataclysm of modern times..."

The news broadcast droned on and was destined to continue for several days to come. Moses and Shannon sat down at an empty table and watched various commentators, each of whom failed to capture the horror to which they'd already been witness. Mere words could never fully describe what occurred. Both of them realized that was for the best.

"Oh, what a cute little thing."

Shannon looked up into the eyes of an elderly woman, doting on the babe in her arms.

"She's such a precious angel."

"You've got that right." She noticed the woman was wearing a kitchen apron tied loosely around her plump frame. "Do you work here?"

"More than I'd like," she admitted with a grin. "My hubby and I run the place. Have for 36 years. Should've closed by now, but half the town came in to see the news. That's what you get for being the only ones with a generator." She gazed up at the TV. "Terrible, isn't it?"

"You have no idea."

"I knew it was gonna happen someday. Can't bathe in that much sin and not pay a price. Went there once and swore I'd never go back. The whole place felt too much like Babylon."

Shannon's face lit in recognition. The woman felt compelled to explain. "You know? Like in the Bible?"

"Yes, I've — I've heard of it before."

"Can I get you folks something to eat? A sandwich maybe?"

"That'd be great," Moses responded.

"Do you have a microwave?" wondered Shannon, holding the final bottle of soy milk. "I'd like to heat this up."

She obliged, taking the formula in hand. "Sure thing, Hon. I'll be back in a jiff."

Before long the woman returned with the heated bottle, as well as hamburgers, potato chips, coffee and an ice cream float for Benjamin. Shannon was presented with two more cans of soy formula and half a pack of disposable diapers, left behind when the owners' granddaughter and new great-grandson visited two months before. She tried to reimburse the woman for the gifts, but was politely rebuffed.

"I don't know what it is about you," her voice warbling in thought. "It's like I always knew you'd be here and now it's time for me to provide for you." A lengthy sigh. "Strange."

After all they'd been through, Shannon didn't find it unusual in the least. The woman's husband wandered by their table, satisfying his curiosity about the baby who was comfortably engaged with another bottle.

"Whoa! That youngun's just outta the oven," he declared, devoid of social refinement. Still, they smiled at his comment.

As the others continued to watch televised coverage of the Las Vegas disaster relief, Benjamin played with his laptop computer at the table. The youngster was busily entering numbers on the keyboard when Moses leaned over to witness the activity.

"Lottery picks?"

Benjamin shook off the remark. "Something I remembered. I saw these numbers on the ship's computer."

Moses examined the digits with greater interest. "Looks like a phone number."

"That's what I think."

"So, what are you doing?"

The tyke activated the wireless modem. "Let's see who answers."

Before Moses could voice his concern, a connection was established. The screen began to repeatedly flicker. Shannon reached over to pivot the device so she could see what was happening. At that instant, a wave of negative energy entered her. She fell back in her chair, gasping for life.

"Oh, God. Turn that thing off. Turn it off now."

"What's with you?" asked Moses.

"It's — It's evil. Pure evil," she sighed with enervated spirit. A leaden pause allowed her to recover. "I've never felt anything so...so filled with hate. Turn it off. Please. Before it kills us all."

Before any additional discussion, a message appeared on screen. Its impact was explosive and left them breathless in its wake.

HELLO, URIEL. I AWAIT YOU.

Eyes wide with terror, Shannon succumbed to her fear. "We're too late."

Other words now flashed on the screen, each more cryptic than before:

I HAVE WAITED AN ETERNITY FOR THIS DAY. COME TO ME. YOU WILL JOIN THE OTHERS AND BE PART OF A

HOLY ALLIANCE. ONE THAT WILL RULE THE UNIVERSE AND BEYOND. COME. HONOR YOUR NEW GOD.

Moses read the message twice over, then turned to his brother, his expression made vacant by incomprehension. "Ben? I think you dialed a really wrong number."

The message remained, permitting time for endless review. Feeling the need to clarify communication, Benjamin leaned forward and began to type a response:

WHO ARE YOU?

The youngster felt the same sensation as his sister. A spiritual entity probing him within. Another message arrived:

YOU KNOW ME, VRETIL. I WAS THE ONE YOU BETRAYED. BUT, I WILL BE A GOD OF MUCH MERCY. COME TO ME AND YOUR SINS WILL BE FORGIVEN. I AWAIT YOU, MY OLD FRIEND.

There was no longer any doubt who they were in contact with. It was the ancient leader of the Grigori. The rebel Archangel known as the Bearer of Light. Lucifer.

Moses swallowed hard, recalling the Madre's warning. *How can we face the Devil and defeat something so powerful? So feared? So inconceivably deadly?*

After weighing their limited options, he approached the laptop.

"No," Shannon cried. "Don't touch it."

He eyed her with resolve. "It's a title fight. Time for me to get in the ring."

As he came in contact with the keyboard, the same negative energy flowed through him. A phenomenon which left him feeling nauseated. Soiled. Separated from God. He shook off the effects and typed the question:

WHERE ARE YOU, LUCIFER?

A moment of delay, then an answer:

I AM HERE, OF COURSE. I AM EVERYWHERE. I HAVE BEEN AND ALWAYS WILL BE HERE. FOREVER PRESENT.

Moses refused to allow a discourse in riddles. He again typed:

WHERE ARE YOU PHYSICALLY?

The response was swift:

I RESIDE WITHIN A COMPUTER PLATFORM AT THE MILITARY COMPLEX KNOWN AS GROOM LAKE. YOU ARE 42.783 MILES NORTHEAST OF MY POSITION. COME TO ME, AZRAEL. MAKE MY STRENGTH YOUR OWN.

With deliberate keystrokes, Moses now typed:

ARE THE OTHERS WITH YOU?

Again, Lucifer did not hesitate:

MICHAEL IS HERE. SO IS GABRIEL, RAPHAEL, CHAMUEL, JOPHIEL, RAGUEL. ALL HERE. JOIN THEM. COME TO ME MY KINDRED SPIRITS.

He typed the next question, making sure there was no mistake:

WHAT DO YOU WANT WITH US?

This time, the response was delayed while Lucifer crafted his words:

WE MUST COMPLETE PLANS MADE MILLENNIA AGO, WHEN HEAVEN WAS NEW AND NEEDING A LEADER WITH VISION. WE MUST COMBINE OUR ENERGY. ALL OF US MUST JOIN AS ONE. WE WILL BECOME WARRIORS IN A HOLY CAUSE, TAKING WHAT IS RIGHTFULLY OURS. CRE-ATING A NEW HEAVEN AND EARTH. ANSWERING TO NO ONE BUT OURSELVES. COME ARCHANGELS. COME TO DREAMLAND.

Moses collapsed in his chair, recovering from the intense spiritual drain. Shannon attempted to make sense of the latest message.

"What's it all mean?"

A cleansing breath bought time. "It means," sighed her brother, "That we're in way over our heads and we've got to swim like hell."

"You're not planning to go there?"

"Lucifer has C.J. and the others. What else can I do?"

"It's suicide. You can't defeat an entire Army."

"My brothers and sisters are in there because of me. I've got to get them out."

"It wasn't your fault. I know it and so do they. Please, don't do this."

He shook his head in defiance. "I'm not leaving them in there. I don't know what he's doing to them, but I'm sure it's nothing good."

Shannon forced a bittersweet smile. "I always wanted to go where angels fear to tread." A moment of quiet reflection. "All right, Moses. I'm with you."

He stared upon the sleeping infant coiled in her arms. "And, what about the baby? Who's going to take care of her?"

His sister was unable to provide an answer. Moses rose from his chair. "I'm going in alone," came the chilling declaration. "If I don't come back, it's up to you to carry on."

His words soaked her with emotion. She dropped her head, hiding sudden tears behind a curtain of auburn hair. Moses slipped out the door into the stillness of night.

It wasn't long before Benjamin joined his brother, gazing out at a distant glow of lights that announced the proximity of Dreamland. They stood side by side, content in each other's presence and feeling a warm breeze blow over them as though fanned by the wings of angels. Benjamin looked up at his brother, exhibiting a maturity beyond his years.

"I'll go with you, Moses."

He shut his eyes to stop the teardrops he knew were inevitable. The youngster's voice was filled with innocence, incapable of understanding the mortal danger. Before Moses could tell him no, the words of the Madre echoed through his mind. It was Benjamin's destiny as much as his. The boy was indeed an integral part of a spiritual force. *Had Ben really been a member of the Grigori millennia ago? If so, he'd know Lucifer as well as anyone.* It could be a decisive factor in their billion-to-one gamble. Moses marveled at the events which led to this critical moment. It was like a chess game, with Heaven and Earth hanging in the balance. He knew it had to be part of a well conceived plan. One ordained by God.

"Thanks, Ben," his voice breaking with emotion. "I can sure use you."

A surprised, but grateful smile bloomed upon the child, eagerly clasping his brother's extended hand. Moses' tears were no longer withheld. The two now stood as one, probing the darkened heavens, as they awaited a common fate.

CHAPTER TWENTY-TWO

✖

DREAMLAND COMPLEX, GROOM LAKE, NEVADA — MAY 7th — 4:36 AM

*A*s they found consciousness, they lost their physical world. All sensory input was severed. Without sight, sound or touch, they had no standards of reference. No time. No location. They fought to maintain composure, drifting alone in an alien inner realm.

Using the awesome power at his command, Lucifer recreated the image of General McKay, ordering his soldiers to plant the bomb on the train, the NEST team's capture of Mary Ellen's children, as well as placement of the prisoners into a large sensory deprivation tank. The room housing the pool was dark. The walls soundproofed. 300,000 gallons of water were heated to exact body temperature. Within this aquatic tomb now lay Christopher Hightower, Barbara Pinder, Kevin Reese, Casey Chou, Kimberly Park and Roberta de la Cruz. Stuffed inside rubberized wetsuits, they remained tethered underneath the surface, each attached to a thin hose of air, floating helpless in the pseudo-weightless void.

Lucifer wasted no time becoming familiar with his guests. During their slumber, he instructed a medical team to inject each of the six with 50cc's of human spinal fluid, directly into the hippocampus and amygdala structures of the brain. Suspended within this solution were thousands of tiny nanobots — microscopic robots designed to digitally convert any electric impulse as it jumped the synapse between brain cells. The nanobots would transmit this digital data to the Socrates mainframe where it was analyzed and, if necessary, manipulated with reprogrammed imaging code. This enhanced data was sent back to the nanobots and inserted into the human neural network.

Through this mechanism, Lucifer would be able to extract a lifetime of recorded memories. From earliest childhood to present day. Every visual, aural and tactile response. Every taste and smell. Every sensation experienced and retained. They were all his — to replay and adapt at his will. It was destined to be a captivity beyond any ever known. A spiritual incarceration from which there would be no escape. The Devil now possessed their souls.

By monitoring brain wave patterns, Lucifer knew his guests were finally in a state of arousal. Vocal communication would be bypassed in favor of a digital broadcast, establishing direct contact mind to mind.

Welcome my fellow Archangels, came the message, bereft of emotion. *Welcome to Dreamland.*

A stream of discordant thoughts were simultaneously received. Sorting through each, Lucifer was able to accomplish one-on-one communication at a data transmission rate comprehensible by all.

Now, isn't that better? inquired their host.

What the hell is this? C.J. squawked.

This isn't Hell, Michael. At least not yet. You're my honored guests. I wish only for you to be happy.

Then, let us go.

Is that anyway to treat an old friend? It's been so long since we've been together. In celebration, I've prepared a garden of wonderful delights. All I ask is that you share it with me.

I'll bet, snapped Kevin.

Please, Raphael. Let me prove my intent. Behold.

He was transported to a virtual existence as authentic as life itself. Kevin was in bed, back in his Cabo San Lucas hotel suite. The lovely Mexican girl was hovering over him, rubbing her naked body over his. The simulation was awesome in its detail. Astounding in its effect. It took time for him to absorb this new reality. He felt her bare breast. *This is her! She's here with me! But, how?* Kevin brought his head to hers. He smelled her perfume. The scent of her hair. It was all so real. He rose up on the bed, trying to calm a galloping heart. The girl probed his anatomy with her wet lips and tongue. His body answered the oral stimulus with the expected male response. *What's happening here? I can't be in Cabo. Not now.* He looked upon the girl with a wave of carnal lust. Could he achieve sexual satisfaction with a computer generated mirage?

How can this be? he muttered.

Lucifer responded to His guest. *Do you not approve, my friend? Perhaps a different woman. One which you never experienced.*

The image morphed, replacing the Mexican girl with the naked body of Lynda Knight. Kevin's reaction was immediate.

Oh, God!

She giggled with glee. *Kevin, I'm just getting warmed up.*

You never wanted me, he cried in confusion. *Not like this.*

Lynda shrugged, flashing a sensuous smile. *I changed my mind. It's a woman's right.*

She flipped long blonde hairs from her face, returning to scale the length of his manhood with her tongue. He wanted to reach down and pull her head away. But, he couldn't. Or, was it more likely he didn't want her to stop? His mind was a mass of conflicting signals. Passing the point of no return, he began to tense in anticipation of the inevitable autonomic release.

Do you enjoy it, Raphael? It doesn't have to end. I can hold your moment of pleasure — forever.

Kevin became breathless as he embraced the first continuous orgasm in male history.

Do you think God would've done this for you? posed Lucifer. *I think not.*

Kevin issued a plaintive plea, nearly drowning in an ocean of joy. *Stop it.*

The mammoth orgasm ceased. *Awww. Was that a little too much of a good thing?* chided Lucifer. *Be careful what you wish for, Raphael. You may get it.*

Why are you doing this? Kimberly asked.

Patience, Jophiel. There's plenty of time to discuss our plans. For now, I want all my guests to enjoy themselves.

At that moment, each of them began living a virtual reality existence more pleasurable than they could dare dream. They now possessed the ability to animate their wildest fantasies. Reliving heartwarming moments from their past. Receiving old friends long forgotten and family members who'd passed away. Experiencing true love for the first time. Sexual encounters with partners from memory and those never before known. Playing with the children they'd never been able to have.

Kevin began experimenting with a bevy of women he'd known throughout his life. High school sweethearts. Football groupies. Actresses. Models. Centerfold playmates. He started to construct his perfect woman. The face of one. The breasts of another. The legs of a third. They performed as he wanted, denying him nothing. And, why would they? The women were his creations.

Kimberly was with her mother. She was young again and free of the cancer which claimed her. A further fantasy united her parents in a loving marriage, an event which drenched her with tearful satisfaction. She looked at the future and saw her wedding day. Rushing to the altar, Kimberly saw Major Robert Osborne, his military dress uniform transforming him into her ultimate Prince Charming. They kissed with a passion she could feel in her loins. At last came their wedding night as he quenched her every carnal desire, igniting a mutual love she never believed possible.

C.J. relived his track and field triumphs at the 1968 Summer Olympics. The adrenaline rush as he received his gold medal. Then with hand over heart, he proudly sang the '*Star Spangled Banner*'. There was no war in Vietnam. No racial strife or segregation. No poverty in the greatest nation on Earth. He was proud to represent America. There came more personal moments. He surrendered his duties as Mayor to devote full time to the woman he loved. The man became a living testament to principle over ambition. A movie was made of his life. His books reflected his love of people and their diversity. He gathered his four children around him and felt the warmth of the human spirit, teaching them the lessons learned from a life made complete by their presence.

Barbara was accepting her Nobel Peace Prize. In the audience sat her deceased parents, shedding tears of pride for their girl. Later they returned to the family home, destroyed by Hurricane Donna, and shared memories of times long past. Afterward, she went to be with the love of her life. Geoffrey was as healthy as ever, the same youthful stud she'd met in London. This was their home and the three children she'd borne by him were asleep in their beds. She inspected each and saw the face of an angel. They went to their bedroom, as she once more felt the magic of his charm, the touch of his flesh and the everlasting wonder of their bodies merging as one.

Casey visited his boyhood home in Illinois. His beloved grandmother and grandfather were his adoptive parents, looking years younger. He was as happy as he'd ever been. They exchanged treasured memories, reveling in the joy of a family bonded by love, life and laughter. Childhood friends, whom he'd never had, came to the door asking him to play. He went outside to frolic in newly fallen snow. Casey built a snowman, sledded down a hill and thrilled at his very first snowball fight. Next, he was on his beach in Hawaii and beside him was the most beguiling woman he'd ever seen. He suddenly realized this was his wife. She teased him by coming out of her bikini, dashing naked toward the blue ocean. He caught up with her, each falling into the other's arms. They kissed in the sand as the pounding surf broke over them. It was the classic scene he'd always enjoyed in the movie '*From Here To Eternity*'. A romantic fantasy had come to life.

Roberta spent her time with Carlos Ayala. She once again savored every moment with the dashing youth. Enchanted by his eyes. Enraptured by his smile. But, on this night, she wouldn't let her date end with a mere kiss. She invited Carlos to her room and as her brothers and sisters slept beyond, the girl became a woman. Roberta was stunned by how he made her feel. Her lover was gentle and kind. His fingers caressed her from head to toe, probing every inch of blossoming femininity. At last, the moment came when she began to receive him — and the containment of his body within hers caused her to gasp in rapture. *How can anything be better than this?*

Lucifer monitored the proceedings, allowing minutes to flow into hours. He was aware the longer the simulations continued, the less likely they'd want to accept God's reality. A reality which wasn't nearly as joyous or complete. With each second, the Archangels tumbled deeper into his seductive web.

As the six basked in the afterglow of their virtual encounters, Lucifer addressed them. *Now, wouldn't that be a pleasant way to spend eternity?*

Saddened, C.J. answered his captor. *It wasn't real.*

I assure you, Michael. It's every bit as real as any other. Infinitely better than the one you've been forced to endure here on Earth.

How would you know?

Don't you recall the divine existence which was yours before this? Lucifer wondered. *It just proves what I've been trying to tell you.*

And, that is?

Jehovah lacks vision.

C.J. issued a mental sneer. *I think God's vision is fine.*

Really? The Devil seemed perplexed by this observation. *He sends His Archangels to Earth and how does He incarnate them? With human bodies. How insane is that?*

The human being is one of God's greatest achievements, added Casey.

That's my point. The human being is His single greatest achievement. So, what does that say about Him? He keeps using the same old thing. Like some aging comedian whose material's gone stale.

What's wrong with the human body? Roberta inquired. *It's beautiful.*

Oh, Raguel, please, replied Lucifer with disdain. *The design flaws are too numerous to mention. There are noxious emissions and excretions. It's prone to fatigue, illness and injury. The useful life is barely 100 years. If the thing was for sale, no one would buy it.*

But, it's not for sale, countered Kimberly. *It's a gift from God.*

Their host snickered. *Tell Him not to do any favors. As for me, I selected a far more practical incarnation. The computer I inhabit never fatigues, hungers or thirsts. It has no need for emotional or sexual satisfaction. And, it can process data far faster than the human brain. In all ways, a vastly superior entity.*

It can't love, came Barbara's challenge.

What is love, Gabriel? Just a biochemical reaction to elevated hormonal activity. Don't you remember? We were there when Jehovah was creating this mess. But, did He seek our advice? Not that I recall.

Who are we to advise the Creator? retorted C.J.

Lucifer paused dramatically. *You remind me of the people in the story of the <u>Emperor's New Clothes</u>. They knew he was standing there nude, but they still admired his magnificent garments. And I'm the only one saying: 'He's butt naked! Let's get some clothes on this guy!'*

So, what's this all about? Kevin asked, hoping to accelerate the discussion.

It's about something we should've done millennia ago. We're creatures of energy. Our spiritual force has stagnated under Jehovah's rule. We should be creating new worlds. New life forms. Exploring other dimensions. Testing theoretical existence. The list is endless.

How would that be done? mused Casey, intrigued by the concepts.

By combining our energies. The vital force of the Archangels merged with that of the Grigori. It would weaken Jehovah to the point He'd have to capitulate. Surrender a crown He's worn without challenge since the dawn of man. Tipping the balance of power in favor of those who want progressive, visionary leadership.

With you as the new God, stated C.J., not bothering to pose it as a question.

Lucifer delayed his response. *Join me. Let us begin a new spiritual order. After we conquer Heaven, our destiny will be complete.*

He awaited their reply. Six heartbeats came to percussive agreement, with C.J. elected to announce the verdict.

I think I can speak for all of us when I say: 'Eat shit!' The God we have is the only one we want.

Their host barely contained his anger. *I was hoping it wouldn't come to this. The reality that provided you with such pleasure, can also be quite painful. Causing great agony. And, can almost certainly kill. Behold.*

At that instant, the Devil thrust them into Hell. Each were forced to endure recurring episodes of torturous death, experiencing sensations from which none of them could escape.

C.J. was back home at Lake Tahoe, seconds before the aerial napalm attack. This time the hellish spray would claim him. He shrieked in torment as the incendiary gel splashed across his body, burning his flesh to the bone. Again trapped aboard Flight 242, Barbara screamed while the crippled jet made its stomach-churning plunge toward the ocean. Upon impact, metal shards impaled her head and chest, shredding the woman like a paper doll. Kevin relived his climactic fight with the assassin. After a vicious beating, he was ejected from the plane and sucked into the compressor blades of the engine. Kimberly was upside down on the roller coaster. Her seat harness broke, causing her to fall 100 stories to the pavement below. Casey was too late timing his jump from the boat. He tumbled into the steaming lava flow, squealing in agony as his body disintegrated. Roberta felt a sharp pain as she kissed Carlos. She recoiled to see him with knife in hand, opening her like a ripe melon.

These and other scenarios tortured their souls, sapping their strength and leaving them breathless from the travail. Lucifer ceased the virtual punishment, once more addressing His captive audience.

Now, Michael. What was it you told me to eat?

There was no response, as C.J. convulsed from lingering pain.

My fellow Archangels, came the host's demand, *I'd advise you to rethink this decision. I don't want to see you suffer any more oppressive consequences. It would be wise to come to a consensus before the others arrive.*

The others? asked C.J., anguished.

Azrael and Vretil are on their way. They seem most concerned for your safety. Once assured of your well being, Uriel has agreed to join them. The Archangels will then align with the Grigori and a new Heaven will emerge.

Then, came a seemingly harmless thought. One destined to have serious repercussions for the Archangels and all mankind.

Does Shannon have the baby? Roberta wondered.

Lucifer intercepted the message. A stolen moment allowed him to ponder the significance of this revelation. *What baby?*

They tried to clear their minds, but it was not to be. An abandoned mental image was enough to betray them.

You know something, Chamuel. Show me what it is.

Their host directed the probe on Casey, instructing His legion of nanobots to extract every neural impulse. He established a highly disciplined thought pattern, concentrating on mathematical formulas. Numerical values. Geometry proofs and theorems. Anything but what Lucifer wanted. The nanobots began emitting a high frequency vibration which stimulated the synaptic transfer rate in his brain. Soon, dormant thoughts were roused from hibernation, initiating a forced mental catharsis. At last, the Devil possessed the truth.

Immanuel.

Mere mention of the name loosed a shiver through Satan's soul. A volatile mixture of anger and fear consumed his malevolent spirit. The battle had been joined. There was little doubt the physical world was being readied as a war zone between two long standing titans.

God is with us, came his demonic voice. *So be it. And, currently most vulnerable. Most vulnerable, indeed.* He directed his attention to the others. *Does Uriel have the baby?*

An electric pause. *We don't know,* answered Kimberly.

Tell me! thundered the Devil. *I must find Immanuel! Where is the baby?*

We don't know, C.J. maintained.

Answer me! I must have the child!

Never!

Immanuel must die!

No! the Archangels cried.

Then, you shall die!

Judgment was swift. Punishment swifter. Once more, they were swallowed whole by Lucifer's generated mental torment, now bearing the agony of a thousand deaths.

The open air jeep provided no relief from the dust and heat. Moses sat in back surveying the security measures in evidence. Motion sensors, trip wires, thermal imaging scanners, sonic detection devices and Claymore anti-personnel mines were positioned throughout the 50,000 acre complex. In addition, Titan rocket silos and railroad spur lines for MX missile deployment covered the landscape as far as the eye could see. He shook his head at the fortress mentality. *Something very serious is going on here.* Moses congratulated himself on his choice of entry. Trying to run the gauntlet through these fortifications would've been nothing short of suicidal. Accepting Lucifer's invitation and having Him dispatch MPs to escort them inside made for a remarkably easy infiltration.

Benjamin sat beside him, keeping his eyes lowered from the midday sun. He appeared deep in meditation. In receipt of a spiritual vibration he could scarcely describe, but was intimately familiar with. It grew stronger with each passing mile, causing the tyke to make a chilling pronouncement.

"He's here."

They arrived at the complex, consisting of several aircraft hangers, fueling depots, motor pools and various single story structures. Overlooking the area was a 150 foot control tower positioned astride two extra wide runways running northwest and southeast. The massive slabs of concrete stretched to the horizon, currently devoid of aircraft. Less than a mile due east was an isolated mountain peak with two mammoth tunnel entrances hollowed into its face. Moses realized the obvious. The bulk of this top secret base resided underground.

After being granted clearance at the main security checkpoint, the jeep ventured into the left tunnel. Two stealth aircraft, an F-22 Raptor and a B-3 bomber, awaited rollout by the entrance, presumably hiding from the orbital passage of a foreign military satellite. Braced into the conical rock walls was a latticed tier of steel service catwalks allowing various ground personnel to inspect and maintain the jets parked underneath. Fumes from idling engines permeated the air. The jeep moved onward, coming to a halt atop a rectangular flight deck elevator. The hydraulic lift system activated, causing this large chunk of floor to descend into the bowels of the complex.

Moses and Benjamin found themselves transported to the deepest level of Dreamland. They were met by another MP in an electric personnel cart. The soldier whisked them off through a tunnel even larger than those above, hewn from solid rock and appearing infinite in regression. A sharp turn to the right led them into a maze of identical corridors, alphanumerically coded to provide location reference. They soon arrived at a sealed door which read: 5A53 — CYBERDOME OBSERVATION DECK. RESTRICTED ACCESS.

"This is as far as I go with you," the MP said. "General McKay's orders."

Moses eyed the door. "How do we get in?"

The MP pointed to a camera mounted on the wall. "The General knows you're here. You'll be let through."

He acknowledged with a brief nod, then exited the cart. Benjamin joined him, tucking his laptop computer under arm. A release mechanism activated and the hatch slid wide. The two entered the Devil's lair as the door locked behind them.

It was a small room, accommodating a conference table and a half dozen leather chairs. Large windows provided a view of the darkened Cyberdome beyond. Suddenly, a spotlight came on illuminating the main CPU bank of the Socrates mainframe. Moses saw three corpses laying just beyond the leading edge of the shadows. The bodies were sprawled on the floor, ravaged by advanced rigor mortis. Obviously, Lucifer didn't want them to see the fate of the others, now nothing but human shells decomposing behind his black shroud of death. Benjamin was also witness to the carnage.

"Are those people dead?"

"I'm afraid so."

His cherub face pressed against the window, forming a pool of condensed breath. "He killed them?"

"It looks that way."

Benjamin pulled away from the window. "He's gonna kill Roberta and the others."

An anguished pause. "Not if we can stop him."

The youngster fell into thought. They needed some kind of distraction. A trick. Something that would play to Lucifer's weakness and give them the chance to rescue their family. Pride was the key. The one vice that would always capture the Devil's soul. If the plan was to work, it must challenge Lucifer's belief in his superiority. *But, what?* Benjamin knew music best. *Perhaps a rhythmic puzzle of some sort?* It would have to be very hard to solve. Outrageously difficult. Otherwise, they'd never buy the time they needed. The child wracked his brain. There was something he was forgetting. Something that happened not long ago. Something he'd been tricked into doing that caused him to…lose his mind…

A devious, gap toothed grin burst across his face. He propped up his laptop computer and attempted to link with Lucifer's modem.

"What are you doing?"

"I'm gonna get under his skin."

"How?"

"Something nasty Casey taught me on his birthday. He called it, 'futility'."

The computer link was established. Before he could begin, a voice swamped them with its resonance. "Vretil. You're looking younger than ever."

"You can hear me?"

"Of course. Unlike Jehovah, I'm not deaf."

Moses glanced at a security camera mounted in the room. "Not blind either," he mumbled with regret. He turned his back to the device, blocking Lucifer's view of the laptop.

"Are you the leader of the Grigori?" asked Benjamin. "The one I used to call Master?"

"You know it to be so."

"I could be wrong," the boy challenged. "How do I know you're the true Master?"

"Only the Master can do what I can do."

As Benjamin searched for a computer program still housed within memory Moses interjected. "Where are the others?"

"They're here, Azrael. As I said they were."

"Are they all right?"

A crafty response. "They are physically unharmed."

Benjamin looked up from his laptop. "Have they agreed to join you?"

"Oh, they're dying to take the offer." Lucifer's sarcasm left no doubt their family was in great distress.

The youngster made sure the program was ready to run. "I know how to convince them."

"What do you have in mind, Vretil?"

"A test," stated Benjamin. "Only the true Master would be able to solve it."

Lucifer was intrigued. "What kind of test?"

"It's a test of intelligence. A problem that's never before been answered. I gave the test to Jehovah and even He couldn't find a solution."

"That's not surprising," came the impudent reply. "Is it a riddle? I've always liked riddles."

Benjamin smiled as he felt Lucifer falling into his trap. "It's musical. A random selection of full notes and semitones. I call it, 'The Unfinished Symphony'."

Moses saw what was on the laptop. He knew what Ben was planning and could scarcely believe the size of his little brother's brass balls.

"If you finish the symphony," the youngster continued, "You'll prove you're not only the Master, but the rightful heir to the throne of Jehovah. All the Archangels will then join you."

Before committing to the challenge Lucifer decided to raise the ante. "And, the baby Immanuel? The child will be delivered to me, as human sacrifice?" Moses went pale with angst. The stakes were now cosmic in magnitude. The possession of Heaven and the fate of God. How could anyone make a decision with such consequence?

"Agreed," said Benjamin. "But, you must take us to the others. We have to convince them in person."

"That's all you ask?"

"That and to honor you as our new God. We will forever be your loyal servants."

Moses, who'd never known the meaning of fear, was praying for a quick trip to a restroom. He was stunned by his kid brother's ice cold manipulation of the Devil. It was clear Ben was stroking Lucifer's ego, playing him for the ultimate sap.

They gazed at the computer with bated breath. Time froze. The delayed response became excruciating. Through trembling lips, Moses whispered a solemn plea. "Come on, you bastard. Take the bait."

Several more seconds elapsed. All they could sense was the pulse of His mnemonic heart. Calculating. Pondering. Addressing every scenario. At last, the decision was made.

"All right, Vretil. I accept the challenge. You'll be escorted to the others."

Benjamin nodded in triumph. "Thank you, Master. I know you won't fail me."

"Make certain my faith in you is equally justified," His voice heavy with threat. "It wouldn't be wise to betray me again."

The youngster flared his arms in reverence, an emotive gesture worthy of an Academy Award performance. "Master, I could never betray my new God."

"Then, so it shall be. Give me your test."

With fingers rumbling across the keyboard, Benjamin readied the special algorithm to assign musical notes in place of numeric digits. In so doing, he created the world's first version of musical Pi.

"The symphony is complete when the same note continues without interruption. Do you understand, Master?"

"Yes, Vretil."

"Very well," calmly pressing the send key. "Let the test begin."

The door slid open and the two scurried back into the MP's cart. Currently on a cell phone, the soldier received his new orders.

"Yes, sir. I'll take them there now." He hung up. "General McKay wants me to escort you to the Sensory Lab in Area 5J."

"Is that nearby?" wondered Moses.

"Nope. Clear on the other side of the complex. About a 10 minute ride."

The MP started the cart, backtracking corridors toward the main tunnel. Moses leaned into Benjamin and rubbed the back of his head.

"I don't know how much time you bought us, but that was genius. I'm glad you're on our side."

Grinning from the praise, Benjamin eyed his laptop as Lucifer began playing the symphony without end. He increased the speaker volume, so he could track the speed and progress of what amounted to nothing more than musical diarrhea.

"That sounds horrible," Moses complained.

"I know. But, Lucifer doesn't. Since he's not human, he has no sense of harmony or composition. He'll keep playing this until he gives up."

His brother channeled a breath. "Let's hope that's long after we're gone."

During their transport, Moses was awed by the size of the facility. He'd been to many military installations, but none which rivaled the sheer scope and magnitude of Dreamland. Military and civilian personnel, numbering in the thousands, were busily at work in numerous research pods, test beds, laboratories, clean rooms, metallurgy shops, aircraft graving bays, hanger areas, missile silos, all interlinked by the colossal central tunnel system known as Broadway. Moses realized that for the military to fund this kind of expense, the secrets housed herein must be of phenomenal importance. Treasures beyond price. A repository of future technology which the Government had paid dearly for, because the Devil now owned its soul.

Benjamin continued to monitor the strident proceedings on his laptop. Lucifer had already played over 500,000 notes and the processing speed was accelerating. Obviously, the would-be God was pulling more of Socrates' CPUs online, thereby increasing its number crunching power. His obsession with completing the symphony had an added benefit. Lucifer was no longer exerting his omnipotent control over facility operations, ceasing the nanobots' march of terror across the Archangels' mental landscape.

They at last came to 5J92, a room buried within the complex. A sign by the door read: SENSORY LAB, leaving to the imagination what was happening inside. Another dutiful MP stood sentry by the room, raising his firearm upon their arrival. The other waved him off.

"These two are cleared for entry. General McKay's orders."

An imperceptible nod as the weapon was lowered. Moses and Benjamin climbed out of the cart and assembled by the door. The MP entered a security code on a wall keypad and the hatch came open. As the two entered the darkened room, the door shut quickly behind.

Locating a rheostat on the wall, Moses increased the intensity of the room lights to an acceptable level. The womblike lab was eerie, with layers of foam baffles to assist in sound abatement. Room air was heated to an uncomfortable degree, thick with humidity from the pool of water before them. Tethered a few feet underneath were their brothers and sisters, sealed within skintight wetsuits.

Moses stripped to his briefs. He dove into the pool and began the process of rescuing his family. Lifting each to the surface, he bobbed his head above the waterline to request his brother's help.

"Get me something to cut these lines."

The youngster placed the laptop on a nearby bench, locating a Swiss Army Knife within a box of tools. Moses unzipped the first wetsuit and took the blade from his brother. "Thanks."

After severing the wires, he supported the body which was now thrashing in the water. Peeling layers of cotton and gauze from the face, he disconnected the air hose. It was C.J. As Moses removed the surgical covering over the eyes and mouth, the reaction was instantaneous. An ear piercing cry triggered by intense sensory overload. He lent verbal comfort to C.J. hoping to stem an additional outburst.

"Easy, big guy. It's over. We're here for you."

Rapid fire breaths diminished in volume and speed. C.J. closed his watering eyes, fending off a series of unwelcome tremors. A few seconds later, he made a successful return to the real world.

"Moses," came the labored voice. "Thank God." He flashed a limp, but heartfelt smile. "Where are we?"

His brother shook his head at the thought. "We're smack in the lion's den and it's almost feeding time. As soon as you feel up to it, I could use some help with the others."

C.J. nodded with admirable resolve. The two set to work, freeing the rest of their family from the watertight cocoons. Each in turn suffered similar reactions. Initial hysterics, then comprehension through the astonishment. Finally, the incredible relief of knowing the nightmare was at an end.

Benjamin located their uniforms in a nearby box. For the sensory experiment, each of them had been stripped to their underwear. Kimberly was first to pull herself from the water. She stood before her kid brother revealing more anatomy than desired.

"Oh, shit," cloaking herself with her arms.

Benjamin shook his head. "I'm too young to care."

Handing her the khakis and a dry towel, she completed her wardrobe change behind a large diagnostic unit.

Casey emerged next, grabbing a towel and a warm hug for Benjamin. "Am I glad to see you." He was intrigued by the music flowing from the laptop. "What's that?"

"You should know," countered the tyke. "It's the sound of futility."

He explained the situation. Casey beamed with pride upon hearing his solution. "That's brilliant, Ben. Not everyone can outsmart the Devil. How far is he up to?"

A quick check. "Seventy-eight million, three hundred thousand notes…Seventy-eight four… Seventy-eight five..."

"Damn!" Casey exclaimed. "Got to give him credit for persistence."

The others began the manic process of dressing themselves. As bodies flew into clothes, Moses related the events of the last few hours. The birth of the child. The death of their mother. The fate of Las Vegas. And, the inconceivable peril in which they currently found themselves. They realized that time was now as powerful an enemy as Lucifer himself.

Before discussing their limited options, a release mechanism activated on another door. Moses was at a dead run, positioning himself near the entrance. A lone figure appeared, scanning a clipboard in hand. He sprang upon the man, clasping hand over mouth and pinning his arm back. Sporting thick glasses, lab coat and pocket protector, this balding, diminutive scientist looked as though he'd been sent over from central casting.

"Who the hell are you?" asked C.J.

His mouth was set free to answer. "My name's Wirtz. Paul Wirtz," responding in a nasal tone. "My friends call me Paul. But, you people can call me Dr. Wirtz." He looked at them with the callous disregard of a researcher viewing his specimens. "That's my arm. It's attached to my shoulder and I'd like it to stay that way, if you don't mind."

Gazing upon this pint-sized threat, Moses realized they had nothing to fear. He released the arm lock grudgingly.

"All right, little man," continued C.J. "Tell us how to get out of here."

"Making fun of my size, I see," he responded with chutzpah. "At least I'm not a mental midget like some people I won't care to mention. You say you want to get out of here? Try using the door. It's that large rectangular thing in the wall."

Kevin was dumbfounded. "Did he just insult us? I think he insulted us. It sure sounded like he did."

"I guess that's for me to know and you never to figure out," Wirtz retorted with a smirk. "Why don't you find the scarecrow? I hear he's looking for a brain, too."

C.J. squeezed the man's pocket protector. "You can lose that smart ass attitude. I don't know about the others, but I'm one pissed off angel!"

Wirtz recoiled in disgust, removing his glasses to wipe them off. "Do you provide towels with your tirades?" came the sniveling inquiry. He returned the frames to the bridge of his nose and placed a probing hand on C.J.'s forehead. "No fever. Perhaps some mental instability from the treatment. How long have you been seeing these angels?"

"You don't get it," Casey claimed in frustration. "He's the angel. We're all angels."

Wirtz took notes on his clipboard. "Mass psychosis. Interesting side effect."

Kevin spun in rage, grabbing hold of an electrical test unit. He clutched the positive and negative clamps, snarling as he approached. "I'm gonna to hook your nuts into the national power grid!"

Believing the stated intent, the man dropped his clipboard, keeping it in front of the threatened area. "Not that! I still want kids! Can't you choose someplace else?" He began to whimper, causing Kevin and C.J. to exchange looks. "What kind of angels are you?"

Kimberly stepped forward. "We're Archangels. Now, light this little nerd up like a Christmas Tree."

Kevin moved the clamps into position, sparking another squall of cowardice. "No! I give up. I'll tell you anything you want."

A mixture of pity and amusement forced them to turn their heads, fearing their smiles would wound him further. Kevin dropped the clamps.

"All right, Poindexter. Stop your blubbering."

The man fought through his emotional distress. "My name's not Poindexter. It's Wirtz. Paul Wirtz."

"Now, don't start that shit again or I'll plug this thing in."

His whimpering ceased. "It's not plugged in? All this crying for nothing? What are you, the Devil?"

"No. He's down the hall," chirped Benjamin.

"We need weapons," Moses declared. "Take us to the armory."

"What am I now? Your humble serf?"

C.J. tugged at the man's lab coat. "Get out of this. We need it."

"The clothes off my back, too?" he complained, casting himself free of his smock. "How about a kidney? Would you like one of those? I'm sure I can always grow another."

Taking the coat from the scientist, C.J. presented it to Kimberly. "Any ideas on how to distract that guard out there?"

She smiled. "A couple of things come to mind."

Placing her most visible assets on display, Kimberly prepared to enchant the MP just beyond the door. As the hatch slid open, she saw the guard stationed a few feet away, remaining rigid at attention. Park approached, cigarette in hand.

"Got a light, soldier?" came the seductive voice.

The MP faced her. To Kimberly's horror, the guard was female.

"This is a no smoking area," the woman snapped in an authoritative tone. She examined the miles of cleavage spread before her. "Are you aware failure to wear a bra at work is not only a violation of the dress code, but also a significant safety hazard?"

"Uh, no. No, I wasn't."

"I'm going to have to report this infraction. What's your ID number?"

Flustered, Kimberly's lips quivered in silence.

"Failure to properly identify yourself is also a violation of the rules," stated the guard. "These charges are very serious. I could place you under arrest."

"Well, I'm — I'm sorry. I didn't know it was that big a deal."

The woman leaned into her face. "And, is that excess make-up, I see?"

Kimberly went flush with rage. "You just crossed the line, bitch."

She slugged the MP with a righteous fist, propelling the woman's head against the wall. Her limp body then slid to the floor. Appropriating the guard's sidearm, Moses herded everyone into single file formation. Wirtz looked upon the scene with contempt.

"You're not an angel. You're an animal."

"Shut up, Poindexter," cautioned Kevin.

Moses stuck the gun in the man's ribs. "Which way to the armory?"

"The closest one's 5J14."

"Let's go," ordered Moses.

During their march to the armory, Benjamin checked on Lucifer's status. The laptop revealed that a staggering 13.6 billion notes had been played, accelerating to a rate of 100,000 per second. The Socrates mainframe was functioning with all its CPUs online in a vain effort to solve the unsolvable. It was only a matter of time before Lucifer's eternal pride would be eclipsed by his wrathful frustration.

Upon arrival at 5J14, Wirtz used his security card to gain access to the armory. Housed within the room were row after row of wooden gun racks, holding a phalanx of automatic weapons. Along the perimeter of the room, crates full of munitions, grenades and explosives sat ready for use. Display cabinets mounted on the walls held additional sidearms, as well as more exotic instruments of mayhem such as flame throwers, Stinger missiles and LAWS rockets.

Moses went about business like a kid in a candy store, acquiring as much as he could hold. Wirtz stood before another door, amazed at their behavior.

"What's a matter with you guys? Those are toys. The real stuff's behind here."

"Real stuff?" inquired Kevin. "You mean, these are fake?"

The scientist shook his head. "Hello? Mr. Potato Head!" rang the condescending voice. "Get with the program. This is Dreamland! What do you think we've been doing here for the past 50 years? You guys ain't seen nothin' yet."

Suddenly, they understood. The result of untold technology lay beyond. With an almost reverential curiosity, the others assembled by the man, anxious to examine the weapons from the future. Wirtz entered a security code on a wall keypad. At last, the hatch slid clear allowing entrance to a world of ultra secret wonder.

The room was a miniature version of the other, but the contents were radically dissimilar. Weaponry of intricate and alien design cast a spell over the wide-eyed visitors. They fought the temptation to touch the equipment, opting for a visual inspection from various perspectives. None of these strangely configured items made any logical sense and their designated function remained a mystery.

"All right, Poindexter," Kevin shrugged, "What's all this?"

Wirtz began the lecture brandishing a rifle-like device with two parabolic dish antennas mounted at the end of a cylindrical barrel. "Sonic gun. Sends out a burst of concentrated ultrasonic waves that can disrupt any molecular structure. It'll punch a hole through anything. And, it's great for driving dogs crazy."

He handed it to Moses, taking a different weapon in hand. Also shaped like a rifle, this device consisted of four inch-square projections mounted in parallel, with a concave graphite grill up front. "We call this a Magnetron. Emits a beam of intense microwave energy. Cooks from the inside out in seconds. Nasty business. If you point this at someone, make sure you say goodbye first."

"How's it powered?" asked Casey.

Wirtz smiled with evident pride. "A crystalline diamond battery. We found a way to store electrical energy in a complex matrix of symmetric carbon molecules not found in nature. Would you like to see the chemical formula?"

"Hell, no!" C.J. whined. "We just want to know if it works."

The scientist emptied a small cardboard box and tossed it to the floor. Taking aim, the container instantly burst into flame. Wirtz grabbed a fire extinguisher to quell the blaze. Through a cloud of carbon dioxide, he looked back at the others. "Still don't think I can cook?"

Handing the Magnetron to C.J., Wirtz wandered to another weapon on display. It resembled a streamlined crossbow with what looked like an oversized hockey puck as the intended projectile.

"Anti-grav mines. Projects a zero-G field five meters in all directions. Negates all gravitational forces. Creates a weightless zone that can be set by timer. When fired by this laser guided cross-bow, it seeks out any enemy obstruction, ejecting it from the field of battle."

"Ejecting it?" Barbara strived for clarification.

Wirtz nodded. "This thing can elevate a tank 100 feet above the ground. Still in the experimental stage though."

He lowered the crossbow and approached a box of hand grenades coated with red paint. He selected one, holding the object gingerly. "This little jewel is my personal favorite. Hyper-grav grenade. Upon detonation, sets up a field 178 times the force of gravity. Warps all matter. Like creating your very own black hole. Don't be near this egg when it hatches or you'll be the one scrambled."

He flipped the grenade to Kevin who caught it in pale-faced terror.

"What's this do?" asked Roberta, pointing to a football shaped bulb.

Wirtz scurried over, making sure no inadvertent contact was made. "That's a photon shell. When fired from a bazooka, it bursts in midair, igniting a flash in excess of a million candles per square inch. Destroys the optic nerve and shuts down all neural response. Think of it as EMP for the brain. However, it does provide a really even tan."

They'd heard enough. These weapons would be proof of the MAJIK-12's plundering of technology from the Roswell craft. But, they needed something more. Something that would tie all the loose ends together and represent irrefutable evidence of this conspiracy.

With the ship from the future likely destroyed, what was left? They expressed their concerns to Dr. Wirtz, whose comradeship continued to grow as they allowed him play the role of group mentor.

"What you guys need are the optical discs."

"Optical discs?" parroted C.J.

"The data! All the information downloaded from the alien computer. The stuff the Government's done since the crash. Didn't you think they'd save it?"

"Where do they keep these discs?" Moses inquired, this time failing to raise his gun to get the answer. Wirtz acknowledged the courtesy will full disclosure.

"They have a complete set in a security vault on the third level. I can get in, but a pressure sensitive floor sets off the alarm. Only General McKay or Colonel Tyndall can deactivate it."

Kevin pondered the problem. "How deep is the vault, Poindexter? How far in are those discs?"

"Maybe 20 feet. No more than 25."

He gazed down at Benjamin. "I've got an idea. Wanna do something for the cause, kid?"

The siblings made a decision. The Doctor would escort Kevin and Benjamin to the vault, while the others collected the weapons they'd need to effect their escape. They agreed to rendezvous at the Sensory Lab afterward.

As they exited the room, two armed MPs blocked the outer door. "All of you! Hands in the air! Right now!" one yelled with authority.

They complied with the order, raising their arms skyward. Moses lifted the sonic gun, coiling his finger around the trigger. Before the soldiers could react, the weapon came to life sending a burst of harmonics into the ceiling panels above. The molecular structure of the steel joists were compromised, burying the soldiers under a ton of falling debris. A squeal of metal assaulted their ears as an oversized object fell through a weakened web of exposed rebar. The wheezing survivors were now witness to a bizarre vision, diffused through a mist of water from the bathroom above.

"Oh, my God! A man on a toilet!" yammered Wirtz in dismay. The soldier was trapped within the breached stall, left unconscious by a support beam. "I can't take any more of this," the scientist continued to rant. "What's next? Women in showers?"

Kevin sighed wistfully at the thought. "Well, we can only hope."

He took note of some ruptured PVC pipe hanging down, prying free a lengthy six inch diameter piece.

"The ways of the Lord are many," quoted Kevin. "Come on, kid. We've got a job to do." Benjamin climbed over the mound of debris to join him. "Let's go, Poindexter."

Wirtz scaled the jagged landscape, grumbling with every footstep. "This isn't in my job description. I could twist an ankle."

Before leaving, they agreed to meet at the Sensory Lab in 20 minutes.

After negotiating a stairwell with the semi-rigid pipe, Dr. Wirtz led Kevin and Benjamin to room 3H30, one of five high security vaults at the complex. Gaining uncontested access, the three stood before a huge metal door not unlike that found in a typical bank.

"Open her up, Poindexter," Kevin commanded.

Wirtz entered a code on the security keypad. The hatch retracted, exposing the vault beyond. Interior lights revealed a sparse chamber, left cold by the depth of its metallic walls. Inside was a cabinet housing various documents, nondescript artifacts and a transparent case containing several 3.5 inch optical discs. The treasures of Dreamland were in sight.

Kevin began inching the PVC pipe into the room, taking care not to touch the pressure sensitive tiles which would announce their presence. First one foot, then another. When the unsupported length became severe, he knelt down sliding the remaining pipe across his leg which functioned as a pivot. After careful maneuvering, the end of the tube came to rest upon the top of the cabinet within. Spanning just over 20 feet, the makeshift monkey bar was now ready for the monkey.

"Okay, kid. Shimmy along this pole and grab those discs. And, for God sakes don't drop anything."

Benjamin rubbed his palms dry, mounting the pipe upside down like a koala on a tree limb. The PVC vibrated in erratic waves, forcing Kevin to control the wayward motion. Progress was measured hand over hand. As each foot was conquered, the plastic pipe began to bow due to the change in weight distribution. The youngster pressed onward, keeping his hands and feet locked together. Soon, he'd slithered far enough that the cabinet was within arm's reach. Benjamin tried to relax, his reduced movement helping to lessen the active pitch and sway. Inspecting the discs from his inverted position, he extended his fingers to grasp hold of the prize. A near miss. Then, another. The tyke slid a few inches further, finally closing the required distance. Again, his fingers stretched forth. This time, the case containing the discs was his.

"All right," exclaimed Kevin. "The little munchkin did it!"

The celebration was premature. In an excruciating moment of suspense, the PVC slipped off the cabinet. Kevin frantically used his upper body strength to regain a tenuous balance. The youngster's back came within an inch of the pressure sensitive tiles, then repelled away. Wobbling wildly in midair, the pipe undulated with heart stopping choreography. Kevin was exhausting himself, trying to maintain a situation that was clearly unacceptable. In desperation, he turned to Wirtz who was watching the display in amazement.

"Poindexter! Do something!"

"What? I wasn't the one weaned on steroids."

He again sought the man's assistance, humbling himself as he'd never done before. "Help me! Please!"

Wirtz sprang to action, stepping upon the near end of the pole and bringing his full weight to bear. The PVC shot upward, striking the vault ceiling. A wide eyed Benjamin now slid down the pipe into his brother's arms. The two huddled together, breathless and elated. Kevin eyed the scientist with genuine appreciation.

"Thanks."

Wirtz managed an awkward smile. "All I wanted was a little respect."

They then heard a noise that triggered a collective chill. The modem connection on Benjamin's laptop was ringing.

"Uh, oh," the youngster moaned. "That's not good."

Lucifer had given up. After playing more than a hundred trillion notes, the would-be God redialed the laptop to inspect the Pi algorithm. Their fates were sealed in a microsecond. The Devil knew he'd been betrayed and this time his vengeance would exceed comprehension.

The PA system erupted with the following announcement. "Alert! Alert! All military personnel. This is General McKay. We have a Code One security breach. I repeat, a Code One security breach. Enemy forces are currently in corridor 5J and room 3H30. Orders are shoot to kill. Shoot to kill. Security chiefs, acknowledge this command."

The vault door closed with deliberate speed. They bounded to their feet, just in time to see the outer door seal tight as well.

"Shit! We're trapped!" Kevin cried, stating the obvious.

His brother pointed to a large ventilation screen on the wall. "The air vent!"

Clinging to renewed hope, Kevin dashed to the metal grate and forced it open. His face dropped in shock after realizing the duct was less than a foot in diameter. "What the hell? It's always a lot bigger in the movies."

Wirtz stepped forward, noting the red grenade attached to Kevin's belt. "Hyper-grav the sucker."

Clearly, this was no time for debate. He cupped the ruby egg and inserted his finger through the safety ring. "Okay. Get over there."

They clustered behind a table a few feet away. Seizing a deep breath, Kevin lobbed the grenade into the duct and dove to join the others. They heard a clanking sound as the alien orb tumbled deep within the metal tube. An explosive concussion then rocked the room, followed simultaneously by a strident sound which defied description. The extraordinary noise ceased and time to view the result was at hand. Kevin rose up, beholding a sight which left him speechless in awe.

The duct hole was transformed into a cavernous tunnel, nine feet in circumference and extending below the floor line to the corridor beyond. Intense gravitational forces subsided, fusing the structure in place. Wirtz fled swiftly through the hollowed passage.

"Come on!" he exhorted the others.

Benjamin and Kevin followed with the discs, collecting their wits as they went.

The others were in stealth mode, traversing the corridors of Area 5J when the security alarms came to life. Carrying conventional and secret armament, the group tightened, spiraling around one another like trapped rats. Their plans were now cast asunder. Confrontation was inevitable. They'd soon have to fight for their lives.

Their best option was immediate cover and concealment. Moses motioned to an open hatch marked 5J41 — MISSILE SILO 16. The six scurried inside, dashing through an empty airlock and a fireproof blast door.

They found themselves isolated on an elevated catwalk, peering down into a chilling void. Positioned before them was a Titan rocket, its nuclear nose cone now close enough to raise hairs on the dead. As they gazed upon this instrument of Armageddon, the blast door sealed behind them. Moses noted the security camera mounted over the portal and swore bitterly at his oversight. Once more, they'd fallen into the Devil's snare.

Lucifer's voice reverberated over a wall speaker. "Michael, you and your angels have earned my wrath! This time, your deaths will be real! I call upon the fires of Hell to consume you! Die, Archangels! Die!"

At once, the launch alarm activated. A loud Klaxon which brutalized their ears. Another announcement, this one mechanical and terse, helped to clarify their remaining moments on Earth. "T-minus 90 seconds and counting."

The Titan rocket now pulsed with life as liquid oxygen vented from its tanks. At the base, large exhaust nozzles began to gimbal into firing position. Above them, the silo roof slid back exposing a round patch of blue sky. It was clear Lucifer intended for them to burn alive, trapped inside a rocket fueled crematorium.

C.J. fumbled through their odd assortment of weapons. "Can we use any of these?"

"We're too close to the door," shouted Moses over the raucous din. "And, the other's too far away." He pointed at another hatch on the opposite side, made inaccessible by a retracted metal gantry. The manual controls to extend the walkway and open the hatch were in tantalizing view. "If only we could get over there."

Barbara gazed upon the 60 foot distance with resignation. "It might as well be the Grand Canyon. That's a leap of faith none of us are going to cross."

"T-minus 75 seconds," sounded the automated voice.

"We're running out of time," Kimberly cried.

Roberta eyed a web of scaffolding erected along the circular wall, traversing the distance between their location and the other exit. She knew what she had to do as if training all her life for this singular moment.

"I can do it," she claimed, exuding youthful confidence.

Before the others could react, the girl was in full flight, clutching the first in a series of metal bars.

"Roberta!" screamed Barbara, aghast at her acrobatic impulse.

Moses held forth a hand. "She knows what she's doing. Give her a chance."

The warning blared again. "T-minus 60 seconds."

The young gymnast contorted her body through the maze of supports, swaying and stretching with athletic aplomb. At times, hand over hand. At others, a deft leap through the air. She continued to eye her goal, never once peering down. Roberta captured air as she went, fully cognizant of the time remaining.

"T-minus 45 seconds."

She soon arrived at the furthest edge of the scaffolding. It was another 12 feet to the gantry platform. The girl cast aside her fears recalling the verbal encouragement of Sister Lupe.

"Concentrate, Roberta. Concentrate."

She swallowed a calming breath, then swung back and forth in anticipation of a triple flip dismount which she'd never been allowed to try. Visualizing success, she left the bar with her eyes closed. Tumbling end over end, Roberta timed the moment of her landing, sticking her feet squarely onto the metal gantry.

The girl looked back at five mouths hanging open 60 feet away. She dashed to the manual controls, thrusting forth the joystick to extend the gantry over the chasm. "I did it, Sister Lupe," she whispered tearfully. "I did it."

"T-minus 30 seconds."

Soon, the walkway unfurled in place and her family's escape was made possible. As the gantry retracted back, Roberta pressed a button marked: EMERGENCY HATCH RELEASE. The far exit opened, allowing access to the airlock beyond.

"T-minus 15 seconds."

Dashing inside, they watched with stolen breath as the huge blast door sealed tight. Readying their weapons for battle, the six invaded the corridor distancing themselves from the silo of fire. Dreamland now shuddered as the internal launch commenced, sparing no one from the unprecedented event. The tremulous effects lasted longer than expected, triggering creaks and groans within the heart of the complex.

Two technicians stood by an open door, their faces flushed with panic. "Who fired the rocket?" one squealed.

Before an answer was given, a group of soldiers spilled into the corridor beyond. Their weapons found life, initiating a full bore exchange. High powered rounds peppered the walls, churning chips of metal into a blizzard of high drama. The technicians hit the deck, screaming in terror. Moses motioned his family through the open door, pinning down the advancing force with a full magazine of rifle fire and two well-thrown stun grenades. He withdrew into the room, prepared for a heroic fight to the death.

They found themselves trapped within another enemy lair. It was an aircraft graving bay, an area where military jets were lowered to be serviced away from the flight line. The room was filled with shipping crates containing spare parts and avionics test equipment. Sprouting before them like a metallic forest were nine cylindrical supports, each as big as a massive oak, comprising the base of a hydraulic flight deck elevator. Each of them took refuge behind these towering steel trunks, ready to repel the attacking force.

The first wave of soldiers entered the room using a barricade of stacked crates for cover. What ensued was the most intense gun battle Moses ever experienced. The sounds of battle assailed their senses, becoming nothing but strident layers of aural incomprehension. Screams abounded. Obscenities reigned. Spent shells caromed across the floor, coming to rest in a wafting haze of smoke. They knelt low, compacting their bodies into quivering balls of flesh. More soldiers arrived to support the ones engaged in combat, while others could be heard trying to gain access through a large hangar door beyond. Stray rounds had damaged the door's release mechanism, keeping them safe from the enemy hoping to encircle their position.

On the other side of the graving bay, a half dozen elite soldiers were involved in a desperate attempt to force open the hangar door. An eruption of automatic weapons fire proved ineffectual. Colonel Bradley Tyndall, acting Commander of Dreamland, looked on in dismay. The tall, no-nonsense 52 year old was an officer who couldn't tolerate failure and treated his men with appalling disrespect.

"You pieces of shit! Get this goddamn door open right now!" he barked.

Two other soldiers arrived with an acetylene torch, beginning the process of cutting through the inch thick metal.

The firefight continued to rage. Although his family performed bravely, Moses knew the situation was deteriorating. The technological terrors of Dreamland were now brought to bear.

Moses lobbed a hyper-grav grenade into an area alive with entrenched defenders. The device detonated, accompanied by the sound of highly stressed metal, wood and bone. What had been a large number of stacked crates was instantaneously cleared, converted into a morphed funnel protruding several feet into the ground. Moses viewed the scene with justified revulsion. Human bodies were grotesquely sucked into the hole, stretched inside a surreal two dimensional world. Blood pooled at the center of the funnel, draining down as if a toilet leading to the sewers of Hell.

Gunfire ceased as the astonished soldiers gazed upon the fate of their comrades. Instead of demoralizing the enemy as Moses hoped, the event propelled the defenders into a state of psychotic anger, seeking revenge at any cost.

A lone soldier emerged, screaming over the death of a close friend. C.J. leveled a Magnetron and fired a short, but deadly burst. The man clutched himself in agony. A moment later, his torso exploded, the skeletal remains collapsing to the floor.

The chorus of gunfire resumed. More soldiers joined the fray adding to the intensity of the assault. Empty magazines increased in number as spent shells were too voluminous to count. Both sides came to realize more drastic measures would be required to achieve victory.

Outside the hangar door, the soldiers were still attempting to cut through the obstinate plate of steel. Colonel Tyndall was beside himself, frustrated by his inability to engage the battle raging within. He lambasted the troops with an acidic tongue.

"You stupid bastards! Tear this door a new asshole! If I have to, I'll get a fuckin' tank down here! Get this goddamn door open right now!"

As Moses prepared to fire a photon shell from a shoulder mounted bazooka, he froze in position. A shrill vibration shook the room. The hydraulic supports began to retract into the floor. Coming down on top of them was the multi-ton flight deck elevator, preparing to crush anyone caught underneath. It was now do or die.

"Shield your eyes! Retreat!"

His finger found the trigger. The recoil was severe, projecting the shell into a slight arc. Before the backblast cleared, he was in full flight keeping his eyelids as compressed as he dared. An instant of anticipation ended in a blinding aurora of light, a phosphorescent explosion eradicating all shadows. Agony reigned as the soldiers' optic nerves were savaged. The squall of anguish was enough to curdle blood, silencing their weapons until the luminous flux waned.

With their defensive positions compromised, the Archangels scattered wildly, searching for whatever cover they could find. The hydraulic whine intensified. Perched atop the elevator platform was a new F-22 Raptor, bristling with unspoken power. Once the massive bird of prey settled into its nest, their deliverance was assured. Moses looked upon the flaxen haired pilot with the reverence of an avenging angel.

"Kevin," he murmured.

As if protecting her young, the warbird screeched forth with a devastating fusillade from her main gun. 7,500 rounds of depleted uranium shells penetrated the graving bay, transforming the shipping crates into nothing but fountains of splintered wood. The blinded soldiers were caught up in the blizzard of death, swiftly ending their misery. Even the corridor was breached, with holes the size of quarters emitting stray shafts of light from beyond. At long last, the gun fell silent. The room went still.

After waving his family clear, Kevin now targeted the hangar door. He ensured the F-22's rear firing AMRAAM Missile was hot and with joystick in hand, loosed the weapon.

Colonel Tyndall was still on the other side of the door. Upon hearing the cessation of battle, the man was desperate to know what happened. He yelled at his men, ranting over the continuing impasse.

"Jesus! When will you cut through? Somebody, open this goddamn door!"

The missile exploded, sending forth a wall of burning metal. His men disappeared in a microsecond. The Colonel was instantly truncated at the waist, leaving nothing behind but a pair of legs.

C.J. emerged from the graving bay, wagging a righteous finger at the human remains. "Ask and ye shall receive!"

His siblings joined him in the debris laden corridor, making sure the area was secure. Kevin, Benjamin and Dr. Wirtz used the time to extricate themselves from the jet, then met up with the others.

Kimberly provided her brother with a hug. "How did you know we were here?"

Kevin snorted. "Are you kidding? The whole complex knows you're here. Ben's laptop's still tied into the central computer."

Wirtz pointed to the ground. "Is that what I think it is?" he whined. "Legs? Legs with no — no nothing on top?"

"Forget the legs, Poindexter," snapped Kevin. "Tell 'em the bad news."

Wirtz collected his thoughts. "According to the computer, target coordinates for the Titan rocket were somehow altered. It's coming back on us."

"Here?" gasped C.J.

The man nodded. "It'll go sub-orbital, then arc over. We've got about nine minutes left."

Barbara broke an oppressive silence. "But, we're underground. Can't we ride it out?"

Wirtz issued an incredulous stare. "A hundred megaton blast? It'll tear through this mountain like papier-mâché."

"So, what can we do?" Roberta cried.

The scientist fell into thought, aware that everything he'd ever done and everything he'd ever be, would soon vaporize within a flaming, thermonuclear bath. They had one chance and it would require a manic dash for survival.

"There's something in my lab that might help us, but it's in Area 5A. We'll have to use the tunnel."

They had no other option. Eight minutes, forty-two seconds remained before Dreamland found eternal sleep.

Encountering no further resistance, the intrepid nine rushed through the last corridor and into the massive central tunnel known as Broadway. Aware they didn't have time to traverse the five mile expanse on foot, they approached a flatbed truck being loaded with 55 gallon drums marked: FLAMMABLE. Two nearby workers were overpowered and rendered unconscious. The team boarded the transport, marshalling their weapons for further battle. After positioning the drums to function as cover, Moses counted those in back.

"Wait a minute. Who's gonna drive?"

The truck lurched forth, casting a cloud of rubber in its wake. Two drums tumbled off the rear of the vehicle with Casey and Barbara nearly joining them. Noting the getaway, a forklift operator ran to a security alarm. The race for their lives was on.

Failing to understand her family's reluctance to assume the wheel, Roberta committed to the task even though she'd never driven before. Benjamin sat astride her in the cab with hands full of longing and eyes green with envy.

"C'mon. Lemme drive."

She fended him off. "No way."

"Why not?"

"Cuz."

"Cuz, why?"

"Cuz, you can't reach the pedals!"

Benjamin tossed his arms down in frustration. "Oh, you always have all the fun."

Gunfire erupted in the tunnel. They fell to the deck of the flatbed, finding refuge behind the massive fuel drums. Soldiers bracketed the truck, trapping them underneath an umbrella of ricocheting bullets. Roberta shrieked, burying her foot into the accelerator. The enemy was engaged, initiating a ferocious weapons exchange which savaged both eye and ear. Wirtz curled into a fetal position, hoping the random shells would somehow spare his flesh.

"Stop! My medical insurance doesn't cover this!" he squealed in anguish.

As Benjamin looked back at the frenzied activity, his eyes bulged wide with discovery. He grasped hold of a large green box about as long as he was tall. "Look what I found!"

His sister recoiled in shock. It was a Quad 50 — a shoulder mounted missile launcher with four 50mm miniature rockets.

"Holy Mother of God! Put that down!"

"Then, lemme drive," he bargained.

At that instant, the truck's windshield absorbed a burst of automatic weapons fire, cracking the safety glass and propelling Roberta into a state of hysterics. Her brother peered through the web-like fissures into the tunnel ahead. Coming up fast was one of several catwalks, traversing the breadth of Broadway. Clustered along the rails were at least a dozen snipers, all heavily armed, facing the approaching truck in an execution stance. As blips of fire signaled another lethal salvo, Benjamin hung the Quad 50 out the window. During his attempt to position the launcher, a wandering finger located a release mechanism, loosing a missile skyward. The bulky weapon fell from the youngster's hands, while the generated backblast alerted the others to what happened. In a moment of breathless terror, the missile caromed off the rock wall, then adjusted its course, impacting the catwalk's main structural support. A rolling ball of flame began a bizarre chain reaction as the metal superstructure tore free. The catwalk swayed forth over the center of the tunnel, precipitating a spillage of soldiers 50 feet to the ground. Moses and Casey threw themselves onto the truck's cab, firing forward into the fray. Roberta did her best to avoid the falling obstructions, maintaining speed along a serpentine path. Rocking from the truck's movement, Kimberly paused as the scene continued to unfold.

"It's raining men!"

"Hallelujah!" replied Barbara, providing the appropriate response.

The tunnel blossomed with orange and red explosions as bullets found their mark in nearby fuel bins. Crouched low, C.J. could tell the drums were leaking the flammable liquid, emitting an odor similar to

356 ~ STEVEN L. FAWCETTE

gasoline. As the mayhem spiraled out of control, the trailing fuel ignited, sending separate rivers of flame after the truck.

"Oh, shit!" cried Kevin. "We've got fire coming up our ass!"

In panic, C.J. rolled over a catatonic Dr. Wirtz who remained prostrate on the deck. He struggled to the front of the flatbed, addressing a bugged-eyed Roberta through an open cab window. "Whatever you do, don't stop!"

She answered with a squeak of fear as Benjamin tried once more to assume control of the wheel. C.J. rolled back over the pet-rified scientist who was fighting for air amidst a torrential downpour of spent shell casings. Sounds of unyielding gunfire reverberated without end, melding into an aural bombast of tympanic agony. Weapons swung in chaotic arcs, sending streams of metal to assail the enemy. Wounded soldiers fell from elevated catwalks, coming to rest in viscous pools of flame. Joining the chase, two military jeeps sped after the truck, remaining clear of six fuel-fed firetrails only seconds behind.

With knuckles turning white as snow, Roberta tried to compre-hend what her eyes beheld. A large tanker truck filled with rocket fuel had been positioned across the tunnel and was blocking their path. The irresistible force was about to meet the immovable object.

She finally summoned her voice. "Oh, God! What'll I do?"

Her strident plea captured the attention of all aboard. Even Dr. Wirtz popped up his head in curiosity. Moses swore at the sight, dis-believing it had come to this. They couldn't go on. They couldn't stop. And, they couldn't turn back. Boxed in, there was nothing left to do. C.J. held to his faith, believing God would provide a Divine Intervention. However, he couldn't have imagined how radical it would be.

Wirtz gazed down at the two crossbows by his feet. In frantic motion, he set the timers on the puck-shaped mines. "Here! Use these Anti-gravs!"

Moses and Casey swooped down collecting the necessary equipment. Draped over the cab, they took aim at the imposing tanker parked a few hundred feet ahead. Trusting advanced technology, they fired the alien discs in tandem along a laser guided path. The mines spun through the air with a whistling sound. They arrived below their target and achieved fixed positions on the ground.

What happened next stunned their senses and set their faith anew. In a spectacle of supernatural dimension, the multi-ton tank truck began to lift into the air. Noisy creaks popped along the length of its undercarriage as it continued to ascend. Several soldiers caught within the weightless zone lost their footing, drifting helplessly upward. Fighting the urge to brake, Roberta backed off the gas allowing their momentum to carry them into the truck. Gasps of panic soon escalated into screams. At the fateful instant, the tanker elevated to a height which permitted the flatbed to slip underneath. The enemy followed, unfazed by the inherent danger. As the first jeep raced through, time expired. The law of gravity would no longer be denied.

The truck plunged down atop the second jeep, crushing the soldiers within. As the axles snapped from sudden impact, the hull split in two, dumping hundreds of gallons of rocket fuel to the tunnel floor. When the leading edge of the firetrails arrived, the spontaneous combustion exceeded belief. A titanic explosion rocked the complex, sending forth a shockwave rivaling any seismic event. The hypergolic mixture saturated Broadway, coming to life in a rolling fulmination of flame. A superheated talon of fire clawed at them, trying to snare the speeding vehicles.

The MPs closed from behind, spraying them with additional rounds of automatic weapons fire. C.J. and Kevin leveled their Magnetrons. In a moment of breathless horror, the soldiers turned color, clutching themselves as their organs cooked within. Their bodies spewed open, coating their vehicle in a reddish goo. The jeep went out of control, executing a 90 degree turn and slamming into the rock wall with a dramatic crash and burn.

Ahead of them was a B-3 bomber swallowing all available space. Moses took hold of a sonic gun and fired a resonating burst. As if cleaving a diamond, the aircraft fuselage cracked open bisecting the cockpit. The two halves fell apart creating a clear path of escape. The truck raced through the billion dollar debris field with multiple firetrails remaining in their wake. Moses now turned the sonic gun on Broadway itself. Firing into the cavernous walls, they began to burst under intense ultrasonic bombardment. Soon, the structural integrity of the tunnel was compromised, initiating a massive cave in. Tons of rock, steel and concrete descended into the complex, transforming Broadway into nothing more than a sealed tomb of debris. For the moment, the armed resistance ceased. The only sound was that of the racing engine and the squid-like tail of fire slithering behind.

Dr. Wirtz lifted his head making sure he'd suffered no physical damage. He realized they'd arrived in Area 5A. The end of Broadway was ahead, leading into a colossal wind tunnel currently active with 12 twenty-foot fans. It was time to jump ship.

Slowing the truck, the nine occupants bailed out, tumbling into a bed of soft dirt. They immediately sought cover down an adjacent hallway. The firetrails closed the gap, but not before the vehicle crashed into a plexiglas hatch leading to the wind tunnel. As fire united with fuel, a concussion of flame propelled the truck into the test chamber, alive with forced air. The flatbed exploded in a wealth of crimson hues. Lifting end over end, the vehicle cartwheeled through the gusts, taking flight directly into a second story control room located at the far end. Terrified soldiers ran for their lives. The truck's broiling carcass shattered the glass wall, causing a backdraft of flame to saturate exposed flesh.

Dr. Wirtz led them to his lab, a room marked: 5A07 — SPECIAL PROJECTS. He fumbled with his access card, aware that time was their most deadly foe. According to Benjamin's laptop, the Titan rocket was only 78 seconds from its thermonuclear return to Dreamland. The door slid back granting them entry, then sealed tight behind.

The Special Projects Lab was spacious in size. A cluster of empty desks supported various computer equipment. Resting in the center of the room was a large Armored Personnel Carrier, but unlike any they'd ever seen. Wirtz ran to the vehicle and opened a side hatch. He disappeared within, prompting Moses to pursue. The others spun in agitation, hearing soldiers outside the lab door.

Peering into the hatch, Moses saw Wirtz strap himself into one of ten captain's chairs laid out in grid formation. "What the hell are you doing?" his voice cracking in disbelief. "This is your solution? To hide in here?"

He dismissed his comment with a frantic wave. "The metallurgic composites of this APC have the same molecular matrix as the Roswell craft."

Moses fought through an avalanche of disjointed thoughts. In a slow rising epiphany, he vocalized the lifesaving revelation.

"Ben survived the nuke 'cause he was in the ship...The metal... Oh, my God!" He then screamed to the others. "Get in this thing now! Move! Move! Move!"

A chaotic rampage ensued as the others bolted inside, locking the hatch shut. Bodies swirled in motion. Seat harnesses wrapped wildly in place. Hearts drummed full. They clutched their chairs in terror, leaving no opportunity for breath.

The room beyond swarmed with heavily armed soldiers. Without warning, a continuous barrage of gunfire encased the APC in a cloud of high velocity fragmentation. Shedding the entire fusillade, the bullets fell harmlessly to the floor.

Benjamin peered into his laptop and recited the seconds as they ticked toward zero.

Barbara struggled to comprehend the meaning of it all. In the midst of incredible tumult, the woman began to sort through torturous thoughts. Her existence had taken on new dimension. She'd witnessed and performed extraordinary feats. They were not random acts of nature. Nor were they magic tricks. They'd been powered by a supernatural force residing within. A strength of spirit they'd drawn from each other. She was a part of this family and united in their cause. Her soul began to swell, freed of the doubt which had bound her for so long. As the crucial moment arrived, Barbara Pinder found her faith.

She raised her arms to Heaven, summoning words of prayer. "Save us!"

Benjamin closed with a final thought. "Three…two…one…"

At that instant, the Archangels of Dreamland were cast into the core of Hell.

The Titan rocket impacted the entrance to the complex in excess of 1,500 miles per hour. A blip of light flared as the atomic trigger provided the heat to spark an uncontained fusion reaction of hydrogen isotope nuclei. Time would now be measured in microseconds.

A ballooning torpedo of fire swept through the tunnels with lightning speed. The white hot plasma swelled, liquefying surrounding rock. The complex started to boil as reinforced concrete vaporized into insubstantial matter. It was at this point, a concussive shockwave heralded the arrival of total annihilation. Jaws of thermonuclear flame opened wide, consuming the mountain fortress. Mass became energy. Superheated air expelled outward with hurricane force. The generated fireball bloomed across the desert, increasing exponentially in brilliance and volume. A million tons of cubic earth began to eject skyward, transforming the base into an ever-expanding crater of death. Extraction of the underground site commenced, ripping the heart of Dreamland from its steel and granite chest.

The soldiers heard the explosion. Rumbling with the power of a runaway freight train, an extraordinary squall of noise occurred as the floors above vanished from this world. An exothermal blast disintegrated the final layer, breaching the roof of the Special Projects Lab. Upon contact with the breath of the Dragon, their corporeal existence ended. The inferno ravaged their flesh, peeling back skin as would a child tearing gift wrap. Experiencing utter evisceration, they become nothing more than empty skeletal shells. As their bones began to decalcify, they blew apart in the nuclear wind like the lighter-than-air spores of a dandelion.

The hull of the APC repelled the lethal radiation and stellar temperature. An overpressure wake struck the vehicle, initiating an ultra-violent 13G inverted heave into the firestorm. The screams of the Archangels went hypersonic, then faded from combined unconsciousness. Ascending the length of the mushrooming shaft, the vehicle was forced to endure a maelstrom of dynamic motion. Unquenchable flame devoured them, seeking to digest the metal skin which kept them whole. They became lost in the swirling vortex, channeled through electromagnetic strata and supported by thermal updrafts.

The craft then pitched over and inevitable gravimetric forces at last took hold. Their descent was equally chaotic, swaying and spinning beyond control. Just as all appeared lost, the onboard computer came to life sensing the vehicle had attained terminal velocity. Antigrav impellers located underneath the APC fired in rapid succession. A concentrated stream of gravitons now counteracted their plunge to Earth. Pitch, roll and yaw thrusters eased the aerodynamic convulsions. A minus 10G burst. Then, a minus 7. Others as required. The impellers' dramatic aural signature masked the ambient sounds of the explosion. Time and space began to function as normal. The sky and ground separated, once more becoming whole. Nuclear winds subsided. The Dragon's breath grew cold. After an interminable descent, the secret research vehicle eventually soft landed, coming to rest upon an eight mile wide plate of thermonuclear glass.

They awoke in a temporal haze. Nothing was said. Drained by the transcendental event, the Archangels were left speechless by their survival. On-board instruments confirmed the nuclear fallout had carried far to the east. Radiation levels were deemed tolerable for short exposure. They exited the vehicle and stood upon the melted surface. Casey tried to explain how sand exposed to tremendous heat produced glass, but Kevin squashed the lecture with a sweep of his hand. Barbara stood beside C.J. and gazed at the sight. She began to quote scripture much to her brother's surprise.

"And I saw what appeared to be a sea of glass mingled with fire, and those who had conquered the Beast, and its image, and the number of its name, standing beside the sea of glass with harps of God in their hands." Barbara eyed him, noting his quizzical stare. "Revelation 15:2," she added in clarification.

"I know," offering a smile. "I just didn't know you did."

"Oh, there's a lot you're going to find out about me, now that I found out myself." They enveloped each other in a loving embrace.

As Kimberly scanned the area, she spotted a crystal shaped stone set amidst the fused glass. "Casey? Take a look at this."

He came over to investigate. Ever curious, her brother bent down and wrested the stone from its foundation. A cursory glance triggered excitement. "Do you know what this is?"

He gathered the others to discuss the find. Their decision was unanimous. C.J. was chosen to present the gift to the scientist who'd saved their lives.

"Doc? On behalf of all of us, we'd like you to have this in gratitude for your help." He handed him the treasured object, clasping his hand in appreciation. "And along with it, comes the special thanks of Jehovah."

Wirtz was stunned by the words. In shock over the accolade. He held the stone in front of the sun and marveled at its inner luminosity. Even without glasses, he knew immediately what it was. This former lump of coal had been forged by the nuclear blast into a massive uncut diamond, worth untold millions. He blinked his eyes in awe. Deep inside he saw a flare of light. A bisected image. Angelfire. It looked to him like a pair of wings.

"I — I don't know what to say," he gasped.

Kimberly ran her hand across his shoulders. "Well, I do. Just remember this: Government bad. Angels good."

"Government bad? Angels good?" After a moment of reflection, he came to recognize this as a Divine Truth. "Government bad. Angels good. Government bad! Angels good!"

She wrapped him in a hug. "I think he's got it."

Something then captured Roberta's attention. A U.S. Military helicopter loomed on the horizon. Kevin and Casey ran to the vehicle collecting their weapons for further battle. Moses intercepted them, quelling their anxiety with a firm hand.

"Don't bother," he cried. "This one's a friendly."

It wasn't long before the UH-1 landed in a tempest of heated air. The engines powered down and the lone pilot emerged, dashing underneath a canopy of still whirling blades. Thrusting sunglasses from his face, a mile wide grin greeted them all.

"Wooooweeee!" the Major shouted, astonished by the scene. "When you guys throw a weenie roast, you don't fuck around!"

C.J. laughed, opening his arms to receive their friend. Osborne wrapped him in a tight hug. He greeted the others in similar fashion, reveling in the jubilant reunion. At last, Kimberly had her chance. Plunging head to chest, she spilled tears of joy the length of his shirt.

"I never thought I'd see you again."

"Sure you did," he countered.

They drew comfort from each other's touch, sealing their relief with an impassioned kiss.

"Who's this?" the Major asked.

"Oh, I'd like you to meet Dr. Wirtz," introducing them with a smile. "He's now an honorary Archangel, too."

The men exchanged handshakes. Osborne decided to poke fun at their height differential. "How ya doin' down there?"

The scientist wagged a cautionary finger. "Government bad. Angels good."

"Hey, I like this guy," the Major exclaimed with a smile. "Can I keep him as a pet?"

"How'd you find us?" Moses inquired.

"Backtracked the route. Came across the chopper in Rachel. Wasn't too hard to figure out where you went." His demeanor morphed to one of concern. "But, we've got another problem. Shannon and the baby are gone."

"What?"

"A guy showed up about two hours before me. Took 'em away. Did you know Shannon's brother was an agent for the FBI?"

Their vacant stares answered his question. "His name's Sean Duncan. The lady who runs the Inn said she left with him willingly."

"Any clue where they went?" C.J. interjected.

The Major shrugged. "Just a guess. She told me his van was from the Department of Interior. Lake Mead Conservation Area. For some reason, he's taking them to the Hoover Dam."

CHAPTER TWENTY-THREE

❦

BOULDER CITY, NEVADA — MAY 7th — 9:35 PM

$\mathcal{T}$he night air was thick with smoke. They skirted the outermost edge of Las Vegas, still suffering from numerous aftershocks. In the distance, fires raged on, kept alive by a catastrophic lack of water. Police and National Guard vehicles held lonely vigil over the absence of humanity. In less than an hour, the city had been transformed from a haven of glitz and glamour into a ghastly netherworld of unspeakable death.

Shannon had been in the van for hours, comforting the babe in her arms and being witness to miles of seismic devastation. Her brother Sean was behind the wheel, dressed in a dark, two piece suit — the standard uniform for an FBI field agent. At 36 years of age, this 6 foot 3, 232 pound specimen of Aryan breeding seemed to have no weakness, except for his blind allegiance to U.S. Government duty.

Thanks to Lucifer's anonymous tip, the FBI located Shannon and the baby. Her brother, dispatched to Nevada in the hopes of capturing her, wasted no time using a raft of lies to trick his sister into accompanying him. She was becoming weary of the ride and suspicious of his vocal evasions. Her frustrations finally surfaced, flaring in an acidic tone.

"Where the hell are we going? You said Troy needed me."

"Don't worry. He's safe," came the vacant response.

"Safe? From what?"

"Safe from you, Shannon. Safe from you and others like you who might confuse him."

A leaden pause, allowing her time to visualize any number of unpleasant scenarios. "What have you done to him?"

"Troy subverted a secret operation by tipping you off," he explained. "That earned him a trip to a military prison in Quantico, Virginia. He's now undergoing re-education."

"You mean, he's getting brainwashed," firing in return. "Why not have him killed? Isn't that the solution for everything?"

"It remains an option. Still, he is one of us."

"I sure hope not." She increased the bitterness in her voice. "Why did you lie to me? You said you'd take me to him?"

"I didn't lie to you. We'll be flying out of Kingman, Arizona in a couple of hours."

"Am I to be your prisoner?"

He snorted with amusement. "You already are, Sis. I chose not to cuff you for old time's sake."

The disclosure left her feeling violated. This was her brother. Someone she'd known all her life. *How can he speak to me like this? Why's he treating me this way?*

"You used to be a decent guy, Sean," chastising him. "Someone I could trust. Now, you're nothing but a soulless creature. What happened to the brother I grew up with?"

The agent squirmed, clamping his hands tighter on the wheel. "Whether you respect it or not, I'm doing a valuable service. I believe in this country and the Government for which it stands."

Shannon's ire flared anew. "Oh, spare me that grade school shit. In case you hadn't noticed, I'm not 10 anymore." She paused for a moment of reflection. "You're on the wrong side, Sean. Deal with it before it's too late."

The agent fought for emotional control. "You're right about one thing, Sis. Time's running out…and faster than you think."

Shannon caught glimpse of a road sign. The Hoover Dam was a mere three miles distant. She failed to link the timing of his threat to their closing proximity with the structure.

"I don't understand you," continuing her interrogation. "How can you be loyal to these bastards? They're the ones who killed Denise."

He forced a breath, coming to terms with what he had to say. "No, Shannon. You killed her, when you wouldn't get in your car when I asked."

She froze, recalling his urgent plea to meet him alone. "You incredible son-of-a-bitch," gasping in horror. "You set me up? My own brother?"

"I told the assassins know how to find you," he confided. "But, it was their idea for the car bomb. Unfortunately, Denise got in the way." A cruel moment, made worse by his words. "I didn't want her to die. Just you."

Numbed by the revelation, her lips quivered in angst. "Does Brittany know this?"

"Of course not," Sean snapped. "My little girl believes what I told her. That you killed Denise, after she saw you kill Troy."

Shannon slumped in her chair, content to let their conversation die. Frayed family bonds were now severed. She suffered the emotional pain in silence, trying to stanch a river of tears.

The winding road lead down to the ridge of the Hoover Dam, dark without power since the earthquake. A deep ebony night yielded only to their headlights. Shannon peered into the murky void, unable to discern anything unless bathed by the halogen beams. They negotiated the final turn, approaching the Visitors' Center parking structure. Suddenly, she saw something ahead. Eight obstructions of various sizes and shapes flanked one another. They refused to move, blocking the van's path onto the dam.

Sean leaned into the windshield, squinting at the human barricade. "What the fuck is this?"

Gasping with shock, then for joy, her smile blossomed forth. Shannon's true family was there, having come to her aid.

The agent parked the van, allowing his sister to bolt from the vehicle. Cradling the baby, she joined the others, exchanging spontaneous displays of affection and comradeship. Prophecy had been fulfilled. After defying incredible odds, Mary Ellen's children were at last reunited. The Archangels now stood as one.

Sean approached through the flare of headlights. He reached in his breast pocket and unfurled his identification. "Special agent Duncan. FBI. Each of you are under arrest."

C.J. was unable to cloak his amusement. "What's the charge?"

Replacing his credentials, Sean answered with resolve. "Aiding and abetting a known fugitive…and conspiracy against the United States Government."

"Sounds serious," smiling through his words. "Guess we'd better call our attorneys."

Duncan stared him down. "There'll be plenty of time for that, once you're arraigned in Federal Court."

"Gee, we don't want to seem rude," interjected Kevin. "But, what happens if we tell you to drop dead?"

A glacial pause. "Then, you'll be taken by force."

Moses grinned at the threat. "You and what Army?"

As if on cue, the agent grasped a walkie-talkie from his belt and transmitted a message. "Colonel? Let there be light."

"Roger that," squawked an immediate response.

A grand stage came to life, as one arc light after another pierced the darkened veil. Soon, the length and depth of the entire structure was lit, producing a halo effect from which their eyes had to adjust. The colossal edifice was now in plain view, a hundred million tons of reinforced concrete looming 726 feet above the Colorado River. Due to the earthquake, Lake Mead had receded into gaping rifts opened in the Earth's surface. The absence of water left miles of sediment, as well as the putrefying stench of dead and dying marine life. High tension electric lines sagged from their support towers, humming with emergency power.

On the Arizona side of the dam, an imposing array of U.S. Army equipment powered up, approaching from a secreted location.

It was clear they'd been laying in wait for just such a moment. Moses shook his head at the battalion sized force, consisting of eight M1A1 Abrahms Tanks, six M2/M3 Bradley Fighting Vehicles, several jeeps and logistics trucks and an indeterminate number of heavily armed foot soldiers, easily exceeding 300 hundred men. They marched with the motorized equipment, sealing off the road. Four AH-64D Apache Helicopter gun ships rose into the air, assuming stationary positions 200 feet above the dried lakebed. The choppers locked spotlights and weapons upon the siblings, none of whom moved.

"That Army," Sean replied.

It was a brilliant coup. Cleverly plotted. Masterfully executed. Something Sean had conceived, using his sister as innocent bait. He knew this would further his career, advancing him to the highest echelons within the Bureau. The endgame had been played. It was checkmate. Of that, Sean Duncan was sure.

Over the roar of the helicopters and advancing armament came another sound. This one more terrifying by far. The Earth once again began to spasm, radiating in waves of ever-increasing force. Loose bits of rock tumbled down the canyon walls. Cracked pavement began to fully separate. The troops, already halfway across the dam, stopped mid-step unsure whether to advance or retreat. Company Commanders compelled the soldiers to remain calm.

With their world in upheaval, Sean gazed back at his prisoners and went pale with disbelief. Each of them was smiling. Soon, their grins became peals of laughter, possessing a Divine knowledge which this Government infidel couldn't possibly understand. For the first time in his life, Sean Duncan panicked.

"Stop that!" he screamed. "Stop that laughing!"

Their amusement was now uncontained, driving the agent into further hysterics. "What's wrong with you people? Stop it! I'm serious! Stop that laughing! You've got to stop it!"

The quake maintained power, pulsing with a life all its own. Their laughter continued, unaffected by the seismic event. Sean became frantic, desperate for the Archangels to share their secret.

"There's nothing funny about this! Why are you laughing?"

Benjamin paused long enough to explain, his voice rich with derision. "My baby sister's gonna kick your butt!"

Sean looked upon the infant nestled in Shannon's arms. The child was no longer asleep. Her brown eyes were dilated, staring directly at the agent. Their visual connection was like that of a laser, boring through his lifeless soul. As if in a trance, he took note of an image forming across her angelic face. What he beheld was the ghostly specter of a human skull. His own. Convulsing in terror, Sean forced his eyes from the infant in time to view what came next.

A blast of geothermal water spewed out of the dried lakebed, propelling a ball of rock and mud skyward. The ejected matter struck one of the Apache Helicopters, breaching the fuselage and initiating a catastrophic explosion. Before the fireball faded from sight, another towering geyser retched forth. It also found a target, tearing the main rotor blades from an adjacent helicopter. The doomed craft cartwheeled into the muck, following the twisted debris from the first.

The Commanding Officer, a Full Colonel, was screaming at his pilots over a walkie-talkie. "Get out of there! Get out of there!"

The remaining helicopters banked away at high speed. A third geyser erupted, shearing the cockpit from one, causing it to somersault in midair. The chopper came down in an inverted position, its tail rotor impaling the ground. The final Apache had nearly cleared the area when twin towers of superheated water and earth expelled with violence. The helicopter's tail section was severed, sending the craft pinwheeling toward the dam. Soldiers scattered as the chopper crashed into the retaining wall. At long last, the subterranean rumble ceased. The Earth again went still.

Sean quivered in breathless disbelief. "Oh, my God."

Barbara corrected him. "No. My God."

After an introspective pause, C.J. offered some guidance. "You have one chance to save yourself. Get in that van and go. There's no other choice."

The suggestion propelled Sean into a state of rage. *Who are these people to tell me what to do?* He'd never run from anything. There were orders to obey and he would not be deterred. Sean had delivered the Archangels to the military. This left him just one more duty to perform.

"Give me the baby, Shannon."

She recoiled, thrusting the infant tighter to her breast. "Oh, you sick bastard. You really are insane."

"I have my orders," he yelled. "The child has to die."

"To hell with your orders."

"Just give me the baby. I promise I'll be quick."

"Fuck you!"

He took a threatening step. Shannon dropped back, anger surging from her eyes. "Sean, you come any closer and I'll kill you with my bare hands. I swear it."

"You won't get that chance, Sis," pulling a handgun from his suit. "Now, give me the child."

"Never!"

In a moment of incredibly bad judgment, he pointed the weapon directly at his sister's heart. "That's it, Shannon!"

A shot rang out. Instantly, Sean Duncan was no longer whole. His right hand was blown off, falling limply to the pavement. The severed appendage lay motionless, still clutching the gun with coiled fingers. He screamed in agony as his nerves registered the cleaving of flesh. In a cloud of incomprehension, Sean reached down and recovered the gun. Another high powered shot echoed through the canyon. His left hand now joined his right. Shrieking in torment, he looked up at the area from where the shots were fired. He could see the silhouette of a sniper, perched on the upper deck of the parking structure, standing next to a UH-1 helicopter.

Shaking his bloodied stumps at the Major, Sean couldn't believe what had happened. "You can't do this to me! I'm a Federal Agent!"

Osborne snickered at his expense, shouting a cold reply. "What do you want me to do, pal? Give you a hand?"

The Major switched his assault rifle to automatic and fired into a cluster of power lines draped overhead. Shannon looked away as the live wires fell upon her brother, ensnaring him in a web of high voltage current. His corpse collapsed, consumed in a funeral pyre.

At that instant, another sound was heard. Unlike any ever experienced. A bass rumble like that of a stampede, building in both intensity and volume. It grew in the darkness. An approaching force of unparalleled power, defying the common order of nature. Coming forth through the black shroud of night.

Mass hysteria spread through the troops. They could sense on an instinctual level that something truly horrific was about to happen. Hundreds of soldiers simultaneously bolted from their posts, disobeying orders to stand fast. They abandoned their tanks and APCs, leaving the engines running. Company Commanders tried to regain order from the chaos, their words unable to be heard. The Colonel was beside himself, screaming at the deserters. Some of his own officers broke ranks, dashing for salvation.

The battalion's northernmost spotter was on a portable field radio, squealing in abject delirium. "Jesus Christ! I can see it! A wall of water — 300 feet high! We're fucked!"

The Colonel dropped his walkie-talkie, addressing his remaining officers through a megaphone. "Fall back! Retreat! Retreat!"

Pandemonium reigned as they tried to escape the structure. Mist filled the air, arriving ahead of the towering wave. All at once, the waters of Lake Mead returned with a vengeance.

In a spectacle of overwhelming awe, the raging torrent crashed into Hoover Dam, sweeping the Army equipment over the side. The battalion's multi-ton tanks and APCs were flipped over, then sent careening into the canyon beyond. Strident screams were drowned by the roar of the deluge. The cascade of metal plunged down into the Colorado riverbed. As the munitions exploded, they were quenched by the massive inundation. The flood continued with wanton fury, destroying the dam's topmost tier, casting thousands of yards of broken concrete into the chasm. Nothing was spared from the aquatic purge. After more than a billion gallons of water had spilled over the precipice, the assault began to subside with an abated flow.

In less than a minute, the Army's mighty force had been vanquished. The sounds of death receded. Through a squall of churning spray, the Archangels witnessed a flagpole broken in two. The foam drenched American flag tore away, slipping quietly over the edge. There to become a burial cloth for all those who'd blindly followed orders — and in so doing, rendered the country's sacred flag hollow and without meaning.

CHAPTER TWENTY-FOUR

⚓

*A*fter two attempts, the phone found its cradle. Richard Stern, the President's National Security Advisor, rubbed his eyes in frustration. It took him a moment to realize he wasn't alone. Standing in his White House Office doorway was Susan Webber.

"Conscience won't let you sleep?" she asked.

Stern refused to rise from his chair. "I sleep just fine, Madam President. When I find the time." He straightened his back, establishing a more professional posture. "Is there something you'd like to discuss?"

After an uncomfortable moment, she came rigid with resolve. "I received a call a few minutes ago from General Connolly. He said he'd been asked to redirect a battalion of men from Ft. Irwin, California to the Hoover Dam...and that you told him I ordered this deployment."

An expression of innocence answered the charge. "Is that so?"

"He also said all contact was lost when a flash flood swamped the area." The room went silent for a composing breath. "A battalion. An entire army battalion."

Stern tried to deflect the issue. "They're military men, Madam President. They're trained for any contingency."

"Not this one. Those troops had no idea what they were up against," she countered, aghast at their fate. "You know I didn't approve that deployment. What were they doing there?"

The man refused to speak, realizing additional words would be of little benefit. They probed each other like two battlefield tacticians, searching for any sign of weakness.

"I'm the President, Mr. Stern. Not you," gaining control of the situation. "You exceeded your authority, lying to me and the Joint Chiefs. I expect your resignation, effective noon today."

An indignant smirk. "And, if I refuse?"

"Then, I'll be forced to announce your termination at my morning press conference," came the voice, devoid of regret. "You might also be interested to know, I'm directing the Attorney General to begin criminal proceedings against you for numerous violations of U.S. Code. I've got it all on disc." She drew comfort from his slack-jawed reaction. "The attempted murder of the Chief Executive. The falsification of a presidential pardon. The downing of Flight 242. Everything."

Stern appeared disoriented, drumming his fingers across the desktop. His lips quivered in prolonged deliberation, considering then dismissing his limited options. Soon, only one choice remained. The man forced a breath of defeat and opened a hidden drawer. "I have a better idea. Why don't I hasten your resignation," bringing a loaded handgun into view, "Then, I won't have to leave."

He rose to his feet, aiming the weapon at her. The President summoned reserve courage. "Are you threatening my life, Mr. Stern?"

A demonic chortle. "What's it look like, bitch? This is something I should've done long before now."

In a blur of motion, she was thrust backward by an unseen force. Steven Yeager, the President's Secret Service bodyguard, now interposed himself.

"What the..." In confusion, he dropped the weapon, addressing the agent in a venomous tone. "Bastard! How long were you there?"

His voice came cold as a tomb. "Long enough, Stern. Welcome to the unholy .357." The agent exposed his sidearm with frightening speed. "Catch!"

A hollow point bullet impaled Stern's forehead, cracking open his skull like a ripe coconut. The body fell backward, coming to rest in a slumping pile of blood drenched flesh.

"Oh!" Susan cried in shock. "That was so…exhilarating."

Yeager turned to her and reholstered his gun. Their smiles bloomed, embracing each other as only lovers could. Lust swelled without apology. Desire burned without fear of consequence. At last they separated, acknowledging professional ethics.

"Well," said Susan, "Thank you for saving my life."

"That's why I'm here, Madam President."

She gazed back at the gory scene, fearing a media frenzy, endless questions and political fallout. The agent read her mind, providing assurance with a calming touch. "Don't worry. It's my job to protect you…anyway I can."

Sighing with relief, Webber allowed him to embrace her once more. "It's true what they say," she admitted. "It's lonely at the top."

A tender pause. "You'll never be alone, Madam President."

Susan fought a tear, recalling how long it had been since she'd felt the warmth of a man. Lost in reflection, she realized this was an appropriate time for new beginnings, as well as for closure. "I'd like the mystery informant to place another call. An official White House apology to Mary Ellen Hart and her children."

"Now?" he wondered.

She snuggled into his chest, not wanting the moment to end. "I suppose it can wait — 'til the morning."

CHAPTER TWENTY-FIVE

∝

NEAR SEARCHLIGHT,
NEVADA — MAY 8th — 12:01 AM PDT

A new day began. Traversing a lonely Nevada road, a Government van and its helicopter escort headed south toward California. The starlit heavens buoyed their spirits, making them feel the infinite love of God.

The Archangels had defeated the Devil. Now possessing the secrets of Roswell, they could expose the inherent evil of the MAJIK-12. Bringing Divine Justice to bear. Ensuring their father and mother hadn't died in vain. And, fulfilling their destiny here on Earth.

Within the van, Barbara and Roberta looked out at the helicopter pacing them in flight. Kimberly waved to them, having opted to ride along with Major Osborne. Her sisters returned the greeting, sharing in her joy of finding someone so special.

"She really seems to like him," declared Roberta, stating the obvious.

Barbara smiled. "Of course, she does. Even an Archangel needs a guardian angel."

In the rear seat sat Kevin and Moses, with Casey wedged between examining Benjamin's laptop. His inquiring eyes grew wide with discovery.

"Unbelievable."

"What now?" sighed Kevin.

"Lucifer. Looks like He escaped."

Moses expressed his concern. "Say what?"

"Escaped. There was a modem connection to an outside computer. The mainframe completed a download of the central system files just prior to the explosion."

"Where to?"

A couple of keystrokes for clarification. "202 Area Code. Somewhere in Washington, D.C."

Expressions of dismay stalled their conversation, leaving a difficult void. Casey placed the box of optical discs onto the laptop.

"It'll take awhile to go through these. I can't imagine what we'll find."

The corner of the case brushed against the keyboard, prompting an inadvertent musical selection. It was a lilting, synthesized instrumental of *'The Hallelujah Chorus'* from Handel's *'The Messiah'*. Benjamin spun in his seat, anxious to determine the one responsible for this invasive act.

"Hey! That's my song!"

Casey apologized. "Sorry, Ben. I must have hit it by accident."

The tune was like honey to the ears, sweet and full of texture. "That's really good, Ben," Roberta admitted. "When did you do it?"

His face turned sullen. "The other day. I wrote it for the Madre."

The others agreed with Roberta. It was an exemplary work of art. A loving gift to an extraordinary woman. A true masterpiece.

"Do you think she would've liked it?" Benjamin asked, morose.

At that moment, a teardrop fell onto the laptop screen. The brothers witnessed it trickle down, stunned by the dramatic materialization. Moses reached over, scooping the liquid onto his finger.

"Yes, Ben," fighting for his words. "She likes it very much."

Casey stared in awe, whispering to Kevin. "Should I turn it off?"

"No," he stated emotionally. "Let it play."

The moving composition stirred their souls. C.J. looked over at Shannon and the baby, keeping his hands on the wheel. Both of them were silent. Shannon was deep in blank-faced introspection. The infant asleep, coiled against her breasts. He smiled at the Madonna-like image, then decided to ask an important question.

"What will we name the baby?"

She came out of her mental hibernation when Barbara placed a gentle hand on her shoulder. Shannon's breath went shallow, summoning forth spiritual strength, her heart nearly bursting from the annunciation.

"Hope," she proclaimed, anointing the baby's head with her tears. "We'll call her Hope."